Genius

Genius

PATRICK DENNIS

NEW YORK

HARCOURT, BRACE & WORLD, INC.

Library of Congress Catalog Card Number: 62-19585

Printed in the United States of America

For
H. D. V.

Genius

I

If you are over thirty it would be presumptuous of me to ask
if you had ever heard of Leander Starr. Anyone with any pretensions to culture could answer immediately that he was
once—and perhaps still is—America's greatest director, rank-
ing with Robert Flaherty, Maurice Stiller, Erich von Stro-
heim, and half a dozen others. There can be hardly anyone
(past the age of thirty) who has not seen his great religious
extravaganza *Ruth in the Alien Corn,* still considered to be
the model for all great Biblical pictures. His wordless documentary, *Yucatán Girl,* involving a deaf-mute Mexican
beauty, a lot of Indian ruins, and the Vienna Philharmonic,
has only to be mentioned in certain circles to bring on a full
minute of reverent hush. And, of course, his witty, brittle,
sophisticated soufflés cooked up for such late and great
comediennes as Carole Lombard and Jean Harlow are still
gems in the revival repertoire.

If, like me, you are beyond forty, there is no need to tell you
that Leander Starr's stage work was regarded with nothing
short of wonder. His direction of comedies for Gertrude
Lawrence, Ina Claire, Francine Larrimore, the Lunts—to
name only a few—was magic. Nor did he bow out at the
drawing-room door. He could take the most impossible plays
of such improbable authors as Marlowe, Webster, Beaumont
and Fletcher, Garcia Lorca, Beckett, and Brecht and turn
them into real Standing Room Only hits. No easy trick.

However, if you are *under* thirty—and half of this nation

is—Leander Starr may take a bit of explaining, for unless you are one of those eager movie buffs who haunt the Museum of Modern Art film showings and the flea-baggiest of cinema art houses, you are not likely to have seen many examples of his superb work. For some years—and for many good reasons— Mr. Starr has preferred to live outside the boundaries of the United States. His work has been sporadic: a couple of pictures filmed in Italy; a psychological Western made in, of all places, the south of France; an all-star historical epic concerning Richard Cœur de Lion at Walton-upon-Thames; and half of a very literate B.B.C. television series based roughly on the Wolfenden Report. Topnotch work, all of it, and still proving that the old master has never lost his touch. But Starr has since seen fit to abandon Italy, France, and England as well as his native shores. In recent years he has been At Liberty more often than not.

While the name Leander Starr spells truth and beauty to many, it spells financial ruin, indebtedness, and bad checks to quite a lot of others. Cut to the bone, his great documentary *Yucatán Girl* runs exactly four hours and fifty-two minutes and is unsalable to the average motion-picture theater. His sparkling comedy, *An Affaire,* may have won four Academy Awards, but it was so ruinously expensive to produce that it broke even only because it generally was shown on a double bill with *Blondie Has a Baby*. Even though his great historical pageant, *The Euphrates,* filled the old Hippodrome to capacity for two full years, it did so at a loss of twelve hundred dollars a week—not including the veterinarian's bills. The first and the fourth Mrs. Leander Starr still scream loudly, publicly, and regularly for back alimony. To my certain knowledge he owes for food and lodging—and very elegant lodgings, too—at the Beverly Hills Hotel, the Ambassador East, Hampshire House, the Plaza, Claridge's, the Ritz (London), the Ritz (Paris), the George V, the Hassler in Rome, and the Hotel de Paris in Monte Carlo. The Department of Internal Revenue is especially anxious to confer with

4

Starr over a small matter of many, many thousands of dollars' worth of back income taxes if he should ever be unwise enough to touch on American soil. He even owes money to me.

I first bumped into Leander Starr—both literally and figuratively—almost twenty years ago in the Edward Hotel in Durban, South Africa. It was during World War II, and I was on my slow, circuitous way to Egypt. In fact Durban was full of people who were all heading to or from some place else. The small resort town had become a sort of halfway house for everybody—rich refugees en route to South America, troops bound from England to the Middle East and India, hospital ships plowing back and forth from God-knew-where to God-knew-where. Everybody's principal occupation was waiting around for whatever ship or plane or train would take them wherever it was they thought they were going and getting a suntan while doing so. And there were worse places to wait.

As everyone was in the same boat—or, to be more specific, *waiting* for the same boat—there was a kind of hectic gaiety about the town. There were the beaches in the mornings, the races and cricket in the afternoons, and bottle clubs like the Stardust in the evenings. The hills around the town were thick with villas named things like *Sans Souci* or *Mon Repos* where patriotic English colonials entertained everything and anything that showed up more or less in uniform. The most un-likely people started up the most unlikely flirtations and friendships simply because they knew—or hoped—that the relationships would be fleeting and that if and when the next P&O boat hauled anchor they would never even see one another again. As I say, it was a pleasant break in the long trip to war, and I passed a convivial month of total idleness there, housed very nicely at His Majesty's expense as a volun-teer in the American Field Service.

As for flirtations, I had done worse than most. The redhead in whom I had invested a great deal of time and money had suddenly produced a strapping and hitherto unmentioned

5

husband in the person of a lieutenant commander off a British troop ship. I had been left holding the bag and my temper while she introduced me to him as "darling Dulcie's Ammedican fiancé, darling" and whizzed off in a smart right-hand-drive Packard to resume domestic relations with the Royal Navy.

Looking lean, leggy and—*I* thought—rather dashing in my British officer's shorts and outsized pith helmet, I strode dramatically into the Edward Hotel, intending to drown my sorrows in gin and lime. It was teatime and the place was thronged. I chose the only available table, a small one in a dim corner, rather regretting that in the darkness my tragic mien was all but lost on the rest of the customers, while noticing with some pleasure that the surrounding gloom somewhat enhanced my tan. (I was very young and could be forgiven a certain theatricality.) However, I was not allowed to brood over my gin for long. The doors flew open and a youngish blonde, very beautiful and rather disheveled, raced in. She gave a wild, hopeless look around the crowded room and made straight for my table. "May I?" she said, and all but fell into the empty chair opposite mine.

"Charmed," I said suavely, rising to my feet and sending that damned pith helmet rolling crazily across the floor.

"Sit down, you fool!" she hissed.

"But my hat . . ."

"I'll buy you a new one. Just sit down and *don't* be conspicuous."

"Well, when it comes to being conspicuous, madame," I began stuffily. Then I got a better look at her. "*Say*, aren't you Monica James?" Having spent half of my formative years watching double and even triple features, there was hardly a movie name I didn't know from the biggest star down to the most minor bit player. Monica James had been a fragile English ingénue of considerable promise in half a dozen Gaumont-British films.

"Yes. Now *will* you shut up?"

"Well, really, Miss James. I simply wanted to say that I have always admired your work. Particularly the last picture you made with Leslie Howard under Leander Starr's direction. It . . ."

"Leander Starr! Don't even mention that beast. He's hounded me from . . . Oh, dear God, here he is! Don't let him see me."

I turned, as did everyone else in the room, and there stood the great Leander Starr, got up to look like Trader Horn. Dark as our corner was, it didn't take him long to spot Monica James. He strode purposefully to the table and said, "Young man, you are in the process of breaking up a happy home. My seconds will call on you this evening."

"Don't be such a blathering ass, Leander," Miss James said.

"Young man, this woman is my wife, and those whom God hath joined together let no man . . ."

"I am *not* your wife!" Miss James said hotly. "I've got my divorce decree right here in my purse and it's the most priceless possession I'll ever own."

"I don't believe you."

"I know you *didn't* believe me," she said, flourishing a paper, "but now I've got it and here it is. My solicitor tells me that I could also have done it on grounds of malicious desertion, insanity, or the fact that you're an habitual criminal. No matter. Adultery was good enough for me."

"Malicious desertion? If it weren't for the gravity of your accusation, Monica, I would laugh. Yes, laugh!" A sweeping gesture. "It is you who deserted me and it is I who followed you across this dark continent, over bush and veld, accompanied only by my manservant and a faithful native bearer, to discover you now in *flagrante delicto* with your American gigolo, while a betrayed husband . . ."

"Now see here, sir," I said, rising to my feet. I noticed he was a couple of inches taller than I and had a longer reach. Miss James brushed aside my hardly begun protestations.

"Leander, you came in on the afternoon express. I saw you

7

while I was at the station buying my ticket. I saw you and I ran like a hare, but not fast enough or far enough. Now get *back* on the express and go away!"

"You're leaving me," he said tensely, grasping her wrist. "You're leaving me in this God-forsaken country, old and sick and defeated and alone. This is the thanks I get for taking you out of the gutter and turning you into a radiant star."

"That's not quite right, Leander," Miss James said. "You did not take me out of the gutter. I'm not a star. And I *have* left you."

"For this callow Casanova?"

"Don't be an ass, Leander. I don't even know the young man's name."

"Nymphomaniac!"

"It's Dennis," I said idiotically. "Patrick Dennis. American Field Service. How do you do, Mr. Starr. I'd like to take this opportunity to tell you how much I've always admired your ..."

Ignoring my outstretched hand, Starr turned regally toward Miss James. "Wanton that you may be, we're going to forget all this. I'm giving you back your rightful position as *the* Mrs. Leander Starr...."

"The *second* Mrs. Leander Starr," Miss James said. "But by no means the last."

"As *the* Mrs. Starr. You are coming with me to the interior of this marvelous land of mystery where I have found the most fascinating tribe of pygmies. Think of the film we can make—you a willowy golden goddess surrounded by hundreds and hundreds of tiny subjects each no taller than...."

"And we'll call it *Little Men*," Miss James said, rising and gathering up her gloves.

"That's a hot one!" I said.

"No thank you, Leander. You go to the pygmies. I'm going back to England. It was an education to be Mrs. Starr for the past two years, but now that I'm educated I'm going home and try to forget the whole bloody mess."

"I won't permit you to return to England. The bombings. The danger."

"That's frightfully sweet of you, Leander, but I'd rather be in the middle of blitzkrieg with Hitler himself than in paradise with you. No hard feelings. Thank you for the tea, Mr. Dennis."

"But it hasn't come yet," I said. Just then an Indian waiter padded softly up to the table, bearing what the Edward Hotel considered to be the absolute minimum wartime tea—tea, hot water, hot milk, cold milk, lemon, bread and butter, hot scones, jam (three kinds), honey, sandwiches, cake, pastries, and a large tart.

"Well, thanks anyhow," she said. "Good-by, Leander."

"Wait!" he shouted, lurching after her. Unfortunately, he lurched squarely into me. There was a frightful crash and the next thing I saw was the great Leander Starr sprawled on the floor, scalded by tea, hot water, hot milk; covered with cold milk, lemon, bread and butter, hot scones, jam (three kinds), honey, sandwiches, cake, pastries, and a large tart. "You pushed me, you blackguard!" he roared. A second later he was up and swinging at me. A second after that we were both out on the Marine Parade, barred forever from the Edward Hotel.

I saw no more of the great man for two days until I was having drinks in the Balmoral Hotel with another beautiful girl. Her name was Caroline Morris, she came from a fine old Philadelphia family somewhere along the Main Line, and she was going to the Middle East as a Red Cross girl. Red Cross girl, hell, she was a recruiting poster! Handsome and lifeless rather than pretty and vivacious, she personified that clean-white-gloves-straight-seams-every-hair-in-place quality so dear to the Red Cross overseas. She was a frosty article and would never have deigned to go out with me if she hadn't been at school with my older sister and knew that we were All Right even if we *did* come from Chicago. To have been connected with Caroline or any of the Morrises, no matter how distantly, automatically conferred social acceptability in her eyes. She suggested drinks at the Edward. *I* suggested the Balmoral. Halfway through the first one I dimly recalled having heard that this living Red Cross poster had recently been the ideal Bryn Mawr girl and a perfect pill, and that before that she had been the perfect Shipley girl and still a pill. Come to think of it, I guess my sister hadn't liked her any better than I did. Still she was beautiful, and lonely American boys away from home were supposed to flip—absolutely flip—in the company of beautiful American girls. I wasn't flipping. In fact I was barely listening to Caroline's rather constipated recital of how ghastly everything had been, coming over first-class from the Philadelphia shipyards. "Hideous food . . . class of people one meets . . . your sister . . . Merion Cricket Club . . . do you know Tommy Huber . . . very dry, please . . . suppose these natives are diseased . . . Mummy and Dr. Ormandy . . ." She was interrupted by a wispy man of indeterminate age who appeared quite suddenly at our table.

"Mr. Dennis, I *do* beg your pardon, but my imployer, Mr. Leander Starr, asked me to stop by."

"Are you his second?" I asked. This didn't seem to be the sort of man who'd be at home on the field of honor—or *any* field, for that matter.

"His sicritary, yes. My name is Alistair St. Regis. Mr. Starr is ever so upset about the misunderstanding of the other day and wonders if he can buy you and your, uh, companion a drink. He'd like very much to apologize."

"Is he related to the Doylestown Starrs?" Caroline asked, showing just a flicker of animation.

"I don't believe so." Then I said, "Thank you, Mr. Uh . . ."

"St. Regis. Alistair St. Regis."

"Thank you, Mr. St. Regis," I said, wondering where he'd ever dug up such a name, "but we won't have time. Please tell Mr. Starr that what happened the other day is perfectly all

right. Just one of those misunderstandings." Mr. St. Regis
hesitated for a moment and then went mincing away.

"Mummy is distantly related to some Starrs on the Eastern
Shore. They breed."

"No. This is Leander Starr. Le-an-der Starr."

"I believe ours are Roger and Maudie Starr. Mummy's actually related to *her* side of . . ."

"*Leander Starr,* the great *director,*" I said much too loudly,
as though she were hard of hearing as well as stupid.

"Oh, theatrical people," Caroline said with a barely per-
ceptible quiver of her splendid nostrils. "Of course, Cornelia
Otis Skinner went to . . ." Her jaw fell open and there stood
Leander Starr in splendid tropical dinner clothes, pure Fred-
ric March.

"Dear boy," he said with a deep bow. "The mountain
comes to Mohammed. I was rather hurt when my valet announced that you'd be unable to have cocktails with me. One
does despise to drink alone and I am a lonely man."

"Oh, but do sit down, Mr. Starr," Caroline said. She looked
a bit shattered, as though she'd just been told that Bryn Mawr
Hospital was a notorious abortion mill, but at least she was
coming to life. Sit down he did, and for the next four hours
he was spellbinding. There seemed to be nobody of any interest he hadn't met and, as a special sop to Caroline, this roster
even included a few Pews and Chews and Cadwaladers.
Caroline was now a different girl. In fact, Starr was so *utterly*
spellbinding that I didn't realize that I'd been left alone,
except for the bar chits, until just after I'd sent him and
Caroline off to dinner in a Zulu rickshaw. That was the last
I saw of either of them for some years. The following day I
was squeezed aboard a troop ship for the long, hot trip up to
Suez.

The next news of Starr arrived in the form of a clipping
from *Time* that my sister sent to me in a letter containing
less sensational social notes:

Marriage Revealed. C. (for Charles) Leander Starr, 35-ish, Hollywood *wunderkind;*
and Caroline Drexel Morris, 22, Philadelphia postdebutante currently AWOL from
the Red Cross; he for the third time, she for
the first; in South Africa last month.

My sister went on, rather gleefully, to say that there had
been a slight stink with the Red Cross authorities and that it
just wasn't *like* Caroline to run off into the bush in full dress
uniform. A very few months later—five to be downright caddish about it—the birth of their daughter Emily was announced from somewhere in Africa, and a few months after
that mother and child were back in Philadelphia suing for
divorce on grounds of extreme cruelty. Within a year the
fourth Mrs. Leander Starr was installed; a year later *she* was
gone and then there was silence.

The war had been over for nearly five years when next I
encountered Leander Starr. By then I was living in New York
with a wife and two children. I had a job in a small advertising agency where I wrote copy for pharmaceutical firms
and, on my own time, what my mother-in-law described as
"little things on the side." In fact, those little things on the
side were what kept us afloat, just. The most recent little
thing—a short, insane dialogue between a right-wing senator
and a method actress—had appeared in a now defunct pseudo-
sophisticated magazine and had won quite a lot of insincere
favorable comment from the Right People. A reputable publisher had asked to see anything along the lines of a novel that
I might have—and I had plenty—and I was enjoying a *very*
minor, *very* short-lived celebrity.

Leander Starr, needless to say, was again heard of constantly. He had returned to America and had overwritten a
long piece for *Life* about his hardships in Africa. The pygmy
picture, *Negrillos,* was packing them in at the Little Carnegie

and kindred theaters. He had taken a lavish suite of offices on Fifth Avenue and was, as variously reported in the gossip columns, negotiating to do a play by Noël Coward, a musical with Mary Martin, an all-Negro *Merry Wives of Windsor*, to found a national repertory company, to film the complete works of Eugene O'Neill, to restage the entire Ring Cycle for the Metropolitan Opera Company, and to marry Hope Hampton. Taking the fullest advantage of our African encounter, I had sent a couple of tentative letters offering him first look at a play I had written. Each letter had produced an answer, very badly typed and spelled, stating that Mr. Starr was currently in Hollywood or London or Bayreuth, where he would remain for an unconscionable length of time, and signed "Alistair St. Regis, Secretary to Mr. Starr."

So it was 1950 before I met Leander Starr again. It was a Wednesday, and I was taking a client and his wife to an expense-account lunch. They were a sweet, grandparently Jewish couple who manufactured a superior brand of mouthwash in New Jersey. He always called me Son and she was forever knitting sweaters for our children and insisting that we remove them from the hot, humid city to their place outside Princeton (which was twice as hot and humid). She adored the theater and we were lunching early at Hampshire House so they could hustle around and catch a matinee of *Gentlemen Prefer Blondes* at the Ziegfeld. We were discussing something wholesome, like toilet training, when Leander Starr burst into the dining room like a comet. "Darling boy," he bellowed, "at last!" Brandishing his copy of *Flair*, from which gatefolds and streamers of tissue fluttered wildly, he descended upon our table and bussed me on both cheeks. Somewhat flustered, I got up, gave him a manly handshake, and introduced him to Mr. and Mrs. Grossman.

"*Enchanté*, Mrs. Grospoint," he said. Then he sat down and ordered a double Martini made with House of Lords gin. "But, dear boy, why have you forsaken me—a sick, lonely, old man thrown to the wolves in this barbarous city."

"That's what I always tell him, Mr. Stern," Mrs. Grossman said. "The idea raising those beautiful babies in a dirty place like this. Why, out by us there are beautiful places going cheap. Sam could help him and with an F.H.A. loan . . ."

"But the talent of you, precious Patrick. I knew it when we met in Capetown . . ."

"Durban," I said.

"Yes, of course, with Deanna Durbin. I knew it then. I saw the mark on your forehead."

"Maybe it was Ash Wednesday."

"The mark of genius. A born writer."

"You should see what he's done for our product," Mr. Grossman said proudly. "New bottle, new label, new spiel on the radio."

"Very high class," Mrs. Grossman added. "And a lovely wife and two gawjus children."

"Ah, Patrick," Starr declaimed, brandishing *Flair*, "I was lying sick in what I hoped would be my deathbed when I read your piece in this pretentious rag. I laughed. I screamed. I clutched my sides in an orgasm of excrutiating glee. I said to myself, 'I *must* find this man again.' Since reading your divine little fantasia I have not slept. I have had my entire staff hunting you down. No stone has been left unturned, and yet the very earth seems to have swallowed you up."

"You might have tried the New York telephone book," I said. "Or possibly Mr. St. Regis could have told you I live on East Seventy-second Street."

"A dark, dirty little place like that," Mrs. Grossman said, twitching her mink indignantly. "With such lovely babies it's a crime."

"Mother, some people *like* the city," Mr. Grossman said.

"That's right, Mother," Starr said, "and if you'll just get on with that chicken salad and not waste the time of America's future Pulitzer Prize winner . . ."

"Mr. Starr," I said pointedly, "Mr. and Mrs. Grossman are old friends *and* clients of mine. I'm in advertising."

"Bah! I'd rather hear that you were pimping. With a gift like yours, chained to a desk on Madison Avenue."

"Actually, it's on East Forty-ninth Street," I said.

"That's what I keep telling him, Mr. Stark," Mr. Grossman said. "He should move out to Jersey, work directly for us. Air-conditioned. Pension plan. Lovely homes. Good schools."

"And the children could use our pool," Mrs. Grossman added.

"*Will* you be still!" Starr thundered. "Dearest boy, leave these savages and come to work for me. When I read this glorious piece of nonsense a whole new concept of the musical revue came washing over me."

"A revue?" I said. Embarrassed as I was, I couldn't help being fascinated. "You mean blackouts, show girls . . ."

"Ah, how few understand me. Even you can be obtuse. No, I do *not* mean a line of strumpets swinging their tits over the orchestra pit." Mr. Grossman choked into his water glass. Mrs. Grossman, fortunately, was a trifle deaf. "I mean something new, something intimate. I mean just four performers—all stars. Darling Gertie Lawrence, dear Bea Lillie, Jack Buchanan, and . . ."

Mrs. Grossman's fork fell with a clatter. "You're in the theater, Mr. Storr?" she asked, her hearing-aid glasses glinting with a new love and respect.

"Yes, Mrs. Grosfeld, I carried a spear in *Aida*. Waiter, bring me another just like this. In fact, make it two."

"Well, perhaps we could talk about it *some other time*," I said. "The Grossmans want to get to their matinee, and I've got a lot to do at the office. If you let me know where you live perhaps I could stop in some evening on my way home and discuss . . ."

"But I live *here* and you're coming upstairs with me now. Call your office and tell them you've resigned. Good day, Mr. Grosgrain, Mother."

As I was propelled out of the room I heard Mrs. Grossman say, "You know he looked a lot like that big movie director, Orlando Starr."

"You know, I believe that's who it was, Mother."

Mr. Grossman was stuck with the check, but they still speak of it as a red-letter day in their lives.

Mr. Starr lived in great style at Hampshire House—as he did every place else—in two large apartments thrown together. The total effect was acres and acres and acres of textbook Dorothy Draper—dark green walls; Regency stripes and cabbage roses; great buckets of white plaster molded into sconces, mirror frames, chandeliers, consoles, and mantels; and a number of large, effusive watercolors by James Reynolds. As a cozy touch, Starr had covered every available surface with signed photographs in tarnished silver frames. King Carol, Nazimova, Marilyn Miller, Marie of Rumania, George Bernard Shaw, Gabriel Pascal, Franklin Delano Roosevelt, Benito Mussolini, and Ernest Hemingway were among those immediately recognizable to me.

"Wow!" I said.

"It's tatty, but it will have to do until I can find something fit for human habitation. Sit down, dear boy, you look dazed."

"I am, rather."

"We'll have something to drink and then get right down to work. St. Regis," he bawled, "where the hell are you?"

"Right here, Mr. Starr, sir." St. Regis bustled in, a needle and thread in one hand, a shirt of Starr's in the other.

"Send for a magnum of decent champagne and get me Gertie Lawrence on the telephone."

"Right away, sir."

"Perhaps I should call my office," I said.

"Yes, dear boy, do that. And tell those whoremasters that you're resigning as of now. Or would you like me to do it for you?"

"Maybe I'll wait until payday."

The telephone rang, and he pounced on it. "Starr speaking. . . . Good. Put her on. . . . *Angel girl!* Drop everything and come to New York immediately. I have the most brilliant young writer under contract and we're all going to do a revue together—just you and Bea and Jack and some competent tonsil artist, say Charles Collins or Al Jolson. . . . Well, then somebody who *isn't* dead. I can't keep track of all these singers. . . . Well, darling, tell Rodgers and Hammerstein you've changed your mind. They'll understand." There was a long pause and I could hear an excited woman's voice at the other end of the line. Starr's face darkened and he seemed to swell up like some sort of angry reptile. "Well! If that's all the thanks I get for hypnotizing you into the only two decent performances you've ever turned in, I'm glad to know it before it's too late. Just don't come grovelling to *me* when you're out of work and forgotten." The voice was still protesting as he slammed down the receiver. "Pitiful creature. Couldn't carry a tune in a bucket. We'll find someone who can sing and is a *star*. Just put the champagne down there and open it, please. St. Regis, sign the check and then get me Bea Lillie. Now, dear Patrick, about our little revue. . . ." The telephone rang again.

It was seven o'clock when I swayed out of Hampshire House, drunk with Starr's champagne and dreams of glory. During the afternoon he had called the White House once, London twice, Hollywood three times, and a number of other places I've forgotten. When Starr wasn't telephoning other famous people, other famous people were telephoning him. One call, from Starr's end of the conversation, sounded like the classic fury of a Woman Scorned; another, answered blandly, cajolingly, and noncommitally, with many vague references to "my accountant" and "my business manager," gave every impression of coming from a collection agency. But I didn't care. By the time the champagne was finished I was in a state of pure euphoria.

"Sweetheart," I said to my wife, "we're in clover." Then I keeled over onto the bed. It wasn't until the next day that I realized we hadn't said one clear or definite word about the intimate little revue.

For the next three months I worked like a stevedore. Although I hadn't been quite foolhardy enough to quit my job at the agency, I had asked for a short leave of absence—a request that was summarily refused. Instead, I was rewarded with three new accounts and the vague promise of a raise the following year. My days were spent writing about the pills and sprays and capsules and gargles our clients forced upon a public of apparent hypochondriacs. My nights and Saturdays and Sundays were taken up with writing what I considered to be devastating material for Starr's intimate little revue. I almost never saw my wife and children, and I was able to pin Starr down to an appointment even more rarely. He was all over the place—Palm Beach or Palm Springs, Houston or Hollywood, Boston or Bermuda. It was always, he explained, to nail down another backer or to sign another star. Late one night when I was trying to get to sleep—not that that was ever much of a problem—I counted up a total of thirty-five stars he had selected to appear in our four-person revue. And they were thirty-five absolute stars whose aggregate salaries would have come to more than a hundred thousand dollars a week in a show that might possibly have grossed fifty thousand. When I mentioned this to him over the telephone he merely said, "Nonsense, we'll charge double."

He frequently called from some faraway place. Once he announced that Cole Porter would write the music, then Irving Berlin, then Kurt Weil, and finally that all three would simply love to collaborate. He declared that Mainbocher had submitted designs for costumes to be worn in skits that I hadn't even written. He would call my office or my home at all hours of the day and night, dragging me out of meetings, out of bed, and—more than once—out of the tub, while my wife growled about wet footprints on the rugs. But when I tried to reach him it was a different matter. The calls to Hampshire House were always intercepted by the ubiquitous Alistair St. Regis who almost always announced that Mr. Starr was out of town or working or sleeping or simply not in. I tried many times to call him at his offices on Fifth Avenue. The telephone there was simply never answered.

Yet the few times I was able to see him, Starr was a stimulating, if peripatetic, collaborator. Dealing with him in his apartment at Hampshire House was a thankless chore, and trying to get him to sit still, to get off the telephone, to state one simple opinion, was like trying to kiss a woodpecker. On three occasions I visited him at his office, always quite late at night when the building was emptied even of its cleaning staff. The home of Leander Starr Productions occupied half the sixteenth floor of an enormous building. The offices were some of the spiffiest I've ever gone through—pale walnut carpeted in yellow with telephones and typewriters to match —and you had to go through quite a series of them to reach Starr's own sanctum sanctorum. It was an eerie experience late at night, and I could never escape the feeling that the big flat modern desks were slabs in a morgue and that I was in the presence of something that was dead. In his office Starr was always cheery enough, bounding about and bursting with enthusiasm. The telephone rarely rang, and when it did he would refuse to answer. Instead, we would sit silently for five rings, ten, fifteen. When the telephone stopped we would go on with our work. Those rare meetings were really stimulating and, odd and irritating as the man could be, I felt a true liking and respect for him.

Finally I had finished enough material to show to Mr. Starr and to the stable of stellar performers he had—or had not— signed to contracts. He was consistently evasive on such minor points.

"Dearest boy!" he shouted over the telephone when I was at last able to reach him. "*How* splendid! *How* wonderful! Come right over and we'll have a good go at the manuscript. Not the office but the apartment, where it's peaceful and quiet."

"Not on your life, Mr. Starr," I said. "I know how peaceful and quiet your apartment is. That's why *you're* coming to *my* apartment. Besides, my wife is dying to meet you. Come for dinner tomorrow night. We'll take the phone off the hook and then you can really look over the stuff."

There was a pause, then he said, "Why, that would be charming, Patrick. Really charming. Have I the address?"

"You have. Seven sharp and don't dress."

"Your wife wants me naked?"

"Exactly. Until tomorrow."

"*À demain.*"

By candlelight, and with the addition of some old Spode and a maid hastily borrowed from my mother-in-law, our apartment looked respectable if not resplendent. There had been deep consultation with the butcher and with Luria's Wines & Spirits. The children had been bathed and fed, mopped up again, and put into the impractical little robes some ill-advised relative had sent them for Christmas. There was nothing to do but wait. So we waited and we waited and we waited. At eight-thirty Mr. Starr arrived in white tie and bearing an immense box of hothouse flowers. "Dear Patrick, forgive my unforgivable tardiness. An *interminable* call from the Coast. It seems that Fred Astaire wants to get back on the stage. Do you think he'd sell any tickets? I wonder." He kissed my wife's hand, embraced both children, inquired as to their names and ages, and then said tragically, "My wife tore my own adorable baby from my arms and ran off with another man. I've never been the same since."

"Which wife was that?" my own wife asked, ignoring my dark look.

"Why, uh, it was . . . Please, I can't talk about it, even today. I didn't mean to burden you with my troubles. After all, you're young, happy, vital, alive. Let us be gay. Perhaps just one more of those delicious Martinis?"

I must say for the old charlatan that he could really charm the birds off the trees without half trying. By the time coffee came in, my own wife was practically sitting on his lap. After he'd swilled down a good bit of brandy and pronounced it excellent, I said, "Now shall we get down to the reading? It's getting late."

20

"Lord, isn't it!" he said, after an elaborate consultation with a Philippe-Patek watch thinner than a dime. "I *must* dash!"

"But the idea was for you to read my material," I said, "here and now without any interruptions."

"And I'm desolate not to be able to, my boy. But I've promised to meet some frightfully rich people at Elmer's—El Morocco, you know."

"I know."

"Well, I mean they're hideously *nouveau* and vulgar and all that—Texas oil—but they're perishing to invest in our show. *Your* show, really. And I can't let you down at a time like this. Give me your manuscript and I swear on my mother's grave that I'll read every word of it before I close an eye tonight. Then I'll give you a jingle *first* thing tomorrow, and we'll get together over lunch and discuss the whole thing. Oh, I know it's all going to be so fresh and new and different and wonderful that I won't even have to read it. It's just that I'm so rotten selfish I want to."

"Lunch then tomorrow?" I said.

"My place. Twelve noon, sharp. Synchronize your watches!" Faster than a smartly struck billiard ball, he was already in the hall swirling his scarlet-lined opera cape around his shoulders. "Oh. Oh, damn! Oh, how could I be such a fool? I've come off without a penny. *Could* you let me have fifty?"

"Cents?"

"Dollars, dear chap."

I had eleven dollars in my pocket and somewhat less in the checking account. My wife, however, who always accuses me of being an easy mark, was positively mesmerized. "I think I have about that much. Just a minute."

"*Mille grazie!*" he said, kissing my wife's hand. He departed with fifty-*five* dollars and, as an afterthought, my manuscript.

It was just noon the next day when I picked up the house telephone at Hampshire House. "Mr. Starr, please," I said. "It's Mr. Dennis. He's expecting me."

"He's not here," the operator said. The usual cheeriness was missing from her voice.

"Then may I please speak to Mr. St. Regis?"

"He's not here either. They've gone."

"You mean they've *checked out?*"

"Not exactly checked out. Just gone."

"Gone?"

"Look, sir, you'd better talk to the assistant manager."

I crossed over to the desk, where the clerk was looking unusually ill and shaken. "I'd like to get in touch with Mr. Starr," I said.

"You're not the only one. So would Hampshire House and the U.S. Government—just to name two others this morning."

"I don't understand. We were supposed to . . ."

"Neither do I, sir. Nothing like this has ever happened at Hampshire House before. He just disappeared—bag and baggage."

I didn't have time for a taxicab. I raced down Fifth Avenue to Starr's office and took the express elevator up to the sixteenth floor. A big black-and-white sign was tacked on to the walnut double doors of the suite. It read:

DISTRICT COLLECTOR OF INTERNAL REVENUE

NOTICE

This property is subject to liens held by the
Federal Government for unpaid taxes. . . .

There was something more about a public auction of property being held on such and such a date, but I couldn't bring myself to read any more.

A building employee strode out of the Starr offices and began fixing a padlock to the doors.

"I beg your pardon," I said, "but I'm trying to find Mr. Starr."

"Who ain't?"

"But isn't there someone on his staff who might know where . . ."

"Never been a staff. He's had this big, fancy place six months now. Never hired the first steno or paid the first month's rent. Night man says this Starr character come in here about three this A.M. all dressed up like a magician, took some papers, and disappeared. Damnedest thing."

"But there's a very important envelope in there that I've got to get." Through the open door I could see file drawers pulled open and papers scattered over the yellow carpet. "It happens to be my property."

"Sorry. Not allowed. Every last paper clip an' Lily cup in there is under the jerstiction of the govermunt. Can't touch anything." With that he closed the door and snapped the padlock.

Too sick to go back to the agency, I walked home. An empty taxi was parked in front of our building, and in the lobby a cab driver was pressing our bell. "Your name Dennis?" he asked.

"Yes," I said. "Why?"

"This envelope was left in my hack out by the airport las' night. I looked inside an' seen your name and address. I figured you might want it back. I even read some of it. Some kind of entertainment, ain't it? The wife an' I thought it was pretty funny."

"Funny," I said. "It's a downright scream." I gave him five dollars and let myself into the apartment. Then I closed the door, hoping I could hold back my tears until I got drunk enough not to care.

For the next five years there was no direct word from Leander Starr, although each Christmas I was the joyless recipient of a minty greeting card, each expressing wishes of the season in a different language—*Buon Natale, Joyeaux Noël,* and so on—from a different country, and each signed "Best Xmas Wishes from your freind Alistair St. Regis," complete with circular i-dots and a scrolled underscoring.

It was only when my first novel was published to gratifying notices and sales that I heard from Starr. It was a long cable sent the most expensive way.

DARLING DARLING BOY EXCLAMATION POINT CONGRATULATIONS CONGRATULATIONS CONGRATULATIONS DOUBLE EXCLAMATION POINT DIDNT I ALWAYS SAY YOU HAD THE MASTER TOUCH QUESTION MARK YOU MUST GIVE ME OPTION ON ENGLISH STAGE RIGHTS STOP I HAVE ALREADY SIGNED A STAR SO FABULOUS SO UTTERLY RIGHT FOR YOUR BEAUTIFUL WORK THAT I DARE NOT EVEN BREATHE HER MAGICAL NAME STOP CABLE YOUR REPLY COLLECT CLARIDGES LONDON FASTEST STOP ABIDINGEST LOVE

LEANDER STARR.

Oddly enough, I laughed. I found that I felt no rancor, no bitterness, no hatred for Starr. It was like hating my children for the time they broke an irreplaceable old Bunny Berrigan record. I was mad as hell, but I knew that they couldn't help what they did any more than they could help being children. It was the same with Starr. Happily, my agent had already negotiated for dramatic rights with a producer who, if less colorful, was more reliable than Leander Starr. I picked up the telephone and called the cable office. "I want to send a collect cable to London," I said, "the fastest, most expensive way. It goes to Leander Starr, Claridge's Hotel, London, England. And the message is just two words."

There was a sharp gasp. "I can't possibly send a message like that, sir. The cable company would never permit it."

"Very well, then," I said, "let's just make it one word and that word is no. N-O, no. And sign it Patrick Dennis."

"Oh. I'm reading your book. I think it's real cute."

"Thank you. Good-by."

"Good-by, Mr. Dennis." Then she giggled.

II

That was seven years ago. When I thought of Starr at all, which wasn't often, I imagined him up to his old tricks, but at least not near me. I had served my time as his victim, had learned my lesson, and had even had the brief satisfaction of what I considered the last word—*No*. I am now slowly recovering from the experience of having Starr, until a few days ago, right next door, right down here.

"Down here" is Mexico City. Now that there is a little money in the bank, now that our children are off at boarding school, my wife and I spend all of our time writing "little things on the side." It is a precarious but pleasant way to earn a living in that it can be done just about whenever and wherever one feels like doing it. The only trick is feeling like doing it. For the past couple of winters we have been coming to Mexico armed with typewriters, Eaton's Corrasable Bond paper, and the best intentions in the world. So far we have tried—with signally small success—Acapulco, that "unspoiled little fishing village," which has become a sort of Mex-Miami; Taxco, which looks suspiciously like a Joseph Urban setting for *Rio Rita* and is crawling with alcoholic Americans on modest trust funds who are all going to commence that play or novel or picture or tone poem *mañana;* and Cuernavaca, where the Americans with larger trust funds start the daily cocktail party every morning at eleven and manage to keep it going until eleven that night—at least. They're all wonderful places to postpone doing any work, but they don't make it exactly easy to scare up the

25

rent money at the beginning of every month. And after very short visits in each famous community, we got to hate them.

This year, things are working out far better. My wife and I are really happiest in places of a million population or more, and so we have chosen Mexico City—or at least its outskirts—where we have the advantages of the pastoral life and are yet only fifteen minutes and seventy-five cents by taxicab from the Juarez section (or the East Fifties of the Distrito Federal) with its glossy restaurants and shops and air of general worldliness. With nearly five million souls in the capital city, we are also a lot freer to pick and choose the people we want to see when we want to see them—and that excludes a great many. A lot of Americans, more or less fluent in Spanish, have tried to crash the Old Mexican Society. They can't, but it would serve them good and right if they could. The O.M.S. is one of the most inbred, parochial, and dismal flocks ever to be seen. At their parties (we have been to just two—the second because we couldn't believe that the first one was really real) the men gather at one end of the room and talk about business, while the women at the other end discuss such stimulating subjects as their children, how lazy their maids are, and the high cost of living. After two or three hours of that, the first glass of tequila is brought out, and a good time is had by all.

Even drearier is that one-hundred-and-ten-per-cent American colony made up of the representatives of such various United States products as refrigerators, calculating machines, farm equipment, soft drinks, and canned goods. What with their D.A.R. and American Legion Post and Rotary Club and P.T.A. and general red, white, and blowsiness, they have always been able to create a miniature Main Street in some of the most unlikely places in the world. Well, they're welcome to it.

Still lower are the Americans who are ashamed of being Americans. They are generally given to beards and sandals, arts and crafts, dirndls and dungarees. They are more native than the natives, denying their children (of which there are many, mostly born via variations of natural childbirth that would shock an Aztec) such bourgeois affectations as shoes and the English language. As the Mexicans will have nothing to do with them, they consort exclusively—and in Spanish—with other Americans who are ashamed of being Americans. They deserve each other.

On the other hand, there is a large and fluid group of perfectly pleasant people who are not much of anything at all. It is a constantly shifting society made up of Americans, English, a few French and Germans, a scattering of South Americans, and a lot of very cheery Mexicans who have lived elsewhere at some time or another and who have more interesting things to talk about than household and finance. They congregate in good, nontouristy restaurants like the Rivoli or the Derby or Ambassadeurs or Bill Shelburne's El Paseo. They give nice large parties and better small ones. If times ever get dull, there are things like vacationing movie stars or minor nobility or con men or just visiting firemen to jazz things up. This clump of jolly, unclassifiable people is called, with heavy scorn, The International Set by all the locals who aren't a part of it. The title makes it sound a great deal grander and racier and clique-ier than happens to be the case. What it actually is, is a bunch of fairly attractive people who like to see one another every now and then, and if you don't take it seriously you can have quite a good time. So much for "down here."

"Right next door" is yet another matter. Right next door happens to be the abbess' suite and refectory of an erstwhile convent. My wife and I are at present rather uncomfortably housed in the vestibule, concierge's office, visiting parlors, and several cells above. The place is now called Casa Ximinez, and it is owned and mismanaged by none other than Catalina Ximinez, star of *Yucatán Girl*.

Señorita Ximinez, or Madame X, as she is unaffectionately known by her tenants, is one of those rare phenomena in the world of movies—the one-picture star. The stories about her are legion and probably libelous. However, from all of the gossip and speculation surrounding Catalina Ximinez, this much is undoubtedly true: In 1930 she was an unknown, unlettered mestizo girl (illegitimate, some say) of seventeen existing as best she could (as a prostitute, some say) in Chichen Itza. Churlish and venal and stupid, she had only one thing to recommend her—she was perfectly beautiful, with strongly chiseled Indian features and masses of blue-black hair streaming down her back. Starr bumped into her (in a brothel, some say), was stunned by the wonder of her face and figure, and that was how *Yucatán Girl* came into being.

When you get right down to it, *Yucatán Girl* is a terribly long and dull picture, notable only for its views of ruins and the fabulous face of Catalina Ximinez, and she had very little to do except to arrange her features into a pattern of imbecility—which was easy for her—and to be photographed running gracefully across the plains—somewhat more difficult. She became Starr's mistress for the duration of the shooting, and then he left her flat. Legend has it that she was paid exactly two hundred dollars for starring in a film that has since grossed millions, but at least she was paid, which is more than many of Starr's associates can claim. However, it didn't much matter. Once her fantastic beauty was exposed to the world, her only problem was one of selection. She became the mistress of an enormously rich Mexican revolutionary general (the mistress of President Plutarco Calles himself, some say) and then set about amassing a fortune of her own.

She was extremely wise to do so. She had absolutely no talent as an actress, and to hear her shrill, rasping cockatoo's voice, one can readily understand why Starr cast her as a deaf-mute. As a matter of fact, cockatoo describes her perfectly—voice, face, figure, mode of dress, and disposition. The Indian blood that brought about her amazing beauty has now brought about her ruin. The fine, high-bridged nose has become an imperious beak. The straight black Indian hair has been cut and crimped and dyed an unsuccessful red. And her straight, slim figure has widened and widened until she looks like an old squaw. Having been told so often —some years back—that she is a beauty, Miss Ximinez is now utterly convinced of it. She is very much the film star, enslaved to fringe and sequins, garish colors and bits of fox fur. No dress is too bright or too tight for her to wear. What I mean is, she's a sight.

But stupid as she may be, Catalina Ximinez has a cagey shrewdness. When her paramour offered to set her up in housekeeping, she was smart enough not to choose one of those bogus Spanish colonial establishments out in Lomas, where all good revolutionary generals and their mistresses go to retire. Instead, she snapped up this ancient disused nunnery for a song and manages not only to live in it in great style with her nutty old mother, but also to rent out half a dozen apartments at roughly three times the going rate. It is here, in the Casa Ximinez, where we are now living.

The Casa Ximinez was once the Convent of the Sisters of Chastity, a small, snobbish, and now defunct order for the unclaimed daughters of aristocratic old Spanish families. The Sisters of Chastity apparently gave up very little else, for even today it is obvious that they were cloistered in extreme luxury. The building is enormous, with barred windows looking blindly out onto the street, and built around a huge patio in the traditional colonial fashion. It is said to date from the sixteenth century, and from the way our plumbing behaves, I quite believe it. The rooms are large and lofty with elaborate tile floors, painted beams, and inadequate heating. It is furnished with pseudo-antiques of the Porfirio Diaz period, which la Ximinez undoubtedly picked up on the cheap at the state pawnshop. In the course of remodeling from priory to apartment house, Madame X has achieved some architectural effects that are eccentric to say the least. In our apartment one is always going up a step, down a step, through somebody else's bedroom, and walking miles to get nowhere at all. The bathroom, for example, opens into the living room on a different floor from the bedrooms. You have to pass through it to get to the kitchen, which is somewhat smaller. Actually, our bathroom is the biggest thing in the whole apartment. On the theory that Americans like a lot of plumbing, Miss Ximinez has gone hog-wild on equipping it. The room contains two wash-basins, a tub, a shower, a toilet, a bidet, a standing urinal, and a tooth basin, all in a virulent dental-plate-pink porcelain with tile to match. Further refinements are a Morris chair, a horsehair sofa, and an imitation Baccarat chandelier. The San Ysidro toilet has been inadvertently piped with hot water, and steams ominously. There is no hot water in either washbasin, just a sad little sigh when you turn on the taps. A most ineffectual Calorex heater blows pathetic, periodic gusts of warm, fetid air into the room from time to time, but as the place measures thirty by thirty, with a very high ceiling and a large, drafty window (affording the casual passer-by tempting views of us in varying stages of undress), it's a little like bathing in an ice palace.

Conveniently adjoining the bathroom is the kitchen on whose renovation Madame X has invested very little time, thought, or money. There is an old zinc sink, a two-burner Acros stove with an oven door that has to be propped shut, and a very small America referigerator with only two ice trays, both of which are permanently frozen into place. As a gay decorative note our landlady has added a bridge table and two little gold ballroom chairs. There is a small amount of native pottery from the Bazaar Sabado, a few mismatched Woolworth cups and plates, and almost no cooking utensils. We used to laugh at our friend Walter Pistole for traveling with his own coffeepot and egg beater. Now I see the wisdom of Walter's ways.

Presiding over the kitchen, and presumably included in the rent, is Guadalupe, our cook and maid of all work. She is about sixty and very fat. She is also the worst cook in the Western Hemisphere. It makes little difference. By setting my alarm for five every morning I can usually get to the kitchen and brew up a decent pot of coffee before she comes shambling down from whichever sordid attic she occupies on the bounty of Señorita Ximinez. To Guadalupe's distress, we lunch on fruit and cheese and Pan Bolillos and Carta Blanca beer, which she can do nothing to ruin. About nine o'clock every evening we put on our city clothes, telephone for a taxi, and go into the heart of the district to some place like El Paseo or La Cava for a decent meal. Yet our grocery bills are staggering.

No day passes that Guadalupe doesn't drag my wife off to the Minimax or the local *tienda* with endless marketing lists: jugs of Casa oil—a particularly nasty sesame-seed oil used for cooking—rice and beans and frijoles and tortillas, Barras de Coco, gallons of pulque, Gloria butter by the ton, Pan Bimbo for toast, and mountains of Nescafé (which my wife insists Guadalupe uses for face powder). And who eats all these groceries? Guadalupe's family. There is her daughter with three children and another on the way (and *still* no husband). There is Guadalupe's sister, who works for Dr. and Mrs. Priddy across the courtyard. There is the *vigilante,* or night watchman, who just happens to be Guadalupe's uncle. There is a cousin who sells lottery tickets during what rare moments he's not in our kitchen eating. There is a drunken son who helps put away Guadalupe's pulque as well as our Scotch, bourbon, gin, rum, and tequila. For two people with light appetites, more food is consumed in our kitchen in the course of a day than in the entire Hilton Hotel chain. There are just about as many people checked in, too. My wife swears that all of them are poor relatives of Señorita Ximinez and that she just keeps them on as servants. (To her horror, my wife found out yesterday that Guadalupe's salary is one dollar a day.) But I don't see how *any* family can be all that big.

The whole of Casa Ximinez throbs with life. In addition

to Guadalupe, her daughter, her three grandchildren, her
son, her sister, her cousin, her uncle, all feeding their faces
in our place, there are her birds—a great reed cage filled
with little *tzinzontles* that bicker and fight even worse than
the humans. There is Perro, Madame X's abominable little
French poodle, who barks for exactly twenty-three and a
half hours every day. There is Loro, her ugly green and
yellow parrot (Miss Ximinez is very direct with animals,
calling them simply the Spanish equivalents of dog, cat,
parrot, and so on—but then Miss Ximinez is very direct
about everything), who gives an awfully good impersonation
of Perro barking and an even better one of Madame X demanding her rent. When he has run through this somewhat
limited repertoire, he flies up into the jacaranda tree just
above my head and screams until Abelardo, the gardener,
comes with a ladder to fetch him down. Less than an hour
later, the whole performance is repeated. It seems to keep
Abelardo a good deal more occupied than the garden does.
Guacamayo, the macaw, lives on a perch across the patio—
but not far enough. By day he is as still as death, blinking
his obscene naked eyelids in the sunlight and searching his
wingpits—if that is the term I want—for lice. Punctually at
midnight he goes stark, staring mad, shrieking and emitting
jungle cries that would freeze your marrow. After dark, cats
prowl and yowl on the roof above, rats scratch and scurry
through the cellars below. Madame X and her mother get
into a screaming fishwifely brawl every night on the subject
of whether or not Mamacita's favorite television program is
disturbing the tenants. Perro joins in. Yellow mongrels out
on the street bark back their replies. About four in the
morning a rooster living *somewhere*—I wish I knew—
nearby commences to crow, and every half hour the *vigilante* rides past on his bicycle and blows a shrill blast into
our bedroom window to tell us that all is serene. (For this
service he charges four pesos a week—thirty-two cents—although he never has change for a five-peso note.)

All in all, it's a silly, pleasant way of life with as many amusements as irritants. The climate is lovely and a lot better than a sleety, slushy winter in New York. We can also piously tell one another that things are so cheap down here we're actually saving money, which is quite true if we overlook—as we resolutely do—the plane fares, the long-distance calls to our children and agents and publishers, and the fact that our expenses continue in New York just as though we were still there.

This year we have been installed in the Casa Ximinez since Epiphany, when the children were sent back to school growling and grousing about the ghastly injustices of being young and having three thousand dollars apiece annually spent on their educations. This makes us the oldest tenants of all, save for Dr. and Mrs. Priddy, who occupy very small quarters on—thank God—the far side of the patio. The P.'s are not to be believed. He is an old poop from Maine who has passed the last sixty-five of his seventy years preparing himself for life. He holds degrees of varying luster from Harvard, Columbia, Heidelberg, Yale, Alabama, Trinity, Clare College, the Sorbonne, U.C.L.A., and God knows how many totally unheard of institutions spread across the face of the globe. The list of initials strung out after his name—and he has them all religiously engraved on his visiting cards, which he deals out as though he were playing six-pack bezique—looks like ANTIDISESTABLISHMENTARIANISM spelled backwards. He is also one of those really tatty Ph.D.'s who insist on being called Doctor instead of Mister, and his wife refers to him solely as *The* Doctor. Having just enough private income to pay for room and board, books, and tuition, he is forever looking one year ahead for the one more degree that will prepare him for a career. Except for homework, he's never done an honest day's toil in his life. He is currently enrolled with the bobby-socks set at the University of Mexico, studying I-forget-what, although he's told me at least a hundred times.

One would think that with so much mileage and tutelage behind him, he might be interesting to talk to. Far from it. He is incapable of speaking or writing a simple declarative sentence. If there is a short Anglo-Saxon word that can be expressed less well by a long foreign phrase, Dr. Priddy always chooses the foreign language. If asked whether he would prefer coffee or tea, Dr. Priddy comes up with a long preamble, a classical quotation, an "amusing little anecdote" attributed to Walpole concerning Boswell and Johnson, a brief analysis of recent findings on the stimulating qualities contained in caffeine, and finally says, "Tea, *s'il vous plaît,* 'The cup that cheers but does not intoxicate,' heh heh heh. Or, as Congreve so aptly put it in *The Double Dealer,* 'They retired to their tea and scandal, according to their ancient custom,' heh heh heh." Oh, he's got a great sense of humor, as he'll tell you in five million words or more. Actually, he's the second most boring person I've ever met.

The *first* most boring person we know is Dr. Priddy's wife, Modesta Lee Drain Priddy. She is a flirtatious Southern belle of sixty-odd who—and I quote—"jest lahves and adowahs innathing quaint." And with Dr. Priddy's lifetime safari through the Groves of Academe ("Actually, the sublime Milton spoke of 'the *olive* grove of Academe' in his *Paradise Regained,* but yours is a common blunder, Mr. Dennis, heh heh heh."), she's seen *ivverything* quaint from the Balkans to Borneo, which she will be only too happy to describe to you in minute detail. She is little and plump— in fact, the word *small* describes everything about both *The* Doctor and Miz Priddy—and prone to peasant blouses, amber beads, cameos, squash-blossom necklaces, beaten silver, turquoises, embroidered shawls, coolie hats, lava earrings, and all the other badges of quaintitude she has been able to barter for in native bazaars and peasant market places for the past half century.

She fancies herself as a one-woman voice of democracy,

who loves and understands peasants the world over. She is wrong. She merely patronizes them, and they know it and resent it—or at least they do down here. And just allow some servant or shopkeeper to treat her as an equal, and she will let everyone know that she is a Drain and Poetess Laureate of Corinth, Tennessee. Childless, she thinks she loves and understands children. But, again, her love and understanding are only patronage. She likes children on her own terms: in native costume performing long-abandoned traditional songs and dances, when they'd much rather be drinking Coca-Cola and watching television. Being poor and greedy, the local children naturally hoped that they might get a few pesos out of the rich Americana. They were sorely mistaken. When the maids at Casa Ximinez beg for shoes for their kids or for a little help in buying the compulsory red school uniforms, Miz Priddy suddenly becomes stone-deaf or delicately vague and forgetful, or, if the bite is *really* being put on her, the outraged spokesman for the huddled masses. As she recently said to my wife, who had just treated Guadalupe's three grandchildren to new shoes, *"Ah* think it's terrible to deprive them of their *pride."* She affects the simpering sweetness of Melanie Wilkes, but just let the proprietor of the Farmacia Corazón de Jesús charge one centavo too much for a bottle of *leche de Phillips* (milk of magnesia seems to be the staff of life in the Priddy household), and the famous Drain dimples disappear while Miz Priddy tells him in her Tennessee Spanish that she's going to call the police.

When speaking English, which she does incessantly and fluently, she has that irritating, coy mannerism affected by some Southern women of making every statement a question by means of vocal inflection at the end of each sentence. "Ah come from Corinth, Tinnesee? Mah family were all Drains?" Drains is right! I suspect the device is intended to inquire as to whether we comprehend and appreciate the importance of each dreary pronouncement. We do. She is also, if you can bear to listen closely, a little hotbed of prejudices. Jews displease her except in Israel ("Wheah they belong?"), dancing quaint traditional *horahs*. Save for such picturesque rites as saint's day processions in full costume, Miz Priddy recognizes no current values in the Catholic Church. The merest mention of the American Negro is enough to erase her cast-iron dimples, although Negroes qualify for occasional roles of quaint folksiness in her tales of native Dixie.

They are great droppers-in. They dropped in on us the first day we moved into Casa Ximinez, scattering their visiting cards, and they haven't stopped since. Our common bond seems to be that we all write. Dr. Priddy in the course of garnering his many, many degrees is the author of countless abstruse monographs and Ph.D. theses, each published by an obscure university press, each averaging an inch of text to a yard of footnotes, and each more stultifying than the last. Miz Priddy, if less prolific, is even less talented. Her literary output amounts to a five-foot shelf of personal memoirs privately published, over the years, by a printer in Nashville, and includes such can't-put-it-down works as *Montenegro—My First Impressions; Going Native—My Two Years as a Portuguese Housewife; My Friends the Fisherfolk of Calabria*. Well, you get the picture.

Miz Priddy is incessantly sticking her nose into other people's business and giving a full report on her findings. It was Miz Priddy who was able to tell us that the couple named Horowitz in Apartamiento 3 were Jewish—or at least she suspected as much. It was Miz Priddy who came up with the scoop that the Catalina Ximinez who owned Casa Ximinez was "none othah than the Catalina Ximinez who appeared in that dowlin' movie *Yew-catayun Gull?*" When the alcoholic who briefly occupied Apartamiento 6 was carried away in a Cruz Roja ambulance during an attack of delirium tremens, it was that old sleuth Miz Priddy who said that she believed he drank. I mean she's alert. And so it was Modesta

Lee Drain Priddy who informed my wife that the mysterious new tenant in Apartamiento 2 was none other than Leander Starr, "die-rectah of that dowlin' movie *Yew-catayun Gull* and othahs?"

My wife came home from some minor shopping foray at the Nueva Mil Preguntas looking wide-eyed and harassed.

"Don't you feel like a drink?" she asked.

"No, not especially," I said.

"Well, make two anyhow. I'll drink yours."

"You look as though you'd seen a ghost."

"I feel as though I had. I was in the Nueva Mil Preguntas when along came old Miz Priddy and said . . ."

"Oh, Miz *Priddy?* In that case I'll make you three drinks. I know exactly how . . ."

"And do you know what she told me?"

"Plenty, I feel sure."

"She told me that the person who moved into Casa Ximinez last night was . . . Well, you won't guess in a thousand years."

"Hernando Cortés?"

"No. I'm serious."

"Pancho Villa?"

"Oh, much worse. It's none other than Leander *Starr!*"

I got up quietly and made *four* drinks.

But if the great man was indeed living right next door to my wife and me, he was being anything but neighborly. As the weather in Mexico City all this winter has been especially warm, we usually work out of doors in the patio. Immediately after my wife and I had downed our restorative drinks we set up office directly beneath Starr's heavily curtained windows. For the rest of the afternoon we played noisy duets on our typewriters. (My output was principally a letter to our son and "The quick brown fox jumps over the lazy sleeping dog," while my wife ran up a scorcher to the Vassar Alumnae Association and several versions of

"Now is the time for all good men to come to the aid of the party.") Every now and then when, from sheer exhaustion, we stopped banging away at our typewriters, we launched into loquacious and totally fictitious dialogue about the brilliant things we were supposedly working on—oh, I tell you, the Lunts couldn't have put on a better show of the madly successful little couple. We had wild bits like:

ME: Would you mind stopping whatever you're doing and casting an eye over this?

SHE: Hahahahaha! Funniest thing I've ever read. They'll love it at Warner Brothers.

ME: Well, they're not going to get it unless I have approval of the director. That's absolutely definite in my contract.

SHE: I don't blame you one bit. That's what I told them at M-G-M. I said, "I want a decent director— somebody young and reliable."

My wife swears that she heard a low moan from inside Starr's apartment, and maybe she did, but her ears aren't half as keen as her imagination. We poured out more drinks and went back to our clattering until we got bored with doing typing exercises. Then my wife led off with another body blow:

SHE: Funny as this piece is, do you think it's quite fair to stop working on that play you promised the Theatre Guild?

ME: Of course I've stopped. I finished it over the weekend and sent it right off to Lawrence and Armina by airmail.

SHE: And you didn't let me read the last act?

ME: How could I? You were at that meeting with Dolores del Rio about adapting that novel for her.

SHE: Oh, so I was. Well, I do hope Lawrence liked it.

ME: *Like* it? They were *mad* for it. They've already

signed Margaret Leighton and Rex Harrison for the leads.

SHE: Perfect!

ME: Now the only problem is finding a director.

SHE: Isn't it always. As I was saying to Josh Logan . . .

ME: Wouldn't you like another drink? *I* would.

SHE: Adore one.

This time, there was the distinct sound of a door being slammed furiously in Starr's apartment and of a voice that could have belonged to no one but Alistair St. Regis saying, "Oh, goodness!"

Between the hot sunlight beating down on us, the many, many, many drinks, the hectic typing, and our bravura performances, we could hardly stagger back into our own quarters at dusk. As I closed the door unsteadily behind me, I saw Alistair St. Regis, wearing very dark glasses and a mass of chestnut ringlets, dart out of Starr's apartment, dash across the patio and into the street.

It was quite late when we glided rather unsteadily into El Paseo for dinner, and at the piano our genial host, William Shelburne, was going out of his Bart Howard set ("Fly me to the moooooon and let me play among the stars, etc.") and into his Cy Coleman and Carolyn Leigh phase ("I have a feeling that beneath the little halo on your noble head, etc."). Although naps, hot coffee, and cold plunges had done something to quell the effects of sun and rum, we were still far from being ourselves, sliding helplessly from great hauteur into fits of inane laughter. El Paseo was thronged, and there was no hope of getting a table right away so we ordered two drinks—which we needed like a case of crabs—and took them to the piano where one could get a splendid view of the Shelburne. But what attracted my attention instead was Alistair St. Regis standing next to me and contemplating his daiquiri with a great sweeping of crimped eyelashes.

39

"*Mis*-ter St. Regis," I said in a small, jovial roar. "This *is* a pleasure and after *all* these years and *all* those Christmas cards!" I thought poor St. Regis was going right up through the skylight, but I clutched his frail arm in order to hold him down and then grandly introduced him to my wife. "My dear," I said grandly, "I want you to meet none other than the great Leander Starr's right-hand man, the distinguished Alistair St. Regis."

"A g-great pleasure indeed, Mrs. Dennis," he stammered. "Goodness, it is late. I must be going."

"Not a-tall," I bellowed. "And do let me buy you another of those."

The piano stopped. "If you would rather sing this song, Patrick," Bill Shelburne said icily, "I'll be happy to accompany you."

"Ever so sorry," I said. "Not my key."

"Pipe down," my wife said out of the corner of her mouth. "You're making a scene."

"Sorry."

"And I really must be going," St. Regis whispered.

"I won't hear of it," I said in a more normal tone of voice. "Why, it's been years since I've had the pleasure of seeing you and dear Leander, and I want to hear about every golden moment of it."

"Your table is ready, Mr. Dennis," Ricardo said.

"I insist that you join us for dinner," I said to St. Regis, who was positively quivering beneath my grasp.

"*His* table?" someone at the piano said. "We've been waiting here since . . ."

Our genial host stopped in the middle of a song. "He has a reservation." (I hadn't.) Then he added darkly, "Sort of a *last* supper." Some performers are just plain touchy.

With St. Regis protesting every inch of the way, we were ushered to a table far, far away from the music, where I ordered a whole lot more to drink and, eventually, even dinner. St. Regis was most unco-operative at first, protesting that he had another engagement, that it was terribly late, that he had promised Mr. Starr to be home by midnight, that he had some letters he must write, that he had a nagging headache, and so on. But he hasn't much head for liquor—or perhaps it was the altitude—and so after being lulled by a few more drinks and a Steak Diane, he eventually relaxed and, albeit guardedly, told me in his affected, prissy manner of the decline and fall of Leander Starr during the past decade.

My sister and I once had an English nurse who was *almost* as ladylike as Alistair St. Regis. Nanny always said "serviette" for "napkin" and "convenience" for "toilet" and "abdomen"—pronounced *ab*-do-men, which sounded even more refined—for "stomach." She also described Al Capone as "most uncouth" and Loeb and Leopold as "two very naughty college boys" and Ruth Snyder as "by no means a lady." Watching St. Regis with his precise table manners —the choreography of knife and fork, the dainty bite-sized pieces, the crooked finger as he raised his glass, the prim blottings of his pursed lips with the napkin (or serviette) —took me right back to the nursery. And when it came to the pretty euphemism, the delicate turn of phrase, Alistair St. Regis made our old nurse sound like Belle Barth. His speech, beneath its garnish of elegancies, bits of bad French, and bogus Britishisms picked up during his years with Starr, seemed to me to be rural Pennsylvania or New Jersey with a liberal larding of elocution lessons—"take a cup of air but only *use* a spoonful . . . pear-shaped vowels . . . when in doubt always choose the *middle* A" and so on. But not put off by the vulgarity of his affectations, I kept plying and prying, and pretty soon the whole story was out. In somewhat more detail than the Recent History of Leander Starr that I have outlined before, St. Regis gave us to understand that the fiasco in Rome concerned an "extremely tem-per-a-men-til Eyetalian screen personidge." The bustup in the south of France was caused by "my imployer's inordinunt love of *Dame Chance*" (pronounced "Damn Shaunnessy") "at the wheel of fortune in Monte Carlo." Upon digging deeper, I learned that Starr had dropped half a million francs which he did not have at roulette (pronounced "roo-lay") and had been forced to flit by moonlight. In English pictures the trouble had been caused by "a drastic differince of opinion between he and a fem-un-un star that shall be nameless" and on television "a misunderstanding concerning the budgit and my imployer's ixpense account." They'd raced in and out of a lot of other countries as well.

Over stingers, which St. Regis had half-heartedly tried to refuse, not that he could do much more by then than keep his head off the table, I got a few more details. The Department of Internal Revenue was still hot on Starr's tail, so that he couldn't return to the States even though he had dozens of good offers in Hollywood. Two wives were after him for back alimony, and he was also up to his eyeballs in unpaid bills all over the world.

"And the tragic de-*new*-mint of it all, Mr. Dennis, Mrs. Dennis," St. Regis said slurringly, "is that had my imployer but heeded my financial advice many years ago, he would today be a gentlemun of great wealth."

"And so what's he doing down here in Mexico?"

"There is no place else that the poor gentlemun can go to, Mr. Dennis. He is a hunted anna-mull. There is a terrible lady that is very wealthy and wants to marry him. . . ."

"Wouldn't that solve *some* of his problems? About *how* rich?"

"Oh, no, sir. Mrs. Po . . . well, I would per-fer not to de-vulge the party's identity, but she is not at all the sort of lady with who Mr. Starr should enter into any kind of personal relationship."

"Better dead than wed?"

"Per-cisely. Oh, I do enjoy your jokes, Mr. Dennis. We was—*were*—residing in Saint Morris, Switzerland, when I read your latest book and I must say that . . ."

"Does Starr owe you money?" I asked.

"Well, really," my wife said. "Talk about nose trouble!"

With a certain noble dignity St. Regis said, "Mr. Dennis, I have been in Mr. Starr's imploy for the past quarter of a century. If he has not been able to recompense me in full during the recent years of financial distress, I know that he will ummediately when he regains his former affluence, for he is a man of honor and his word is as good as . . ."

My wife had a terrible coughing fit and had to be thumped on the back. I guess she was feeling no pain either.

"But if Starr isn't paying you, how can the two of you afford to live in a clip joint like Casa Ximinez, and how can *you* afford to come to a place like El Paseo?"

"While you're about it, why don't you ask Mr. St. Regis the results of his last Wasserman test, *dear?*" my wife said.

"Fortunately, Mr. Dennis—or perhaps I should say *un*-fortunately—my Awnt Bessie, that raised me after I lost my folks, passed away and left me as her sole heir. She was a beautician in Alhambra, New Jersey. I have always admired beauty-ful things, Mr. Dennis—good restaurants, stylishly dressed ladies and gentlemin, lovely florial arrangemunts, elegunt surroundings. That is why I selected the apartmunt Mr. Starr now occupies, and once a week I allow myself the luxury of dining at a . . ."

"*You* chose the Casa Ximinez?"

"Yes, sir. It has a certain jenny-say-coy about it. Señorita Ximinez owes my imployer a great debt. She was nothing but Iztic trash before my imployer developed her stellar potentials."

"She still is," my wife murmured.

"Mr. Starr's great cinema, *Yucatán Girl,* was made down here. The climate is selubrious. My imployer is a sick man, Mr. Dennis, frankly between you and I, he has lost the will to work. A certain influential Mexican producer—you may know the name—a Señor Aristido González has contacted Mr. Starr about filming a . . ."

43

"González?" I said. "Why, he's almost as crooked as . . ."

"Therefore, I took it upon myself to bring Mr. Starr to Mexico so that he can regain the fortune and reputation that are so rightfully his."

"Do you mean to say that out of the money your uncle left you . . ."

"My awnt. Awnt Bessie."

"Out of the money your aunt left you *you're* picking up the tab for Starr's visit to Mexico?"

"It . . . it seemed the least I could do, Mr. Dennis."

"But why?"

"Because, Mr. Dennis, Mr. Starr is a great director, and I have always wanted to be an actor."

He rose unsteadily to his feet, swayed dangerously, and was helped tenderly out of the restaurant and into a taxi by two solicitous waiters.

III

The next day was a Saturday, and from the way we felt, one that will live in infamy. Many visitors to Mexico City find that being eight thousand feet up makes a single drink do the work of three. My wife and I are constituted differently. We've discovered—or at least like to believe—that we can drink much more at that altitude than we can at sea level, that we get along on far less sleep and that we never have hangovers. However, that Saturday was a dazzling exception.

I woke up well after eleven feeling exactly like death. And it didn't make things much better to find a pot of cold, muddy coffee parked on the bedside table. (Guadalupe always brings the coffee at seven thirty, regardless of whether we're asleep, awake, or even there.) I lowered one tremulous leg out of bed, got weakly to my feet, skidded and landed on the cold tile floor. It was then I realized that I had a shattering headache. I picked myself up, too dispirited to curse, and shuddered into my robe. I looked at myself in the tin-framed mirror and recognized what I was seeing—a gigantic hangover. The red-to-yellow eyes, the pouches beneath them, the crease across my forehead from lying flat on my face, the beard awry from having been slept on the wrong way—all the signs of the real sockdolager. Other signs were the suit I had been wearing, hung up much too meticulously; the shoes, the shirt, the socks, the tie all arranged on a chair as though I might have been trimming a window at Brooks Brothers. Sober, I'm far more casual about undressing. True, we had been drinking way out of our league most of the day and all of the night before, but this was the kind of morning-after that hadn't happened to me for years. I shook four aspirins out into my trembling hand, popped them into my mouth, tried to swallow them, found that they were stuck halfway down my throat, discovered that the water carafe had been emptied—or, more likely, had never been filled—washed the aspirins down with half a cup of Guadalupe's frigid coffee, gagged, and then staggered down the stairway, through the library, across the hall, the length of the living room, and into the pink bathroom to throw up. So began my day.

My wife, who felt little better, was already up and swaying over the kitchen stove where she was wanly trying to brew up a fresh pot of potable coffee. The noise and the crowds were unbelievable. Guadalupe, her daughter, and grandchildren were all quarreling violently over something that I took to be the cost of a first-communion dress. I can't imagine why, when they knew perfectly well that Mr. and Mrs. Sucker would end up paying for it. Guadalupe's cousin, who sold lottery tickets, and her uncle, the *vigilante*, were having a second breakfast of rice and beans, *pan dulce, café con leche,* and pulque. The *tzinzontles* were chattering furiously in their cage. This may have been because a stray cat had wandered in and was contemplating them hungrily through the bars. Perro was barking from some place in Madame X's cavernous apartment, and Loro had flown up into the jacaranda tree and was screaming while Madame X's mother was screaming for Abelardo to bring a ladder and get the parrot down. Out in the street there was a terrible cacophony of bugles and drums and every now and then the clanging of a glockenspiel. It happened to be a hundred school children all dressed in white, flourishing red, white, and green Mexican flags, and all shouting at once while two hysterical schoolteachers tried to shout above the noise. It was Flag Day or Revolution Day or something like that. Mexico has even more parades than New York City, and I can never keep track of what illustrious occasion it happens to be. All I wanted that day was for everyone to shut up and go. I made a lunge for the *News* and grabbed it just as Guadalupe was about to wrap her grandchildren's lunches in it. We subscribe to two newspapers—the *News* in English for us and the *Zócalo,* a sort of Spanish-language *National Enquirer* or *News of the World,* overflowing with murder, violence, and scandal, for Guadalupe. But we hardly ever get to see our own newspaper before Guadalupe has lined her bird cage with it. When it comes to the *Zócalo,* however, she washes her hands carefully, sits down for two hours to read every word of it, then presses it with a warm iron and sends one of her grandchildren out to resell it.

After an eternity our coffee was ready. My wife and I picked our way through the rush-hour traffic and lurched out to the patio. It was a lovely sunny day—it's *always* a lovely sunny day. I set the tray down on a rickety tile-topped table, and we fell into our chairs. I looked up at the cloud-less sky and saw a swarm of vultures circling the Casa Ximinez.

"They're back," I said.

"Who?"

"The vultures."

"They always know before we do," my wife said, lifting her coffee cup unsteadily to her lips.

"Well, I hope they take me first. It's been a pleasant life up till today. Now I'm ready to go."

"And I want to go with you."

"I don't suppose the children will miss us much. They're practically grown up and much more self-sufficient than most."

"More self-sufficient than I am," my wife said, a terrible tremor sending a shudder through her entire body.

"My will is in order. There's enough money socked away for our funeral expenses . . ."

47

"The vultures will make that unnecessary. That's what they're *for*."

". . . and to finish the children's education," I said, fighting back a wave of flatulence. "My sister will be a good guardian."

"Probably better than we've been. At least she's not a lush. What *do* you suppose got into us yesterday?"

"About a gallon apiece—not counting ice cubes. Well, there'll be no work done today. I'm going to get this coffee down—if I can—and then back to bed. I suggest you join me."

"Oh no you're not," my wife said. "You've forgotten what day this is."

"It's Flag Day or Insurgents' Day or Revolution Day. No matter, the local parade just begins here. They'll be gone in a couple of minutes and then we can . . ."

"I wasn't speaking of fiestas. Today is the day we're going to the Maitland-Grims's for lunch."

"Oh, God," I said, "why?"

"Why? Why, to meet Lady Jones or Lady Joy or Lady Somebody. Bunty's handwriting is so affected I couldn't make it out on the invitation. Anyhow it's to meet whatever visiting V.I.P. she's hooked."

"Perhaps it's the Loelia, Duchess of Westminster, or the Duchess of Argyll. They're everywhere. Well, I don't care. I don't think I can go through with it—not Bunty and not today."

"Neither do I," my wife said, "but I'm afraid we're going to have to. The Bunty Maitland-Grim Celebrity Service has spread the net all over the district for Lady Whatever. She's tried to trap Dolores del Rio and Mr. Riley to represent Drama; the Juan O'Gormans as Architecture and Horticulture; the Denis Bourkes are to portray Gay Society and Procter & Gamble. Dr. Julia Baker is to come as Medicine and a Patroness of the Arts."

"It sounds more like a pageant than a party. Do you suppose she nabbed any of them?"

48

"I don't know, but she got us. We're to represent Contemporary Light Fiction, and it's too late to . . . Oh Lord! Here it comes again!"

I turned around and saw Madame X and her old harridan of a mother bearing down on us. Although the tenants of Casa Ximinez lease their apartments by the month, we pay in quarterly installments every Saturday at twelve noon sharp —and in cash, no checks. In this way I figure that Madame X collects thirteen months' income every year instead of just twelve, as some months, such as this March, have five Saturdays instead of four. The paying of rent to the mistress of the manor has become a tradition like May Day in Moscow or Dr. Scholl's Foot Comfort Week. Madame X gets dressed to look as much like a streetwalker as possible, and with Mamacita functioning as a combination lady in waiting, duenna, and cashier, she makes her majestic progression to each of her serfs, starting with Apartamiento 1 (ours) and eventually winding up at Number 6. Then she gets into her antique Hispano-Suiza touring car, with Abelardo at the wheel, and is driven off to some expensive restaurant such as Passy or Jena or Quid where, every inch the movie queen, she makes a grand entrance, lunches in solitary splendor, and then has a big scene in gutter Spanish over the bill. We caught her act one Saturday at La Cava, where they have the added advantage of a circular staircase to descend, and it was priceless. The only trouble is that most people can't remember back thirty years to her only film, and the few who can don't recognize the grotesque she has become.

On this particular Saturday, Madame X was in the pink —and I mean exactly what I say. She was wearing a tight pink dress of some very sleazy-looking material, cut in such a way that her buttocks and navel were in perfect bas relief. With each step the skirt would ride up a bit higher, treating us to a splendid view of knee caps and of rose-colored stockings sheer enough to display a virile forest of black stubble. Her legs were never Catalina Ximinez's best point. Her neckline plunged down far enough to afford a glimpse of

49

the grayest pink brassiere I've ever seen. She wore a lot of pink-glass jewelry; long pink gloves from which one varnished fingernail protruded; and pink satin slippers slightly run down at the heels. This ravishing getup was topped off by a boa, muff, and busby of soiled pink fox. Perro was tricked out with a pink suede collar and leash. In comparison with this molting bird of Paradise, her mother looked as though she had just stopped in to say good-by on her way to the poorhouse. Being completely toothless, Mamacita had the face of a nutcracker. She wore a rusty old black dress, thick black stockings, and high black Keds. What hair she had left was pure white and skinned back in sparse strands to a meager little knot, her coffee-colored scalp shining through. When outside Casa Ximinez, her head was always covered by a black *rebozo,* which was perhaps all to the good. Mamacita carried her customary black reticule into which the rent monies were dumped and from which she produced whatever change was forthcoming.

"Buenos días!" Madame X said in her cockatoo screech, gold fillings glinting in the sunlight. (We were her favorite tenants of the season, as we had taken the largest apartment for four full months and because we remembered to have our pesos on hand every Saturday.)

"Buenos días," we muttered colorlessly.

"Ai aff come for de . . ."

"I know," I said, getting painfully to my feet, "the rent. *El aquiler.*" I went unsteadily toward the apartment and my wallet.

" 'Ow gude you spik the Spanish," Madame X screamed. Actually, I speak about half as much Spanish as I speak Urdu. I toiled back with two five-hundred-peso notes and handed them to Madame X, who counted them twice and then handed them to her mother. Mamacita also counted them and then popped them into her reticule.

"Tonk you, señor," Madame X said with a flirtatious wriggle. "Olues Ai say to Mamacita—to my mowder—Ai say

Señor y Señora Daneece exactly dey luke lak Maximiliano y Carlotta." Then she repeated the sentiment in Mayan—or at least I guess that's what she said to the old crone—and they both went off into fits of giggles.

So far so good. Now there was nothing left but for Mamacita to get off the only four words of English she knew. I could see the pleated lips, the toothless old gums, working up to her gala performance. She licked her white whiskers delicately, wound up for the pitch, and then let us have it. "Mai . . . dotter . . . beeg . . . star." Having pulled off this amazing accomplishment, she cackled delightedly with a fine show of brown gums. She would repeat it six times that day, just as she did every Saturday—once for each apartment. Having collected from us, they moved on to Apartamiento 2 —the current home of Leander Starr.

Terrible as we both felt, we sat there in the patio and watched with a certain fascination as Madame X and Mamacita approached the door of Number 2. It was closed, and the apartment looked very, very vacant. Almost kittenishly, Señorita Ximinez knocked. There was silence. She knocked again. Still no reply.

"You don't suppose they've jumped the rent again after seeing us?" I muttered to my wife.

"Are you insane?" my wife said. "That nice biddy who works for Starr couldn't have jumped over the doorsill last night. He was in far worse shape than we were."

Catalina rattled off something to her mother in Mayan, was handed a pass key from the depths of the reticule, unlocked the door, and entered the apartment. There was an ear-splitting scream that started Perro to barking and started Loro on his famous imitation of Madame X demanding the rent. From the depths of Apartamiento 2 we could hear the familiar, somewhat hammy voice of Leander Starr roaring, "Madame, *what* are you and that bag of bones doing in my quarters?"

"Starrr!" Catalina screeched. "Leondorrr Starrr!"

Mamacita fled from the apartment, reticule flying, fell to her knees on the patio, and crossed herself three times. She was followed by her daughter, who had gone ashen beneath her rosy panchromatic make-up. Leander Starr was not far behind.

From what St. Regis had told us the night before, I had rather expected a wizened, shriveled old man—white or bald, perhaps even toothless, and certainly drained of any and all fire. No such thing. Starr still came on strong. Always resembling some well-known matinee idol, Starr had now entered his Basil Rathbone phase. He was still tall, still dark—although in the bright sunlight there was a suspicious green and purple opalescent sheen to the black of his hair. Far from looking seedy and threadbare, he wore white silk pajamas and a scarlet dressing gown cut along the lines of something you might expect to see on Prince Albert or Napoleon III.

For once la Ximinez was beyond speech. She could only tremble and say "Starrr."

"I can readily see, *Miss* Ximinez, that your fifty years away from the jungle have done nothing to improve your deplorable morals. You are still forcing your way into the rooms of innocent men. Or is it this seductress whose body you are trying to sell?" He indicated Mamacita, and she crossed herself again. "Now be off or I'll have the police on you. *Policia!*" he shouted dramatically.

"Starrr," Catalina began. "Ai gived theess plas to a Señor San Ray-hees. Alice—somet'ing lak that—San Ray-hees? This my house. Ai own."

"St. Regis is my valet. Surely you don't think I can bother with dreary details, like hiring a little *pied-à-terre* in this Indian village. If, as you say, this hovel really belongs to you, I would like to point out certain shortcomings in the appointments. There is, for example, a very large cockroach in my bathroom." The Ximinez grasp of English was not enormous. She spoke just enough to get by and then only after having rehearsed it to herself—as I do with Spanish.

She also found it more blessed to give than to receive when it came to conversation, and so it was obvious that she had understood almost nothing of Starr's denouncement. He seemed to sense this and translated in very bad Spanish. *"Una cucaracha en el cuarto de baño. Uno ratón en la cocina. Disgustamente!"*

"Ai fix, Starrrr," Madame X whimpered. "Ai fix right now. Dees day. Ai come only for the rent. You pay now. Ai fix."

"Do you mean to say, Miss Ximinez, that you can stand there got up like the whore of Babylon and ask me to *pay you money* for quarters unfit for human habitation? It's risible! When my financial advisor, Mr. St. Regis, returns, you may take the matter up with him." He drew himself up to an impressive height, took a deep breath, and then bellowed, *"Now go!"* Mother, daughter, and dog took to their heels. Without stopping to collect another centavo's rent from anyone, they scuttled the length of the patio, slammed their heavy carved door, and clanged the bolt into place.

Lost in admiration, we burst into applause. "Bravo!" I shouted. "Viva Starr!"

Starr bowed briefly in our direction. "Ah, Dennis, dear boy. Mrs. Dennis. I had heard that you'd retired down here. Still writing?"

"Oh, yes," I said. "Still directing?"

He ignored my question. "A pity that you weren't able to put enough away for your declining years. I felt—to my great regret—that your recent, um, outpourings lacked the vigor and vitality of your earlier work. But I suppose that's true of all you writers. Look at poor Willie Maugham. Well, now that you know where to find me, the two of you must look in for cocktails. Say this evening, when my butler returns. Sevenish? And now if you'll forgive me, I have a severe migraine and must lie down in a darkened room. *Hasta la noche.*" With that he was gone.

"Well, I'll be damned," I said. "I'll be double damned."

An hour later, after a warm tub and a therapeutic beer, we were dressed up in our party clothes and on our way to the Maitland-Grims's. My wife, all gloves and nose veils, looked like Joan of Arc at the stake, and there was even a certain grim-jawed stoicism about me. I suppose suffering does ennoble.

Many, many years before the war, when I was just old enough to be taken to wholesome musical comedies, there was invariably in every show a foppish, ersatz young Britisher named Freddie or Reggie or Ceddie. His lines were pretty well limited to fatuosities like, "What-ho . . . Right-oh . . . Pip-pip . . . Oh, I say." He was always the son of a duke or, at the very least, of a belted earl. He never got the joke or the girl. And he was known in the theatrical trade as the Silly-Ass Englishman. I have never seen such a person in real life, and I doubt that one ever existed off Broadway. If there ever *were* such types in England, death and taxes have taken their toll.

But in this age of women's rights the Silly-Ass Englishman has been replaced by a very real and all-too-common female counterpart, the Silly-Ass Englishwoman. You can see her in Mayfair, Belgravia, Chelsea, and Knightsbridge. Her picture is forever in the *Tatler*—not attending good, staid English affairs like hunt balls or point-to-points or art exhibitions, but at those functions that are inaccurately described as "fun," such as roaring-twenties parties, gambling-club openings, and twist contests. Youngish, foolish, and usually pretty, the Silly-Ass Englishwoman grasps at any new wrinkle of fashion as though it were a life jacket. Becoming or not, she adapts herself to *it* rather than it to *her*. If skirts are too short and heels too high (as they certainly are this year) hers are shorter and higher. If lips are very red, she looks as though she had been caught sucking blood from a jugular vein. If lips are pale, she zincs hers until her teeth take on the patina of old rosewood. She lives in a mews cottage or a service flat done up by Michael Inchbald or

David Hicks. She exists only for new faces and new places, and you can be sure that her poor old mother would turn in her grave could she but know, because the Silly-Ass Englishwoman has either stepped down or stepped up from the place where she was born to become the heart and soul of a new class of English society that never existed before —and anyone with a modicum of charm or a good deal of money is welcome.

Bunty Maitland-Grim, our hostess of the day, personifies this new phenomenon. She is somewhere between thirty and fifty years old. Her father could have been anything from a dock hand to Lord Chamberlain, but from her accent you could never tell exactly when or where she started. She is small and has a lovely figure, although her feet are rather large. I suppose she is a brunette, but over the years we have seen her brown, black, ash blond, piebald—that was '59 when women were having their hair chemically streaked to make themselves look like shaggy zebras—gold and silver. This winter she is back to a rich, sable brown, puffed and teased and tangled high around her head as though she might be wearing—for some reason known best to Bunty— a successful chocolate soufflé. From beneath two tattered draperies of hair her pointed little face peers out, the eyes lined and extended almost to her ears, the lids stained an iridescent green, which makes one imagine the advanced stage of conjunctivitis. As the day wears on, the many coats of mascara have a tendency to smudge. Powdered flour-white, with a pinkish daub for a mouth, the Bunty of this winter gives you the unsettling feeling that you've seen her somewhere before. And of course you have. It's Marcel Marceau. But Bunty has no gift for the mime. Her mouth is never still, calling out idiocies overpunctuated by no-longer-fashionable catch phrases like "Oh, but darling . . . too divine . . . a *fun* party . . . sheer heaven . . . too blissful . . . ghastly bore."

We have known her—very slightly—for five years now.

55

Bunty knows *everyone,* always very slightly. Her latchstring is a lasoo. If the Pope himself happened into London, Bunty would think nothing of ringing him up, introducing herself with the sublime assumption that of course His Holiness had read about her last Come-As-Your-Favorite-Courtesan party in the *Daily Express* and asking him to rush to her place in Hamilton Mews for Bloody Marys with Edith Sitwell, Billy Graham, the Queen Mother, and Sabrina. "Then, ducks, we'll all run round the corner to Les A. for a bitey." After which she would blithely call the others and promise them the Pope. The odd thing is that quite a lot of people are so stunned that they accept. Look at us.

Married to a totally colorless older man of impeccable background and impressive income, Bunty has been leading the life of an international gypsy for the past fifteen years. She is in London for the season, in a dismal country house called—appropriately—Grim Place over weekends, in the South of France during August, and in a series of warm, westerly places after Christmas. Nassau, Jamaica, Palm Beach, Bermuda, and a lot of other resorts have all contained the Maitland-Grims from time to time. Taxes or foreign holdings or something like that have quite a lot to do with their constant peregrinations. However, Bunty has developed a pretty fiction that Major Maitland-Grim (retired) writes. I've noticed that everyone we meet who does absolutely nothing says, if asked, "I write." This could mean, I suppose, a laundry list, a post card, or a begging letter to the bank. However, the statement "I write" has come to mean full-time bum.

Henry Maitland-Grim has never been known to say anything more than "Hello," "Yes," "No," "Please," "Thank you," and "Good-by." With Bunty always on, he's lucky to get that much inserted into the record. Bunty always speaks for him—"Oh, but darling, poor Henry is working himself to the sheerest rag what with all his research on the Maitland-Grim family in Jamaica" (or Bermuda or Nassau or

Trinidad or wherever; in this year of grace the Maitland-Grims seem to have been conquistadors with four centuries of roots entangled in the eroding soil of Mexico). What Major Henry Maitland-Grim actually does do, other than pay the bills and put up with Bunty and the inconvenience of a wooden leg, is drink. They say that Bunty, not the leg, drove him to it, and I can believe that. Mind you, it's not a loud, showy, obvious kind of alcoholism. Henry is far too refined and too repressed for anything like that. He just puts on a tidy little package upon arising every morning and keeps working on it throughout the day. I can't say that I blame him. With Bunty around, it's essential.

This year, Bunty has leased a very large, very grand house in San Angel, which is Spanish colonial with a vengeance, its forbidding façade belying the enormous amount of space inside and behind. But she has managed in a matter of weeks to wreak her own subtle forms of destruction. The two suits of conquistadors' armor standing in the *salón de entrada* now sport flower leis and hats from Chez Elle. The collection of pictures that ranged from Velasquez to Tomayo have all been removed and replaced by the derivative fashion-magaziney dabs and daubs run up exclusively for Bunty by her large stable of Chelsea painters. Everywhere there are flower arrangements consisting not so much of flowers as cabbages and grapes and seashells and—in one especially unforgettable display—a pearl necklace. For a very brief period Bunty fancied herself as the peer of Constance Spry and got poor Major Maitland-Grim to set her up in a very expensive flowershop in Berkeley Square, where she attended only the grand opening and, two months later, the grand closing. However, she is still filling her husband's riding boots with lilies and larkspur, raiding kitchens for buds of garlic and colorful onions in her perpetual quest of the outlandish. It is, as far as I can see, her only domestic talent.

We were the last to arrive, and Bunty was at her most frenetic, all got up in tight gold-lamé trousers, high-heeled gold mules, and enough necklaces and bracelets to sink her if she'd fallen into the swimming pool. "Darlings, you're so naughty being so late!" Bunty has never been on time for anything in her life. "But I mustn't be too cross, must I? I know you've been up since the screech of dawn writing some absolute bit of divinity." We let her greeting go by without comment and submitted to her welcoming kisses. She's a great kisser and has been known to kiss total strangers on the hunch that they *must* have met somewhere. "Now, darlings, do let me introduce you all round, then Henry will get you something to drink. I'm having a simply heavenly thing I invented last week. It's called the Bunty Bomb, and it's tequila with lime juice in a tall glass and you pour champagne over the top of it. Or if you'd rather have something else . . . Oh, here you are, darling. Do let me introduce you to two of my oldest chums in the world. Lady Joyce, this is Patrick Dennis, who writes all those divine little books, and this is Mrs. Dennis who does—well, I don't know quite what she does do, except count piles and piles of lovely mon every day. In fact I can't fancy why you've never met before. Really, my dear, you can't travel an inch without being absolutely *inundated* with his books. I do believe that they give them away with passports and visas and things. As I said to . . ."

"But Lady Joyce and I have met," I said. "Aren't you Monica James—the former Mrs. Leander Starr?"

"Why, yes," Lady Joyce said. "But I don't believe I remember where."

The label "starlet" never quite fitted Monica James except to imply that she was an up-and-coming young actress. But actress she was and not the usual ball of fluff whose only performances are limited to publicity shots, cheesecake art, and producers' bedrooms. She was blond and very beautiful in the way that only English girls are beautiful, with a lovely skin, a slightly aquiline nose, and the kind of carriage that made one believe that she rode expertly. In the twenty years since I had seen her, she had become even more the idealized *Country Life* frontispiece. She was still very much the pink and white silvery blond, but the years had caused her excellent bones to be a bit more pronounced. Her hair, which my wife swears has never been near the dye pot, was arranged in a classic, becoming manner, very flattering and suitable to her age, which was somewhere in the middle forties. Her dress was fashionable and obviously expensive. It was the kind of outfit that she could put on ten years from now and still look aristocratic and smart. By way of ornamentation she wore the only strand of real pearls in the room and two very impressive rings. One wondered how she and Bunty could ever have come to know one another.

Cocktails went on for a very long time, as they always do at Bunty's, and over my glass of weak whisky (my wife and I had intelligently refused the Bunty Bomb) I watched Lady Joyce, poised and confident, being charming to the odd collection of mismatched people Mrs. Maitland-Grim had ensnared.

About half past three, luncheon was announced, and save for a meandering centerpiece of orchids and artichokes, the long refectory table looked very elegant with its Mexican silver service plates and goblets. Bunty had also shucked the plain white jackets off her two menservants and had replaced them with loose hanging green and orange striped beach shirts from Lila Bath ("So divinely native, darling"), which gave me the uncomfortable feeling that I must eat very rapidly so that the help could get off for a swim. Otherwise everything was very grand.

Lady Joyce was seated between Henry Maitland-Grim and me, and from the look of our host, he had had at least two Bunty Bombs too many. He'd retreated into his collar and was simply not relating. I mean it was all he could do to sit at the head of the table and toy with his lunch. As for carrying any conversational ball, he was less articulate than ever, an occasional cultivated grunt being about his only contribution. This left Lady Joyce to me exclusively, and there have been worse fates.

"I'm sorry I mentioned Leander Starr when we met today," I said. "I didn't mean to embarrass you, but I was so surprised to see you again after all these years. . . ."

"But you didn't embarrass me at all," she said. "Besides, it was *interesting* to be married to Leander. I mean there were perfectly ghastly times and he was the most impossible man to live with, but he was never dull."

"And, uh, Lord Joyce?"

"I'm afraid he was just a baronet, not a peer. He's dead."

"I'm sorry."

"So am I. He was a dear man—much younger than Starr and completely different. Daddy was so pleased when I married him. He pulled every possible string so that he could conduct the ceremony himself. My father was the vicar in our little village, you know, and Joyce was the son of the local squire. It was just a little slice of Jane Austen. He represented everything that was dear to Daddy—old family, good schools, wing commander in the R.A.F., love of the land, successful cattle breeding, Adam furniture, an interest in local affairs."

"Are you very good at opening bazaars?"

"To tell you the modest truth, I'm perfectly splendid at it. After all, I made a round dozen films before I retired, and in every one I was a vapid ingénue named Lady Caroline or the Honourable Victoria. It got so that I could do those roles without even reading the script, and of course it carried right over to Boar Hall—that's the name of our place, I'm sorry to say. You know there are quite a lot of us Pams and Jills and Sybils—all nice young girls from nice hard-up families —who caught the acting bug, got it out of our systems, and wound up with nice young men in club ties who had been patiently waiting for us. Even Bunty had a crack at the stage, you know."

I glanced at our host who was dozing over a plate of

prawns and couldn't imagine him—or anyone else—patiently waiting for Bunty to do anything but shut up. "Wasn't it ever a bore at Boar Hall—I mean after Starr?"

"Deadly. Oh, I don't quite mean that. After Starr it was a bit like having a lovely long rest in a very posh nursing home. Lots of lovely fresh milk and eggs and acres of flowers and splendid rooms simply crying to be done over and enough money to do them up properly. Yet, even the nicest nursing home can pall after a while. But my husband was so sweet and so proud of 'the splendid way you're taking hold, old girl' that I'd never have dreamt of letting on. And then I had a baby to fuss over until he was packed off to school. Don't worry, I'm not going to show you pictures. He's enormous and he rows. There have been unhappier lives than mine."

"And now that you're the Dowager Lady Joyce?"

"Well, that's just it. Nothing. We have an excellent bailiff, and the place takes care of itself. My son doesn't need me. So here I am. Not wanted on the voyage."

"I find that very difficult to believe."

"But it's true, alas. I'm in the country just enough to keep the place up for my son and to let the villagers know that the lady of the manor hasn't forgotten them—not that they'd care, they've got very modern. For the rest of the time I've got a nice-enough flat in a madly fashionable part of London, equidistant from Harrod's and Victoria Station—my two ports of call. And there I suppose I just lead the London life."

"À la Bunty?" I asked, knowing from the dulcet snore at one end of the table and the gibbon's chatter at the other that I would never be overheard.

"Oh, dear no. Nothing half so spectacular. Luncheons for four, little dinners for eight, and lots of good works—the English Speaking Union, the Distressed Gentlefolks Aid Association, King George's Pension Fund for Actors and Actresses."

I couldn't help noticing that a youngish American man, whose name I hadn't quite caught, shot a look across the table at Lady Joyce.

"You never think about going back into the theater?"

"Oh, I think about it a lot. But I wouldn't—couldn't really. You see the stage was dashing and daring and cute and forgivable for Monica James when she was a chit of eighteen. But for Lady Joyce who opens bazaars and has an almost-grown-up son it wouldn't do at all. Besides, I was frightful. I've seen some of my old films on television, and I was so embarrassed just sitting alone and seeing me make an ass of myself that I had to shut the set off and have a stiff drink."

"You were better than you think, and the pictures you did for Starr . . ."

"Ah, Starr was a different matter. Childish and selfish as he may have been, he could get a performance out of anyone. Even me. In his perverse way he was really a genius. But who can live with a genius?"

"And you've never seen him since your dramatic escape from South Africa?"

"Just once. It was around the time that Starr got into some fearful scrape in England. It was during some dismal period between the cattle show and our hunt ball—two gala functions you may be sure. My husband and I were staying at Claridge's (he usually liked Brown's but Claridge's was a sort of treat for me because I'd been such a grand old trump and given up a trip to the Continent so that he could buy a vicious underslung Aberdeen-Angus bull—you've no notion how hideously expensive they are, but I'm told that this one has more than paid for himself in fees). Well, anyhow, we were all dressed up—thank God—and having supper, and I was just wondering whether I'd been a grand enough old trump to order caviar or had I best stick to the dressed crab when I looked up and saw Leander charging at me like a —well, like a bull. I seemed to have bulls on the mind at that point."

"What did you do?"

"Do? Well, what could I do? I'd had no warning, no rehearsal, not even Starr to direct me. And need I tell you that my husband simply was not of the *Design for Living, ménage à trois,* why-can't-we-be-friends turn of mind at *all?* So after Leander had kissed me—and with such feeling—I introduced my two husbands in my best garden-party manner and prayed that Leander would go away or die on the spot —or that I would."

"Did he?"

"No such thing. He called for a chair, sat down, took over the ordering, and set about to charm us outrageously while the champagne flowed. So finally, after picking at a Dover sole for what seemed to be a year and a half, I thought if *I* go, *he'll* go, and it will only be a matter of months before I'm forgiven and we can settle down into Boar Hall with the new bull and go on as though nothing had ever happened. So I got up and said, 'If you'll forgive me I have rather a headache, but don't hurry on my account, dear.' So I went upstairs and got into bed with Graham Greene."

"I beg your pardon," I said.

"One of his books. Something about a man from Havana. I was so undone I really couldn't keep track of it that night. So I waited and I waited and I waited, thinking of some terrible brawl going on out in the street and how the Joyce name would be dragged through the mire all because of some little upstart of an actress like me who married above her station. Eventually I just dropped off from sheer exhaustion only to be awakened at five o'clock in the morning when my husband came rollicking in so drunk he could hardly undress himself. Well, he and Leander had closed Claridge's and then gone off to some bottle club—I leave you to guess who paid. My dear, he'd just never met anyone so charming by half as Leander. Couldn't understand *why* I'd ever left him. In fact he found Leander so *utterly* charming that he'd gone and lent him five hundred pounds! I was fit to be tied! And yet you know I wasn't really cross at Leander. I've never been able to stay angry at him, even though there were times when I'd have happily shot him right through his black heart. I think I was angrier at my husband for being such a fool."

"And for not being sufficiently jealous and outraged?"

"That, too, I suppose. Poor Leander. I wonder what's become of him."

"Would you really like to know?" I asked.

"I'd give a great deal to know where he is to-day."

"About how much?"

"What do you mean?" she asked.

"I think you've come to the right place."

"I'm afraid I don't understand," she said.

"Starr is here. On the q.t. He lives right next door to us, about a mile from here. In fact, we're going there for drinks this evening."

"And did you also know you were taking a guest?" she said.

"No. Who?"

"Me."

Luncheons in Mexico start late and last long, but none so late nor so long as Bunty's. Although she's dealt a death blow to every solid old British tradition inbred in generations of Maitland-Grims, she still clings tenaciously to the most tiresome of all—that one where the ladies withdraw, even in the afternoon, leaving the men to heavy, unwanted dollops of port or brandy and to the heavy, unwanted conversation of each other. And so instead of our being allowed to make half an hour's polite conversation and go home for a much needed nap, Bunty rose shortly after five and said, "Henry's a wee bit *hors de combat,* so will you do the honors for the boys in library, darling?" I don't know quite which darling she meant, me I guess, as she was staring near-sightedly in my direction. "The loo's through a divine secret panel next the fireplace. I hope you can find it." I hoped so, too.

The library was a dim cave tricked out with leather-bound volumes of greater age than value or interest, some antique swords and shields, an arrangement of avocados, gourds, and gardenias (with rhinestone dew), and an enormous painting of an elfin Bunty by Marcel Vertès that looked more like an advertisement for Schiaparelli products than a portrait. I won first prize for finding the "loo" and from the display of toothbrushes, straight razors, shaving bowls, and hangover cures spread out on the marble shelves, deduced that Henry had abandoned Bunty's boudoir and was obviously bedded down on the big ratchet sofa in the library. I wondered if Bunty had exiled him or whether the move was voluntary because Bunty talked in her sleep also. Either way I couldn't work up much sympathy.

When I returned to the merrymakers, Henry Maitland-Grim had been gently settled into a great oak chair of the Inquisition Period. It couldn't have been less comfortable if it had been fitted out with electrodes, but our host was past caring. The honors with the decanters were being handled by the young American who had sat across the table from me at lunch. "Port or cognac, Mr. Dennis, sir?" he said with a winning smile.

"Neither, thank you." For some obstinate reason—vanity, perhaps—I don't care to be called "sir" by people who are over twenty-five and this one certainly was. "Could I have a glass of water instead?"

"Certainly, sir." A fine, showy bit of work with the ice tongs, an authoritative glugging of the Garci Crespo bottle, and I was served. It was a great performance that might have accompanied cherries jubilee in a posh restaurant, but it was just a bit too stagey for serving up a glass of water. Then he fastened me with a sincere brown-eyed gaze and, with a splendid show of teeth, said, "I don't really know any of the fellahs here, do you, sir?"

"I've met them before."

From a glance at the male contingent, "fellahs" was about

the last thing you could apply to them. Bunty hadn't been able to bag any social lions that day and had had to satisfy herself with a shrill English milliner who hadn't made much of a go of his hat business in London and, under the wing of a naughty old Mexican gentleman, was thriving down here where hats are almost never worn. There was a youngish Spaniard (Cuban, it turned out later) with a very grand name overflowing with de's and la's and los's and y's (not quite his own, it turned out later) who, under the patronage of a naughty old Mexican lady, had recently opened a decorating establishment on the Calle Niza. There was also a very intense young American playwright-producer-director, much heralded by the many local little theater groups as the new Samuel Beckett, whose off-Broadway play in New York had been roasted by three of the daily newspapers, ignored by the other four, and closed after one performance. The nice thing about Mexico is that there's always room for one more and if you don't do whatever it is you do very well wherever it is you come from, you can always bluff your way down here. It is the haven and the heaven of the second-rate. Bunty certainly had the scrub team out on the field today.

The young American gave the "fellahs" a faintly scornful glance—not that I blamed him—and then treated me to a sincere grin of friendly admiration. "Your books have certainly given me a great deal of pleasure, sir. I've had a lotta laughs."

"Thank you," I said. I don't know why it always embarrasses me to have people compliment my books—I'd be furious if they came right out and said they hated them—but it does. Eventually he'd get to *his* eccentric aunt; everyone does.

"I was especially nuts about one I ran across in the Knickerbocker Club library, and I couldn't help thinking of my own aunt—great-aunt, that is—old Mrs. Chauncey van Damm up in Tuxedo Park. She was quite an eccentric." He began to launch into an anecdote about this lovable eccentric and

Mrs. Twombley in an electric car and I knew I could shut off my hearing-aid, so to speak. In a few well-chosen words he'd got his point across very nicely: fine old club; fine old family; fine old fortune; fine old address; fine old friends. But then if he'd done his name-dropping so well, why had I noticed?

The anecdote and the electric car came to a halt in a morass of mutually insincere chuckles. He flipped open a very gold cigarette case stamped B van D. I thought instantly of BVD's, as I'm sure everyone else does, and refused. He lighted a Yetl *(con filtro)*, coughed piteously, treated me to another winning smile, and said, "Is Lady Joyce an old friend of yours?"

"Not really. I just met her a long time ago." I'd thought of going into the meeting with Starr but discarded it as none of BVD's business. I also found myself not liking him as much as I should, considering the effort he was making, and damned myself as a hungover old crab, patronizing a perfectly well-mannered younger man who was only trying to be polite. Still, I didn't exactly warm to him. I hate to be charmed.

"It's a very fine family in England," he said. "Very old. Irish, actually."

"Is it really?" I said, wondering just when I could get the hell out and go home.

"Yes. You've got to be terribly careful down here."

"Careful of what?"

"You meet so many phonies." His fine brown eyes swept the room. Much as I wanted to, I could not gainsay him. If I'd liked him better, I could have filled him in on countless petty scandals from the recent past concerning the small armies of bogus dukes and countesses, con men, and cagey little hustlers who had made minor killings on the Mexican social circuit. But I didn't.

"Are you working on something now?" he asked smoothly. I've always felt that if the answer were "On the blonde across the street" or "Why, yes, I've just perfected a bomb that will blow us all to kingdom come next Tuesday," the only reply would be a smiling "That's nice." The only thing more boring than the question "Are you working on something now?" is the answer. However, we were both saved by the clattering entrance of Bunty.

"You naughty boys! If you're going to spend the whole day telling horrid stories, at least come in and tell them to us." Her husband gave a loud snort and then slumped back into his coma. "Poor Henry, he's simply exhausted from all his research. Well, come along this instant, the rest of you, you've been together long enough." How right she was.

The ladies were all looking a bit heavy-eyed, but too done-in to protest when Bunty, in her terrible Mayfair-accented Spanish, squealed to her beach attendants, "Pedro! Mario! *Mas* Bunty Bombs *por favor!*" Overloaded with food and drink as we were, we could only hope to take a couple of sips, pour the rest of the Bunty Bomb into one of the horticultural excrescences, and make our getaway.

My wife oozed across the room, giving me one of those private let's-get-the-hell-out-of-here looks. She was followed by Lady Joyce, who did much the same. "I've been having such a nice talk with your wife," she said. "In fact, I've made her promise to take me along to Leander's." She lowered her voice and added, "My only other alternative is to learn the twist with some ghastly American chums of Bunty's. No offense meant."

"We know exactly what—and probably even *who*—you mean. And I can't say that we blame you."

"I think the twist might possibly—just *possibly*—be passable," my wife said, "if you're underweight and under twenty-one, but . . ." She stopped. Suddenly, silently, BVD, all splendid teeth and eyes, was in our midst. "I do hope you'll stop in and see me sometime," he said smoothly. "I've taken a flat on the Hamburgo—just bachelor digs, you know—right near the American Ambassador's house. If you've got a pencil . . ."

"I'll telephone for a taxi," I said.

"But do let me drop you off," he said. "My car's right outside."

"Oh, don't bother to do that," my wife said.

"It's out of your way, anyhow," I added.

"Very far?"

"Well, it's about a mile from here. We could walk when it comes to that."

"Not in these heels on those cobblestones," my wife said darkly.

"Then I won't hear of your not coming," BVD said generously.

There were farewells and embraces and promises of getting together immediately with Bunty. Bunty was quite put out with Lady Joyce for leaving with us, but after an interminable amount of small talk we made our escape. In a moment we were all in an opulent Continental Phaeton, gliding grandly homeward through the tortuous streets and alleys of San Angel.

The car, which he drove expertly and effortlessly, struck me as quite a lot like young BVD himself—glossy, expensive, conservative, if any contemporary American automobile can be described as faintly conservative. As with its owner, I only wished I liked it better, and again scolded myself for being such an unreasonable old crank.

It was only a matter of minutes or so before we reached the great carved doors of Casa Ximinez, which our transportation officer professed to find fascinating. "I've always been crazy about these old places," he said with a winning grin.

I knew what was coming next. My wife was about to rise to the bait like a trout. She can no more resist handing out the empty invitation than she can stop breathing. "Wouldn't you like to come in and have a drink?" she said, and she seemed slightly staggered when, instead of saying some fatuous thing like Thanks-but-I'm-late-for-an-appointment-in-town, BVD treated us all to a charming smile and said, "I'd love to—but just for a minute." I cast my wife one of our intramural God-damn-you-to-hell-with-your-great-big-mouth looks and graciously opened the door to Number 1.

While I struggled with the ice trays and took orders for drinks, our young male guest was showing Lady Joyce around the place quite as though he'd lived there for all four centuries, pointing out various architectural features and commenting learnedly on the various periods of Madame X's fake antiques. I did, however, derive a certain wry pleasure from discovering that in almost every statement he was totally incorrect.

Once again I called myself every kind of mean, cantankerous, unreasonable old bastard and tried to convince myself that I was jealous of his good looks and good manners. It's so rare nowadays that anyone gets to see anything like good manners that I purr with pleasure whenever I'm around a truly polite person who displays them. Just my hangover, I decided.

By the time the drinks were passed around, he was seated decorously on the sofa playing Do-you-know with my wife and Lady Joyce, and it seemed that he knew just *everyone*.

Through the window I could see St. Regis in a white jacket bustling about the patio arranging chairs and tables, bottles and hurricane lamps, and plumping up a great vase of rather weary-looking gladiolus. "I see," I said almost too pointedly, "that St. Regis is just about ready for us."

"St. Regis!" Lady Joyce cried. "Darling old Albert Schmackpfeffer!"

"I beg your pardon?" I said.

"Alistair St. Regis—né Albert Schmackpfeffer of, oh, where was it, something like Montevideo, New Jersey. . . ."

"Alhambra, I believe."

"Yes. Exactly. You don't mean to tell me that that old hound Leander still has him hoodwinked into thinking he's going to have his name in lights when the poor little man couldn't act his way out of a cupboard. Really, that Starr is insupportable."

"Do you mean Leander Starr, the famous director?" BVD said, all eager interest.

"Yes," I said. "That's where we're going. In fact, we're a bit overdue."

"How I'd love to meet him."

"And I," Lady Joyce said.

"Perhaps, then—if I won't be intruding—I'll just say hello and then be on my way back to town."

"Well . . ." I began.

"Yes, Mr. ah . . ." Lady Joyce fumbled for his name.

"Van Damm," he said charmingly. "But just call me Bruce."

"Very well," I said, defeated. "Finish your drinks and let's get going." In Indian file the four of us, with BVD—"just call me Bruce"—and me making a great to-do about who would precede whom through the door.

IV

I suppose it was a regrettable little streak of malice that led me to take Lady Joyce to her ex-husband's place for drinks. I was hoping that Starr would be embarrassed or nonplused or at least upstaged for once in his life. It just goes to show how little I knew my Leander Starr.

St. Regis, however, reacted enough for two. He bustled out and all but genuflected in front of our mystery guest. "Oh, Miss Monica—Lady Joyce, I should say! Such a pleasure to meet up with you again after all these years. I wrote to you when I read of your marriage and again when that poor gentleman passed over."

"I know you did," Lady Joyce said. "I shall always treasure your letters."

"And I your replies," St. Regis said prettily.

"You're looking splendid, Albert—forgive me, Alistair. Not a day older."

"And you likewise your ladyship."

"Silver threads among the gold, I'm afraid."

"Oh, I've had very much the same problem, your lady-ship, but now with the beautyful range of Miss Clairol colors on the market, I'm able to mix up just the shade it always was."

"Even a bit redder than it used to be," Lady Joyce said, but her tone was one of an artist appraising another's work and entirely without malice.

"Oh, do you really think so?" St. Regis said, dismayed, his hands fluttering to the thin underbrush of chestnut curls.

"Perhaps I'd best tone it down a bit next time. But now do let me prepare you all a nice refreshment. Mr. Starr has had so many urgint long-distince calls today that he hasn't quite finished dressing."

"Is he still lacing himself into that waist cincher?" Lady Joyce asked, not unkindly.

"Oh, your ladyship!" St. Regis went off into fits of giggles and tittuped over to the bar.

With almost a fanfarade of trumpets, Starr appeared in the doorway, paused for the expected ovation, and then advanced upon us. "Can I believe my eyes? Is it some trick of the setting sun—some magic of the candlelight or is it . . . *is* it . . ."

"Yes, Leander," Lady Joyce said. "You can sit down now. It is."

Starr took both of her hands in his, bowed low over them, kissed the backs and then the palms. "My golden girl. My lovely Monica. Younger and more beautiful than ever."

"About as young as Dame Sybil Thorndike, Leander, but thank you, anyhow. You're looking fit."

Actually, Starr was got up like the cruel ballet master or as though he were about to fight a duel in the Bois de Boulogne. He wore narrow black trousers, an elastic cummerbund, which did wonders for his waistline but did tend to leave a roll above and below, pumps, and an extravagantly full white silk shirt left open two or three extra buttons to display what was still a splendid chest. Knowing that he was somewhere in his mid-fifties, I wondered unkindly whether he'd ever had his face lifted.

I was about to introduce our hanger-on, but young Mr. van Damm was miles ahead of me, shaking Starr's hand, spilling a few judicious bits of sincere flattery and saying "Just call me Bruce, sir." On second thought, Bruce would have a drink—"But just one, sir, then I must go."

In a moment we were joined by still another uninvited guest—Catalina Ximinez. Although she and Mamacita and

Perro had been put to flight earlier in the day, Madame X had apparently marshaled her forces for an all-out attack to get her rent. She had changed from the skin out and was this evening a discordant symphony in ice blue with a *ma'kech* gamboling across the hills and valleys of her bosom. A *ma'kech*, by the way, is a Mayan lucky bug, a live beetle, wearing a jeweled harness and leash, which some Mexican women of more exotic tastes than most pin onto themselves. When not being worn, the poor creatures live in small boxes where they feed off a lifetime supply of a special kind of wood. They are considered tremendously chic in certain circles (I felt sure that Bunty would have one before long), but the sight of them scampering around, tethered to the fronts of dresses, still makes me want to call the Society for the Prevention of Cruelty to Animals.

Whether she knew it or not, and I suspect that she did, Señorita Ximinez couldn't have picked a better time to hit poor Starr for the rent money than when he was on full display. All unctuous charm and coy smiles, she sidled up to Starr like a killer crab and said, "Ah, Señor Starrr, Ai see your lights burning as Ai about to go to deener party and Ai say to myself 'Now Ai weel stop by for the rent to save poor Señor Starrr from have to bring it to mai house.' "

"My dear," Starr cried. "How radiant you look tonight, except for that cockroach on your knockers. Tell me, is that the one you got out of my bathtub today? They look remarkably alike."

"Abelardo has fix everything. Now the money pliz?"

"But my dear, do let me introduce you round. It's not every day that these poor Anglo-Saxons are privileged to meet the shimmering star of *Yucatán Girl.*"

"Leander! You don't mean it?" Lady Joyce said. Her tone was one of stunned incredulity that this henna-rinsed tub of lard could actually be the smoldering remains of that breath-taking Indian beauty of thirty years ago. However, the Ximinez, not overly familiar with the subtleties and nuances of English, took it as her due and began to soften

74

a bit. Not enough, however, to forget the original purpose of her mission. "Very pliz to mit you," she said, giving Lady Joyce the up and down. If Madame X was out of movies, she was still *at* them a good deal, and her interest in the former Monica James as a more prolific actress as well as one of many former Mrs. Leander Starrs, was more than casual. "And now, Señor Starrr, if Ai may trobble you for . . ."

"Ah, *malheureusement*," Starr began, striking his forehead a stunning slap, "I *knew* I'd forgotten something today. I meant to go to the bank, but with my severe migraine headache . . . Dennis, dear boy, *do* you happen to have a spare five hundred pesos? You *did* say five hundred, did you not, Catalina, *mi corazón?*"

"Nine hondred," Madame X said dangerously.

"Ah, si si, they're spelled so much alike. Dearest Patrick, do you happen to have a thousand, say?"

I was about to reply, quite honestly, that I didn't, when St. Regis got into the act. He did it so badly, so baldly, that I could understand why he had never seen either "Alistair St. Regis" or "Albert Schmackpfeffer" in lights, but at least the day was saved. "Oh, Mr. Starr, sir," he said, "seeing that you were predisposed, I took the liberty of stopping by the Banco dee Mexico y Laundress and withdrawering a bit of pin money from your extinsive English holdings." With a flourish, he produced a roll large enough to choke a horse (in very small denominations), counted out nine hundred pesos, and all but flung them at Madame X.

"How too good of you, St. Regis," Starr said. A deft flick of his hand and the roll of bills was in his pocket before St. Regis could get it back into his own. Miss Ximinez and Bruce van Damm were duly impressed, as anyone with half an eye could see. To the rest of us it was an old, old story, its only variation being that for once Starr's rent was actually paid. "Don't bother with the receipt now, Catalina *querida,* just send that toothless old Indian hag around with it *mañana.*"

"Mamacita?" Madame X said, her jaw dropping.

75

"Whatever quaint Mayan name you call your help. Now do sit down, Pocahontas, and join us. What'll it be, champagne or pulque?" The bar boasted rum and beer. Imported champagne runs about thirty dollars a bottle in Mexico, but Starr, now that his rent was paid and his pocket bulging with poor St. Regis' money, was feeling very grand.

"There is no champagne, sir," St. Regis said, taking his cue. "They had such inferior stock at the shop that I knew you'd rather not serve any at all than to offer your guests an inferior year."

"Quite right of you, St. Regis, but do cable tomorrow for a few dozen cases of Taittinger *Blanc de Blancs,* 1953. Air France can drop it off, and you can pick it up at the airport. The duty shouldn't be too much."

"Only about three hundred per cent," my wife murmured.

"Easy come, easy go," Starr said with an airy gesture. "And now, Malinche, what will it be?"

"*Cerveza, por favor,* señor," Madame X mumbled. When thoroughly squelched Señorita Ximinez has a tendency to lapse into the language and manner of a back-country servant girl.

"Pour the lady a beer, please, St. Regis, then you may have the evening to yourself. We'll just pig it here—self-service and all that sort of thing. We don't mind being carefree peasants, do we?"

"Do come off it, Leander," Lady Joyce said tolerantly.

"It would be a pleasure, sir," Just-call-me-Bruce said.

"Lak de old times, Señor Starrr," Madame X said with a soft little belch. She seemed to have forgotten entirely the brilliant dinner party she had said she was about to attend and spread a *taco* thickly with *guacamole.*

"So, St. Regis, if there's some little thing you'd like to do this evening . . ."

"Oh, that's ever so kind of you, sir," St. Regis said. "As a matter of fact, Dolores del Rio is playing quite nearby. Something about the sin of a mother, I believe. I've always admired her ever so. Haven't you, your ladyship?"

"Very much," Lady Joyce said.

"Darling Lolita," Starr said dreamily, with a look that implied volumes of erotica.

"Gee, do you know Miss del Rio, sir?" Bruce said.

"Ah, what can I say?"

"You might say, Leander," Lady Joyce said tartly, "that you and Miss del Rio once shook hands at an Academy Award dinner during the late thirties, but as she was under contract to another studio and much too smart to get involved in one of your harebrained schemes, that's about as far as things went."

"My poor, precious Monica," Starr said sadly. "I see with regret that your enforced retirement from the screen owing to advanced senility has done nothing to soften what was always at best the tongue of an adder."

Lady Joyce laughed delightedly. "Oh, Leander, bravo! It does me good to be insulted by you once again—*now that you're a harmless old man.*"

"Well, at any rate," St. Regis said nervously, "I've been a fan of Miss del Rio's ever since *Ramona.*"

Catalina Ximinez, who had come to think of herself as the Eleanora Duse of Latin America on the strength of one film, allowed her lip to curl. "Gemme nudder beer, pliz," she said loftily.

"Oh, and St. Regis, before you go, would you just lay out my blue mohair and a suitable tie? This high, clear air has done such wonders for my poor head that perhaps I might even venture out to dine tonight, if these lovely ladies would deign to accompany me. My two radiant stars—tempestuous Catalina and serene Monica. Daddy and his girls."

"Won't that be fun," Lady Joyce said. "Just like D. W. Griffith and the Gish sisters." But I didn't notice her saying no. Miss Ximinez rolled her eyes appreciatively.

"If, indeed, there's any place suitably festive in this provincial backwater. I've been too ill to take more than a little broth."

"Oh, yes, indeed, sir," Bruce van Damm said eagerly. "El

Paseo is very nice, or Delmonico's or Ambassadeurs. Or if you care for dancing we might try the Capri or Jacaranda. . . ." I noted the *we*, and I also promised myself that not for rubies would I go any place but to bed that night.

"Ah, dancing. By all means dancing. And perhaps la Ximinez would favor a lonely old man with her famous paso doble."

Madame X favored him with a tarnished smile, a coquettish waggling of her finger, and slapped back the rest of her beer.

"Well, just see that everything is in order before you go, St. Regis," Starr said. He peeled a five-peso note off the roll and handed it over. "Enjoy your film and treat yourself to a little snack afterward. *Buenas noches.*" Movies in Mexico City cost four pesos, that left poor old St. Regis with a cool eight cents to spend on anything his little heart desired. I could see he was going to have a whale of a night.

"Thank you, sir. And a very pleasant evening to all of you."

"And now," our genial host said, "just one more little half drink, and then we're off." Two hours and four drinks later, after a good deal of pleading with us to join them, the merrymakers piled into the Van Damm equipage and set off, while my wife and I struggled wearily off to bed.

My wife was dispiritedly brushing her hair by the time I'd doused the living-room lights, cleaned my teeth, and scaled the circular staircase. "Sixty, sixty-one, sixty-two, sixty-three, sixty-four, sixty . . . oh, to hell with it. I'd rather be bald." She got into bed, took up a pencil and pad, and started to work on her five topics. This is an old practice of hers. Right after a party where there has been drinking and just before going to sleep, she writes down five subjects she's discussed and the person she's discussed them with to prove to herself that she hasn't lost her grip on reality. They are unofficially known as "Mother's Conversations at Midnight," and gathered into one sizable volume they would form the greatest compendium of fatuosities ever bound between covers. Whenever I look for a piece of paper, I'm bound to turn up a flyblown, coffee-spotted old thing with such cryptic messages as:

> Elizabeth—Hems taken up?
> Jack—Marcia's etopic pregnancy—pity.
> Cyril (?) —London, Americanization of.
> Mrs. G.—Hal's drinking.
> Couple from Rye—Progressive schools.

She feels that this sort of thing keeps her on an even keel. It would only confuse me more the following morning. There are some things I'd rather not know.

"What was the name of that attractive young man?" she asked.

"Alistair St. Regis—né Albert Schmackpfeffer?"

"No. Not that poor old auntie. The one who was so charming at the Maitland-Grims's with that fantastic car. You know."

"Oh, him," I said. "You mean Van Damm—Just-call-me-Bruce."

"Yes, that's the one. Didn't you think he was nice? You rarely see young people with such lovely manners nowadays. He'd be awfully good to have around as an extra man in New York. We always need them, and he's tall and good-looking and personable and polite and not queer, I don't think, and . . ."

"And loyal, trustworthy, helpful, friendly, courteous, kind, obedient, cheerful, thrifty, brave, clean, and reverent."

"Didn't you like him?"

"No, not especially."

"That's just because you didn't have a chance to talk to him."

"I don't expect to cry myself to sleep on account of that."

"Well, *I* thought he was charming. I used to go to school with a Marie Louise van Damm. Very top-drawer."

"And what happened to her?"

"Oh, she married somebody. I ran into her at a luncheon for some dreary worthwhile cause a couple of years ago."

"And?"

"Well, I said hello and Marie Louise said hello and she told me her married name, which I've forgotten, and I told her mine. . . ."

"Which she's forgotten."

"Well, naturally. Then I said I'd been meaning to send her a wedding present and she said she'd been meaning to send me one and we both said why not just forget the whole thing and that was that."

"You do spend stimulating days in New York. I've always wondered about what you did."

"Well, I suppose she and Bruce must be related. That's all."

"Did Marie Louise have an eccentric aunt in Tuxedo Park who did strange things with a Detroit Electric and Mrs. Twombley?"

"Well, as a matter of fact, she did. It was her grandmother. They also had an electric boat. That's because people in Tuxedo have to drink the lake water."

"Isn't that interesting. Well, good night," I said, kissing her. I rolled over and closed my eyes. "Don't keep the light on too long. It attracts bugs and also Dr. and Miz Priddy."

"She had a younger brother, but I think he was killed in Korea or else in an automobile crash or maybe it was a motor accident *in* Korea."

"Mm-hmmm." I heard no more. I was sound asleep.

The night went by as usual. Perro barked; the cats yowled; Mamacita, left to her own devices for the evening, tuned in to a stirring drama on XHTV at top volume; the *vigilante* blasted his whistle into our window at regularly spaced intervals; and promptly at midnight the macaw went mad. Otherwise it was as still as the grave.

And then at one o'clock all hell broke loose. As ours is the first door one encounters upon entering Casa Ximinez, my wife and I have been the victims of many little surprises intended for other tenants. So far this year we have been showered with five dozen red carnations addressed to nobody and bearing the cryptic message "Because of last night —Always—Jimmy"; a set of pottery casseroles from the Bazaar Sabado to Miz Priddy; a full-length white-fox coat for Madame X, which makes her look like a pregnant polar bear; great masses of dry cleaning from the Tintoreria Francesa all intended for other people; a very dapper little Mexican lawyer who told me that if I'd simply sign this document I'd be legally divorced from Andrea Morganthau Blackburn; and a series of flashing-eyed call girls. On this particular night we received a set of matched luggage (blue) and a ravishing eighteen-year-old daughter (white).

The pounding and clanging began at one o'clock.

My wife switched on the light, pummeled me into wakefulness, and said, "Are you expecting anyone, dear?"

"Naturally," I said, "I've invited Dr. and Miz Priddy, Bunty Maitland-Grim, and President Lopez Mateos in to make fudge. I always entertain at this hour."

"Very funny. But are you going down to the door or must I?"

"Why should either of us bother? We're not expecting anybody. It's just some drunk. He'll go away eventually."

Still the pounding on the great carved door, the pealing of the iron bell.

"It could be a telegram," my wife said. "Perhaps something's happened to one of the children."

"Nonsense, I've told both schools never to telegraph, always to call long distance."

"Well, something could have happened to Mother."

"That'll be the day."

The racket still kept on.

"Well, if *you're* not going to see who it is, *I* am."

"Oh, all right!" I got crossly out of bed, put on my robe —inside out—shuffled into my sandals, and began the long trek to the front door.

"All right, all right, all right," I said, struggling with the sixteenth-century bolts and bars and latches and with the twentieth-century Yale lock. Finally I got the door open, and a beautiful brunette threw herself into my arms and cried "Daddy!" After I'd been soundly kissed, she disengaged herself, stood back, and drank me in. "Oh, Daddy, I knew I'd recognize you anyplace—even with your beard."

"Well, young lady," I said, "that's more than I can say for you—even without yours."

"Just put my bags inside, please," she said to a seedy-looking cab driver. Then she consulted her Berlitz phrase book and said, *"Las maletas aqui, por favor.* Daddy do you have any Mexican money to pay the driver? My plane was so late that the money-changing place at the airport was closed. And I waited for you for more than an hour. Didn't you get my telegram, Daddy?"

"Nobody ever gets a telegram in Mexico and will you please stop calling me Daddy."

"Don't dream of stopping, young woman," my wife said, appearing from nowhere in a black negligee that makes her look like a kept woman. "In fact, go right on. I find this very interesting."

"Daddy! Is that your . . . your *mistress?* Mummy said you . . ."

"We've been sleeping together for the past fifteen years, and now if you'll be so kind as to get the hell out of here, we can go right back to bed together. We're insatiable— when it comes to getting a decent night's sleep, that is."

"Daddy!" Her lip trembled, and tears welled up in her enormous eyes. Very pretty.

"Now listen to me, young lady, a joke's a joke, but I've had a long, taxing day, and it *is* late and . . ."

"Excuse me," she said, "but *aren't* you Leander Starr?"

"Leander *Starr?* I've been accused of some terrible things in my life but never of . . . My God!" Suddenly everything fell into place. The dark prettiness of the girl, the slight Philadelphia accent, the marked resemblance to the icy Caroline Morris of twenty years ago. "You're not . . ."

"My name is Emily Starr. I'm Leander Starr's daughter."

V

"Well," my wife said the next morning after Guadalupe had slapped a trayload of coffee onto our bed and shuffled out, "aren't we going to have a nice surprise for our neighbor today. Yesterday an ex-wife, today a long-lost daughter."

"That's us, chock-full of tricks and treats, every day in every way getting better and better. Where will it end?"

"I think I was right to make her spend the night here. Who knows what time Starr got in, or in what condition?"

"Or with whom. I think perhaps I'd better go over and prepare the old maniac for a great big, grown-up daughter."

"And *I* think that perhaps *I'd* better stay here and prepare that great big, grown-up daughter for a great big baby of a father."

"They've never met?"

"Not, according to Emily, since she was a baby in the heart of the pygmy country. So her impressions of him can't be very vivid."

"Don't worry, they will be. What's she doing down here anyhow, after all these years?"

"Well, I don't quite know. She was so exhausted last night that she wasn't making much sense. Dozed off two or three times while I made up her bed. But I gather that she's had some disagreement with her mother and stepfather over some boy back in Philadelphia. So she's taken it into her head to rush down to Daddy for moral support."

"She's chosen a frail reed at best."

"I wonder what the mother can be like."

"Simply beautiful. A perfect mannequin."

"You mean she was a model?"

"Good God, no. Caroline Morris would never do anything so common as kick her train around the Philadelphia branch of Bonwit Teller's. She's very Main Line, very Bryn Mawr, very Assembly. When I say mannequin, I mean that Caroline has the same beauty, the same warmth, and the same intelligence as a window dummy. At least that's how she was twenty years ago, and I think she was too set in her ways to change."

"How in the world did a girl like that ever get mixed up with a man like Starr?"

"You've come to the right place to ask. Actually, I introduced them. Just count on the Patrick Dennis Lonely Hearts Introduction Service—'Someone for Everyone,' that's our motto. May I have about half a cup more of that molten lava?"

"You can take the whole pot for all of me. But how could a sheltered, gently reared girl from Philadelphia ever wind up with a madman like Starr?"

"Well, you're a sheltered, gently reared girl from New York, and you thought he was pretty special."

"But I didn't marry him."

"He didn't ask you to. And Caroline didn't stay married to him for very long."

"She's now a Mrs. Strawbridge living somewhere between Paoli and hell."

"That's more the Caroline Morris speed—the Academy of Music, the Merion Cricket Club, the flower show, and doing good works in a Peck & Peck suit with tweed hat to match."

"I once had a very pretty suit from Peck & Peck. You always *said* you liked it."

"Well, I think I'll throw on *my* Peck & Peck suit and go over to warn Starr."

"At eight o'clock in the morning? Emily won't be up for hours. She was half dead when I tucked her in last night."

"I think that Starr may need more preparation than most. He's never been exactly what progressive schools call a 'participating Daddy,' you know."

"If you go over there now he'll kill you, and I wouldn't blame him."

"My first exclusive may kill *him*. It's nip and tuck."

I waited until a little after ten when I saw St. Regis fussing around the patio cleaning up after Starr's party of the night before and trying to pump just one day's more life into the bowl of rotting gladiolus.

"I guess I'll go over and beard the old goat now," I said to my wife.

"I think you'd better. I hear just the faintest stirrings up in Emily's bedroom."

"Here I go. This is going to be the corniest script since *Daddy Longlegs*."

"Good luck," she said.

St. Regis had just executed a dainty little pirouette, landed a bit unsteadily, and was standing more or less in the third position of ballet over the remains of the bowl of *guacamole*.

"Good morning, St. Regis," I said.

"Oh! Oh, good morning, sir. Isn't it a lovely day. A real *bueno dee-o,* as the Spanish say."

"Enjoy the picture last night? *The Sins of the Father?*"

"*La Pecado de uno Madre,*" he corrected more sternly than accurately. "Oh, it was beautyful, Mr. Dennis. Miss del Rio was marvelous and just like a young girl. Amazing. It's about this lady that is involved in an accident and goes right ahead and has a daughter . . ."

It seemed as good an opening as any. "Speaking of daughters, is Mr. Starr in?"

He looked quite stricken. "Oh, good heavens, no, Mr. Dennis."

"You mean he's not back from dinner yet?"

"Oh, goodness, I mean he's back but . . ."

"Would you please tell Mr. Starr I'd like a word with him."

"Oh, I couldn't do that, sir, my imployer would be most disturbed."

"Not nearly as disturbed as when he hears what I've got to tell him. Just inform him that his daughter Emily is asleep in our apartment."

St. Regis' lower jaw dropped dramatically, a pearly upper plate following a split second later. With a little click, he hastily closed the whole aperture, setting the flawless dental work back into position. "His *daughter,* sir? She's just a baby."

"She's eighteen, she's no baby, and she's right here waiting for dear old dad. Now do you want me to go in there and tell him or will you?"

"Wait right here, sir, please. Don't go away."

"I wouldn't dream of it."

St. Regis swayed weakly into Starr's apartment while I, thoroughly enjoying myself, stretched out in the sun to wait. Nor was there much delay between St. Regis' disappearance and the fireworks. Suddenly a roar issued through Starr's bedroom window that sent Loro flapping hysterically up into the jacaranda tree. "St. Regis," Starr bellowed, "how many times have I told you *not* to enter my room until I ring for you. You have embarrassed a . . ." There was stillness for a tiny moment and then Starr's stentorian *"What?"* Another short silence and then Starr on again, stronger than ever. *"Will* you get out of here you fat sow! Now, St. Regis, start in again."

Hardly a second had elapsed before Catalina Ximinez scuttled wildly out of Starr's apartment, hair awry, wearing the white-fox coat, bare feet thrust into her pumps with a few bits of last night's rumpled ice-blue finery tossed over one arm.

"*Buenos días,* Señorita Ximinez," I said.

87

She cast a wild hunted look in my direction and then rushed stumbling to her own quarters.

A moment later Starr appeared on the balcony above me, buttoning himself into some silk pajamas. "Mr. Dennis," he said, but the voice had lost quite a lot of its Shakespearean boom, "would you be good enough to come up here and explain the exact nature of this . . . this gigantic hoax? I fear that my valet has taken leave of his senses."

"All righty-roo, Leander," I said.

Starr's apartment, while not comprising as many rooms as ours, was even larger. I entered a living room as dim and vast as Howe Caverns, made a wrong turning into a kitchen, where I saw an ironing board set up with half a dozen of Starr's suits waiting to be pressed and a copy of *The Joy of Cooking*.

"*Will* you hurry, man!" Starr shouted from the upper reaches.

Accustomed to the gloom at last, I found a great, meandering stone staircase and started climbing it. Halfway to the top I saw an ice-blue garter belt, which I picked up and draped over one shoulder like Miz Priddy's dyed squirrel scarf. In the upper hallway there were three vast studded doors. One was open and I could see Starr, supine on a great, carved walnut bed, like a dying infante, having his wrists chafed by St. Regis. "In here, man, in here. And be quick about it. And what in the name of God is that truss you're wearing?"

"This?" I said, holding Madame X's garter belt up daintily. "I found it on the stairs. Is it yours or does it belong to St. Regis? No matter. It's terribly pretty."

"Put it down, for God's sake. You don't know where it's been."

"Oh, I'll bet I do."

St. Regis giggled, and Starr shot him a malign glance. "Now, Dennis, my valet here tells me that some creature who claims—mind, I say *claims*—who *claims* to be my child has, in my absence, taken advantage of both your hospitality and your gullibility. It's obviously some opportunist who's after my money."

"After your *what*?"

"Just who does this . . . this girl claim to be?"

"She claims to be Emily Starr out of the former Caroline Morris Starr who is now a Mrs. Strawbridge residing in some verdant *banlieue* of Philadelphia. And I see no reason to doubt it. She's the image of Caroline."

Starr shuddered. "That impossible woman. Tell me, dear boy, is . . . is Emily as pretty as her unfortunate mother?"

"Prettier, I should say. More yielding."

Starr shuddered again. "She could hardly be less so. About how old?"

"Eighteen she says."

Starr ruminated on the age, consulted with St. Regis who counted up on his fingers. "Yes, that would be just about right. What a colicky baby she was and plain as plain."

"She had lovely hair, Mr. Starr," St. Regis said. "I used to arrange it myself."

"She still has," I said. "In fact she has lovely everything."

"But what, in the name of God," Starr said, "does she want of me? Surely not money. Her mother's people were very well off, although there was some talk of disinheriting Caroline when she married me."

"I wonder why," I said.

"Very provincial people, the Morrises. Although I never had the dubious pleasure of meeting them. But why, after all these years, does this child descend upon me?"

"I don't quite know the details, Leander, but she seems to have had a falling-out with her mother, and she's come to you for the advice of a wise father. God knows why."

Starr got off the bed and strode to the window where he posed dramatically gazing out over the patio. It was perhaps a mistake as the light coming through his sheer pajamas silhouetted a considerable fullness at the waist.

I was about to say something unkind about his gaining weight when my attention was caught by something on the bedside table. There were some blue-glass earrings that I remembered as having been especially tasteless when worn by Catalina Ximinez the night before. Next to the earrings was a small bit of black fur about as big around as a silver dollar. It seemed to correspond exactly with the tiny bald spot now visible on the crown of Starr's head. I quickly put on both earrings and slapped the hairpiece onto the middle of my forehead, where it clung precariously thanks to a residue of spirit gum. There was a horrified squeal from St. Regis. Starr spun around.

"Me Yucatán girl," I said. "Is this fur piece yours, or did Miss Ximinez leave her merkin?" St. Regis bent double in a gale of giggles and, almost on all fours, left the room.

"Now see here, Mis-ter Dennis," Starr fumed, "if you think I intend to be insulted by a third-rate gag writer like you when I am beset by trouble and aggravation, you are mistaken. I shall thank you to vacate my quarters forthwith."

"Okay, Leander," I said, removing his toupee from my forehead. "Here's your yamilke. Where shall I deliver the body?"

"No. Wait. You've got to help me. After all, you're a father, too."

"Like to see some photographs?" I asked. "I just happen to have . . ."

"No. I'm serious. What shall I wear?"

"Your rose taffeta with the green sash perhaps."

"No. Really. I'm new at this father sort of thing. I want to make a good impression."

"Well, that's going to take more than a toupee and tailoring. Face reality for once. The girl hasn't come to a fashion show. She's got a problem, and she wants a father to help her."

"Yes, yes, yes. But how do you think I ought to play it. Robert Young? Lewis Stone? Paul Scofield? Should I let myself go gray at the temples?"

"They've been like the driven snow under that shoeblacking for years. But why do you have to play it as anything? I suggest that if you just be yourself the poor girl will be so let down that she'll go home on the next plane."

"Dennis, dear boy, I beseech you—as one father to another . . ."

"Don't give me that jazz, Leander. At least I've had more practice at the father act. I'll bet you've never sent your poor daughter a birthday gift or even a post card since the day she was born."

"I'm a very busy man."

"Busy at what, dodging the bailiff?"

"Amelia was torn from my arms—literally."

"Her name is Emily. She's waiting next door to see you for what amounts to the first time in her life. Now get into your King Lear costume and come on over. Don't worry. You'll manage to ham your way through somehow. My sympathies aren't with you, they're with her." With that, I marched haughtily down the stairs, leaving Starr to his plight.

I was so angry with Starr for his obtuseness, his terrible vanity, his bone-selfishness, his complete lack of feeling for his only child, that I kept thinking of my own daughter in the same plight as Starr's and resolved to be especially paternal and tender when I saw Emily. For some reason I envisioned her as looking small and crushed in a suit of Dr. Denton pajamas and just possibly a hair ribbon. My heart all but bled for this innocent, trusting, fatherless child, soon to come face to face with a bogus old monster like Leander Starr who would obviously make her life a living hell, rob her piggy bank, and abandon her.

But when I got into our apartment I saw quite a change. My wife had been able to force her way through the teeming humanity in our kitchen, find a silver coffeepot that was almost shiny, cook up an omelet that was *not* swimming in Casa oil, and serve it all up prettily on a tray along with a clean napkin and some kind of local exotic flower leaning a bit top-heavily from a bud vase. Daintiest thing she'd done since I had pneumonia in 1950. However, I could tell by a certain tell-tale whiteness around her lips that all was not going well with our guest.

If Emily, from fear, bewilderment, and exhaustion, had seemed the little lost lamb a few hours before, a good night's sleep, breakfast, and the knowledge that help was on the way had quite restored her to one of the most positive, prim, and unpleasant young women I had ever met. If there is anything I dislike more than gaucherie in the young, it is total self-confidence—and Emily had it.

"I'm sorry," my wife was saying, "I don't smoke, but my husband has some Filtrons someplace around the house."

"I suppose they're some Mexican imitation of American filtered cigarettes. It's amazing how people all copy us. Look at the Japanese."

"Not now, if you don't mind," my wife said.

Far from the fluffy, slightly disheveled, endearing child she had been the night before, Emily was got up in something very white and starched and crisp that made me think somehow of a dietician or a domestic-science teacher or a public health official. Not that she wasn't still pretty, she was, but there was a sort of antiseptic, touch-me-not, no-nonsense-please quality about her that struck me as far from pleasing.

"Oh, good morning," she said, eyeing my rather casual outfit. "Do people dress like that for church in Mexico?"

"I'm sure I don't know," I said.

"I don't suppose there *are* any Protestant churches down here, but then with a name like Dennis you're probably . . ."

"There are several—Episcopal, Lutheran, Christian Science, you name it."

"*We* are Episcopalians," she said primly.

"I thought as much. However, this morning I have been worshiping at the shrine of Leander Starr."

With that she perked up a bit. "Oh, was he surprised?"

"Surprised hardly describes your father's emotions, Emily."

She gave me a look as though I had been overly familiar by not addressing her as *Miss* Starr and then said, "I can't see the attraction of a country so inefficient that important telegrams aren't delivered."

"Have you tried to dial Washington from Philadelphia recently, *Emily?*" I said.

"We don't know anyone in Washington nowadays. We're Republicans."

"We're not," my wife said. "More coffee?"

"No, thank you. I find it rather strong. But I suppose it's quite stale by the time it gets down here."

My wife looked as though she were about to explode.

"No, Emily," I said. "It's grown in Latin America, so we're really a lot closer to the source than Philadelphia is. In fact, it's mixed and ground to order at the *tienda* every day. We *like* it strong."

"I see," Emily said, somewhat chastened. I believe that she sensed for once that she had been rude, and no daughter of Caroline Morris' would ever be rude—unintentionally.

"You're very like your mother, Emily," I said, not entirely meaning it as a compliment.

"Oh, do you know Mummy?" she said with some surprise. "I don't believe I've ever heard her mention you."

"Probably not. You see I introduced her to your father."

Emily snickered, caught herself, and stopped. I could well imagine what Caroline had had to say about Starr during the girl's formative years. "How did you know Mummy?" Emily asked with just a hint of suspicion.

"She was in school with my sister."

"Boarding school or college?"

"Both."

Emily thought that over for a moment and then became slightly warmer. As with her mother, if you had ever shared the same school, the same dentist, or, I suppose, the same bed, you became more respectable if only because of sheer proximity. She gave me a chilly little smile of approval. "And I thought you were just a friend of Daddy's." Then she turned to my wife and said, "Did you know Mummy, too?"

"No. She's *years* older."

There was a lull. Then Emily looked at her wrist watch and said to no one in particular, "I wonder what can be keeping Daddy?"

"I suspect that he wanted to shave and dress and spruce up a bit to see you after all these years," I said. For all I knew he'd cut his throat and I wouldn't have blamed him.

She looked at her watch again. "Does he always sleep this late?"

"I don't know. I've never slept with him."

Emily looked horrified, and my wife, ever the conscientious hostess, said, "As you know it was quite late when he got in. The hours down here are somewhat more Spanish. No one dines before nine or ten and . . ."

Her travelogue was interrupted by Emily. "I suppose he runs around with a lot of women. Mummy said . . ."

"Actually, your father leads a very quiet life," I said. "Yesterday was the first time he's left his apartment since he came to Mexico. He hasn't been well," I added lamely, my sympathies suddenly having switched from daughter to father.

"What seems to be the matter with him?" Emily asked in the tones of a consulting specialist who suspects a patient of malingering.

I was about to add, "You, for one thing," when a shadow fell across the breakfast table. We all turned, and there was Starr standing majestically in the doorway, white at the temples and corseted to a fare-thee-well. From his imposing height, I also suspected lifts in his shoes. He was dressed as a happy compromise between a corpse and an undertaker in a morning suit that, like Starr, in spite of its age and general dilapidation, still had a good deal of dash. Pressed to his heart he carried a small prayerbook.

"Forgive me, my darling baby, for not rushing here in dishabille as was my first instinct. But then I thought, No, and betook myself instanter to our sweet little Anglican

chapel to offer up a humble father's prayer of thanks to
Our Lord for delivering safely to me my adorable girl-baby
daughter."

I could have thrown up.

"Oh, Daddy!" Emily said, rising weakly to her feet.

Starr advanced three giant steps into the room. Emily
rushed to him, and the old fraud let the prayerbook (which
I noticed upon later examination was inscribed "To Albert
Schmackpfeffer with love from Aunt Bessie") fall with a
leathery plop, and gathered Emily expertly into his arms. I
gave my wife a sharp kick under the table, but when she
looked in my direction I saw that her eyes were filled with
tears. I excused myself.

When I returned, St. Regis, in full butler's regalia, had
been added to the dramatis personae and was gathering up
Emily's matched luggage while saying a lot of tiresome things
about how he hadn't seen her since she was crawling and
how he'd have known her anywhere. If Starr had been stag-
ing an Oscar Wilde revival, the role of the paterfamilias
couldn't have been played with a higher gloss or greater
élan. Emily, while still reserved, was obviously charmed by
the stagey mannerisms of the old phony.

"Well, I'll tell you what, my darling daughter, how would
you feel about seeing a bullfight?"

"Oh, Daddy, I never have. Have you?"

"Constantly. A real *aficionado*. As a boy, in fact, I seriously
considered a career in the ring."

"The ring, Daddy?"

"Bull!" I said. "The bull ring."

"Just so, dear boy," Starr said a bit uneasily. "And then
we might dine at that place Mr. Dennis is so fond of. Del
Paseo, dear boy?"

"*El* Paseo. And it's closed on Sundays."

"What a pity. Well, some other place. St. Regis, after
you've stowed Miss Emily's luggage away, do get out the car."

"The car, sir?"

"Oh, drat! I forgot that the Rolls is being serviced. Dear

Dennis, do you suppose we could borrow the *voiture de maison?*"

"The what?"

"You know that old pile that belongs to our gracious hostess, Señorita Ximinez."

"Well, after all you've done for her, Leander, I'm sure she'd be enchanted. I believe you have some things to return to her anyhow."

"Um . . . yes . . ." he said edgily. "St. Regis, would you just take . . . uh . . . Miss Ximinez's belongings round to her flat and ask if her car is available. Surely you could drive it."

"That old foreign . . ."

"The very one. Now be quick about it, St. Regis. A father doesn't get to greet his long-lost daughter every day. Come along with me, darling, and Daddy will show you to your room. You must forgive this jiggery-pokery old place. It's just a temporary *pied-à-terre* until my agents find a suitable house. Good-by, *mes chers,* and thanks so much for looking after my little girl."

"Good-by, Mr. Dennis, Mrs. Dennis," Emily said with almost a curtsy. "Thank you very much, and I do hope that we'll meet soon again."

"I'm almost certain that we will," my wife said. "Good-by, and have a pleasant afternoon."

"Good-by, Daddy Warbucks," I said.

Starr closed the door and we were, at last, alone.

"Well," I said with a sigh.

"Miss Emily *is* something of a prig," my wife said.

"Come again?"

"Prig. P-R-I-G."

"Oh."

"But even so she's not really bad."

"Indeed she's not. She's dreadful! Just like her mother."

"Yes, but at least she's had the guts to escape from Mummy."

"*Mummy* is right, and Emily is just like her: Embalmed."

"No, not quite. What you say is correct, and there were

times this morning when I could have reached across the table and slapped her arrogant little face. I'll grant that she's narrow, snobbish, disapproving, and a lot of other unpleasant things, but that's simply because of the way she's been brought up. Underneath there's something lively that's just itching to be let out. I can tell. Remember, I'm a woman and I *know* other women."

"I'll bear that in mind," I said.

"But what amazed me was Starr himself. The change that having his daughter here has made in him. I was moved almost to tears."

"I was moved even further."

"I had no idea that he was such a deeply religious man."

"Such a what?"

"Well, that bit about dropping into the Anglican chapel for a prayer. Where is the Anglican chapel, by the way?"

"Did you come down in the last rain? There *isn't* any Anglican chapel. The nearest thing to it is Christ Church, and that's miles from here on Artículo 123 right in the heart of town. And Starr wasn't there. He was in the sack with none other than Madame X—for old times' sake, I suppose."

"I find that impossible to believe. There was such a . . . well, spiritual quality to him this morning. I could almost smell it."

"That was the spirit gum holding on his hairpiece. And the odor of sanctity came from the moth crystals in his morning suit. I'm amazed that anyone like you—on to the old charlatan for years—could fall for such a performance. The cutaway, the prayerbook. Really!"

"I feel," my wife said piously, "that he wanted only to show his daughter that he was a well-bred and religious man —if only to counteract the terrible things her mother must have said about him."

"Well, he doesn't happen to be either. He's a self-centered old megalomaniac, and when the novelty of this heavy father act wears off—as it will in about two hours—he'll be the same shabby deadbeat he always was. Remember, I'm a man and I *know* other men—especially this one."

My soliloquy was interrupted by the coughing and choking of Madame X's old Hispano-Suiza pulling up out in front of the Casa Ximinez. St. Regis, in archaic chauffeur's livery, was at the wheel looking terrified. In a moment Starr appeared with Emily on his arm. She was very white gloves and picture hatty, while Starr was still in his courtly Adolph Menjou phase. He helped Emily into the car with an air of gallantry and a little half bow that made me want to kick him in the pants. Then he climbed aloft—and considering the age and height of that old touring car, I mean just what I say—and executed an airy gesture of command. The car lurched hideously and leaped forward with such violence that their heads were snapped backward to the folded-down roof. Then they were off in a cloud of white dust. "There they go," I said, "Elsie Dinsmore and Daddy-dear."

"I still think it's sweet," my wife said with a little less certainty.

"I only hope that St. Regis can afford this little family outing. I also hope that we might be left alone just long enough for me to take a bath." I started up the stairs, unbuttoning my shirt at the same time. When I was about halfway up, our bell started clanging.

"I knew it was too good to last," I said, trudging the long, long route to the door at the front of the building. I undid all of the locks and bolts and opened up. Standing there was a small, rather untidy-looking man. He wore rimless glasses, a small wispy mustache, and he carried a shabby, bulging briefcase that looked as though it had seen a lot of travel.

"Yes?" I said.

"Mr. Starr?"

"Now don't tell me that you're his long-lost son?"

"You *are* Mr. Starr, aren't you?"

"No, thank God, I'm not." I had the feeling that I was sitting through a motion picture—possibly one written, produced, and directed by Leander Starr—for a second time.

"Isn't this the Casa Zzzziminezzz?"

"This is the Casa Hhhhiminez, but you have the wrong apartment. Mr. Starr is in Number Two—straight through the patio and then to your right."

"Thank you, sir."

"But he's not there. He's just left."

"Left the country?" the man asked rather too sharply.

"No, alas, left the Casa Ximinez. I don't know what time he'll be back, and what's more, I don't . . ."

"Maybe you can tell me, is there any kinda ho-tel or tourist home—a motel like—around here?"

"Not really. The San Angel Inn is fairly close, but I don't know if they can take any guests at the moment."

"You suppose there'd be a vacancy here? I mean in the Casa Zzzziminezzz?"

"I think there may be. I'm not sure. You'd have to ask Miss Hhhhiminez. Her apartment is across the whole back of the patio. You can't miss it. Good . . ."

"Expensive?"

"Miss Ximinez?"

"No, this place. The Casa Zzzziminezzz."

"*I* think so."

"About how much?"

"You'd have to take that up with Miss Hhhhiminez. Now if you'll excuse me . . ."

"You know this Leander Starr?"

"Certainly. Who doesn't?"

"Has he been livingue here longue?"

"Mr. Starr? I really couldn't tell you. I'm afraid I can't help you at all, Mr. . . . uh . . ."

"Guber."

"*Goober?*" He did look rather like the Planter's Peanut man, only not as jaunty.

"Yes," he said, handing me a business card. "Mr. Guber of the Department of Internal Revenue. Be seeingue you."

VI

In her definitive book *The Death and Life of American Cities,*
Jane Jacobs deplores the sterile, planned, lifeless neighborhoods and favors those sections that just "grew" and throb
with people and activity twenty-four hours a day. Mrs. Jacobs
would jump for joy if she could see our *barrio.* Although
Casa Ximinez presents a blank face to the street and exudes
a totally false air of somnolence and tranquillity, the rest
of the neighborhood absolutely seethes with activity. On
one corner is the *tienda,* reeking of coffee and garlic and
onions and cabbages. Opposite is the Corazón de Jesús Farmacia, which I also suspect of being a numbers parlor. The
Nueva Mil Preguntas variety store occupies a choice corner
on the way to the Insurgentes, and in between are the Vog
(sic) Salón de Belleza, where my wife's back hair was singed
to steel wool, two doctors, a dentist, a public bath, a flower
stall, a dressmaker, and a sordid bar. In other words, there are
always plenty of people around, and it takes very little to
collect a crowd at any hour.

It was the lavender hour of that same Sunday when one of
the largest mob scenes in the history of our *barrio* gathered
around the biggest, most thoroughly awful Cadillac limousine ever created. One could hardly blame the locals for
staring. The car, like the hour, was lavender—but with an
iridescent finish—and almost as long as an ocean liner. It
had chromium in all of the usual places and in about twice
as many *un*usual places, plus two radio and telephone an-

tennae soaring upward like buggy whips. This infernal machine was manned by a crew of two—chauffeur and footman—dressed in blue-violet liveries that made me think mostly of the old Northwestern University band. On the doors of the tonneau were violet initials, C. P. (Cerebral Palsy? Communist Party?), large enough to read at a hundred yards. It was some sight.

The footman leaped out, forced a clearing in the crowd, and opened a rear door, revealing to the admiring multitudes an interior of fuchsia tufted satin. A loquacious giggle was heard, and from this amaranthine excrescence stepped Leander Starr, looking disheveled and furious. He was followed by Emily, who still looked prim and starchy but with a certain thin-lipped, irritated expression that reminded me more of her mother than of the girl-with-a-crush who had sallied forth with her psalm-singing Prince Charming a few hours earlier. Last but not least emerged a vision even more striking than the automobile itself—a woman of indeterminate years wearing a short pleated skirt, a white cardigan lavishly trimmed with multicolored paillettes and mink, and bracelets to each elbow.

Through the open window I could hear Starr, for once almost at a loss for words. "Um . . . well, uh, thank you very much, uh, Mrs. Pomeroy. It was most kind of you."

"Why, Leander," the woman shrilled. "You certainly know me well enough to call me Clarice. And you must, too, Emmy."

"Uh, yes," Emily said in a voice you could chip with an ice pick.

"Well, uh, Clarice," Starr spoke the word as though it were an obscenity, "after your great kindness we mustn't detain you any longer. Thank Mrs. Pomeroy, Emily."

"Oh, no, you don't, Leander," the woman said with a soubrettish wag of the index finger. "Now that I've saved you, I demand my little tribute. You've gotta ask Clarice in for a wee droppy. One for the road." She giggled inordinately.

My wife joined me at the window. "Who's the comic Valentine?"

Suddenly it came to me exactly who it was. "That is California's answer to Bunty Maitland-Grim. Her name is Mrs. Worthington Pomeroy and she is the sole heiress to Wonderlax, whose famous motto, 'Down and Out' once won for me a ten-dollar raise."

"And that car?"

"The rewards of regularity. Millions of satisfied Wonderlax users who have, to quote some of my own brilliant advertising copy, 'thrown off the shackles of constipation and joined the regulars.' Surely you haven't forgotten my television commercial featuring a distinguished gray-haired man in white tie and an aristocratic actress in a rented tiara sitting in an opera box:

> HE: Cynthia, you look ravishing tonight.
>
> SHE: Thank you, Gregory, and I'm simply adoring *Tosca*.
>
> HE: You have such *joie de vivre*, Cynthia, joy of life, as it were. Everyone at the club marvels at how you do it. They say you're a wonder.
>
> SHE: Wonder is only *half* of my secret. The *whole* truth is *Wonderlax*. Every morning upon arising, my maid brings me a refreshing, foaming glass of Wonderlax to combat the problems of . . ."

"I remember," my wife said. "Just hearing it made me quite ill."

Suddenly Starr caught a glimpse of us at the window and shouted at us, waving both arms like a drowning man hailing a passing ship, "Dennis, dear boy. Just the one I wanted most to see. Do join us and this charming lady"—he all but choked on the words—"for a drink."

"I'm sorry Leander, but . . ."

"I *won't* take no for an answer. If you can't join us, then *we'll* join *you*."

"If you can't lick 'em, join 'em," my wife murmured.

"We're not dressed for it," I said weakly, comparing my Mexican cotton shirt and slacks with the opulence of Starr's morning suit, the confidence of Emily's good little white, and the grandiloquence of Mrs. Pomeroy's whatever-it-was.

"Nonsense, darling boy, come as you are. I *need* you," he added pointedly.

"Please join us," Emily said in a desperate tone of voice that made me feel momentarily sorry for her once again.

"Let me fix my face, and we'll be over," my wife said, totally defeated.

When we got to Starr's apartment, the lamps in the vast living room were lighted, Emily was sitting uncomfortably on the edge of a high-backed Spanish chair, Mrs. Pomeroy had spread herself and her belongings on the sofa and was lavishly powdering her nose, and Starr was wandering about helplessly as though he'd never seen ice cubes or liquor or soda before. The room was furnished in the same sort of fake antiques as our apartment, plus a lot of life-sized carved wooden *santos* with missing hands and a tremendous silver chandelier—the only genuine thing in the place—which had undoubtedly been left over from Casa Ximinez's convent days.

". . . simply adore it, sweetie," Mrs. Pomeroy was saying. "So quaint and old world. Woo hoo!"

Introductions were brief on Starr's part, but the response was effusive on the part of Mrs. Pomeroy. "Oh, this is indeed an honor and a pleasure. I just can't tell you how many hundreds of copies of your books I've purchased as gifts for my friends. I've got a copy of everything you ever wrote in every guestroom in every home I own—in Santa Barbara and New York and Monny Carlo and the apartments in London and Paruss and Rome." It was an impressive list of real-estate holdings, and I tried to figure what my royalties would have been but gave it up, not knowing the number of guest-rooms each establishment contained. "I'm not much of a reader, but I never miss one of your books. Woo hoo hoo! Folks all say you must be writing about me! Woo hoo!" I shuddered involuntarily. People have said a lot of unkind things about my books, but I've never been accused of writing science fiction.

"Thank you, Mrs. Pomeroy," I said. "But you know we have met before."

"Really, sweetie? Where at? Practically everybody I know is a sillebrutty, but I never would of forgotten you."

"It was when Mr. Pomeroy was still alive. I used to write the advertising copy for Wonderlax. I remember what an active part you took in the campaign."

She squinted near-sightedly at me through her stubby, beaded lashes and then said, "Why, sure, sweetie. Now I remember perfectly. And I said to Mr. Pomeroy, I said, 'Daddy, mark my words, that young man's a comer.' Oh, I remember now."

The Pomeroy memory was perhaps not as effective as the product. Fifteen years ago the first Mrs. Worthington Pomeroy had been an entirely different person—a fey, withdrawn, quiet woman in her sixties who spent most of her time pondering the ponderous works of Mary Baker Eddy, perhaps in an attempt to believe that Clarice did not exist. But Clarice did, indeed, exist—first as the late Mr. Pomeroy's secretary, then as his mistress, and finally, blatantly, as his out-of-town wife. On all of Mr. Pomeroy's business trips—and they were far and frequent—Clarice simply went along, all matched luggage and mutation mink, registered as Mrs. Pomeroy, leaving the genuine article behind with her well-worn copies of *Science and Health*.

It was in the old advertising agency where first we met. For some years Wonderlax had done a roaring trade as the poor man's purge, and social barriers aside, one alimentary canal is pretty much like another. But Clarice wanted to change all that by giving America's biggest laxative the social cachet of a cure at Baden-Baden. Useless for me to suggest to her that the elite did not discuss the condition of their bowels at polo matches, regattas, hunts, embassy balls, dinner parties, or any place else; the newspapers, magazines, billboards, and airwaves of the nation were soon jammed with people of distinction—pink coats, ball gowns, parures, and commodore's stripes—discussing their new regularity joys. While I doubt that Society went flocking to its collective friendly-neighborhood pharmacist in search of amazing new Wonderlax (made with miraculous scientifically proven SH-70), it gave the poor a new self-respect to think that they shared the same problem and the same cure with the Vanderbilts, and business went on as usual. What was even more important was that it helped to assuage Clarice's yearnings for Class. Fifteen years later, now as the authentic widow Pomeroy, she was still yearning—and she still had a long way to go.

Shortly after plain old Wonderlax had been internationally launched as *the* physic of the chic, the first Mrs. Pomeroy admitted error and died—"Went over," I believe is the term —of a massive and mercifully quick stroke. A year to the day after that, Worthington Pomeroy, who was only a moderately dirty old man and helpless in the web of a tarantula like Clarice, laid a memorial wreath on the Pomeroy mausoleum and then hotfooted it to city hall to make an honest woman— and a rich one—of Clarice. She must have been good at reading electrocardiographs, if not books, because he died a month later of a coronary aboard the *Clarice,* if not aboard the lady herself, leaving her sole heiress to just everything.

Nor did the Worthington Pomeroy fortune begin and end in the bathroom. The old boy, whose only extravagance was Clarice, had invested shrewdly in stocks and bonds, annuities, and real estate with an eye to such artful tax dodges as municipals and oil wells and depreciables. Clarice had come a long way from the typing pool, but, as I said, she still had a long way to go.

I was roused from my remembrance of things past by Starr's bellowing "Damn!" from the kitchen.

"Excuse me," I said. "Maybe I can help our host. What's happened to St. Regis?"

"Oh, that's a long story, Mr. Dennis. Woo hoo!" Clarice's capacity for self-amusement seemed boundless. She patted the sofa and said to my wife, "You jess sit next to me, sweetie, and we'll let the gentlemen wait on us. I love that creation. It's from It'ly I'll bet."

"No, I bought it at Ohrbach's," my wife said.

I went to the kitchen where Starr was wrestling with ice trays, like ours, firmly frozen into the refrigerator. He gave the machine a vicious kick and was rewarded by a cascade of melons rolling out and bouncing off his somewhat dusty shoes. This was followed by a volley of such eloquent profanity that I quickly shut the kitchen door if only to spare Emily's young ears.

"Here, Leander," I said. "Let me."

"Oh, thank you, dear boy. I can't tell you what a day this has been. One *mauvais quartre d'heure* after another."

"I can imagine. And how are things going with you and Emily?"

"It's uphill work, my dear Dennis. The Matterhorn! She's a pretty little thing but a stick. Well, what can you expect with such a mother?"

"Yes. A pity *you* couldn't have raised her."

"Oh, please, dear boy, don't mention such a ghastly prospect—not even in jest. What a mechanical gift you have! So that's how you get ice cubes out of those things and into the bucket. Amazing!"

"Even more amazing is how you and your daughter managed to set out for a simple afternoon at the bullfight and end up with nobody but nobody but Clarice Pomeroy. How do you manage to get into so much trouble with so little effort, Starr?"

"Oh, darling boy," Starr said, lowering his voice to the merest death rattle, "this has been a day of the sheerest hell. First my shattering encounter with a child I haven't seen since . . ."

"Sorry, Starr, that was your *second* encounter. First came Catalina Ximinez. What did you ever do with that blue garter belt?"

"Don't be facetious, Dennis—*or* caddish. *Miss* Ximinez and I are very old friends. After all, I took her out of the jungle and made a star of her. She will always owe me an enormous debt of gratitude. Then there was the meeting with Emily—oh, the drain on my emotions! And then that ghastly bullfight—sitting in the blazing sun and watching them torment that unfortunate animal. I thought I'd be sick."

"Why, Leander," I said, pouring rum—which was all he had to serve—into the glasses, "I thought you were an old *aficionado,* considering the arena as a career, I believe you said."

"Please, dear Dennis. We kept a cow when I was a boy in Iowa. Her name was Flossie. But she died of natural causes. Gas. And then driving home in all that traffic on the Insurgentes . . ."

"Yes?"

"Well, Catalina's wretched old car broke down completely —tires or something like that. And then . . . Oh, I can't go on."

"You must," I said. "I'm spellbound."

"Then what should come along but this orchid calliope, containing none other than the one woman I have been trying to escape from for the past five years—Madame la Veuve Pomeroy."

"Just how did you and Clarice happen to meet?"

"Oh, it was an ill-fated dinner party in Monte Carlo some

years back. I was in the south of France doing a film, when some frightful Greek people—well, they were backing the picture, but otherwise they had *no* pretensions to culture. Frightful social climbers . . ."

"Well, if they thought that Clarice was *up,* they must have been pretty low."

"Oh, they were. But . . . well, I mean they'd been so niggardly about the budget for the picture—three million stinking bucks, and then they wanted to pay it in drachmas."

I was beginning to get the drift. "Go on," I said.

"Well, there was Mrs. Pomeroy—oh, she was younger then, more attractive, slimmer. She gave me to understand that she was quite well off. . . ."

"She gives everyone that impression, Starr. She'll come right out and tell you if you have any doubts. So you sold her a bill of goods and . . ."

"I simply saw her home to her vulgar villa, accepted a glass of champagne—quite a decent year, but pink, *malheureuse-ment*—and attempted to discuss with her the tax advantages of investing in my film."

"And?"

"My God, that frightful woman has stuck to me like a fungus ever since."

"She did invest?"

"No, *caro.* And when one thinks of all that gelt. Why, she's wearing enough jewelry today—*pour le sport,* mind you —to cover me twice over."

"You mean all that ice she's wearing is real?"

"Yes, more's the pity. If there's a Korvette's for diamonds, she's found it. And now . . ."

"And now?"

"And now when I have the onus of Emily heavy upon me, what do I do but break down on the Insurgentes and run into the one woman I've been trying to avoid. Fate is *too* cruel."

Much as I was enjoying the old fool's discomfort, I couldn't find it in my black heart to tell him that someone whom he was trying even harder to avoid—Mr. Guber of the Department of Internal Revenue—had also appeared.

"The drinks are ready," I said, "shall we take them in before the ice melts?"

"Just a moment, *carissimo,* I'm not *quite* ready." With that, he tipped up the rest of the bottle of Ron Castillo and emptied it. "Right," he added miserably, "in the middle of the Insurgentes."

"Right," Mrs. Pomeroy was saying as I carried the tray of drinks into Starr's living room, "in the middle of the Insurgentes. My dears, it was too amusing. Woo hoo hoo! I was coming home in my Caddy—I call my Cadillac my Caddy—from spending the weekend with Mimi and Pedro Gomez-Gottschalk in Cuernavaca—surely you must know the Gomez-Gottschalks, Mrs. Dennis, sweetie; *she* was a St. Louis Niemeyer, and *he's* very big in Peruvian emeralds."

"I don't believe I do," my wife said. "Thank you, I need this," she added as I offered her a drink, in a tone that only husbands and wives understand.

"Well, sweetie, *I'll* see to it that you meet them. They have this dee-vine villa right near Bobsie Hutton's in Cuernavaca. I always call her Bobsie, isn't that cute? Woo hoo hoo!" (Nobody who *knows* the former Barbara Hutton ever calls her any such thing, but that, of course, was beside the point with Clarice.) "I had the most dee-vine time. I'll tell you who was there. . . ."

While she was telling us, I passed the drinks around. Emily gave me an especially grateful glance. If she had found us perhaps bohemian and non-Main Line earlier in the day, she now gazed on me as though I were Vere de Vere, and snobbish as it may sound, as compared to Mrs. Worthington Pomeroy I *was*.

". . . and there was this funny old-fashion foreign-type car all steaming over, sweetie, *and* with a flat tire. So I picked up the telephone and said to my footman . . ."

Starr sank into a chair with a soft moan.

"And lo and behold whom should it be but my old beau Leander and his cute little girl. Emmy, do you know that your daddy never ever told me he had a cunning little Philadelphia day-butante for a daughter? I'n't he naughty!"

"I . . . haven't . . . come . . . out . . . yet . . . Mrs. . . . Pomeroy," Emily said in measured tones. I began to dislike her again. But not quite as much as I disliked Clarice—after all, I had known Clarice *when*.

"But ummagine, to run inta my old sweetie-pie, Leander Starr, right on the Insurgentes. Why, I didn't have any idea that he even was *in* Mexico. And that funny old car!"

"The Hispano-Suiza was always a superior motor," Starr said. "At least in my day—*and yours*."

". . . adorable place. I mean it's quaint. You gotta gimme the gran' tour. Woo hoo hoo! I mean I'm staying in this dinky little suite in the El Presidente, and I'd hate to tellya what I'm paying per day." Within thirty seconds Mrs. Pomeroy had overcome her reluctance and was able to tell us, to the last centavo, exactly what she was paying, including quarters for her car, chauffeur, footman, and maid. "But I kinda think I'd like to move out here. I mean, sweetie, it's convenient and yet it's quiet and a lot cheaper. And you don't run into a lot of American tourists."

"*We're* American tourists," my wife said. It was lost on Clarice.

"Well, so'm I, sweetie," Clarice said democratically. "I don't s'pose you know of any vacant house around here?"

As a matter of sorry fact, there were, at the time, five houses ranging from ten to forty rooms for rent within a stone's throw of Casa Ximinez, including one, said to have belonged to Cortés, just around the corner. "I . . . I don't really know," my wife said, and choked into her drink.

"You know, sweetie, I believe I know your mother," Clarice said to my wife, with a friendly pat on the thigh. "She's a dear friend of *my* dearest pal, Nellie Poindexter Dane.

We've lunched many times at the Colony—the Club, I mean, not the rest'rant."

It was my turn to choke. My mother-in-law is a saint. She has never said an unkind word about anyone in her life—except Nellie Poindexter Dane and *me*. Somehow the picture of my mother-in-law, Mrs. Dane, and Clarice breaking bread *anywhere* was like seeing my wife's mother handcuffed to a common streetwalker in a paddy wagon. I excused myself and went to the kitchen. Starr joined me almost immediately.

"My God," he said, "isn't there some way to get this . . . this woman deported?"

"No, Leander, but there are plenty of ways to get you invited to leave."

He opened a new bottle of Ron Castillo, took a swig, and handed it to me. I did likewise.

"But, Dennis, my dear, I *can't* leave. In the first place I'm in a little . . . uh . . . income-tax difficulty back in the States. . . ."

"So I understand."

"And now I have this totally strange daughter suddenly descending on me with all sorts of adolescent problems to be ironed out. . . ."

"I'm sure you can cast yourself as a male Abigail van Buren."

"I don't even know what they are yet. We were going to have a long, quiet talk tonight—that is before Medusa came onto the scene. Now you can't get a word in edgewise."

"The problems will keep till tomorrow."

"And then there's this picture I'm planning to make down here. It could be another *Yucatán Girl*. It's called *Valley of the Vultures*. . . ."

"Oh, it sounds like a perfect scream. Something light." I took another swig and passed the bottle back to Starr.

"My dear young man, I promise you it is art, art, *art*. It could be done on a shoestring—just a few hundred thousand."

"Pesos or dollars?"

"Dollars, of course. A small crew, a dozen professionals, and the rest inexperienced natives but with marvelous facial planes. I was discussing it with Catalina Ximinez last night. I even went so far as to suggest that she might invest in it."

"That must have been some discussion. Will she?"

"Not unless she's in the starring role."

"Which is?"

"A peasant girl of eighteen."

"Maybe you could tamper with the script a bit and have her go for fifty. And then there's always Mamacita."

"Don't be facetious, dear boy. Can't you see I'm desperate? By the way, you've done awfully well lately. I don't suppose . . ."

"Right! But what are you whining about? Fate and a flat tire have landed you the biggest sucker in the business— Clarice. I'm sure you can talk her into it. You're in clover."

"Oh, you fool, you fool, you *fool!*" Starr tipped the bottle back again and then set it down with a thump. "Are you so blind that you don't recognize what that woman wants of me?"

"Same thing they all do, I suppose. God knows why. Well, old Worthington Pomeroy thought she was pretty special. We all have to make sacrifices for our art. All cats are gray at night."

"Oh, yes, there's that. But Clarice wants more. She wants *marriage!*"

"Woo hoo!" Clarice called. The kitchen door opened, and she waved coyly. "Now that's enough boy talk; you fellahs come right in and join we ladies. I understand by the way, Mr. Dennis—do you mind if I call you Paddy?"

"Terribly."

"Well, I understand that you know my dear friend Bunty Maitland-Grim."

"Oh, are you friends?"

"Well, I mean I've met up with her you know like on the Riviera and like at a party at my friend the Countess of . . ." One thing about Clarice was that she always answered every question in depth, dropping names of people, places, restaurants, hotels—complete with rates—and always a *petite histoire* concerned mostly with the financial or social connections of the names she was dropping. In the long run it turned out that she didn't know Bunty at all, but would like to have us arrange that wild sweet coupling. But then Clarice never came right out and admitted not knowing anyone you cared to mention. If you asked her if she knew Queen Nefertiti, she'd tell you first that they'd lunched at Laserre last week and then work her way around to begging for an introduction.

As a matter of fact, it was both unkind and unfair of me to compare Clarice Pomeroy with Bunty Maitland-Grim. While they share many irritating qualities, now that I know them both better I can see certain unsubtle differences, and Clarice suffers by comparison. Outlandish as Bunty's getups are, she sometimes manages to look rather nice. Clarice is first, last, and always the retired madam. Both collect people furiously, but Bunty, with an eye to who might be interesting or amusing, gets the better ones. With Clarice it is grim social climbing—and not very high at that. She has no discrimination; her conquests consist of shabby or shadowy titles, the not-quite café society who are seated on the wrong side of El Morocco, and people who have nothing except money—they make a deadly crew. Bunty is extravagant and generous. Clarice is extravagant, but every penny she pays out is expected to bring back returns. Bunty is an ass and a fool. Clarice is an ass, but she's no fool; she is grimly calculating. But I guess that the greatest difference is that Bunty, for all of her shrill silliness, has a good heart. Clarice has none at all. But then I neither knew nor cared about these differences at the time. My only aim was to get the hell out of Starr's hornet's nest.

I gave my wife that on-your-feet-and-fast glance and said, "Well, thanks so much for the drink."

"Oh, you're not going," Starr said desperately. It was more a command than a question.

"Oh, yes, we are. Good-by, Mrs. Pomeroy. Nice to see you again."

"Oh, but it's not good-by. Now that I've found you, I'll be darkening your doorstep again. As a matter of fact, sweetie," she said, turning to my wife, "maybe you and I can do a little house hunting together."

"What?" my wife said.

"Yes. I'm getting sick of the El Presidente. I have this dinky little suite, and I'd hate to tell you how much they charge for . . ."

"You already have," Starr said.

"So I thought for the same amount of money I could find something real nice in this neighborhood."

"Oh, but would you be staying here long enough to make it worth while?" my wife asked, a certain tone of dismay entering her voice.

"*Keen sobby,* as the Spanish say. After all, I have houses in . . ."

"Santa Barbara, New York, and Monte Carlo," I finished for her.

"Uh, well, yes," she said, "and there's such a nice set down here." She reeled off a roster of local names that comprise the outhouse aristocracy of the Federal District. I wasn't surprised that she knew them.

"Well, I'm afraid I don't know much about local real estate," my wife lied—and badly—edging toward the door.

"Or maybe you and hubby can come in for a little drinkie tomorrow about eightish? I'm having the new ambassador from . . ."

"Uh . . ." my wife began miserably. She has never learned the art of the social lie, although I tell her that the mark of a truly creative writer is to be able to make up a plausible little story on the spur of the moment. Mark Twain always used to preface his social lies with "Oh, I'd love to, but . . .," and in the space of those five words he could invent a perfectly valid excuse. It's good practice for a novelist.

"Unfortunately we're having people in for dinner," I said.

"Or Tuesday, I'm giving a luncheon at Passy for my dear friend the Marquesa de . . ."

"Uh . . ." my wife began.

"Isn't that too bad," I said, "that's the day we're taking a picnic to the pyramids of Teotihuacán with Dr. and Miz Priddy."

"We're *what*?" my wife said.

"Or on Wednesday," Mrs. Pomeroy continued, undaunted. "I'm having a dinner dance at the Jacaranda in honor of my beloved old chums, Baron and Baroness . . ."

"What a shame," I said, "that's just the night we promised to go to the movies with *our* dear chums, Maximilian and Carlotta—Max and Lottie—Weintraub." I was pleased to note that that one produced a stifled giggle out of Emily, a gasp from Starr, and yet slid over Mrs. Pomeroy like mineral oil.

"We-ell," she said, "I'm not doing anything on Thursday. . . ."

"Oh, but we are, more's the pity. Katy Walch is showing lantern slides of her trip through Yugoslavia."

"Well, on *Friday*," she said determinedly, "I'm giving an intimate little . . ."

"Isn't that the night the Bourkes asked us to play bridge?"

"Why, uh," my wife began. Then she, too, got the bit between her teeth. "Bridge Friday, poker Saturday, and canasta on Sunday. The Bourkes are inveterate gamblers."

"Well, tell me," Mrs. Pomeroy said dangerously, "what day or night during March *are* you free?"

I knew I was licked. "Oh, hell," I said, "we'll come tomorrow."

"Dee-vine! Eightish in my suite at the El Presidente. Shall I send my car for you?"

"Please don't. Well, goodnight." Seeing poor Starr's ravaged face, I added, "Can't I see you to your car, Mrs. Pomeroy?"

"Oh, no. The night is young. Woo hoo hoo! I'll just have another little drinkie and dish old times with Leander and Emmy. *A demain!*"

Thoroughly trounced, we made our escape.

"Well, I never," my wife said in the privacy of our bedroom. "Unzip this, would you. I can't imagine what single women do about zippers down the back."

"They could always wear the dresses hindside-to. You never what?"

"Thank you. I never in all my born days met anything to equal Mrs. Pomeroy. I mean she's a real, man-eating shark. Well, she's not going to get me."

"Oh, yes, she is."

"Oh, no, she's not. I'll have a headache, a delicate female complaint, a sprained ankle—I'll break a leg if I've got to."

"And be lying in bed immobile where she can prey upon you all the easier? Give it up. She's tougher than we are. Admit defeat gracefully."

"I'll be rude."

"She can be ruder."

"But, except for another name to drop, what is the frightful woman after?"

"Don't you know?"

"No."

"She's after Leander Starr."

VII

"There's just the faintest likelihood," I said to my wife the next morning, "that I might get a little work done today. It's been some time, what with one thing and another, since I've done a tap, and what with the children's spring vacations just around the corner, the federal income taxes, the New York State income taxes, and a few frivolous whims such as eating regularly, we could use some money. Do you suppose that if I put my typewriter out in the patio and hung up a big Do Not Disturb sign anyone would pay any attention to it?"

"I doubt it," my wife said, "but you might try. At least I won't be around to disturb you. I'm going into town to get my hair done, have a girly lunch with Katy, and then go to Sanborn's for a lot of interesting things like emery boards and vitamins and 4711 soap, and maybe I'll just see if Lila Bath has anything I can wear. What with Emily and Bunty and Lady Joyce and Mrs. Pomeroy switching around in their fine feathers, I'm feeling very much the little brown wren. Have we got any money?"

"No, but the National City Bank does, or you can always cash a check at El Paseo if that's where you're having lunch. And promise me you won't come back until you can do it in a purple Cadillac with a mink and sequin sweater."

"Here's my cab. Good luck."

I put on my Mexican working clothes from the High Life (rhymes with Fig Leaf) haberdashery, gathered up my paper and typewriter, and went out to the patio. All was typically serene at Casa Ximinez. Guadalupe was feeding her daughter, the *vigilante,* and the cousin who sells lottery tickets in our kitchen. Out in front, Madame X and St. Regis were having a heated quarrel over the Hispano-Suiza with Mamacita joining in occasionally in Mayan. A mechanic from the local garage was acting as interpreter and referee. Perro was barking, and a crowd of two or three dozen interested spectators had collected around the car and the tow truck, participating to the fullest. The gist of the argument seemed to be that St. Regis had been woefully negligent versus the point of view that the Hispano-Suiza was thirty-five years old and in run-down condition. I suspected that the truth was somewhere in between.

I set up office on the rickety little tile table under Loro and the jacaranda tree, and tried to reread what I had written some days before. It was a light, frothy piece for a famous women's service magazine that will buy any piece of fiction, no matter how bad, as long as it's wholesome and the author's name is sufficiently well known to beef up the front cover. They have a something-for-everyone formula that is one hundred per cent foolproof. While the ladies in the fiction department put away about a quart of gin apiece at lunch every day before dashing off to their analysts, the stories they insist on printing are simon pure. Nobody smokes, drinks, swears, or has any problem deeper than will-virtuous-Penny-get-dashing-Hillary-away-from-scheming-Marcia. The readers all know that she will, in three thousand carefully chosen words, but they've been happily reading the same story for more than half a century and still gurgle with pleasure and excitement when goodness and honesty triumph over wickedness. In the nonfiction department, however, anything goes, and the closer to pornography the better. Sandwiched in between fashions, recipes, beauty hints, model rooms, and stories of such a purity as to make *Our Sunday Visitor* look like *Playboy* are articles that would curl your hair—"Syphilis in Our Nursery Schools," "Is Your Daughter a Teen-Age Prostitute?" "The Orgasm and You." Still, I don't have to read the magazine, just write for it, and one sweet, simple story (prefaced by a warning to the subscribers that I am very wicked) pays an awful lot of tuition.

I began reading:

Salli♣ dabbed a bit of powder over her tip-tilted nose♦ and gave her reflection a long, violet♠ gaze.

"Gloriosky,"❋ she said to herself, "twenty-two♥ tomorrow and still an old maid.✍ If only Mr. Right would come along."◑

Fitting a sheet of paper into the typewriter and a cigarette into my mouth, I wound up for the big scene of pure hilarity, where Salli tries to get to Mr. Right's heart through his stomach—oh, let me tell you, there's a chuckle on every line in the kitchenette episode, culminating in a girdle-splitting, button-popping explosion of the pressure cooker that leaves broccoli all over the ceiling. (The kicker, quite naturally, is that he hates broccoli but loves Salli. He's just been too shy to admit to either.) But before I'd struck the first key, I was conscious of another presence. I turned and saw both Dr. and Miz Priddy. "Ah, Mr. Dennis. 'Then, rising with Aurora's

♣They like diminutives of Victorian names such as Candy for Candace, Debby for Deborah, or even Vicky for Victoria. However, spellings of the Italianate School—Patti, Susi, Jeri—are enjoying a tremendous vogue at the moment, and who am I to lag behind the times?

♦No short-story heroine is ever permitted an aquiline, Roman, Semitic, or pug nose, although rhinoplasty is a favorite subject of the beauty editor: "Do You *Like* Your Nose?"

♠A favorite color now because—or in spite—of Elizabeth Taylor. Violet eyes have totally replaced green and turquoise.

❋Most girls would have said "Balls!" but one bows to reader mail from the Bible Belt invariably ending, ". . . . cancel my subscription to your salacious magazine, which I have consigned to its rightful place—the *fire!*"

♥As the median subscriber's age—if not intelligence—is twenty-two and a half, no heroine is ever older. This is known in the trade as "creating reader identity."

✍Can one wonder?

◑Need I tell you that in the very next paragraph the doorbell will ring, and there will be snub-nosed, freckled, rangy Jeff or Greg or Tad, with his happy-go-lucky grin, who has inadvertently come to the wrong apartment, leaving brittle, mean-mouthed Claire or Sandra or Sybil tapping her aristocratic foot on the floor above? Well, it's a living.

light/The Muse invoked, sit down to write,' as Swift said of poetry."

"This isn't poetry. It happens to be crap. Good morning. Playing hookey from old Mexico U?"

"A diller, a dollar, um, a ten o'clock scholar. No, uh, today I am absenting myself from my seminar to accompany Modesta to a nearby village—well off the beaten tourist track —where the natives have a most unusual private celebration of considerable ethnical . . ."

"Good mawnin' Mr. Dennis? Yes, this little village is about thirty miles away? It's said to be very picturesque?"

"Good morning, Mrs. Priddy," I said. "Well, if it's that far, you mustn't let me detain you. Some of the roads in those out-of-the-way places can be . . ."

"While discussing our little, um, peregrination with, uh, my, uh, associate and, uh, heheheh, co-conspirator, Dr. Moreno y Moreno, he told me of a little known short cut whereby one can save . . ."

"The children all weah these masks? And there's a procession from the cathedral around the Zócolo? And then they invoke the . . ."

"A cathedral, by the way, Mr. Dennis, of more than routine interest in that it dates from the viceroyship of the Conde de Revilla Gigedo during the last quarter of the eighteenth century—the, uh, Age of Enlightenment, as it has been so aptly called—and contains a reliquary which is said to . . ."

"Well, you must tell me all about it when you get back. But I don't want to hold you up."

"Ah expict you know we've got a new tinant?" Miz Priddy said. "He seems very unusual to me?"

"Oh?"

"Yes, Ah asked our maid to find out his nay-yum? It's Guber?"

I became suddenly more interested than usual in Miz Priddy's endless total recall. "Oh?"

"Yes. He doesn't exactly seem to be ouah kind?" Although

I resented being lumped with Dr. and Miz Priddy even if it was meant as a compliment, I was suddenly all ears. "He seems to be that Noo Yoke-Miami type? Ah don't have to tell you what Ah mean? He took the very smallest apartment?" (The one Miz Priddy couldn't get, as a matter of fact.) "Numbah Fo-ah? He haggled something awful about the price? That whole race does that?" (But certainly not with the ardor of that smiling Southern belle, Modesta Lee Drain Priddy.)

"Speaking purely technically, Modesta, and in the interests of pure semantics, 'race' is the incorrect appelation . . ."

I stopped listening and thought about poor Starr. Here he'd come all this way to avoid paying up his back taxes, and now the revenue boys had planted their own hawkshaw right across the patio. Not that I had much sympathy for Starr. I don't like paying taxes any more than the next man, but at least I do it. Still, with all of his other problems, Mr. Guber did seem to be the last straw. I looked across the patio and saw Mr. Guber emerging from his apartment dressed in a seersucker suit that looked exactly like a pair of pajamas.

". . . and so, my dear, even after five thousand years of ritual circumcision, the prepuce is, uh, still, uh, very much in, uh . . ."

"I believe this is Mr. Guber coming now," I said, "perhaps you'd like to discuss his circumcision with *him*."

"Oh, de-ah, you don't suppose he heard?" Miz Priddy said with a fluttering of her Roman-striped shawl.

"I'm sure I don't know. Let's ask him, shall we?" I said.

"Heavens, Modesta, we must, um, needs make haste." Consulting his watch, Dr. Priddy let fly with one last platitude. "To quote the wise old Virgil, 'Sed fugit interea, fugit inreparabile tempus.' Or loosely translated, 'Meanwhile time is flying—flying never to . . .' "

"I'm familiar with the quotation," I said. "But it is flying and you'd better fly with it." With that they were gone, Miz Priddy tripping over a stone as she looked guiltily back at Mr. Guber.

Turning back to Salli and the broccoli, I was able to type nearly half of a side-splitting line before I was interrupted again. "Top of a morningue," a voice said. I turned and there stood Mr. Guber, bifocals gleaming.

"Oh, good morning, Mr. Guber," I said guardedly. "I see that you're staying here."

"Yes. It's very costly, but I prefer to be within walkingue distance. On per diem expenses he can be very diff-fi-cult about cab fares."

"Who can?"

"Uncle Sam." Although I haven't had so much as a parking violation in my entire lifetime, I shuddered.

"Comfortable here at Casa Ximinez?" I asked.

"Definitely. Very Spanish. Reminds me a good bit of the Roney Plaza."

"Well, yes," I said. "Mexico *was* a Spanish colony. But then I guess Florida was, too," I added lamely.

"I haven't ever had the pleasure of travelingue to Spain, but I was down in Cuba on a case fi'-six years ago. That's very Spanish, too."

"Do you travel much?" I asked conversationally.

"All the time."

"Just a vagabond, I suppose."

"No. Business. Tax business. Shirl, that's my wife, says why have a lovely home in Teaneck—that's in Jersey—if I'm never in it. But I say . . ."

"Do you mean the government really sends men *outside* the country to . . . to . . ." I could hardly say it ". . . to collect income taxes?"

"Definitely. Only the big cases, though. We have a permanent-type office in Paris, France, just to keep an eye on any conspicuous spendingue."

"Isn't that interesting," I said weakly.

"Seen Mr. Starr this morningue?"

"Oh, good Lord, no. When he goes away for the weekend, sometimes he's not back for . . . well, for weeks."

"You dint say he was gone for the weekend yesterday."

"Didn't I? Well, I'm sure he won't be . . ."

"St. Regis," Starr bawled from his bedroom above our heads. "St. Regis! I want my breakfast."

"What was that?" Mr. Guber asked sharply.

"Th-that? Why, that was Miss Ximinez's parrot, Loro. See? He's perched up there right above us." Mr. Guber squinted upward toward where Loro was dozing. "Amazingue," he said.

"St. Regis! My breakfast," Starr bellowed louder than ever. By now the argument on the street had reached such a crescendo that St. Regis couldn't have heard a fifty-megaton explosion. However, Perro's incessant barking from the street suddenly inspired the parrot up in the tree to an imitation. As an encore he finished off with his impressions of Madame X, saying, *"Buenos días,* I aff come for de rent."

"That's some bird," Mr. Guber said. "Ve-ry ver-sa-tile. Shirl—that's my wife back in Teaneck—has a parakeet but she can't teach it to say anythingue."

"Well, that's life," I said desperately. "Some can, some can't."

Mr. Guber looked up into the purple jacaranda blossoms where Loro, having located a particularly delicious covey of vermin under one wing, was pecking away at himself. "Astonishingue! Uh, speakingue of breakfast, is there some kind of coffee shop in the vicinity?"

"Hasn't Señorita Ximinez assigned a maid to your apartment yet?"

"I don't expect to be here longue enough for that. Too expensive. But if there's a cafeteria or some kind . . ."

I began to see a way out for Starr. "Well, there's a bar-cum-chili-parlor across the way. . . ."

"That ought to be good enough."

"Oh, no, it won't. Very dirty. Lot of low types. Drunks. *Mean* drunks. And they hate Americans."

"Well, I'm not a drinkingue man myself. I mean I haven't got anythingue against it—in moderation. Rye and ginger ale at a social gatheringue—somethingue like that—but . . ."

"No," I said firmly. "It wouldn't be neighborly to send you

across the street. I'd never be able to forgive myself if anything happened to you." He looked dismayed. "But, I'll tell you what, Mr. Guber. Why not try San Angel—the German restaurant. That's very nice. You can pick up a taxi at the corner and . . ."

"A cab. About how much . . ."

"Oh, the merest pittance. One peso, fifty—two pesos at the most."

I could almost hear the comptometer of his mind clicking. "That would be about sixteen cents—few mills less. About the same as a New York subway."

"Exactly—and so much more colorful and interesting. You'll like San Angel. Don't hurry back. Look around. Very old. Very quaint. Very picturesque." I was beginning to feel like Miz Priddy.

"Well, thank you very much, I'm sure. But I can't waste any time on sight-seeingue. Business first, pleasure later. The German restaurant in San Ongue-hell."

"That's right. The drivers all know it. *Buen provecho!*"

"Thanks a lot. So longue."

I waited until he was out of sight, then I gathered a handful of pebbles and threw them up at Starr's open window.

"Ouch!" he cried. "Merciful God, am I to be shot as well as starved?"

"Starr!" I hissed as loudly as I dared. "Starr!"

He apeared at the window, hair and dressing gown flying. "What kind of practical joke is this, Dennis?"

"Starr," I said. "I've got to tell you something. It's important."

"Oh, very well," he said. "Just let yourself in, and while you're about it would you mind bringing a pot of coffee, some hot—not cold but *hot*—milk, croissants with *sweet* butter, and some simple confiture—I don't suppose you have any . . ."

"No, Starr," I said. "Not here. Any place else, but *not* here. Now throw on some clothes and . . ."

"Well, it will take me some little time, dear boy. There's

124

my tub, and I can't find my valet to shave, massage, *or* feed me. Then I run through a set of calisthenics—one likes to keep fit, you know. . . ."

"Starr, listen. Just put on anything *and* your dark glasses and come with me. I'll explain later."

"Oh, all *right,* if you must have your childish dress-up games. I'll be down shortly. Damn St. Regis!"

Starr was downstairs in a remarkably short time. I couldn't help noticing that he had left off his girdle and the tiny little patch of hair, nor can I say that, informal as his outfit was, he was dressed as inconspicuously as I would have liked under the circumstances. He was wearing skin-tight white sharkskin trousers, kelly-green espadrilles, and a blazing red shirt of voile so sheer that you could count every hair on his chest from across the patio. He had, however, put on the biggest, blackest pair of wrap-around glasses I had ever seen. All very chic on Capri or at St. Tropez or even in Acapulco, but if that was Starr's idea of disguise, he'd have been a lot less noticeable stark naked in our little suburb.

"You look like the Mexican flag," I said.

"And you look like a pile of . . . Do you realize, my dear Dennis, that not one morning since I've been in this misbegotten place have I seen a pot of coffee before I've seen you? Friendship is one thing but breakfast is another. Now do let's tuck into a decent meal before I'm forced to listen to your trivial chitchat. I'm told there's ra-ther a nice little Bierstube at San Angel, we might stroll . . ."

"Oh, no! Anywhere but there. It's an ex-Nazi hangout."

"Very well, then. You're the great gourmet. You suggest something. What is all that caterwauling out in the street?"

He soon found out. The crowd had thickened to an alarming size. Señorita and Mamacita were both screaming at the tops of their lungs. St. Regis was all but in tears, and even the garage mechanic was hard put to control his passions and the small command of English he reserved for interpreting. Perro barked hysterically throughout.

"What," Starr said, drawing himself to his full height, "is the meaning of this disgraceful street brawl? St. Regis, I have needed you and you have failed me."

"Oh, Mr. Starr," St. Regis said, "it's just awful! I mean the things this cheap—I mean the terrible things Miss Ximinez is saying. Oh, she's accused me of . . . Oh, I'd hate to say what *not!*"

"Starrrrr!" Madame X shrieked. *"El automóvil—mi Hispano-Suiza, un automóvil importado y muy caro—no anda! El motor no marcha bien. Tiene un desperfecto; la batería no funciona; se necesita reparar el carburador; necesita bujías nuevas; la llanta necesita un parche. . . ."*

"Quiet, you dizzy bitch! *Silencio!"* Starr's roar of command somewhat stilled St. Regis, Catalina, Mamacita, and the crowd. "Ask for a mechanic, Dennis, there's a dear."

"Hay un mecánico allí?" I said automatically to the mechanic.

"Sí, señor. Yes. I am mechanic."

"Here's your man, Leander."

"Now just what does Señorita Ximinez seem to be saying, my good man?"

"The Señorita Ximinez is saying that her motorcar is Hispano-Suiza, imported and very expensive. Also, she is saying that it does not run. The engine has a how-you-say to knock?"

"A knock?" I said helpfully.

"Thank you, yes, señor, the engine knocks. It is not marching properly. The battery fails to function. It is necessary to repair the how-you-say *carburador?"*

"Carburetor?" I ventured.

"Exactly. Thank you, señor. It is necessary to repair. Also it is needing replacement of the . . ." he gestured toward the sparkplugs. "As well the tire wants a . . ." Another gesture told us that it needed patching. "The Señorita Ximinez say also that you take her car to *corrida de toros* one day past and you must pay."

"*Absolutamente!*" Catalina screamed. She had been hanging on the mechanic's every word and had more or less followed his translation. "Hispano-Suiza, very rare. Cost much. Now is *roto*. You pay."

I glanced nervously up and down the street. A parade couldn't have drawn such throngs. Wet, bare bodies were hanging out of the windows of the public baths, women in rollers had come out of the Vog Salón de Belleza. I could hardly have chosen a worse time to spirit Starr quietly away.

Mamacita's brown old India-rubber face began to work, her adder's tongue shot out to lubricate her whiskers, her leather lips. "Mai . . . doter . . . beeg . . . star!" she screeched with pride and then chortled happily.

"*Y también yo deseo seis llantas nuevas,*" Madame X shouted.

"*En garde,* Starr, she's trying to screw you out of *six new tires!*"

"I've had enough of this," Starr said with enormous dignity. "My dear fellow," he said to the mechanic, "will you please tell Señorita Ximinez that the car is almost as old as she is, if such a thing is possible." The mechanic did. It brought down the house. "You may also tell her that I happen to know where she got it and when and, more importantly, *how.*" Catalina gasped at this juicy bit of translation. The audience was loving it. "Please add that the car shook like a reducing machine—*comprende usted* 'reducing machine'?— and rattled like castanets, and if she thinks I'm going to do anything but repair that glassy-smooth old tire that burst she's insane."

The crowd got an enormous charge out of this translation. Besides being impressed by Starr's bravura performance, the neighbors were more or less anti-Ximinez, disliking her for the airs she put on, albeit a former screen star and general's mistress. "And now, St. Regis, please leave this degrading scene and prepare Miss Emily's breakfast. When she awakens please tell her that *I shall return.* Come, Dennis." Like General MacArthur he marched up the street. Over Madame X's rage and the taunts of the crowd and the barking of Perro, I could hear the poor mechanic saying, *"No podemos arreglarlo hoy. No tenemos los accesorios correspondientes, Señorita Ximinez. Puedo arreglarlo por el momento."* No question about it, the scene had been all Starr's.

". . . very idea," he muttered, "of that Indian sow trying to hold me up for a whole new car. No wonder she never got anywhere in pictures after I made her name a household word. Greed, I tell you, dear Dennis, pure avarice—that's why that ignorant, grasping savage never got ahead." I fought down the impulse to point out that Catalina Ximinez—greed be damned—was by now several million dollars ahead of Starr. I also knew that he'd have to unwind before I could tell him anything. We strolled on for about a quarter of a mile into a woefully shabby section quite unfamiliar to me, when finally Starr said, "Dear boy, I can't go another step until I've had *some* nourishment to sustain me—at least a cup of coffee. I do think you might offer me that much before I have to listen to your problems."

We went into the only available place, a dank, dark little café that reeked of stale beer, fresh urine, and rancid grease. A couple of drunken Mexicans were at the bar and so were a couple of beatnik Americans naïve enough to think they were wallowing in true Mexican culture. We sat down at a damp table. On the wall above us some discouraged American had written, in a burst of poesy:

> *The flag is a rag.*
> *The Bible's a book.*
> *Mother's a hag.*
> *And God is a crook.*

It was that kind of place. Out in back I could see a slattern filling the mineral-water bottles from a rusty tap. Starr ordered coffee, eggs, beans, and *tacos*. Having witnessed the water trick, I settled for a beer and elected to drink it straight from the bottle. "I hope you've got a strong stomach, Starr," I said, wincing at the disgusting mess on his plate. Starr said, "I believe in letting my every organ know who's boss. Keep the stomach too busy to feel sorry for itself and you'll never have any trouble. And speaking of trouble, what seems to be your problem, dear fellow?"

"Well actually, Leander, it isn't my problem at all."

"Then you make a dreadful mistake in meddling. Worry only about your own problems and you'll never . . ."

"It's *your* problem."

"Oh?"

"Yes, I'm afraid so. There's a man down here looking for you from the Department of Internal Revenue. A Mr. Guber." Starr went gray beneath his tan, whether from the information or the meal I didn't quite know. "I put him off yesterday when you and Emily were at the bullfight, and I managed to get him out this morning. But of course he'll be back. He'll have to come back. He's taken a little place in Casa Ximinez. He's living there."

With surprising aplomb Starr said, "Ah, Mr. Guber. Poor Irving. Sometimes I fear that he has formed a deep homosexual attachment for me—unfulfilled, of course. You know, dear boy, when I once considered directing *Les Misérables,* I was struck by the notion that it might add a bit of piquancy to that old chestnut if the inspector—cold, bureaucratic, literal, apparently without feeling—was actually, unbeknownst to himself, a seething sinkhole of the most *unusual* emotions and had the hots for Jean Valjean. Well, naturally, that was too daring for Twentieth Century-Fox during . . ."

"Starr," I said, "I got the distinct impression that Mr. Guber is after a good deal more than your fair white body."

"Oh, indeed he is, dear boy. More thousands of dollars than I care to recollect. And he's been after them for years. Ever since, uh . . ."

"Ever since you skipped the country?"

"Since I went away for reasons of health. Oh, my yes, the

times I've had with Irving Guber—Italy, Switzerland, France, Belgium, Greece, England. A more perceptive individual could have gained the equivalent of a college education just pursuing me from pillar to post. So now the grand tour has led the two of us down to this sewer?"

"You don't seem very concerned, Leander."

"Why should I be? I can't be extradited. Mr. Guber is hardly big enough or strong enough to kidnap me and drag me across the border. And even if he could, what would the government get? They've taken everything I had to leave behind—a house in Beverly Hills, my office furniture, even attached my bank account."

"Was there much in it?"

"Oh, quite a lot. Ninety dollars, give or take a few cents."

After all my pains to shield Starr from Mr. Guber, I began to feel a bit miffed by his cavalier attitude. I have noticed before that whenever anybody voluntarily takes it upon himself to "save" someone from an unknown fate, he expects a kind of blubbering gratitude as his due and becomes resentful if that unknown fate turns out to be anything less than disgrace, imprisonment, or hanging. "Well, in that case," I said hotly, "perhaps you could ask him to share your apartment. With his per-diem expense account he could at least defray the rent bill. That might help poor old St. Regis!"

"Ah, good, virtuous, hard-working, respectable Dennis," Starr said. "You must think me a vain, selfish, unreliable, frivolous old man, had you only the rude honesty to say it."

"I have both the rudeness and the honesty to say more than that, Starr. I think you're a deadbeat and a crook. In fact, I know it."

"Well! If you think I've come here to be insulted by . . ."

"I also know that you're at the end of your rope. Snaky as you are, you haven't got a pit to hiss in. That old simpleton St. Regis is keeping you in food and lodging and pocket money as well as waiting on you hand and foot. You can't go home, and there isn't a civilized country on the face of the earth where you're not wanted by every hotel and restaurant and tailor and loan shark—not to mention the police. You're finished, Starr. Everybody knows it. The only funny—or maybe I mean sad—thing is that you don't know it too."

"Now listen to me, you middle-aged leprechaun . . ."

But I was too annoyed to listen to any more. "You've run as far as you can run. Now you're down here living it up on your valet's money—taking people to night clubs, doing the big pitch for the daughter you've neglected, clasping that prayerbook and gassing away about Rolls-Royces and God and a lot of other things you've forgotten ever existed. And just who the hell do you think you're fooling? Me? My wife? Your ex-wife? Ximinez? Emily?"

"I think Emily was ra-ther impressed."

"But for how long? She's not an imbecile."

"Dennis, dear boy, could I allow my own child to believe that I was . . . that I was all the things you said I was?"

"No, I don't think you could, any more than you could be a normal, affectionate, flesh-and-blood father who cared whether she lived or died. Not you, Starr. You've got to be the last of the big-time spenders whooping it up until the boom falls, and then little Sara Crewe ends up in the garret dreaming of that wonderful Pappa and the diamond mines that never were. But in the meantime by all means go right ahead impressing the girl with the pretty fiction of how big and rich and famous you are—how very much in demand, but don't say by whom. With any luck she may be summoned back to Philadelphia before you're kicked out of Casa Ximinez, and she can spend the rest of her life looking back to that paragon of a father who devoted two or three days of his invaluable time exclusively to her. Leander Starr—the father of us all—the great producer-director who's as dead as Kelsey's nuts in every picture studio from here to . . ."

"Stop it!" Starr shouted. "Stop it! Stop it! Stop it!" To my amazement there were tears streaming down his face.

"Starr," I said, "I'm sorry. I got carried away. When you get right down to it, I'm not much of a father, either."

"Have you a hankie? I seem to have come away without . . ."

"Here," I said. Disgusted as I was with him, I was also ashamed and contrite.

"Thank you, Dennis," he sniffed. "I'll have my manservant launder it and . . ."

"Oh, go soak your head," I said, snatching the handkerchief back.

"What you say is by and large correct. I have been self-indulgent and foolish. I have neglected my child. I have been shamefully indiscreet and careless when it comes to money matters. *But I am not forgotten.* If you don't believe me—and I can sense that you don't—take a look at these." From his wallet Starr produced a stack of letters from every major motion-picture studio and every television network in America. I took my time reading them, suspicious always of a trick or, at the very least, a grandstand play on the part of Starr. They were authentic. I recognized the names, signatures, and styles of the heads of almost every company. Far from forgotten, Starr had been offered the director's job on every major property scheduled for production during the next two years. Not only were the salaries staggering, but even better for a man in Starr's delicate position with the government, there were all sorts of complicated deals involving shares of the profits, percentages of grosses, spread-out payments. "But, Starr," I said. "Why don't you say yes to one or two or three of these offers? Not one of them is more than a couple of months old. Something must still be open. Within a year or so you could be right back to where you used to be. You could pay up your honest debts and . . ."

"Don't be absurd, child. With the income-tax people hanging over me like a sword of Damocles? With the first Mrs. Starr—I was hardly more than a boy when I married her— and her wretched lawyers waiting for God knows how much back alimony? With Ilonka—that was my fourth ghastly mistake; promise me you'll always avoid Hungarians—wailing like a Tzigany for *her* blood money? Go back to America with my hat in my hand, an old has-been trying for a comeback, looking like a beachcomber?"

"Well, a Fire Island beachcomber, perhaps," I said, taking in, once again, his bizarre costume.

"No! Damn it, man, I won't do it. I *can't* do it. When Starr returns, Starr returns in style—in splendor!"

"Oh Lord, here we go again: the maharaja returning to the imperial suite on a spangled elephant. Starr, these are the sixties, not the twenties. People have forgotten all that red-carpet nonsense. Surely you've had enough of life à la Ritz by now to know that it's phony—nice, but not worth the price." I handed the letters back to him, satisfied that they were the real McCoy. "In these days of inflation and taxes all these people ask of you is a superior job of work, not a super new standard of living."

"No," he said quietly. "I've got to come on strong. . . ."

"I wouldn't worry about that if I were you."

"But you're not me. You've had all the advantages."

"All I could *pay* for," I said pointedly.

"The social graces, the best schools, a rich family . . ."

"What are you talking about, *rich*? My father was a broker in Chicago. He still is. Real estate. But he's not rich, although he yells about the Democratic party as though he'd been . . ."

"*I* was raised on a pig farm in Iowa and a mighty poor pig farm at that."

"Well, you could fool me—not that you haven't before."

"How do you think I feel when I'm with people like . . . like Emily's mother? Like Emily herself?"

"You've always seemed to have the situation well in hand."

"But it's been an act."

"You could have played the Palace with it, Leander."

"But it takes costumes, scenery, props, and I can't go on without them."

"So you plan to stay down here at pig level?"

"No. When I go back to the States—and I'm going soon— I'm going back with money in the bank."

"How, Starr? Just tell me how!"

"There's this Mexican picture. I mentioned it to you last night. It's called *Valley of the Vultures*. The script is patchy, but that can be fixed. I could do it in a couple of weeks—a month at the longest, knowing what I know. It would cost nothing. Nothing, I tell you. With me at the helm I could turn it into the biggest grossing art film ever made—and for nickles and dimes. All I need are those nickles and dimes. By the by, dear boy, I don't suppose that you or your charming wife might happen to have a bit of loose capital to . . ."

"No, Leander," I said. "Not a dime *or* a nickel. Unlike you, I've put every penny into my children or my sugar bowl, where I can't get at it, so that fifteen or twenty years from now I *will* be unlike you."

"Well, it was just a shot in the dark."

"You missed."

"But I do have other opportunities down here. Of course you know the famous Mexican impresario, Aristido González?"

"I know *of* him and it isn't good. He's about as solid as quicksand and . . ."

"Ah, here we go again. Whenever we get on these boring matters of mere money, you begin to sound like a threatening letter from Emily's maternal grandfather. Let us get on to a more aesthetic tack, while I tell you something of the artistic *meat* of *Valley of the Vultures*. Oh, and by the way, dear boy, now that I've breakfasted—and *abominably!* I don't know *how* you locate these appalling *bistros*—perhaps you might consent to join me in something stronger. *Mozo!*" he called, signalling to the torpid barman-waiter.

Fight it though I would, I found myself once again hypnotized by Starr and his dreams of glory. Two hours later, we jostled our way over the roaches and out of the café, arms clasped as though we had never exchanged a cross word, both of us hellbound for home where we could *really* tackle the script and the technical problems of *Valley of the Vultures*.

We swayed congenially for a few paces along the street, when our grandiose plans for fame in filmdom were interrupted by the bartender who tapped Starr rudely on the shoulder.

"*Ole, señor, la cuenta!*"

"What is it, my good man?" Starr said.

"The check," I said. "He thinks it ought to be paid."

"Oh, what a dunderhead I'm becoming," Starr said, after a pretty pantomime of slapping at his pockets. "I've left the apartment without a sou. Dennis, *carissimo*, could you? *Would* you?"

Together we wobbled congenially through the deserted streets, parched in the heat of the day, back home, paying loud and elaborate compliments to one another. It was only at the portal of Casa Ximinez that I developed a certain drunken caution. "What if Mr. Guber should be waiting for you?" I asked.

"Who, good old Irving? Irv? Why, darling child, we'll simply cast him as the leading vulture. He'd be superb!" We laughed immoderately, grasping helplessly at one another for support.

The patio was mercifully empty. We made our uneven way toward Starr's door. "To work, to work, dear Dennis!" he shouted.

"Wait, Leander, wait. I'll bring my typewriter so that any time we arrive at a brrrrrilliant idea, I can get it down in white and black." I weaved toward the table and glanced at the fifteen or twenty words I had written that day. From the jacaranda branches above, Loro had dropped a large but eloquent literary criticism on Salli, Mr. Right, and the broccoli.

VIII

I followed Starr into his apartment, where St. Regis was industriously polishing the dozens of silver frames that surrounded Starr's collection of photographs of the dead Great. "I see you've got the rogue's gallery out again," I said. St. Regis giggled.

"Ah, yes, *mi amigo,* they make this torture chamber a bit homier, and then I thought they might interest my daughter. By the way, St. Regis, where is Miss Emily?"

"Oh, she's gone out to lunchin with a young gentilmun, sir."

"A young gentleman? How does she know any young gentlemen down here?"

"Why, he came to call on *you,* sir. I don't recall the name, but I seen—*saw*—him here the other night. Ever so attractive, lovely dark eyes, beautyful manners and great big, ellygunt opin car."

"Who in the name of . . ."

"Just-call-me-Bruce?" I said. "Bruce van Damm?"

"Why, yes, Mr. Dennis. That's iggzackly whom it was."

"Oh, well," Starr said, "he seemed nice enough. Mannerly. Do the child good to get out with some young beau."

"Young Mr. van Damm isn't losing any time, is he?"

"Ah well, Emily's a sensible girl—too sensible. She'll come to no harm. St. Regis, be a pearl and bring down all the material I've collected on *Valley of the Vultures."*

"Oh, Mr. Starr, you don't *mean*—you *can't* mean that we're going to get rolling on a new ixtravaganzia?"

"I mean just that, St. Regis. Now, do hurry." St. Regis skittered up the stairs two at a time.

"Have you discovered what problem brought Emily down here?" I asked.

"Oh, just some trivial girlish thing. Don't worry, it isn't anything ghastly like making a grandfather of *me*. It's simply that there's some young man up in Philadelphia—oh, very proper and old family—who wants to marry her. Naturally her mother's pushing for it. She's got the whole thing mapped out like a rocket launching: first the coming-out party; then announcing the engagement; then a proper waiting period; then the gala wedding. It's just Caroline's sort of thing."

"But is it Emily's?"

"Well, she doesn't know."

"You mean she doesn't love the stallion Caroline's picked out?"

"Oh, nothing that melodramatic. She thinks she does, but she isn't sure. She *is* smart enough to realize that she's very young and that she's seen nothing of life except what Caroline and Mr. Strawbridge wish her to see. And that's precious little—Philadelphia all winter and some dismally respectable watering place all summer—and always with the same people."

"Is she fond of her stepfather?"

"She seems to be. But her main problem is that she wants to get away by herself for a time and think. See something of life."

"Well, she'll certainly see it with you."

"I do hope so. In moderate doses, of course. But this young Bruce van Whatever . . ."

"Damm."

"*Now* what's the matter?"

"Van Damm. That's his name."

"Oh, yes. He doesn't seem to me much different from any of the proper young Philadelphians she's gone to dancing school with—pure vanilla. *I* would have suggested a more radical change."

"Don't be too sure that Just-call-me-Bruce won't be more of a change than she's bargaining for."

"What do you mean, Dennis?"

"There's just something about him that rubs me the wrong way. I've got nothing to go on with Bruce van Damm but . . ."

"Here it is, sir," St. Regis said, puffing down the stairs with a great rubbish pile of papers. "All I could find, at least."

"Splendid, St. Regis. Just set it all out in the patio, and Mr. Dennis and I will get down to work."

"Oh, and remember what you promised, Mr. Starr."

"What's that?"

"A part in it for me. I've been rehearsing my Spanish, too. *Obblay oo-stead Espaniel.*"

"Oh, yes. Well, we'll see. And do bring out some drinks."

"Yes, sir!"

Starr's "files" covering *Valley of the Vultures* were a mare's nest of extraneous bits of paper that spilled over the edge of the table and fluttered to the ground. Notes had been written on the backs of old envelopes and checks, on hotel stationery and menus from all over Europe, on bills and dunning letters, on timetables and laundry lists. No archivist in the world would ever have been able to sort them out. Not so our Starr. Drunk as he was, disorganized as his material was, Leander was all grim purpose and pure efficiency. He knew exactly where to lay hand on every fact and figure, and he knew just what he was talking about. And he talked fast.

For a man who in his day had been known to insist on using vintage champagne instead of ginger ale "for authenticity"; who had blown up a fleet of full-sized Spanish ships instead of miniature models "for scope"; who, instead of using catsup, demanded real blood corresponding to the actors' types (at fifty bucks a pint) "for realism"; who would cheerfully order his cameraman to shoot a thousand feet of film and scrap all but a yard of it, Starr could be amazingly down-to-earth when it came to filming a picture.

My knowledge of the intricacies—even the terminology—of film making isn't good enough to this day to allow me to record more than isolated snatches of Starr's machine-gun delivery. But it certainly was impressive and, I know now, to the point. "Do it on a shoestring, dear Dennis, have to. . . . Cut plenty of corners. I know which ones. . . . Get around the unions as best we can. Dispense with a make-up crew. This is a picture of *life,* not Elizabeth Arden's. Any slap that needs applying I can do myself. . . . Do my own cutting, do my own mixing. I've forgotten more about it than the most expensive men in Hollywood ever knew. . . . Forget the studio rentals, the light rentals. We'll work on location, by daylight. Hot, harsh, grueling sunshine. It won't be pretty, but it'll be real. . . . I'll be my own script girl—or you can. . . . Know the best camerman in the business, ex-party member, can't work in the States, can't get papers to work down here, poor bastard. He'll do it for peanuts. . . . Shooting schedule all laid out on this idiotic, whining letter from my tailor. Cut to the bone. Three weeks flat—maybe two. . . . A shoestring, man, I tell you, a shoestring. Hundred thousand dollars maximum!" On and on he went.

About the only subjects I felt capable of commenting on were the strong Mexican unions, the impossibility of shooting anything (except perhaps one's self) in the genuine Valley of the Vultures—an arid wasteland that lies parched and gasping for a breath of air in Guerrero between the Sierra Madre and Taxco—and money.

"Starr, Starr," I said, "this is all fine. I'm with you. I'll go over the script, do anything I can to help you. But stop referring to a hundred thousand dollars as 'a shoestring.' If that's a shoestring, Starr, you haven't got an inch of dental floss."

"Maybe not, dear boy," he said, slopping rum and soda into our glasses. "But I'll get it, by God, I'll *get* it!"

"Where?"

"Catalina Ximinez, that's one place."

"Madame X? After what you said to her this morning? After you kicked her out of bed yesterday?"

"Yes, damn her, yes. She's got it—plenty more—and she'll give it, too."

"She'd be a horse's ass if she did."

"Of course she's a horse's ass. She wouldn't be an actress if she weren't. And like all the rest of them, she's perishing to get back in front of the camera."

"You mean you'd have that bulbous old squaw *in* the picture? As what, a squashed totem pole?"

"As anything. She can think she's the star for all of me. She's too stupid to read the script and too vain to know the difference. I'll cut her out later—or at least trim her part down to size."

I was about to ask prudishly if that was quite honorable, but I knew that such a naïve objection would fall on deaf ears. "But she's lost her looks, her voice would shatter bottles, she can't act, and she's retired."

"Don't worry your young gray head about that, dear boy. I don't want looks. Hollywood is full of pretty, stupid marshmallow faces. I can have a voice along the line of Elvira Rios' dubbed in. I can pull a performance out of a stone—and don't you forget it. As for being retired, there is *no such thing* as a retired actress. Rich or poor, good or bad, they'll all go on and on and on until they . . . And speaking of *rich,* retired actresses, just turn and look at what Fate has dropped into our laps."

I turned and saw my wife entering the patio with Lady Joyce.

"Monica James?" I said. "You're insane. She'd never . . ."

"Be quiet and leave this to me. Well, hel-lo! Two lovely ladies come to bring a little beauty and cheer into the lives of two lonely men. Mrs. Dennis, darling Monica!"

"Oh, come off it, Leander. What are you after now?" Lady Joyce said.

"Look what I found under the next dryer," my wife said. "We had our hair done together, we lunched with Katy Walch, we shopped and we shopped and we shopped, and now we're dying for a drink." She glanced at me. "From the look of *you*, you suffer from no such problem."

Ignoring her loftily, I said, "Lady Joyce, how nice to see you again. Do sit down."

Her Ladyship, who was looking smashing in yellow linen with one go-to-hell emerald pin, sat down and crossed her ankles elegantly. Observing the mess of rubbish on the table, she said, "Why, Leander, from all those grubby little bits and pieces of paper spread out before you, I'd almost wager you were planning another film. What fun!"

Starr gathered them all jealously to his bosom, spilling better than half. "*If* you please, Monica, this is something that concerns only Mr. Dennis and me."

Lady Joyce picked up a paper that had fallen to the ground. "Hmm. Kilgour, French & Stanbury. 'Dear Mr. Starr,' " she read. " 'We must now press for settlement of the enclosed greatly overdue account amounting to . . .' "

"The other side, you dense cockney!" Starr snapped.

"Oh, yes. 'Shooting. First day: Exteriors hacienda. Pedro, Don Jaime, Pilar and extras, cornfields . . .' "

"Give that to me," Starr said, snatching it from her. "There's nothing there that would interest you at all. Now, my dear, what can I offer you to drink?"

"Gin and lime, I think, Leander."

"That sounds good," my wife said.

There was nothing on the table but rum and only about an inch of that. "Dear Dennis," Starr said. "We seem to be out of gin. Have you a drop in your diggings? Also lime and ice. And *if* you should have any Scotch, some bourbon, perhaps a dash more rum?" I got up to raid my own supply of liquor. "Now, ladies," he continued suavely, "let's not waste valuable time talking about this stupid picture. Besides, it's just a silly little spur-of-the-moment thing to be done locally next week. No more than charades in the attic, ac-tually. Now tell me, what interesting things have you done today? Shopping?"

By the time I had done battle with the ice trays and collected bottles and glasses and limes and soda, Lady Joyce was leaning forward in her chair, gazing spellbound at Starr. "And is it to be one of these wide-screen, glorious-color, cast-of-thousands affairs, Leander?"

"Certainly not, my dear. That kind of crap is too big for this picture, and *I'm* too big for *it*. *Valley of the Vultures* is to be one tiny, perfect gem of despair in pure black and white. Chiaroscuro. A black as black as the rich soil of a century ago, a white as white as the dust of today. Ah, here come the reinforcements. Do let me mix something for you."

"Patrick can do all that," my wife said. "Go on, please."

"Yes, Leander," Lady Joyce said.

"Oh no. I don't want to bore you with this trivia. Too bad I didn't think of it twenty years ago, Monica. There's a part in this—Doña Ana—that would have fitted you like your skin. Well, I suppose we could get someone like Diana Dors to play it."

"Diana *Dors?*" Lady Joyce said indignantly. "Well, *really* Leander!"

"Beggars can't be choosers, Monica. Was it my fault that you abandoned the boards for Burke's *Peerage?* Howsomever, you *have* retired and probably for the best."

"Well, it was hardly enforced retirement, Leander. I suppose I always could go back if the role interested me."

"Oh come now, Monica, with a boy in college—a baronet in his own right. How would he feel to see his poor old mum cavorting across the screen in a low-budget Mexican art film?"

"Well, Leander dear, it's not exactly as though I'd chosen to resume a career as a stripper in Soho. I mean there are films and *films*. It might be rather a lark, and one does get bored sitting about and listening to Bunty's chatter all day."

"It would pay nothing, Monica, *literally* nothing. No, Monica, it's just not your sort of thing. It might have been fun, but . . ."

"Well, Leander, if you really can't find anyone suitable down here and think that you might trust me to handle a very *small* role . . ."

"We'll discuss it at some other time, my dear. Gin and lime I believe you said?" While Lady Joyce was scrutinizing her face in her mirror, searching for little telltale lines, Starr tipped me a prodigious wink. Even *I* knew that the old charlatan had her in the bag.

Everyone except Lady Joyce had begun talking about other things, when our little gathering was joined by Emily and Just-call-me-Bruce van Damm. I must say that they made a handsome couple, and Emily seemed to have a good bit more bounce than heretofore. She was looking very much the all-American, Lord & Taylor girl (Bala Cynwyd branch), while he was very brown and toothy and cashmere jackety. They reminded me a little of those idealized illustrations of the young lovers in the magazine I was *trying* to write for. Emily was duly introduced to Lady Joyce, and Bruce went just a bit too far by bowing low over her Ladyship's hand. I told myself with a malicious satisfaction that he couldn't have spent much time in higher English circles. Drinks were made —by me—while Lady Joyce went into well-bred raptures over the beauty, charm, and grace of Emily.

"Good heavens, Leander, this young beauty is your *daughter?* It's incredible. Your mother must be very lovely, my dear." Starr shuddered. So did I.

Then to get the conversation to less painful topics Starr took over. "Well, child, what did you do today? See sights? Pyramids, museums, cathedrals, monasteries?"

"Oh no, Daddy. Bruce took me to lunch. It was a heavenly place with a garden. What was the name of it, Bruce?" She cast him a look of the sheerest devotion.

"I—I don't remember, Emily," he said. But he exchanged the same rapt look, and the plain old Emily sounded more like a caress.

"And then Bruce showed me his apartment. Oh, it's wonderful!" My eyebrows shot up. It did seem to me that a *bien elevée* young lady from Philadelphia's finest just didn't go prancing up to the apartment of a man she'd met for the first time. Then I decided that I had a dirty mind.

"Oh, it's just a place to hang my hat," Bruce said magnanimously. "Like my little hole in the wall in Gracie Square. That's what I call home back in New York. I always live in crazy places." Crazy they may have been, but I noticed that on either side of the border they never happened to be located in neighborhoods that were what sociologists describe as "depressed."

The conversation was steady but scattered. Lady Joyce kept her eye rather beadily on Starr, while Emily trained her gaze on Lady Joyce and Bruce stared almost exclusively upon Emily. That left nobody for me to look at but my wife, and as we'd been seeing each other for some years, I looked into my drink and wondered just when I'd have time to finish that mawkish magazine story.

Suddenly we were interrupted by a loud "Woo-hoo!" and everybody gave up gazing at one another and stared at the entrance of the patio. And well they might. There stood Mrs. Worthington Pomeroy dressed to kill. Built along the lines of a pouter pigeon, Clarice was got up in a sheer dress of colors my grandmother used to describe as "pigeon's breast," busy with beadwork and stoles and floating panels. She was wearing *all* of her bracelets today, along with an immense flowered hat, clear plastic pumps, and a plastic bag into which many innocent butterflies had been laminated. One could see through it, and I was casually able to observe a gold-and-ruby cigarette case, lighter to match, a book of Wonderlax matches (in case the lighter failed), a soiled handkerchief, a Benzedrex inhaler, a dirty comb, some eyedrops, and quite a lot of other accoutrements of Clarice's eternal allure.

"Hello, neighbors! Woo hoo hoo. You'll never guess what I've been doing all day."

"Molesting native children?" Starr suggested.

"Woo hoo hoo! No! I've been house hunting and I've finally

taken the Casa Ortiz-Robledo. It's simply dee-vine and it's *just* around the corner!" How right she was. The place was an ancient pile bigger even than Casa Ximinez. "And that's why I just bursted in: to tell you that my party tonight has been moved. Woo hoo hoo! I tried to telephone you, Paddy, but I couldn't find you in the Anglo-American Directory."

"That's because we're not in it," my wife said.

"Or even in the phone book."

"We don't have a telephone," I said. As a judgment our telephone started ringing. I knew it would go on ringing until Guadalupe stopped eating and waddled off to answer it.

"Well, I just came around to tell you that I'm already moved inta my colonial mansion, so that's where my party will be tonight. Shall I send the car for you?"

"As it's fifty paces from here, you'll hardly need to," I said. Then I noticed her looking with increasing curiosity at Lady Joyce, and I decided I'd better do the big thing—if nobody else would—and make a few introductions. "Lady Joyce," I said, "this is Mrs. Pomeroy."

"Oh, say, aren't you a pal of my dear friend, the Duchess of Gault?"

"I've met her," Lady Joyce said.

"Well, I do hope you'll come to my party tonight. It's for the new ambassador from . . ."

"That's very kind of you, Mrs. Pomeroy, but I'm afraid the Maitland-Grims are having some people in and I'm expected to be on hand."

"Bunty Maitland-Grim, sweetie?"

"Yes."

"Oh, I wish you'd bring her. I'd love to meet her." Mrs. Pomeroy caught my eye and then added, "Again."

"I'm sure she'd be very interested in meeting you, too," Lady Joyce said, "but their people are coming quite early. In fact, I must be going along to change. Thanks ever so much. Good-by, Leander," she said, sadistically kissing the little bald patch on the crown of his head. The gesture was lost on neither Emily nor Clarice. "Do call me about . . . about what we were discussing. I *might* be interested. Thank you and good-by." With that she was gone.

"And Emmy, I hope you'll bring yer boy friend. I don't believe I've had the pleasure?"

"Mrs. Pomeroy," I said, "this is Mr. van Damm."

"Just call me Bruce," he said.

"All rightie, Bruce, if you'll call *me* Clarice."

"That's very nice of you, Mrs. Pomeroy," Emily said. Once again her voice had taken on that chill, disapproving tone. "But . . ."

"We'd love to," Bruce said with a sincere grin.

"Dee-vine. Anytime after eight. Well, good-by now. I've gotta get home and get all dressed up." She pranced out of the patio, her fat little feet bulging over the vamps of her plastic slippers.

"Get dressed *up?*" my wife said.

"Daddy," Emily said a bit petulantly, "*must* we?"

"Yes, my darling daughter," Starr said wearily. "We must. At least *I* must."

Clarice's cocktail party in the grandiose Casa Ortiz-Robledo was interesting only in a clinical way. The ambassador and his lady did not show up. In fact, I soon got to notice that to be one of Mrs. Worthington Pomeroy's guests of honor was an almost sure way to achieve a cold, a virus, a stomach upset, a pressing business engagement, or an urgent trip out of town about an hour before the festivities commenced. What did show up was Mrs. P's usual ragtag and bobtail of international riffraff. The titles from Georgia, Montenegro, Ruthenia, Bosnia-Herzegovina, and other defunct countries had turned out in full force. In addition there were Clarice's rich —the dull rich, the vulgar rich, the rich who were dull *and* vulgar. Most of their names were attached to oil or manufacturing, to chain stores or discount houses, to well-known brands of packaged foods or patent medicines. If you could not make the commercial connection immediately, it didn't matter, because Clarice was always on hand to supply the complete rundown on exactly who one was and what one did. Rounding out the jolly throng were the old Mexico City hands—the nonacting starlets, the nonwriting writers, the nonpainting painters, the drifters and grifters and con men and remittance men who would go any place where the food and liquor were free. It was the sort of crowd that made you feel absolutely certain that someone would be pushed into the swimming pool before too long.

Clarice was wearing a scarlet-lamé dress with a fringe skirt ("Stick around, sweetie, we're all going to twist later"), an ugly diamond-and-ruby necklace that accentuated the shortness and thickness of her neck, and all of the bracelets. As a final fillip, she had put on a platinum-blond wig, arranged in the tangled fashion of the moment. I can only suppose that the effect she was striving for was one of sheer, youthful glamour. But all that the skittish pile of white hair did was to make her look like a very bawdy old lady.

Although taking up residence only a few hours ago, Clarice was very much in command of the enormous house. There were two bars, circulating maids and waiters, an endless table piled high with that inedible party food (although I could have told her that some of her guests would eat *anything*— were, in fact, counting on her dabs of crab and cheese and caviar and you-name-it as substitutes for dinner). A mariachi band in dusty ruffles played in the patio.

We arrived with Starr and Emily and Bruce about nine, and one look at the assembly made us feel drastically underdressed but indescribably tasteful. Emily's jaw dropped when she saw the crowd gathered in the huge, beamed drawing room that had been built for grandees and their ladies. "Just like the Philadelphia Assembly, isn't it?" I said. She giggled and squeezed Bruce's arm.

Clarice leaped like a seal at feeding time when she saw the conservative element—so to speak—standing in the doorway, and it wasn't long before we had been introduced—with business, social, and family (if any) connections catalogued—to half a dozen poisonous people. My wife and I were allowed to drift by ourselves among a horde of old harpies, each of whom told me explicitly that *she* was the original Auntie Mame. Starr naturally got detached from us and very firmly attached to Mrs. Pomeroy, who clung to his black-silk sleeve as though she were going to be swept away. From every part of the great room I could hear her, the joyless laugh, which punctuated nearly every sentence, resounding like a trumpet voluntary. "An' I wantcha ta meet the famous pitcher director Leander Starr, an' this is his cute little day-butante daughter from Philadelphia, an' this is Mr. Bruce van Damm. Woo hoo hoo!"

"One hour," I muttered to my wife, "and then cut for home."

"Must we stay *that* long?"

Through the noise and the smoke and the crowds I kept watching Starr. When it came to the social graces, he certainly had them. Even in this throng of flamboyantly overdone ignoramuses, he stood out in his anonymous black suit and string tie. Even people who had never heard the name Leander Starr (for this set didn't give one the impression that they were great patrons of the arts) seemed to realize that he was Somebody. Women fawned on him. Men looked nervously, enviously, suspiciously at him and then consulted one another as to who and what he might be behind hammy, glassy-nailed hands. This was his first public appearance since he had arrived in Mexico, and he was really mowing them down.

After what seemed the equivalent of a summer in St. Louis, our hour was up. *"Now,"* I said to my wife. "And don't stand on one foot and then the other making your farewells. A simple 'thank you' and 'good-by' will be sufficient."

"Don't worry," she said.

We fought our way across the room to where Clarice, still clinging to Starr, was explaining the charm, wealth, and chicté of a couple who were very big in plumbing, and we bade our adieux. "Oh, don't leave yet, sweetie," Mrs. Pomeroy said, grasping my free arm with her free claw. "We're all going to twist."

"Well, not quite *all* of us," I said. "I have to be up very early in the morning." I didn't.

"Indeed you do, darling boy," Starr said. "For tomorrow you and I are going to call on Aristido Gonzáles."

"Oh, are we?"

"Yes, dear boy."

"Daddy," Emily interjected. Once again, and against my will, I began finding Emily self-righteous, cloying, and tiresome. "Daddy, couldn't we *all* go?"

"*You* may, my dear. Mr. and Mrs. Dennis will see you home, I'm sure. *I* will have to stay for a bit."

"But, Daddy . . ." I could have slapped her. Had the girl no idea what her father was suffering, what he was up against? Well, no. Naturally, of course, she hadn't. Nor could she conceive of any such thing in her neatly ordered orderly life.

"I say no, child. Mr. and Mrs. Dennis will see you home if you're *that* anxious to go."

"Bruce is here, Daddy. He'll take care of me."

"Blessings on you child. *Hasta mañana.*" He pecked her forehead chastely.

The four of us walked home together, my wife and I sedately leading the procession.

Some hours later, unable to sleep, I was found at our bedroom window by my wife. "What are you up to?" she asked gently.

"Just enjoying a view of the patio, dear heart," I said.

"What are you, some kind of nut or something?"

"Be still, love, you're disturbing them."

"Who?"

"Oh, put on your specs, you old fool. *Them.* The fair Emily and Just-call-me-Bruce."

She did, and then she gasped. "You filthy old voyeur," she said, "you *are* getting on!"

"Well, at least I can see with the naked eye the naked . . ."

"You come back to bed this instant, or I'll report you to the . . ."

"*I* ought to report them to the . . ."

"You have a filthy, evil, depraved, sick mind. Mother always said so."

"I don't know what your mother would know about it unless she, too, is a filthy, evil, depraved, sick . . ."

"Oh, be still! They're just young, innocent lovers—the two of them—while you're a vile old married . . ."

"I grant you, my dear," I said with dignity, "that I am vile and old *and* married. But I beg to differ with you when you say that *they*—or at least *he*—is the unshorn lamb you like to imagine. *I* say—and I am a voice bleating in the wilderness—that *he* is a thoroughgoing . . ."

"And *I* say that you are a drunk, bleating in the wilderness. Come to bed."

I did and that was that.

IX

Having had trouble getting to sleep the night before, I had even more trouble waking up the following morning. It was past ten when I was aroused by Starr's pounding on the bedroom door. In my frenzy to scramble out of bed, I knocked over the omnipresent breakfast tray with a crash. I said an ugly word, stepped into a shattered cup, said a still uglier one, threw a robe around myself, and opened the door to Starr. He was dressed for a guards' luncheon or a conference in Downing Street—stiff collar, bowler, gloves, and a smartly furled umbrella, although the first drop of rain was still a good two months off.

"Good Lord, man, do you intend to loll about all day? Your wife's been up and about for hours. Now do hurry. We can't keep an important figure in the Mexican cinema such as Aristido Gonzáles waiting."

"Sit down," I mumbled, "while I get some fresh coffee and take a shower."

"We haven't time. Besides, you *look* clean."

"Well, I'm not."

"Perhaps no one will notice. Now do put on something with a bit of dash." He opened the closet door and began pawing through my suits. "I say, haven't you *anything* with any style to it at all?"

"Not down here. Your kind of drag isn't worn much—off-stage, that is."

"Tattiest wardrobe I've ever seen."

"Well, at least it's paid for."

"Here, this will do." He tossed me a Glen Urquhardt plaid suit, originally woven with Siberia in mind. "And wear the waistcoat, too. If there's anything I can't endure it's American men with their bosoms hanging out of their suits—shirt bosoms, that is."

"Are you crazy, Starr? It'll be up in the eighties today."

"We must all make some sacrifices for art, dear boy, and with Gonzáles a certain air of formality is *sine qua non*."

"That and sitting on your wallet, from all I've heard," I growled. I threw off my robe and burrowed through a drawer for a clean shirt.

"Good heavens, man," Starr said. "Are you gray all over?"

"Yes. Are you dyed all over?"

"Don't be cheeky with your elders and do hurry. We can't keep González waiting." After Starr had gone through all of my neckties, criticising each as he let it drop to the floor; after he had recommended a splendid little place on the rue Castiglione specializing in foundation garments for gentlemen; after he had called me ten kinds of a slob for not having brought a bowler, an umbrella, and chamois gloves to a land of sunstroke and palm trees, he pronounced me passable— "But do try to keep to dim corners, dear boy, and by all means keep your mouth shut. *I'll* do the talking."

"That'll be a nice change for all of us," I said. He steered me down the stairs and permitted me to give my wife a chaste kiss.

"Will you be home for lunch?" she asked.

"I . . . uh . . ."

"Certainly not. My dear old friend González will undoubtedly lay on a superb spread. *À bientôt, chérie.*"

We got out into the street, and I said, "Is it within walking distance or should we take a taxi?"

"Don't be ridiculous, my dear fellow. God, how can one be as naïve as you after forty years in this vale of tears?" He pulled a tiny gold whistle from his pocket and let fly with a piercing blast. From around the corner Mrs. Worthington Pomeroy's hideous lavender Cadillac appeared, complete with chauffeur, footman, fuchsia-satin upholstery, and the air conditioning going full tilt.

Starr settled into the car and gave the address. "Would you like to have that chinchilla lap robe tucked around you, Gramps?" I asked.

"Don't be facetious. You know, this car wouldn't be bad—in a different color. Although in the long run a Rolls *is* cheaper."

"Doesn't Mrs. Pomeroy want her car today?"

"Not today. She has a new toy. That enormous house. So she graciously consented to lend it to me."

"In exchange for a pound of flesh?"

"Just about. Now remember, don't be all apple-cheeked American boy when you meet González. Latins don't understand that sort of thing. Dignity and decorum. Follow my lead." He drew a very grand cigarette case from his breast pocket and snapped it open under my nose. It was empty. "Drat! *Do* you happen to have a decent cigarette on you, good fellow? My valet grows more careless with every passing day. Thank you!" He settled back into the tufting, smoking with elaborate nonchalance, but I could see that he was nervous.

Mrs. Pomeroy's vast equipage rolled sedately out to the Pedregal section—all very posh—and came to a halt at a severely modern, although somewhat scaly, wall, pierced with a "moderne" wrought-iron gate that made me think a bit wistfully of the scenic designs of the late Joseph Urban. There was a short, pretty ballet involving Starr and the footman, who opened the door, bowed low, and all but tugged his forelock as he helped us down—or rather *up*—from the great underslung car.

Starr pulled at the bell chain, and we waited. He pulled again, and still we waited. Then he yanked at it furiously, and the chain came off in his hand. "Damn!" he roared. A moment later a pale boy of about twenty, with thick lips and thick glasses, appeared on the other side of the gate. He looked sleepy and stupid and unbelievably suspicious.

"*Qué desean Ustedes?*" he asked guardedly.

"Is Señor González in?" Starr asked.

"I don't know," the boy said in perfect English, with a slight Oxford accent, which seemed comical considering the rest of his appearance. "Who wishes to see Señor González?"

"Mr. Starr. Le-an-der Starr. I have an appointment."

The youth cast a questioning glance at me, his eyes looking as big as prunes through the thick lenses of his spectacles.

"Mr. Dennis," Starr said. "My associate." This was the first I had heard of my new position. I had volunteered to help Starr with his script ("patchy" had hardly begun to describe it), but I had never realized that I was to be so closely involved in *Valley of the Vultures.*

"My father is expecting you, then?"

"Nat-u-rally," Starr declared.

"Come in, please." He undid several bolts and locks and, with a terrible screech of rusty hinges, opened the gate just wide enough for us to enter crabwise. It seemed a far cry from that highly touted "*Mi casa es su casa*" Latin hospitality. We walked up a longish, rutted gravel driveway through what must once have been a beautiful garden of the naturalistic school. However, nature had taken over with a vengeance, and the place was choked with weeds and wild vines. A large reflecting pool scooped out of lava rock was clogged with leaves and scum, a swarm of insects humming over its few inches of opaque, stagnant water. Before us loomed a severely modern (some years back) flat-roofed house that reminded me of Frank Lloyd Wright's more daring experiments of thirty years ago. The boy stood aside sullenly at the front door, which looked a bit like the entrance to an old Trans-Lux Theatre, and allowed us to go in first.

The *salón de entrada* was a large, stark, whitewashed cube with a lava-paved floor and great slabs of roughhewn lava sticking out of the wall to form a staircase leading to the upper quarters. A similar cantilevered lava-slab arrangement led downward. In fact, no two rooms seemed to be on the same level. On the walls were enormous, postery-looking figure studies—mostly female—painted by artists such as Diego Rivera, Frida Kahlo, José Orozco, and David Siqueiros during their rare nonsocially significant moods. Like the house, they served to remind one of how drastically fashions had changed.

Here and there one could see a large white rectangle where, mercifully, one of these masterpieces of the thirties had been removed. An enormous old dog of no known species came growling at us from out of the gloom. The boy cursed at him in Spanish (second person familiar). The dog disappeared into the darkness with a yelp.

"Down this way," the boy said glumly.

We followed him down the lava slabs into an immense high-ceilinged living room. Again, it was pure Frank Lloyd Wright with, now and again, a hint of Luis Barragán, Carlos Mérida, and Juan O'Gorman of many years ago. The room was very sparsely furnished with overstuffed chairs that looked as though they had been dredged up from the smoking saloon of the old *Normandie*. The predominating colors were mustard and chartreuse in furry, textured weaves. There were grayish smudges on the arms and backs of all of them. Stumps of candles were everywhere. "Be seated, please," the boy said. "I will tell my father you are here."

I sat gingerly in one of the chairs; there was the twang of a broken harp string, and I was poked viciously by a spring.

I got right up again and strolled to the fireplace. It was filled with old newspapers, letters, candy wrappers, and cigarette butts. Over the mantel was a portrait as big as a blanket. It was, again, by Rivera and depicted a sloe-eyed beauty in native costume. It reminded me of nothing quite so much as an old poster urging one to visit the Southwest via Union Pacific.

"Know who that is, dear boy?"

"She looks fairly familiar."

"That's Concha Malagár—González's wife. That boy's mother. Famous actress in her time. Toast of Latin America."

"Too bad the son doesn't favor her," I said. "What's become of her?"

"Dead. Suicide."

There was a shout from outside. "Ay! Starr! Leandro! *Aqui. Estoy en la piscina.*"

"What's that?" Starr asked.

"He says he's in a pool. What is he, a piranha fish?"

We went outside through some dirty sliding glass doors and down another long, curving flight of lava slabs. Like the grounds in front, the garden must, at one time, have been sensational. Now it was hopelessly overgrown with bits of rubbish scattered here and there. At the bottom was a large swimming pool, more or less kidney-shaped. It seemed empty. The sides of the pool were slick with scum, and the murky water, clotted with algae, looked as though it hadn't been changed or filtered in years. Suddenly, with a great snorting and splashing, the fattest man I've ever seen bobbed to the surface. I could think of nothing but a hippopotamus wallowing in ooze. "Ah, Starr! *Querido* Leandro! I come out." With a thrashing and churning of the filthy water, Señor González wallowed over to a slimy ladder and struggled up to dry land. He was as naked as the day he was born and about a thousand times as repulsive. He carried at least three hundred pounds on the narrow frame of what should have been a slender man. Great, pendulous breasts swayed to left and right with every movement, huge folds of blubber cascaded over his hip bones, his belly was a great flap of fat that hung halfway to his knees. He was covered with short, black hair through which the water coursed in a million little rivulets. He waddled around the edge of the pool toward us, shedding water, his flat wet feet going "splat, splat, splat" on the lava pavement. "Leandro! *Querido* Leandro!" In traditional Mexican fashion he threw both arms around Starr, hammocks of hairy flesh swinging from his biceps. Starr, his splendid London suit drenched, freed himself agilely and introduced me. I was fortunate in receiving only a suetty, wet handshake and a *"Con mucho gusto."* He stepped back and shook a bit more water off himself, setting his mountains of blubber to dancing obscenely. Then he grabbed his little pig's snout between thumb and index finger and blew his nose. *"Le gusta nadar?"* he said, gesturing invitingly toward the filthy pool.

"No, thank you," I said, fighting to keep my stomach down, "I don't believe I'll go in swimming today." Starr gagged.

"Pliz be sitted," González said with a gesture toward two rump-sprung canvas chairs. Water had collected in the seat of one. Starr chose the other, and I was delighted when the rotten canvas seat split, leaving Starr's chin between his knees and his rear on the warm lava pavement. González had a good laugh over that, his sagging dugs and prolapsed stomach bobbing hideously.

"For God's sake, Dennis," Starr snarled, "get me out of this flytrap." I was grateful for the opportunity to avert my eyes from our host. By the time I'd extricated Starr from the ruined chair, González had put on what had once been, I suppose, a white turkish towelling robe. It was now a grimy mass of pulled threads, gray as an old floor mop.

"Come, Starr, señor," González said, "we all sitt over here." He sank into the mildewed cushion of a rusty old glider that screamed with agony at his weight. Then he put his spindly little legs, interlaced like a road map with varicose veins, up on the tile table in front of him and surveyed his distorted feet complacently. He suffered under the delusion that toenails took care of themselves.

"Thees mai son, Heff."

"I beg your pardon?" I said.

"Thees mai son, Heff. I name him for famous American actor and dear friend, Heff Chandler. Now dead." He crossed himself piously.

"Oh, I see. Jeff Chandler."

"*Sí. Exactamente.* Poor Heff. My friend. My brother." Then he rattled something in rapid-fire Spanish to Heff. As far as I could gather, it had to do with going out and buying some tequila. Heff's fat lip curled, and he snarled, again in Spanish, "With what?" There was an embarrassed pause. "Ai weel need Heff for interpretation. Mai Eengleesh ees . . ." a gesture.

Heff began to translate in his stilted English. "My father says that he will need me as an interpreter as his command of . . ."

"Yes, yes, child. Both Mr. Dennis and I were able to follow. Now, Aristido, about *Valley of the Vultures* . . ."

"Ah, *sí, sí,* but first permit *pequeña memoria* of last night. I have weeth me the most beautiful blonde. Like the Marileen Moron she was." (A sinuous gesture down his obese body to indicate her figure.) "She come to my house, she plead me for to take her to my bed. I say no. She beg. She cry. I say perhaps. She take off the dress. . . ." Overcome, he lapsed into Spanish with Heff translating in cold, clipped, precise English.

"My father says that the young lady disrobed. He stroked her torso like a rare musical instrument—a violin or a cello. She moaned with pleasure, beseeching him to possess her bodily. Again he refused. When she was mad with desire, he ultimately relented. In due course she entreated my father to cease his violent passions. My father, being somewhat weary from having had his will, carnally, with two other beautiful women during the early part of the day, fell into a deep slumber. When he awoke this morning, the young lady had departed. But on his pillow she had left a superb diamond pin as a token of her extreme gratitude." The son finished with a soft sigh of disgust. The father, waiting patiently for the end of the translation, beamed with pleasure. I was flabbergasted. The picture of Señor González in bed with anything more than a hot-water bottle was quite beyond the wildest flights of my imagination.

"Good for you, Aristido," Starr said with a stagey chuckle. "Still the same old devil with the ladies, aren't you. Now about this film. I have the script and the cameraman." Heff carried on his simultaneous translation rapidly and dispassionately. "However, I am working on a very small budget. I will have to avoid a great many unnecessary luxuries if the film is to be made at all. It is here where I will need your help—your connections in the Mexican film industry."

González held up his hand for silence and once again erupted into Spanish. "My father is saying that several years ago, when he was on his yacht anchored in the Nile at Cairo, an emissary from a certain royal house of Europe came aboard and commanded my father's presence before his ruler—an internationally known princess of indescribable beauty. Heavily guarded, my father accompanied the—uh—the equerry to the villa of her royal highness. She received him quite disrobed but for high pay-tent leather boots with scarlet heels. In her right hand she carried a long whip. This royal personage explained to my father that she had attempted to achieve pleasure with all the greatest lovers in Europe, and all of them had failed her. She then gave him a love philter that was said to assure a state of complete tumescence for forty-eight hours. She led him into an adjoining chamber, which was hung entirely with black velvet. The floor was buried deep in *fraises du bois*. . . . Excuse me, sir, *fraises du bois* in English is . . ."

"Strawberries," I said, stifling a yawn.

"Oh, yes. Thank you, sir. The princess then ordered my father to remove his clothing. . . ." Heff droned on and on with all the emotion of someone reading a bank statement aloud. I stopped listening. This time González's chapter of personal history was taken almost word for word from a bit of pornography I had once picked up in Cairo for five piasters. It was entitled *Such Nise a Prinsess* (sic) and was noteworthy more for its typographical errors than its erogenous impact. The story finally ended, as I could have told González in advance, with the beautiful princess throwing herself at his feet —I had to avert my eyes from his feet; those in crushed strawberries were more than I cared to picture—and offering him her kingdom if only he would sign on as royal stud. Having selflessly refused, he was rewarded instead with his weight in diamonds.

"Whot cood Ai do, Leandro? Theese dame had me there seex days. Ai, whot a wooman!"

"Heheheh, haven't lost any of your old fire, Aristido," Starr said. "Now about a studio, in case we should need one. There are the Churubusco Studios. They're the biggest and the most expensive, or the San Angel studios. Now could you possibly intercede and ..." Again the gesture for silence.

"Excuse me, Mr. Starr. My father inquires as to whether or not you recall a certain Spanish actress named Estrellita who appeared in his last motion picture...."

"Forgive me, please, Heff," I said, "but when did your father produce his last film?"

González was champing at the bit to get on with his venereal reminiscences, but the son turned politely to me and said, "I do not know exactly, sir. It was before I was born."

"Thank you," I said.

"She was a dazzling brunette with breasts like melons. However, my father continues, one evening after the other actors had departed from the studio, she summoned my father to her dressing room...."

"Pardon me," I said, "I'll be right back." González glared at me for cramping his act, but I felt sick. I relieved myself in the shrubbery and, perhaps ten minutes later, returned to the stinking pool. González, glistening with sweat, was winding up another romantic exploit. Starr looked hot and impatient, the son martyred and impassive.

"... at the end of two weeks in that hotel suite in St. Petersburg, the grand duchess with tears in her eyes offered my father a check for a million rubles, but my father was too proud to accept it."

"If we could get on with the problems of producing Mr. Starr's movie ..." I said pregnantly. Heff translated. Through the folds of fat, González's evil little eyes focused a look of sheer hatred upon me. He grunted a fairly long sentence in Spanish. Heff colored slightly, paused, fingered his collar uneasily, and began speaking to me. I was conscious of his embarrassment and of his digging for euphemisms to make whatever it was his father had said sound a little better. "My father says, sir, that it is his understanding that North American men are not really manly and that they indulge in sexual relations not for pleasure but only for procreation. He asks if this is true and if you do not have some personal erotic anecdote to relate."

I smiled and said, "Please tell your father that in the United States sex is like money—the people who really have it don't talk about it." There was a full second of silence. Starr was the first to break it with a loud, throaty laugh, and then Heff broke up completely, one shrill, hysterical scream following another. He held his sides, he slapped his thigh, he rocked to and fro in his unsubstantial seat, and finally fell out of it and rolled on the wet pavement. The tears flowed, steaming up his glasses, punctuated by great choking sobs and gasps. I had no idea that I'd been that funny. Starr was ho-ho-ho-ing, but his laughter was nothing compared to the performance Heff put on. The only person who did not seem amused was González. He turned the color of a sunset and gave me a look of unadulterated loathing. I returned it. After a bit Starr's laughter subsided, and he wiped away a tear or two with a splendid linen handkerchief. Not so the son; he was still gasping on the ground. It was embarrassing. At long last González got to his feet—agilely for such a big tub of guts—and roared *"Váyase! Váyase y deje de molestarme. Salga!"* Heff got to his feet with an effort and, bending double, all but crawled up the lava steps, still heaving and shaking. At the top he turned around and tried to stand erect. "Forgive me, gentlemen, but I must ask to be . . ." One glorious squeal of sheer glee, and he bolted for the house.

"Loco!" González growled, tapping his fat head. "We continue alone. Now about the *película*—the ceeneema . . ." In pidgin English, in snatches of Spanish and French, Starr and

González got down to business. Everything was to be an idyllic partnership based on the trust, love, and understanding born of their many years of beautiful friendship. They were, "how-you-say," brothers. No unions, no working papers, no permits would be needed. González had connections with every bigwig in the Mexican film industry as well as the Mexican Government. González would arrange everything—the film, the processing, laboratories, the negative, work prints, rushes, dubbing, the works. Starr—dear, good, kind, lovable, wonderful Starr—need only leave everything in González's hands. After all, who was the most famous film producer in Mexico? González. Who was Starr's best friend? González. Who was the boon companion of every influential person or family in the country? González. Who was the best little fixer of everything in the whole hemisphere? You got it, González.

It was after one o'clock when Starr completed his arrangements and got up to go. I followed González on the climb upward, trying not to see his great rump undulating beneath his sour-smelling robe. Back in the house, Starr said, "By the way, do you mind if I use the telephone?" Without waiting for a reply, he picked up the receiver and jiggled the cradle. *"El teléfono está descompuesto hoy, Leandro.* He don't work. Must have fix."

Suddenly Heff appeared at the top of the stairs. "My father says, gentlemen, that our telephone is out of order. It does not work. It is silent, gentlemen, and it has been silent for longer than a year." Then he shot a glance at his father, snorted wetly, bent double again, and disappeared.

González waddled as far as the front door and treated Starr to an all-enveloping farewell *abrazo* and said a few more effusive things about being brothers. I didn't get so much as a handshake or a word of farewell. And I didn't mind. We walked down the overgrown driveway, negotiated the bolts and locks on the rusty gates, climbed aboard Mrs. Pomeroy's terrible car, and we were off.

"Quite a character, Aristido," Starr said. "May I have a cigarette, dear boy?"

"Starr," I said. "Have you lost your mind?"

"Don't believe I know what you mean, dear boy."

"Look, Starr, this is your chance to do something decent so that you can go back home. Don't louse it up by getting involved with a lard-ass like González."

"Now listen to me, González is the biggest producer in Mexico."

"If you mean in pounds and ounces, I'll go along with you. But he hasn't taken so much as a snapshot in more than twenty years. You heard what his son said."

"Heff is an unhappy, neurotic child who is jealous of his father's . . ."

"Of his father's *what?* His looks? He's a deadbeat and a fraud. His reputation is so bad that even *I've* heard of it. That filthy house, no telephone, no water, no light . . ."

"Your lamentable weakness, dear boy, lies in the undue importance you attach to earthly things. Aristido is my brother, you heard him say it."

"Yes, and I heard him say that Jeff Chandler, Gary Cooper, Clark Gable, Ernest Hemingway, André Gide, Pancho Villa, and a lot of other people are his brothers. They just don't happen to be around to deny it. But I'm around to tell you that your brother is a crook, and you'd better look elsewhere."

"You just dislike him because he doesn't like you." Starr chuckled. "I must say that was a sly dig you got off at him. I mean sex is amusing, but it's a frightful bore to hear about. Like travel."

"I'm glad he didn't like me, because I don't like him or trust him or respect him or believe him or . . ."

"Ah, you say that now, but if you could only see him . . ."

"If I could only see him being turned slowly on a spit and basted at regular intervals, I'd give a barbecue for all of Mexico City—and we'd have plenty of leftovers. Now shut up, and I'll take you to El Paseo for lunch."

There was a general buzz of recognition and/or appreciation among the Junior League ladies as Starr entered the

163

restaurant, not that his St. James Street outfit wasn't enough to stop traffic up and down the Paseo de la Reforma. He was introduced to William Shelburne, the owner, graciously accepted a drink on the house, changed the location of our table only twice, and then said cordially, "Mr. Shelburne, do come and have a drink with us when you have a free moment."

Starr ordered expansively and expensively, passed favorable comment on the food, and didn't send a single dish back—high praise indeed. He talked rapidly about a number of unimportant subjects—the unsung merits of certain South American and Alsatian wines, the excellent quality of Austrian gloves, the necessity of having empty pockets if one's suits were to hang correctly—anything to avoid the subject at hand, Aristido González. But when Bill joined us, I took matters into my own hands. "Bill," I said, "you know everybody in town. What do you know about a certain film producer named Aristido González?"

"Please, Patrick," Mr. Shelburne said with a pained expression. "I never discuss my ex-customers."

"*Ex*-customers?" Starr said, his eyebrows rising.

"That's right, Mr. Starr. I wouldn't let González in the back door of my restaurant." A waiter came up and said something in rapid Spanish. "Excuse me, Patrick, Mr. Starr. There's a crisis in the kitchen. Enjoy your lunch."

"You see?" I said a little smugly to Starr. "That may give you some rough idea of how your 'brother' is regarded locally." But if I'd hoped to discourage Starr with a few well-chosen words and considered opinions, I was wrong. Instead, his back was up. He was so stubborn that he would have gone into partnership with Satan himself rather than admit that he could have been guilty of any crime so heinous as an error in judgment. "You Anglo-Saxons simply do not understand the inner workings of the Latin mind—least of all the mind of a great creative such as Aristido. Our contract is sealed. We commence work immediately."

"Speaking of contracts, Bill knows a very good law firm that can . . ."

"Insult my friend González with a lot of legal mumbo-jumbo? Are you out of your mind? The *abrazo*—the embrace—is all the contract I need with an old bosom buddy like Aristido. Now you leave this to me. I know what I'm doing. Why don't we have some of that delicious-looking mocha roll and then call for the check. We have a lot to do this afternoon."

"Such as what?"

"We have to nail down three ladies of considerable financial means—my former wife, Monica Lady Joyce; my former star, Catalina Ximinez; *and* Mrs. Worthington Pomeroy."

X

From the chill interior of Mrs. Pomeroy's car, Starr placed a telephone call to his apartment—or rather, he had me do it. In Mexico it's often easier to reach Paris than the house around the corner.

"Ah, St. Regis," he said into the orchid mouthpiece, "you certainly take your time answering the telephone. . . . Never mind. Excuses won't do, punctuality will. Any calls? . . . Oh, Mr. Guber, eh? In person? Well, that must have been nice for you. So many old times and places to remember together. What did you tell him? . . . Good. . . . Anyone else? . . . Ah, Lady Joyce. . . . *Three* times? Just fancy. Hang on a moment." He nudged me and said, "Do you know where Monica is staying?"

"Yes. With a couple named Maitland-Grim. They've taken a big house in San Angel. I know where it is."

"St. Regis," Starr said back into the telephone, "please return Lady Joyce's call and tell her that I'm on my way to her house right now. And how is Miss Emily? . . . Oh, off with Mr. van Damm again? Well, I suppose that's all right. Bathing suits and all, eh? Well, *Mens sana in corpore sano.* . . . Nothing. Now call Lady Joyce and then get back to your waxing. The floors are a disgrace." He hung up and said, "Please direct the chauffeur to wherever it is that darling Monica is staying. Tell me about these Mainland-Grits; are they rich?"

"They're not exactly on the dole."

"Good. Splendid. Now, dear boy, if you'll stop chattering like a gibbon, I shall attempt a very brief siesta."

The Maitland-Grim household was having after-luncheon coffee around the pool—clean, clear, sparkling, turquoise-blue water with an ever-fresh supply gushing from the mouth of a bronze dolphin. Lady Joyce, rather shrouded in a long-sleeved dress, was protecting her skin from the sun in the shade of a pepper tree. Bunty, the color of a mulatto, was wearing a minuscule bikini and so many coral necklaces, bracelets, and anklets that they covered more of her brown skin than the bathing suit did. Bunty was talking. Henry, an empty glass at his side, his coffee untouched, was asleep in a deck chair. The introductions brought Bunty Maitland-Grim to the boiling point of effusiveness, and she was suddenly able to recall having met Starr at the 400 in London, or could it have been last winter in Davos, or was it at the Cannes film festival, or was it possibly at the Laird of Something's shoot, or was it Biarritz last August or . . .

"Last Year in Marienbad?" I suggested.

"Yes, of course, darling. Oh, you're joking!" She went off into peals of laughter, "Well at any rate, I'm so frightfully glad to meet you now. You must tell me when you can dine. We live so quietly here, what with poor Henry's grueling work. His book, you know. Do let me call for some drinks. And wouldn't you love to go in for a bathe?"

"I don't think we're dressed for it," I said, feeling my shirt clinging to my skin under the heavy coat and vest. The pool certainly looked tempting.

"Oh, Henry's got some old things you could wear. Or we could all plunge in nudie. I'll promise not to look."

"I'm afraid we shan't have time, Mrs. Maitland-Grim. Or may I call you Bunty? I feel that I know you so well."

"Oh, please do . . . Leander."

"I've simply come to try to dissuade dear Monica from investing in *Valley of the Vultures.*"

"*Investing?*" Lady Joyce said, as though the word were strangely foreign.

"Yes, my dear. You knew, of course, that the film was to be a co-operative venture where all the principals involved put up the original production costs and then share in the profits—a sure yield of three or four thousand per cent. But I couldn't allow you to do it. It's too chancy—especially now that you're a widow and in reduced circumstances."

"Well, Leander," Lady Joyce said with just a note of irritation, "what with the taxes and one thing and another, I haven't perhaps all I might *like* to have, but I'm able to make ends meet, and the role, as you describe it, does sound . . ."

"No, my dear Monica, I can't permit it. I could search to the ends of the earth without finding another actress who would be half as good as Doña Rosa as you and fail. But I cannot let you . . ."

"I thought you said her name was Doña Ana," Lady Joyce said.

"Doña Ana-Rosa, actually, my pet, but I could never forgive myself if you squandered your widow's mite—*and* your matchless talent—on a film that was one shade less than a classic and an all-time box-office winner. No, Monica, my advice to you is to take your few pounds and shillings and stick them into a nice, safe, tax-free building and loan society. Then you will never be in want, and I shall never be tortured by sleepless . . ."

"Now, see here, Leander," Lady Joyce said warmly, "I think that *I* know more about the state of my finances than you do. I mean I should jolly well *expect* to recoup my initial investment and perhaps a bit more. But my *second* husband was a far cry from a spendthrift, and he did leave me amply provided for. That and what I was able to put by whilst I was making films—not that I ever got paid for the ones I did with *you* . . ."

"Oh, and mayn't *I* put just a teeny-tiny bit in?" Bunty asked. She wriggled sinuously, showing off her superb figure. "I know I could get Henry to advance me my next quarter's allowance. . . ." Henry snorted from his chair and dozed off again. "And I *have* had experience. Oh, nothing like Monica's. But I did study at the Royal Academy, and I had rather a cunning bit with the old Crazy Gang just after the war—of course I was a mere child. But they gave me a specialty number. As for my hair . . ."

Half an hour after we arrived we left, Starr carefully folding two checks, drawn on Barclay's Bank, into his empty wallet.

"Talk about the soft sell," I said.

"Sell? Sell? My dear boy, I paid that call simply to dissuade the ladies from parting with their money. You heard me beg them, plead with them. Is it *my* fault if they absolutely *forced* their checks on me? Oh, and by the way, Dennis, when you go over the script, be sure to write in a fairly hefty part called Doña Rosa-Ana and something not too taxing for that old Tiller girl. Casa Ximinez, *por favor!*" he shouted to the driver.

Although my wife and I lived at Casa Ximinez, we had never been received, so to speak, in Madame X's own lair, which sprawled across the entire rear of the building. A real-estate agent had shown us the two or three available apartments in Casa Ximinez, expressed his complete agreement and admiration for our exquisite taste when we chose the most expensive, and sent Abelardo to fetch our new landlady. After a most casual lease had been signed out in the patio, Miss Ximinez had snatched our deposit and disappeared back into her own quarters to remain, heard but unseen, except on Saturdays when she collected the rent and on the rare occasions when she ventured out of the compound. For some odd reason I felt that I was invading a cloister—or perhaps I mean a seraglio. Not so the intrepid Leander Starr; he marched briskly across the patio, averting his face only slightly from the general direction of Mr. Guber's little flatlet, and thumped at the big double door. To my surprise the door was opened by what I had considered to be our own maid, Guadalupe. She had been on her hands and knees scouring the elaborate tiled floor of Madame X's *salón de entrada,* and here I'd always thought that when she wasn't eating she was sleeping. I asked in my inimitable mixture of English and Spanish for Señorita Ximinez. "You wait. *Espéreme aqui, por favor,"* Guadalupe said. *"Por poco tiempo.* Little time. I go."

Starr strode across the wet tiles, slipped, flailed his arms, and went over backwards. I caught him just in time. *"Cuidado!"* Guadalupe warned unnecessarily. *"El piso está mojado.* Wet floor." With that she raced up a soaring flight of stairs—very grand indeed. I strutted gingerly about, gazing down a wide corridor that led to a series of rooms, one bigger and more opulent than the last. Madame X's taste was eclectic to say the least. Staring in each direction I could see French rooms, Spanish rooms, Italian rooms, English rooms —all as fake as fake could be, I suspected, but very elegant and impressive when seen hurriedly at a great distance. In a moment Guadalupe was back. "You wait. Little time. Here," she said, opening a door. "You wait. *Aqui con la señora."* She ushered us into a dim little room filled with old tubular chromium furniture that looked as though it had come from a defunct U.S.O. lounge. The walls were covered from floor to ceiling with pictures. There were great, gory bleeding hearts; graphic crucifixions and *Pietàs;* highly tinted studies of saints—Sebastian, Catherine, Julia, Lawrence, Lucy, and a lot of others—undergoing tortures of the most agonizing sorts. (We never know when we're well off, do we?) They were painted on canvas, tin, zinc, wood, velvet, satin, and *moiré,* and all of them were—speaking aesthetically as well—hideous. One wall, which had been reserved for art of a more earthly nature, was papered with old stills of Catalina Ximinez clipped from fan magazines of thirty years ago.

In the center of the room sat Mamacita, bouncing gently up and down in a chromium and red mock-leather armchair, her Keds rhythmically slapping the floor. The television set was on, and Mamacita was watching what I guess was a popular Spanish-language soap opera. It was too colloquial for me to follow, but it was certainly filled with violence, passion, and characters who were very definitely good guys or bad guys. During the very few minutes we waited there, we were treated to a knifing in a night club, a hospital room, a deathbed repentence, a vow of vengeance, armed robbery, and an attempt at what I *think* was the abduction of a six-year-old girl dressed for her first holy communion. Mamacita bounced up and down more excitedly as the action grew more hectic. At the end of every scene she burst into applause, and she emitted a deep sigh of regret as an endless string of commercials appeared on the screen. During a very poignant commercial for a powder against, I guess, diaper rash, Guadalupe scratched on the door. "Señorita wait you now. You come, pliz." Starr and I got up.

"Es bueno, no?" I said to Mamacita, indicating the television screen. Mamacita displayed her gums, thought for a moment, and then drew her lips back into a square.

"Mai . . . dotter . . . beeg . . . star," she said. The program resumed, this time with a heavily veiled villainess of the Theda Bara school, offering what must have been a drugged cordial to the heroine. Mamacita continued her gentle bouncing, and we tiptoed out.

Starr and I followed Guadalupe up the resounding stone stairway, past suits of armor, tapestries, and portraits of seventeenth- and eighteenth-century dignitaries so imposingly patrician that they couldn't possibly have been forebears of la Ximinez. I can only suppose that they, as well as the building itself, had been grabbed by Catalina's general during the antireligious, anti-upper-class uprisings of the middle twenties.

Finally we were ushered into the presence of Señorita Ximinez herself. For some reason she had chosen to receive us in her bedroom, and it was immediately apparent that she had been smitten by those movie magazine articles entitled "Homelife of the Stars" a long time ago and hadn't been cured yet. The room was made up of equal parts of mirror, white bearskin, gilt furniture, and rose silk. Madame X herself lolled on a circular bed, peering ludicrously out from beneath pink-acetate draperies that fell in dusty swags from a baldachin of molting ostrich plumes. She wore a magenta negligee garnished with silver fox—and lots of it. To surround herself with the menagerie of exotic household pets that were once the obligation of every movie queen, she had hastily summoned in Perro, still yapping but gussied up with a bedraggled magenta bow; Guacamayo, the insane macaw; a very pregnant old cat that had at some time been white and almost angora. The cat and Perro were not hitting it off very well. As a final touch Señorita had pinned the *ma'kech* by its jeweled leash to her bodice, where it foraged happily away at a large grease spot. There was an undeniable scent of sweat and musk.

" 'Ow nice off you to come," she said, flashing her golden-glinted smile and languidly extending a stubby, not quite clean, hand, one talon of which had been hastily patched with adhesive tape. It was quite a show, and Catalina Ximinez must have felt that she was being overpoweringly seductive. Still, I would have been more aroused by a visit to a geriatrics ward.

"Catalina, *querida*," Starr said, seizing her hand and kissing it. "How lovely! *Hermosa!*"

"Car-fool," she said coyly, "mai duenna." Turning, I noticed that Guadalupe had been engaged to remain in the room—standing primly with her hands folded across her stomach—to convey the impression that this aging concubine, bedmate of a gangster and of Starr himself, was very much the sheltered ewe lamb of a proud old creole family. It was on the tip of my tongue to suggest that *her* duenna might be excused to clean *my* kitchen, but then I didn't want to cramp Starr's style.

And Starr's style had altered quite a lot from that of his visit to Lady Joyce and Mrs. Maitland-Grim. His florid, stacatto delivery had been toned down to the simplest basic English, plus the 250 "-ion" words that are almost identical with their Romance-language counterparts. Armed with this vocabulary, he almost crooned it to Madame X as though she were a very sick child troubled by insomnia. He remarked upon the beauty and bouyant health of her mother, the old lady's ardent passion for things cultural. Madame X accepted this with a winsome *moue*. He inquired as to the state of her automobile. With a pretty pout, Madame X allowed as how the damage had not been as severe as first anticipated and added that, rare, costly, and delicate as the Hispano-Suiza was, a patch on the tire and a bit of tinkering with the motor had rendered the machine roadworthy for another thirty or forty years. Then Señorita Ximinez hospitably passed around a tarnished silver dish of toxic-looking pink candies that gave off a repellent odor of roses, plucked up a soiled artificial gardenia, and sniffed at it langorously —an open invitation to silicosis—while Starr got down to the point.

"My dear Catalina—*querida*—since you appeared in *Yucatán Girl* I have received letters—thousands of them—from your admirers all over the world—*todo el mundo*—desiring to see you again in a motion picture."

"Oh? May Ai see dem?"

"They are in my bank in Paris, *desafortunado,* with all of my dearest possessions. And they are all in foreign languages—even some in Chinese."

"*Ah! Los chinos! Que divertido!*"

"I now have another beautiful Mexican story. . . ."

"Ah, yessss?"

Flattery could get you *almost* everywhere with Catalina Ximinez, but it was slow going. Vain and gullible as she was, she still had a certain crafty shrewdness that was difficult even for an operator like Starr to get around. While she cared not at all about the script itself—which was fortunate, as there was nothing in it (as yet) that she could conceiva-

bly play save an old mestizo hag—she was insistent that whatever role she play would be that of a beautiful young aristocrat and that it be the starring role, with billing to match.
She also suggested singing a song or two, and made a few
tentative stabs at how her dressing room was to be decorated
and by whom. It was pretty fancy talk for an aging carica-
ture of the jungle girl whose only histrionic experience had
been expressing mute attitudes of bovine placidity in one
film thirty years ago, but I suppose that Starr was right:
Once bitten by the movie bug, they never get over it.

He was clever enough to let her do most of the talking
without ever saying a definite yes or no to anything, so that
she soon began answering her own questions to her own
satisfaction and, eyes sparkling, cockatoo voice rising in excitement and triumph, she envisioned herself as the greatest dramatic actress in Latin America—a star of such magnitude as
to put tried and true performers like Dolores del Rio, Maria
Felix, Katy Jurado, and all the rest of them into total eclipse.
By the time she got down to money, she was so entranced by
the idea of her name in lights that she would have paid to
be in the picture, which was exactly what Starr had in mind.
She became suddenly more realistic, as I was sure she would,
but she had already done most of the damage herself. How,
she probably figured, could a picture in which the unforgettable, the unutterably beautiful Catalina Ximinez makes her
triumphal return to the screen fail to earn millions? Starr
could hardly disagree with her, and he pointed out that as
long as she had such confidence in herself and, of course, in
the picture and him, a percentage of the profits paid out
over years and years and years of return engagements would
be a far sounder business investment than a flat salary of the
five million pesos she had originally suggested. That was the
clincher.

She sent Guadalupe for pen and paper, and on two pink
pages, reeking of cheap scent, drew up a simple agreement
in Spanish, which she could barely write. She signed. Starr
signed. I witnessed the signatures as did Guadalupe, who

placed an "X" on the place indicated, and then rubbed her thumb with the pen and left a smudgy print beside it to prove that it really was her signature. Instead of a check, she gave Starr her whole investment in currency—after having deducted that week's rent—and demanded a receipt. Catalina Ximinez was in the bag. All that remained to do was to leave and to think up *some* sort of part she could possibly play. Starr made elaborate leave-takings with heel clickings and hand kissings. I took the limply extended hand and shook it so fervently that it set Madame X's head to rocking like a Chinese figurine's. Out in the corridor we ran into Mamacita lurking in the shadows. Once again she said, "Mai . . . dotter . . . beeg . . . star." With that we were off.

Out in the patio Starr riffled ostentatiously through the wad of banknotes he had received from Madame X and crammed them into a pocket.

"I see that you don't mind much about the hang of your suit as long as you've got *plenty* of money in your pocket," I said.

"Filthy stuff," Starr said, "a check would have been so . . ."

"Hey, Starr! Mr. Starr!" We turned and saw Mr. Guber wearing his underwear and standing in his doorway.

"Why, Mr. Guber," Starr said. *"Bienvenido!* Welcome to Mexico. Vacationing I suppose?"

"Wait a minute, Mr. Starr. I want a word with you."

"So sorry, but I'm late for an engagement just now. *Adiós.*" Quickening his pace, he said, "Come, dear boy, don't dawdle."

Mr. Guber raced out of his apartment, met the horrified eye of Miz Priddy, glanced down at his hairy legs, and dashed back into the apartment.

"Buenas tardes, gintlemin?" Miz Priddy began. "The Doctor and Ah have jist attindid the most *in*-tristing licture on . . ."

"You must tell us all about it someday," Starr said. "Hurry, Patrick."

By the time Mr. Guber had put on some trousers and got

out to the street, the Pomeroy limousine was rounding the corner on its short trip back to Casa Ortiz-Robledo. Starr tipped the chauffeur and the footman each five hundred pesos and walked into the house as though he owned it.

From somewhere the English-language channel was blaring away on a television set. Following our ears, we came to a darkened room and stood in the doorway. Flickering away on an enormous screen were a stately pair of models climbing gracefully up one of those rolling metal stairways that lead into the maw of an airplane. The woman on the screen was wearing a sable coat and said in cultivated tones, "Yes, Derek, I always fly nonstop Mexicanadian Super Jet. It takes me direct from my hacienda in Mexico City to my ski lodge in the heart of Montreal." The man with her, dressed for the Royal Enclosure at Ascot, said, "How right you are, Daphne, and in just five pleasure-filled hours. Imagine!" "Oh, but that's not all, Derek, the large, roomy, reclining seats on Mexicanadian and those delicious Mexicanadian meals aloft, brought to you by courteous, attentive Mexicanadian flight stewardesses—caviar, *pâté de foie gras, filet mignon,* and the finest vintage wines." "Not to mention Mexicanadian's delicious cocktails, aperitifs, and cordials, Daphne." In unison: "That's why those in the *know* always *go* Mexicanadian!"

"I like it," a familiar voice said. "It's got class."

"Yes, Mrs. Pomeroy, but it's not selling any tickets."

"I *still* like it." In the gloaming I saw Clarice squinting at the television set through her lorgnette.

"Well, Clarice," Starr said, "are we interrupting your favorite kiddies' program on the boob tube?"

"Oh, Leander and Paddy. Woo hoo hoo! I didn't even hear you come in. You can turn it off now, Mr. Overton." The lights went on in the room, revealing Clarice in a pair of stretch slacks that had been stretched to the bursting point. "Just in time for a little drinkie. Have fun on your picnic, Paddy?"

"What?"

"Din'tchew say something about going on a picnic with some people name of Purdy or something like that?" I realized that Clarice never missed a trick.

"Oh. Oh, yes. I just left Miz Priddy." At least I was being perfectly truthful for a change.

"They any relation to Priddy Petroleum Products? She was a Gerstadt and he . . ."

"Oh, no. Miz Priddy was a Drain—and still is."

"Then I wouldn't know 'em. What'll it be?"

"Uh, Clarice," Starr began a bit uneasily, "I wonder if we could discuss the, uh, matter I mentioned to you last night?"

"Ya mean . . ."

"I mean my *film*."

"Well, you couldn't of picked a better time to do it, sweetie. Mr. Overton, meet my dear friends, Leander Starr, the great director, and Paddy Dennis, the writer. I'm sure you heard of 'em both. Mr. Overton handles my financial affairs in Mexico."

Mr. Overton was one of those young men who just happened to be born old. He looked at us over the tops of his spectacles as though we were in the police line-up (and I must say that in Starr's company I often felt as though I soon might be), ignored our outstretched hands, and bowed briskly from the collarbones. "How do you do?" From the tone of his voice it sounded like an unfinished sentence that might well have read, "How do you do things like murder, extortion, arson, rape, check kiting, and second-story work, and still manage to stay out of jail."

"Wait a sec while I put on some music," Clarice said. "Paddy, you mix up some dakkeries, sweetie." Clarice, who had gone Latin with a vengeance, put "Fiesta del Cha Cha Cha" onto an enormous record player, turned the *alta fidelidad* on full volume and wiggled her behind, occasionally calling out "Cha-cha-cha!"

Mr. Overton looked displeased but, raising his voice, laced

right into Starr. What with Clarice and *las orquestas* Aragon,. America, and Enrique Jorrin, I couldn't make much of what was being said, but ominously businesslike phrases like, ". . . your capitalization . . . bank references . . . a full financial report, naturally, Mr. Starr . . . legal representation in this country . . . meeting with the attorneys of the other backers . . ." kept looming up over the bongo drums and maracas. For someone who hadn't the slightest notion of what such difficult terms as "audit," "profit," and "loss" meant, Starr bluffed his way better than could be expected, but I could sense that he wasn't making much of an impression on Mrs. Pomeroy's Mr. Overton—or at least not a good one. Clarice didn't seem to be paying much attention, constantly jumping up to change a selection or to make the overpowering noise still louder or higher or deeper, but I have since learned that Mrs. Pomeroy, addlepated as she may seem, allows very little to escape her.

At eight-thirty I rose wearily to my feet. "I'm sorry, but I really have to go," I said. Starr shot me a look of pathetic desperation.

"Oh, stay, sweetie. I'll send the car fer yer cute missus an' we'll make a regaler party of it."

"I'd love to," I said dishonestly, "but," I added quite honestly, "some friends of ours are here from Acapulco on their way back north, and we've promised to have dinner with them."

"Bring 'em all."

"I'm afraid I couldn't. They've got to catch the late plane for Chicago."

". . . and so you see, Mr. Starr, that I would be totally unable to advise Mrs. Pomeroy to go forward without a complete examination by our Mexican certified public . . ."

"Good night, and thank you," I said. "Good night, Leander," I added with special feeling.

It was early—for Mexico—when my wife and I got home that night. There was a big moon and it was unusually warm and still, so we decided to mix nightcaps and drink them out in the patio. We had just sat down when the light flashed on in Starr's living room and the door opened. A voice I could recognize as Bruce van Damm's was saying, urgently, insistently, "It's early, Emily. Couldn't I stay just a little . . ."

"No, darling. Really, no," Emily whispered. "Daddy's out, and I don't know when he'll be home. He might not like it. So go now. Please. Please before I . . ." Just what she was afraid of doing I shall never know. The two of them went into a fervent embrace that cleared up quite a lot of questions in my mind.

Chivalrously I coughed a couple of times, cleared my throat, and lit a cigarette, brandishing my lighter as though it were the torch of the Olympiad. Instantly they sprang apart, assuming the stiff, unnatural attitudes of the models who pose for etiquette problems in Elinor Ames's "The Correct Thing."

"Well, good night, Emily," Bruce said, in a well-bred baritone.

"Good night, Bruce. Thank you for a lovely evening."

"And tomorrow?"

"I do hope I'll be able to say yes. I'll ask my father."

"May I call you?"

"Please do."

There was a pretty handshake—one almost expected a dancing-school bow and curtsy—and Bruce came marching in our direction like a guardsman.

"Good evening, Bruce."

"Oh, good evening, sir. Mrs. Dennis? I had no idea you were here."

"So we gathered," my wife said. "Good evening."

"Good evening *and* good night. I didn't know how late it was getting. Well, *buenas noches*." With that he was off.

A few moments later, Emily, lipstick replenished, hair freshly combed, wandered out to where we were sitting. "Good evening. I haven't seen either of you all day. I seem to be out of cigarettes and wondered if I could . . ."

"By all means," I said. "If you wait a minute, I'll go in and get you a whole package." She'd become so much more human that I refrained from adding that they were just a Mexican imitation of American filtered cigarettes.

"Oh, no. Please don't. Just one. Then I'm off to bed. Thank you. You don't happen to know where Daddy's been all day, do you, Mr. Dennis?"

"I certainly do, because I've been with him almost every minute of it. He's been racing around town getting his new picture started."

"Is Daddy *really* going to make another movie? How thrilling! And Mummy always said . . . Well, I'm very glad he's going to be active again. He was gone before I got up, and he wasn't home when I came back to change for dinner, and I just wondered. . . ."

"Have no fear. Your poor father is dining with Mrs. Worthington Pomeroy."

"Oh." Her face became hard and disapproving once again. "Mr. Dennis. Do you *like* Mrs. Pomeroy?"

"Lord, no. Nobody does."

"Then what do you suppose Daddy sees in her? She's common and vulgar and loud and pushy and . . ."

"Money, my dear."

"What?"

"Money. Your father's interest in Mrs. Pomeroy is purely a business one. He wants her to invest in his new film. There's nothing between them."

"Oh, I see." She seemed vastly relieved. "Well, it *is* late," she said, faking a little yawn, "and I *am* tired. I went swimming today at some club—I forget which one—with Bruce." Her voice seemed to throb when she mentioned his name. "Then he took me to El Paseo for dinner. . . ."

"Your father and I lunched there today. Very good."

"Yes. Mr. Shelburne told me so, and he sang *our* song." I didn't dare ask what it was, and Emily seemed to sense that she had been indiscreet. "He's very nice."

"Bruce?"

"No. Mr. Shelburne. Oh, Bruce is very nice, too," she added casually, but her knees seemed to buckle at the mention of the name. "Well, thank you for the cigarette. I hope Daddy will be home soon."

"I'm sure that he hopes so, too. Good night, Emily."

"Good night."

We were just about to call it a night when a slumped-over form appeared at the entrance to the patio and sagged weakly toward our general direction. It was Starr.

"Leander," I said. "We've been wondering about you."

"As well you might, dear boy, darling girl. Not that I got any moral support from *you*. Oh, no. *You* can go out skylarking with some totally fictitious friends from Sheboygan I believe you said. . . ."

"Chicago. Truly. Russell Straley and Grace Dodge."

"Chicago, then, leaving me to face the music."

"Mrs. Pomeroy's Mr. Overton did seem to lack any appreciation for the artistic nuance."

"Mr. Overton is a thoroughgoing schmuck. I've met hundreds of them—dried-up little bookkeepers with not the faintest notion of how one creates a masterpiece. The best thing to do with them is to throw them out."

"Did you?"

"Certainly. I let him go through his song and dance, said 'Don't call us, we'll call you,' and personally ushered him out of Clarice's ostentatious house."

"Then you didn't get the money? That's a shame, Starr."

"Shame is the correct word. However, I *did* get the money."

"Why, Leander!" I said, jumping up to shake his hand.

"But I also got something else. A fiancée—Clarice Obendorfer Pomeroy."

XI

We were breakfasting in bed the next morning when a great avalanche of mail arrived—most of it actually intended for us. There was an air-mail rush, rush, rush letter from my agent, informing me that the fiction editor of that refined women's magazine was calling me a word they would never dream of printing, that the June issue was going to press at any moment and that if that wholesome story about Salli, Mr. Right, and the broccoli wasn't in New York by the end of the week I could start looking elsewhere for eating money.

We had letters from both children—a standard weekly assignment at their schools—both saying, for once, almost the same thing, namely that their spring vacations started late this year but lasted longer and that they would arrive in Mexico City on Friday, April 13. *Someone* would put them on a plane—my daughter wrote that their grandmother would do it; my son seemed to think that a master from his school was going to see that they got aboard—and would we please arrange for tickets and tourist cards.

"Well, it will be nice to see the children again. Easter and all that sort of thing."

"Mmm-hmmm," my wife said from the depths of a letter. "Mother says it's been a very mild winter in New York."

"That's too bad." If there's anything that annoys me, it's to go some balmy place and then discover that there hasn't been snow up to the rooftops back home. "Any good dirt?"

"When does Mother ever know any good . . . Ooooo!"

"What?"

"Well, here's a *fairly* hot item—not that it hasn't happened before. Mother says: 'My dear old friend, Mrs. Elsworth Barney (Lucy Brooke as was, we were in school together), took her son Lucien on a cruise . . .'"

"Hardly his first if what I think about Lucien Barney is true."

"Shut up. '. . . on a cruise of the Caribbean, and when they returned Lucien discovered that a young man he had befriended had disappeared taking Lucien's lovely new car, a lot of clothes and jewelry, and many valuable things from the apartment. You know what exquisite taste Lucien always had.'"

"But not in his boy friends, apparently. How many times does this make?"

"Three that I know of. There was that Panamanian soccer player, the gifted Irish playwright, and that standard piece of rough trade who was going to enter the Mr. America contest."

"They earned it. What else?"

"Well, Mother's very cross at Mr. Bernstein and the whole Philharmonic for the new things they've been playing this year. She also says that your *sister* is going to put the children on the plane."

"I see. Anything more?"

"Yes. 'P.S. In answer to your question, I have *never* had lunch with Nellie Poindexter Dane and never *would*, so I *couldn't* have met your fabulous Mrs. Pomeroy. And if she's a friend of Nellie Dane's, I wouldn't *care* to, although I do know some very *nice* Pomeroys—much younger—in Bronxville. Again, love. Mother.'"

"Somehow the picture of Clarice and your mother never quite came off in *my* developing tank."

"And the picture of Clarice and Leander Starr? He must be out of his mind."

"So must she. She's got all the dough in Deauville, which Starr would only spend. She's getting a little long in the tooth to think too much about a bash on the Beautyrest, she hasn't got the intellect to care about any movie much beyond the Ma and Pa Kettle series. What do you suppose she's after, granting that Starr *is* attractive to women?"

"Are you out of *your* mind?" my wife said. "I'll be happy to tell you what Mrs. Pomeroy wants. Ready? A. Starr is very attractive. B. He needs money and she must know it—she's not an idiot. C. From the way she's been sniffing around Emily, she's obviously dissatisfied with her own social set. She has plenty of money, and now she wants to go places where money won't take you—or at least it won't take *her*. She's too vulgar for Real Society, too square for the International Set, and too stupid for the Intellectuals. But if she had a lion like Starr on a leash, he could lead her into groups where she wouldn't ordinarily be allowed to pass the canapés. And with Emily as the adoring stepdaughter to launch her in Philadelphia . . ."

"*Emily?* Emily hates her guts. You heard her last night. She wouldn't launch Clarice in the Delaware River."

"But Clarice doesn't know that. Besides, Emily adores her father. She's proud of him, too. No matter how she feels about Clarice, she'd hardly spit in her father's eye because of his common wife. I think Clarice realizes that, too. Remember, I'm a girl—you're a boy."

"I still can't believe he'll go through with it."

"He may have to."

"Making this picture is very important to him—vital. And he can't do it without the Pomeroy bankroll."

"That's Mrs. Pomeroy's magic hold on him. And she knows it. Do you suppose I ought to send her a dozen hand towels as a sort of engagement present?"

"Marked His and Its. And I'll send *him* a dozen hairshirts. But let's hold off. As you said, I'm a boy, and I'd bet my last dollar that Starr is one old boy who can wriggle out of it some . . ."

The bedroom door burst open, and there stood Starr. He

was dressed the way successful male novelists used to dress for their dust-jacket photographs a quarter of a century ago —stout tweeds, foulard ascot, and pipe. All he lacked was a noble hound at his side. "Great Scott, man," he said, "here it is eight o'clock, and you're still abed. We've got to get to work on a script conference immeejutly. Good morning, my dear," he said more affably to my wife. "That coffee looks uncommonly good."

"Well, it's uncommonly bad, but if you'd like some you're welcome."

"Splendid. I'll just have a cup while Patrick dresses. Get along with you, boy."

A few minutes later we were sitting out in the patio at Starr's insistence. "Nonsense, dear boy, the sunshine, the fresh air, the songs of the birds will inspire you."

"I'd be a lot more inspired if I know that Catalina Ximinez couldn't overhear every word we say about her part, which, as far as I can see, doesn't even exist."

"Nonsense. That savage can't understand English."

"She understands more than you think. Then there's your friend and neighbor, Mr. Guber. He's still longing to see you."

"I'll take care of him in my own good time."

No sooner had I put out the typewriter and paper, plus Starr's scratchings and scrawlings, than he said, "Jesus, but it's hot! Excuse me while I slip into something a bit more comfortable. I don't know how you writers work in these clothes."

"We don't," I said.

"I'll be right back." With that he disappeared into his own apartment.

I settled back to read what Starr *thought* was a screen play and the dog-eared article that had inspired it—a very red and very old-fashioned piece culled from *New Masses* many, many years ago. "Good morningue," a voice said. I looked up and there was Mr. Guber, bulging briefcase, seersucker suit, and smelling strongly of a manly after-shaving lotion.

"Good morning, Mr. Guber," I said.

"Mr. Starr around?"

"Why, no."

"Now listen, I just two minutes ago saw him."

"Do you see him now?"

"No. Where's he gone to? I'm gettingue awfully sick of hanguingue around here just waitingue on Starr."

"He's gone to the bathroom," I said. "If you'd like to join him . . ."

"In that case I'll wait. By the way, just what are you to Starr?"

"Why, didn't you know, Mr. Guber? I thought everyone did. We've been lovers for the past fifty years."

He thought it over for a moment and then said, "You're kiddingue."

"Have it your own way then."

"Well, you cert'ny seem to cover up for him. You and his daughter and that *fagele* butler he's got. How come he can afford to keep a butler an' still not pay up his back taxes?"

"You'll have to ask him that. Maybe the butler keeps him."

"Very funny, I'm sure. Highly amusingue. However, by your unco-operative attitude you're impedingue the course of American justice. The Department of Internal Revenue. Ever think of that?"

"I think of it constantly, Mr. Guber. But have no fear. My taxes are paid. If you have any doubts, just get in touch with the excellent Mr. Badian of 355 Lexington Avenue, New York 17."

"Oh yes. A sterlingue outfit. But you wun't fall under my jurisdiction. P through T, that's me."

"I beg your pardon?"

"That's my section of the alphabet for delinquent taxes—only the *big* money, though," he added patronizingly. "I handle the letters P, Q—not much there of course—R, S, and T."

"Good for you, Mr. Guber. My but U, V, W, X, Y, and Z must be a lead-pipe cinch."

"We all help each other out. I got plenty others to contact down here. Starr's not the only delinquent to run off to Mexico. But of course Starr's the biggest."

"Starr's the biggest what?" Wearing bathing trunks no larger than a diaper, Starr strode across the patio conscientiously lifting his chest and pulling in his stomach. "Good morning, Mr. Guber. We meet again."

"Well, Mr. Starr, I've cert'ny been runningue after you from pillow to post."

"And now that you've found me?"

"Could I have a word with you alone, Mr. Starr?"

"There is nothing—no matter how intimate—you cannot say in the presence of my great and good friend, my constant companion, Mr. Dennis." He patted me affectionately on the head. "Isn't that right, darling boy?"

Mr. Guber gave me a look that left no doubt that he was beginning to believe my earlier statement.

"Knock it off, Leander," I said. "Mr. Guber's only interested in your money."

"Well, yeah. Now look here, Mr. Starr, this has been goingue on for ten years. At six per cent, the interest is mountingue up every day to the tune of . . ."

"Mr. Guber, I am penniless. But here, I give you the very clothes off my back." He fumbled with the top of his bathing trunks.

"No, wait a minute, Mr. Starr. Uncle don't want that. We just want some assurance that you mean to pay up. Why, just to get you off of the books we'd be willingue to settle for . . ."

"Mr. Guber, as you well know, I am destitute. Howsomever, I shan't be in a few weeks—in a very few weeks. I'm shooting a picture at this very moment. A superb film. When it is released I shall be able to pay you in full and to return to my native soil with my head held high. But until then you are wasting your time—your time *and* mine—with these meaching entreaties upon my bounty, which for the time being . . ."

"But, Mr. Starr, you were shootingue a picture in It'ly and in France. . . ."

"And I could have paid you *double* at Monte Carlo had but the *noir, pair, première douzaine* come up, as it was supposed to, instead of that God-damned double zero. I would have broken the bank and settled for Grace Kelly. My intentions were the noblest, Mr. Guber. Do be fair."

"And in England?"

"I wasn't paid. Now, Mr. Guber, I must get on with my film. If you'd care to ransack my quarters, please do so. But be careful not to awaken my daughter. Or if you'd like to sit here with Mr. Dennis and me—silently, that is—while we confer, you are perfectly welcome to do so. Do be seated," he said, indicating a chair splattered with parrot droppings. "Now, dear Patrick, to get on with the basic script. You *do* feel that with a few essential changes we have the germ of a story here?"

"Now listen to me, Mr. Starr . . ."

"Shhhhhhh. I told you, Mr. Guber, that I would have to have a deathly hush. Now I thought we could work in a series of flashbacks to utilize those performers who *must* be used. . . ."

"Now listen to me, Starr," Mr. Guber said angrily, "I'm sick of your bluffingue. First you talk how poor you are, then you talk what a big picture you're makingue, then I see you ridingue around in a big Cadillac, throwingue away money in fancy rest'rants and night clubs like you're rich as Creases. This time I'm callingue your bluff. I'm goingue out for breakfast now, and when I come back I'm sittingue right in that chair and listeningue to every fumblingue word. And if you really are makingue a picture—the veracity of which I sincerely doubt—I'm even goingue to be *in* it. So you and your—uh—friend better write a good part for Irvingue A.

Guber, U.S. Department of Internal Revenue!" With that, he picked up his briefcase and stomped out of the patio.

"Starr," I said, "I think he means it."

"He might be good as the evil priest, dear boy. Keep him in mind."

"Now *about* that evil priest, Leander, and that nude bathing scene when he assaults the girl. There's an organization called the Legion of Decency still very powerful with American film makers, and they may well have more than *one* objection to the entire concept."

"Really, dear boy? How so?"

Starr's grasp of a story line was tenuous at best. Heretofore, he had happily shot several hundred miles of film, spliced the best parts of it together, and had it acclaimed as art. It may have been art, but it wasn't economy, and I had fairly rough going explaining to him that first one started out with a story that had a beginning, a middle, and an end, with settings and characters and the words they were going to say all systematically written down on paper before the camera work even commenced. Grudgingly he agreed.

Politically he was a babe in arms. When I pointed out that the article he had cribbed his story from was pure Communist propaganda—and very naïve and old-hat propaganda at that—he was stunned. "But it's right there in black and white, dear boy, as any fool can see."

"Any fool can write anything and any other fool can print it and still more fools can read it, but that doesn't necessarily make it true."

"But my dear young man. There it is—the history of Mexico. The land torn from the Indians by the decadent Spanish nobility, who forced the former owners into slavery and sent all the gravy back to Spain."

"That's not what the most impartial modern historians say, Starr."

"Then working this fine, fertile land to the very bone—

or whatever you call it—threshing all the corn, bottling the olives. . . ."

"Spain forbade the growing of olives in Mexico, Leander. There wasn't an olive tree in the country until the nineteenth century."

"Well, what-*ever!* And the landlords, with the help of a corrupt church, allowing the soil to erode. . . ."

"How could the church be responsible for soil erosion?"

"Well they didn't *irrigate* it, you fool!"

"Did you expect them to sprinkle holy water over the whole Valley of the Vultures?"

"And then, just as it says in Jaime What's-his-name's piece, the people, the poor, the downtrodden arose. They threw out the corrupt Spanish grandees. . . ."

"Who had been out for more than a century."

"Be still! They kicked out the lecherous clergy and their concubines, and with their leaders they took this arid desert and transformed it once again into a fertile valley *of* the people, *by* the people, and *for* the people! There, now how does that sound?"

"Sounds pretty pinko to me." Mr. Guber had quietly returned from his breakfast and was sitting in the shade of the jacaranda tree. "And speakingue of pink, you're invitingue a ve-ry se-vere sunburn, Mr. Starr."

"Oh, shut up, Irving!"

"Starr," I said, "have you ever *seen* the Valley of the Vultures?"

"No, but I can well imagine it—rolling terrain, fields of golden grain, neat red barns. Pity we *can't* do this in color."

"Starr. I've driven through it a dozen times. It's a dust heap. There's no water, nothing. The only green thing you can see for miles is cactus."

"Well, that's colorful."

"Even the vultures are ashamed of it. Now, I suggest that you get into the shade and into this handy little book, Mc-Henry's *A Short History of Mexico.* There's a germ of truth in some of the things you've said, but I think you ought to have the facts. The history of Mexico is so turbulent and so terrible and so tragic that it's almost comical. But I think you should have a better grasp . . ."

"Oh, so now you want me to do a slapstick comedy! Custard pies and . . ."

"Just take this book, sit in the shade, and I'll try to pull some of your elements and *all* of your leading ladies into a story."

"I'll sit where I damned well please and I please to lie in the sun."

"You're gettingue awfully red, Mr. Starr. No pun intended."

"Shut up, Irving!" With that Starr threw himself down onto a hot tile bench and began reading *A Short History of Mexico* with a prodigious rustling of pages. I got down to work. Mr. Guber simply sat—waiting.

It was almost three o'clock when I'd finished the barest sort of outline. Mr. Guber was nodding in his chair, and Starr, lying supine in the blazing hot sun, had dozed off at around the constitutional presidency of Benito Juárez (1858-61). "Hey, Starr. Leander," I called. My answer was a dulcet snore. Playfully I picked up a small, flat pebble and tossed it. It landed neatly on Starr's bare stomach. With a roar of agony Starr shot up into the air. "Ouch! Dear God! I'm on *fire!* I'm burning *up!*"

"Anythingue wrongue?" Mr. Guber said, snapping back to consciousness.

"Oh good Lord, *look* at me! I'm burnt to the bone! Absolutely barbecued!"

"Hmm, front *and* back. That's not good. This friend of mine, Melvyn, he's stayingue at the Fountain-blew in Miami. So he goes up to this beautyful solarium—very modrun—on a day the sun isn't even shiningue. . . ."

"To hell with Melvyn! What about *me?* By God, Dennis, you're to blame. I'll sue you for every last . . ."

"Come on now, Leander. I'll fix you up." I took him by

the arm, and he screamed with pain. "Ooops, sorry. Come with me now, Daddy fix."

I filled our big pink bathtub with tepid water, a box of baking soda, and—moaning and groaning—Leander Starr. "Now just sit there and soak," I said. "It won't cure you, but it *will* help. And so would a drink. What would you like?"

"Prussic acid, if you've got any."

"You'll really be better off with gin. Mr. Guber?"

"Rye and ginger ale? Scotch and Seven-Up?" He finally settled for rum and Pepsi-Cola. "Very refreshingue," he said.

"Now that we're all here and you're feeling better, Leander, I'll read the very rough outline *I* ran up while *you two were sleeping.*"

Starr lolled back in the tub with a gasp of pain, Mr. Guber settled himself on the morris chair, while I, perched delicately on the pink toilet, read aloud the framework of *Valley of the Vultures.*

Given an impossible story and an improbable cast of characters, it hadn't been easy to turn Starr's material into much of a story. But I had seen enough of Starr's work to realize that the less plot the great man was encumbered with, the better the picture would be as a result of his diabolical tricks —mad camera angles; wild zoomings upward or downward of the lens; mystifying close-ups of such unexpected and mystifying things as a slice of bread, a human navel, an animal's eye, an insect; odd lighting effects. Starr was essentially a "trimmings" man and such a gifted one that audiences were perfectly satisfied with the trimmings, never minding—or even noticing—that the basic fabric was cheesecloth. Instead of one story, which Starr had never had to begin with, I gave him three intermingled stories. The first is set in the sixteenth century, when a wealthy Spanish grandee migrates to the valley with his lovely English bride, Doña Ana-Rosa (Lady Joyce), and her silly maidservant (Bunty Maitland-Grim), builds a great hacienda and promptly dies leaving his widow and baby as sole heirs to the fertile acres. (I was by no means certain that the Valley of the Vultures had ever been anything more than a wasteland, but I felt sure that there would be very few moviegoers who could remember back to the fifteen hundreds and call me a liar.) Doña A-R builds up the village, the church, cares for the Indians, etc., etc., etc., and also gives her descendants a good excuse for being able to speak English. She dies leaving a fertile valley of peace and prosperity as her own monument. Episode Two takes place during the bloody revolutions of the nineteenth century. The family is richer than ever but somehow gone to seed, having grown decadent, lazy, proud, and arrogant. French and Mexican marriages have largely removed the English strain—except, happily, for the dialogue. The current owner, soft and sybaritic, spends most of his time lolling in smart clubs in Mexico City or whoring with the village girls. His vulgar mestizo wife (Catalina Ximinez—but a part to be written in such a way that she could play it straight and be twice as terrible) is the real power, grasping and ruthless. Comes one of the many revolutions—with both sides treated dispassionately as neither all right nor all wrong—and the owner is killed, the fine old colonial mansion all but burned to the ground, leaving the mean mistress of the house swearing vengeance. Episode Three, time the present. The family grandeur is all but vanished, the current generation little more than scavengers on the depleted land. The beautiful daughter (played by whom, Clarice Pomeroy?) wants to marry a fine young Indian boy who is an engineer, but the stiff-necked, tradition-ridden elders won't hear of it. Trouble and strife. Picture ends with girl and Indian hoofing it toward the big town and a better future, leaving the wasted acres to rot behind them. I'm afraid I can't tell you the moral, but if Starr wanted a saga of pure despair, I'd certainly given him one.

"Brilliant, dear boy, brilliant. Ouch!" Starr said from the tub.

"But kinda depressingue. I always like a happy endingue myself," Mr. Guber ventured.

"You fool, don't you see that it *is* a happy ending? Young love, new blood deserting a dead past to find a new way of life."

"That's pretty radical stuff. But I guess it isn't actually subversive."

"And you see, Starr, the whole thing is tied together with these vultures wheeling around in the air and..."

"Yes, yes, I see it. And watching and waiting to pounce. And then we could tie up each segment with an *enormous* vulture that actually comes down and enfolds the characters in his black wings."

"That would have to be one smart bird, Mr. Starr, and a very large one, too," Mr. Guber volunteered.

"We'll find a big one, shoot him, have him stuffed and rigged on wires."

"It's against the law to shoot vultures in Mexico, Leander. They act as a sort of free-lance sanitation department."

"Well, in that case . . . Wait! I've got the perfect one. St. Regis! I've always promised him a part. We can trick him up in black tights and a feather boa—he'd love that—and this way no one will be able to see his face or hear his Marjorie voice. He could be symbolic."

"And maybe instead of wastingue all kinds of money on settings you could maybe use parts of the Casa Zzzziminez. It sure *looks* fancy."

"That's a very good idea, Mr. Guber," I said.

As the afternoon went on, all three of us grew more and more enthusiastic. Although Starr was hopeless when it came to creating a story from scratch, he was marvelously inventive when it came to adding dramatic highlights, subtle twists, and nuances. Even Mr. Guber was helpful in the role of Irving Average Audience. Perhaps he had never heard of *Yucatán Girl* or *The Euphrates* or any of Starr's immortal triumphs, maybe his favorite performers *were* Debbie Reynolds and

Lassie, but whenever Starr's flights of fancy—*and* extravagance—took him too far afield, Mr. Guber could always be counted on to make the flat-footed statement that would bring our director right back to home base. We talked on and on, scribbling down notes, making suggestions and countersuggestions. We might have been talking still, except that toward dinnertime my wife rapped impatiently on the door and announced that she'd like to go to the bathroom. It was then that we helped Starr out of the tub, wrapped him tenderly in a towel, and sent him groaning home to the tender ministrations of our star vulture, Alistair St. Regis.

I was so busy banging out a rough shooting script that I saw very little of Starr for the rest of the week. Others saw quite a lot of him, because about all he could wear was Noxzema. But from my vantage point in the patio I saw almost all of Mexico coming and going.

Every morning a great ape of a woman, folding massage table tucked under one hairy arm, would skulk ominously across the patio, and from the open windows of Madame X's rose-colored bower there issued a two-hour concert of slappings, moans, curses, wails, and loud supplications to Our Lady. Every afternoon two minions from the Vog Salón de Belleza arrived with mysterious reticules, wheeling a great glistening hairdryer, and the same slapping and cursing and screaming would carry on until five o'clock, when all the lights blew out and the general uproar from every apartment in Casa Ximinez would inform me that our landlady had been sufficiently beautified and was being set out to bake to a fine glaze. A week earlier, Señorita Ximinez had been quite willing to cross the street on the rare occasions when she felt that her hair, face, and nails wanted attention. But now that she was once again the movie queen, beauty came to *her*. Whatever the results, they remained a closely kept secret, even to the amazing extent of entrusting Abelardo (under Mamacita's surveillance) to collect the rents on Saturday.

Emily Starr gave the impression of being apart from Bruce

van Damm only when she was asleep. The great glossy Continental Phaeton pulled majestically up to Casa Ximinez every morning at about ten to spirit Emily away, and she never got back until well past midnight.

"Nevah did see such a comin' and goin' in all mah bawn days?" Miz Priddy would remark two or three times each hour. To compound the congestion in the patio, she had also taken it into her head to rehearse a couple of dozen local urchins in a song, dance, and chant said to be indigenous to the area around Oaxaca. It didn't make working any easier, and the routine was even more unpopular with the children themselves than it was with me.

But the person who reviewed the longest and steadiest parade of visitors was, of course, Leander Starr. Sitting gingerly on the edge of a chair girded with a Hermès scarf (his skin was so tender that he could not lie down, and the soles of his feet so burned that standing was extremely painful), he held court all day long. A constant procession of actors, technicians, designers, model makers, wig makers, came and went from eight in the morning until eight at night. Miserable as he felt, Starr was a glutton for work. He sat at a table covered with sheets of figures and seemed to know the answers to everything before he even asked questions of his steady stream of visitors. Whenever I finished a scene and Starr was not closeted with some segments of the Mexican film industry (over the atonal bleating of Miz Priddy's urchins, the screeching of the parrot, the agonies of Madame X, and the clatter of my own typewriter, I could hear Starr's confident, knowledgeable questions and answers through the open window), I would rush it in to Starr, wait for him to read it and comment upon it. Wild as his sense of narrative was, whenever he made a criticism or suggested a change, he was invariably correct. When it came to a sense of dramatic values, no one could match him.

Among the callers I was summoned to meet were Lady Joyce and Bunty Maitland-Grim. Even they, with an eye to facing the camera, looked slightly enameled and mysteriously constricted from thigh to bosom. Lady Joyce did what I considered a flawless reading of the role of Doña Ana-Rosa. Then Starr gave her a violent chewing-out and, holding both her temper and her tears, she gave a far better one. As all I had given Bunty to do was to squeal and giggle from time to time, she was born letter-perfect in her part.

The contraband cameraman, a Mr. Lopez, was an American of Spanish extraction. Black-listed in the States as a former Communist and unable to get working papers in Mexico, he was the soul of co-operation; and now the most militant of *ex*-Communists, Lopez planned to shoot the whole picture under the pseudonym of "Joseph R. McCarthy." Desperate for work, he was willing to supply the camera and his own superb services for a flat one thousand dollars instead of the one and twenty per day that is the official rate for Mexican cameramen. I quite liked him in spite of his misinterpreting every faintly liberal statement as coming straight from *Das Kapital*. Where Lopez had once worshiped from afar Eugene Dennis, Earl Browder, Joseph Stalin, and Mother Bloor, he was now so far to the right as to be almost in outer space. "Ya don't t'ink dat's a li'l pinko, dat scene where Doña Ana-Rosa won't allow the overseer to lash da farm hands? . . . Dis is pretty commie, here in de uprising." While he spoke elegant and fluent Spanish, I can only think that Mr. Lopez learned his English while organizing the waterfront. However, he was so desperate for the job that he was willing to overlook my dangerous Marxist tendencies when I implied disapproval of such conservative old institutions as slavery, share cropping, illiteracy, and *droit du seigneur*.

A daily visitor was my great favorite, Aristido González, accompanied always by his pitiful son, Heff, to serve as interpreter, secretary, and body servant. González was the sort whom you may dislike on first meeting, but once you got to know him you really despised him. I had thought that clothes might make the man, but I was dead wrong. On his first visit

González oozed and flowed like lava from a very small taxi-cab, wearing a shiny old black suit that must have been made for him at least fifty pounds ago. There was a heated discussion over the fare, and Heff was dispatched to borrow ten pesos from St. Regis.

Quite against my will—and quite against González's—I was dragged away from my work and into the first production meeting, where "Mexico's Number-One Producer" was able, in his subtle little ways, to make it quite clear that I hadn't exactly grown on him either.

While he wallowed on Starr's sofa, pensively scratching and picking at his mountainous flesh, he spoke with great authority and Heff obliged with the simultaneous translation in his precise Britishese. "My father will undertake the function of producer for one thousand American dollars per diem."

"Splendid, splendid," Starr said.

"I happen to have ascertained," Mr. Guber, who was never far from Starr, interjected, "that the goingue rate in Mexico is seven-fifty a day."

This was translated back to González and brought on a fit of histrionics that made me think of a bull elephant with a mouse up his trunk. After a lot of translation back and forth, Starr said, "That is the going rate for just *any* producer. Mr. González is, however, exceptional."

"But that includes a sound stage, lightingue, and a crew for the interiors?" Mr. Guber asked with a surprising suavity. I felt a sort of warm kinship with him. For a human adding machine whose only interests in life were back taxes, Teaneck, and Shirley, Mr. Guber had not only proven to be a very sensible—although uninvited—script analyst, but he had also learned, *somehow*, the financial ins and outs of Mexican film making.

There was another outburst from the sofa and some more translating. "It has been agreed, Irving," Starr said haughtily, "that in the interests of realism we will not employ a studio. You yourself suggested that Casa Ximinez would do admirably for the few interior shots."

"All right already, but why pay for a studio you won't even be usingue?"

After some more polylingual pyrotechnics it developed that González would furnish whatever lights were needed, but that he was too influential to be bullied by a lot of corrupt technicians' unions and would supply whatever unseen personnel was needed out of his own bottomless generosity and purse.

González was annoyed to discover that Starr had already engaged the magic camera of Mr. Lopez, but Starr held his ground firmly. Cans of film would be supplied by González at one hundred dollars per thousand feet. But they only cost fifty, so how come, Guber inquired, when it wasn't even in color? This was very special film. Another scene and finally a compromise at seventy-five because Starr was González's brother. Laboratory fees and rushes could be arranged through González's all-reaching influence at two pesos per foot of film each. But, Mr. Guber said, consulting a very thorough set of notes, the usual rate was one peso—or ten cents a foot at the most. But this was very special artistic work. Surely the great Leander Starr wouldn't be satisfied with anything but the best. Another tantrum and another compromise at one peso, fifty centavos the foot. Extras—and we would need hundreds of them, according to González—would cost one hundred pesos a day. Here I got into the act and said that the script had been written so that we would *not* need hundreds of extras, but twenty or thirty at the most and only for a few days. González glared at me and then at Mr. Guber, who announced that extras hired through S.T.P.C., the official syndicate, cost only fifty. Another tirade. Did Starr want a lot of stupid, syphilitic Indians? Yes, dear boy, as a matter of fact that was exactly what Starr did want. A new tack: Did Starr think he could get decent performances out of such clods? It was the wrong tack. Yes, by God, Starr could get a performance out of anything *alive!* While Starr was trying to be careful about costs, such picayune topics as the salaries of extras, the cost to the penny of processing a foot of film bored him. He was growing impatient, and González took

199

Starr's restlessness as a cue to heave his bulk up from the sofa, throw a paw around Starr's bare, anointed shoulder—a gesture that brought forth a roar of pain—and announce, through Heff, that *he* and not a *judío* from America—an epithet which Heff did not translate—knew about making movies in Mexico, and that his old friend, his brother, should leave everything to him. End of first meeting.

But not quite the end. Mr. Guber excused himself to write up a report to the Internal Revenue folks back home. I said that I had to get back to work. We said good-by to Heff. González snubbed us petulantly by turning his fat back to us and breaking wind, whether intentionally or not I shall never know. Five minutes later he strutted through the patio on his built-up heels, wreathed in smiles and puffed up like a turkey cock.

On the occasion of González's second visit, there was no question of taxi fare. He was unloaded by his son from a very large, although somewhat banged-up, Mercedes-Benz and resplendent in a pearl-gray rayon suit with a pink acetate lining; on the third visit he sported neon-blue shantung and lizard-skin shoes; on the fourth, milk-chocolate gabardine and a white-on-white silk jacquard shirt. Poor Heff, while a lot neater and better dressed than his father, consistently appeared in the same threadbare gray flannel.

I was always summoned to their meetings, and Mr. Guber, who wasn't letting Starr far out of his sight, always happened to be there. We were about as welcome as a crash diet as far as González was concerned. However, there were few moments of discord. I had selected the Carretera del Desierto de los Leones for most of the exterior shots because it was very near to Casa Ximinez and contains almost every kind of scenery from grubby wasteland to fine trees, ravines, fields, and forests. There was no argument there, and González assured us that he would arrange everything with the national-park authorities. With the removal of such non-sixteenth-century accessories as lamps, radios, and telephones, various corners of

Starr's apartment and ours would do nicely for the interiors, and the patio of Casa Ximinez with its tiles and arches and faded frescoes and picturesque wellhead was a treasure-trove. Mr. Guber did say, "I still don't see why there should be any studio costs when we're gettingue all the settingues for nothingue," but his remark passed by, ignored by all but me. Heff modestly translated his father's suggestion that he, Heff, be put on the payroll at two hundred pesos—or fifteen dollars in United States currency—a day as interpreter, and no one saw fit to quarrel with that. Otherwise, money was never again mentioned, and although our relations with González *père* were not exactly cordial, we got on without any fisticuffs.

Starr, tolerant as he was of the odious González, did show his teeth, however, when it came to casting the young girl. On his last visits, González, more resplendently dressed with each appearance and sporting big Upmann Havana cigars, led in a constant parade of chippies vying even with him for brightness of dress. The effect was rather like a eunuch presenting a line-up of dubious virgins for the potentate's pleasure—and what girls! I've seen tramps in my day, but the selections of Señor González looked like the lowest hookers ever to work the Plaza Garibaldi. I could hear Starr ranting and raving through his open window. "No, no, no, Aristido! Maria is supposed to be a young, intelligent, virtuous, pretty, religious *girl*—not like these tarts who'll never see thirty again. Translate, please, Heff, and tell your father to get these doxies out before we have to call the fumigators."

There would be an indignant high-pitched uproar from the González starlets, none of whom understood English, and then González would say in his own brand of English, "But Leandro, oll nize ladies. From very gude Creole families. Oll make love. Oll got teets like . . ."

"I don't care if they're built like the she-wolf of Rome. Get them out of my apartment and back to whatever cathouse they came from. Out, out, *out!*" Starr's denunciation would be followed by a cacophony of furious invective from les girls, who would march indignantly across the patio, heels ringing, rumps rolling, bleached heads held high—the very picture of outraged virtue—while they cursed González for a fraud and a pimp and a cheat and a liar and a number of other more or less accurate things in a brand of Spanish never heard in the throne rooms of the viceroys of Mexico.

Even Mr. Guber was quite undone by the procession of hustlers. "Mr. Dennis," he'd say, bug-eyed, "I've never seen anythingue like it—one *nafkeh* after the other. My understandingue of the story is that Maria is supposed to be a good Catholic girl and not like these hoors, you should pardon the expression."

"I believe everyone understands that except Mr. González, Mr. Guber."

"I presume that your estimation of Mr. Gonzáles is nothingue to rave about, either, Mr. Dennis."

"You presume good, Mr. Guber, as my brother Ernest would say."

"Ernest? Oh, Ernest Hemingueway. Do you think he and Mr. González were really related?"

"Don't be an ass. González's mother was Rin-Tin-Tin's sister."

He thought that one over and then laughed. "Very amusingue. Droll. You got quite a sensayuma, Mr. Dennis. I got to admit it. Well, I should worry so longue as González has the money."

"Who told you that?" I asked sharply.

"Why, Mr. Starr. Well, time for my siesta. Be seeingue you."

But during that hectic week of planning, the most constant visitor of all was Mrs. Worthington Pomeroy. In her role of being lovely and engaged, this matronly fiancée, showing the tenderest concern for poor old Starr, was in and out three or four times a day, dressed now like an ingénue in a Victor Herbert operetta. She would arrive at any hour of the day or night, her footman bearing hampers of goodies, iced buckets of champagne, books, flowers, chocolates, unguents—anything she could think of as an entrance fee to Starr's working quarters, where she could be heard billing and cooing and clucking and driving the poor man almost to frenzy. She had been quite bad enough as heiress, social leader, and patroness of the arts, but as the young girl in love Clarice was unendurable. She even resorted to babytalk at her worst moments, and to hear Starr referred to as "lamby pie," "honey-bunny," "snuggle-buggle," and by endearments even less apt was enough to make one sick.

Engrossed as he was in his work and still suffering from his terrible sunburn, Starr would explain, civilly enough, why he shouldn't come to Clarice's for lunch, why he couldn't attend her cocktail party, why he wouldn't be able to take her dancing, why he was unable to go to Acapulco for the weekend, why it was impossible for him to watch her being fitted for negligees at Marisa's, each excuse tinged with an added note of annoyance. But when it came to monumental irritation, Starr had met his match and more in Mrs. Pomeroy. The kitten had claws. She would sulk, she would pout, she would whine, and eventually she would scratch. It had been some years since Clarice had not had her own sweet way in almost everything. It was her custom to pay her money and take her choice, and the only times that didn't work were with the people she couldn't buy. However, she *had* bought Starr—signed, sealed, and delivered with a lifetime guarantee—when she had invested in *Valley of the Vultures*. But now that the merchandise wasn't performing properly, didn't live up to its advertising, proved something less than indestructible, Clarice was showing all the signs of the dissatisfied customer. It was then that Starr would become surprisingly humble. "But Clarice, my dear, I am in great pain. The doctor says this is a second-degree burn."

"Don't be sil, sweetie, what kinda man are you? It's just an ole sunburn. See?"

"Ouch, God damn it!"

"Oh, so now you swear at me!"

"Clarice, when you pinch, the pain is excrutiating."

"So all right, yer burn'll be gone next week. *Then* can I give a dinner party? Or a luncheon? Or *something?* I want to announce our engagement. You could bring Emily and that cute Brucie and the Maitland-Grims and maybe Dolores del Rio and Lady Joyce and . . ."

"*Do* you think it would be in the best of taste to invite my ex-wife to an engagement party?"

"Who cares about that? She cert'ny don't seem to. Besides, she's big in London. Can we say Monday?"

"But Clarice, that's the first day of my picture."

"So? Start Tuesday."

"Clarice. This film is costing a great deal of money."

"You're telling *me?*"

"Not only your money, uh, darling—although you mustn't think me ungrateful—but other people's as well. It involves the work of a lot of talent. I can't let them down and go tooting off to lunch. This is very important. . . ."

"Fer cripes' sakes, it's *just* an old movie!"

On and on and on would go these discussions to which I was the most unwilling—but still rapt—eavesdropper. There would be tears and threats and tantrums, until finally Starr would beg for her time and patience, buy her absence of a few hours with a vague promise and a tender caress, and Mrs. Pomeroy would stamp out of his apartment, her eyes flinty, her mouth set, only pretending to be placated. "Poor old Starr," I kept thinking.

It was late Sunday night when I finally hammered out the last page of the rewritten shooting script—not that Starr wouldn't rewrite it a dozen more times in the process of filming the picture—and my wife had lovingly put aside her own work to make six extra copies (she is the one in the family who can put in carbon paper so that you don't need a mirror to read what's been typed). Starr's apartment was blazing with light. The door was open, so I walked right in. Starr's sunburn, owing to the constant lardings applied by St. Regis, was now a deep Indian brown. At last able to wear clothes, he was making the most of his color with a stark-white shirt and white shorts. He looked splendid. Mrs. Pomeroy was also there, dressed something like Mary Pickford in *Poor Little Rich Girl*. She did not. She looked sore as hell, her rather heavy face, relaxed from the constant calisthenics of bright little smirks, doughy and disconsolate. From force of habit, she grimaced slightly when I came in, and she said, "Hello, sweetie. Long time no see."

"I've been busy. Here, Leander. Here's the final revision *and* six copies, just in case mine blows away."

"Are you in on this too, Paddy?" Mrs. Pomeroy asked dangerously.

"N-not really. Just a little help with the script."

"Well, how long do *you* estimate this pitcher's gonna take?"

Starr looked uneasy to say the least. "W-why, I really couldn't say. I don't know anything about making movies. Ask Leander."

"I just did," she added darkly, "an' *he* says . . ."

I suppose he'd put it at several decades and I wouldn't have blamed him, but Mrs. Pomeroy was never able to give me his considered estimate. We were interrupted by the arrival of Emily. She looked sort of soft-boiled and dreamy-eyed, but when she got a glimpse of Clarice sitting there in dimity ruffles and sausage curls dangling down her neck, Emily snapped out of it and reverted back to the Puritan girl I knew and did not love. "Oh, good evening, Mrs. Pomeroy, Mr. Dennis."

"Hello, sweetie," Clarice said, counterfeiting very badly a sort of girl-to-girl good nature. "Been out with yer cute fellah?"

"Bruce and I went to the bullfights, had dinner, and came home early. I wanted to talk to Daddy." Having cut Clarice down to size, Emily now cut her out of the conversation entirely. "Feeling better, darling? I see you're able to put some clothes on."

"Much better, dear, thank you."

"I thought you might be alone," Emily said. I realized that her curtness was not directed toward me, but I could take a hint even if Clarice couldn't.

"Well, I'll be on my way. . . ."

"Stay where you are, dear boy," Starr said sharply. It wasn't an invitation to remain, it was a command.

"Good night, Daddy," Emily said, making her way to the stairs. "Good night Mr. Dennis, Mrs. Pomeroy."

Clarice turned on her mechanical simper. "Just a sec, sweetie," she said. There was an edge to her voice I didn't quite like.

"Yes, Mrs. Pomeroy?"

"I thought I ast you ta call me Clarice. Didn't I?"

"Uh, yes. Yes, you did. But . . ."

"But *what*?"

"Well, somehow it doesn't seem respectful, Mrs. Pomeroy. Just not right."

"That's right, sweetie, it *isn't* right. At least it *won't* be right. Because a few weeks from now you can just call me *Mother*. G'night all." She flung her furs around her shoulders and made for the door.

Anxious to be out of the line of fire at *any* price, I said, "Can I walk you home, Moth . . . uh, *Clarice*?"

"No, you can't! Whaddya think I keep a limmazeen for?" With that she was gone. Emily stood on the bottom step looking as though she'd just been slapped. I cleared my throat uncomfortably and wished that I were dead and buried. Starr was silent.

"Is this true?" Emily said at last.

"Uh, now, darling, don't jump to conclusions. Nothing definite has been decided."

"Daddy, you're lying to me. It's written all over your face."

"Well, darling . . ."

"Don't 'darling' me! And as for *you* . . ." Emily turned on me with blazing eyes. "As for you—Daddy's great old friend, and Mummy's, too. Not one week ago you had the gall to look me in the face and tell me that Daddy and that woman were only interested in *business*."

"At the time it was true," I said miserably. "Really it was."

Having dismissed me as something beneath contempt, she turned again on Starr. "So it was just money you were interested in? Just an investment?"

"What Mr. Dennis says is entirely correct, child. But Mrs. Pomeroy—Clarice—seems to be playing for higher stakes."

"Do you mean to tell me you'd marry that shrew just to get her to invest in your picture?"

"Some very successful marriages have been based on . . ." Starr gave up on that one. "Emily, I have misled you badly. I find myself temporarily embarrassed. I have been for some time. Starting this picture tomorrow is my big chance. I can get out of debt, go back home, begin all over again, make something of myself once more. But I couldn't let you know that I was on my uppers—flat, stony broke. Clarice has millions. She . . ."

"Do you mean to say you'd marry a woman—just any woman—for money?"

"I didn't say I was *going* to marry her. I'd hoped to postpone things until I'd made enough to pay her back—with interest, of course—and then call this thing off. But this was a matter of . . . Emily, I wanted you to be proud of me."

"And of course this sort of thing makes me *very* proud. If you needed money, couldn't you have come to me—your own daughter? I've got loads of it—Grandpa's, Grandma's, Uncle Julian's. I'd have *given* it to you rather than know that you'd . . ."

"Emily, I didn't know. I . . ."

"Of course you didn't. You didn't know whether I was dead or alive—or *care*—until I came down here. Maybe if you had known you'd have paid a little attention to me—just for the money, *naturally*." There was a stunned silence. Even Emily seemed shocked at what she had said. Then Starr cried, "My God, Dennis. Don't you *see* it?"

"Don't I see what?"

"Maria! There's our *Maria*! Not one of those sluts González keeps bringing around. *Emily* can play Maria! The fire, the facial planes, the burning eyes. I've had a leading lady right under my own roof and . . ."

"*Oh!*" Emily screamed. She raced up the stairs and slammed her door.

"Leander," I ventured, "do you think this *quite* the moment to go into casting when Emily is . . ."

"Emily is superb! Can't you see her as a Mexican daughter of the soil?"

"I saw Katherine Hepburn as a Chinese daughter of the rice paddies—*Dragon Seed,* I think it was called—but it was still Bryn Mawr to me."

"But *I* can get a performance out of her. You saw how magnificent she was tonight. I'll talk to her."

"I think you'd better do just that—and fast."

"Yes, I must, while this fiery mood is still with her."

"It's not the mood I'd choose, exactly," I said. "Well, good luck with the picture. If there's anything I can do . . ."

"Anything you can *do*? Well, I expect you out in the patio at six o'clock tomorrow morning."

"You *what*?"

"You heard me. You don't talk me into making this film against my better judgment and then dump me on the very threshhold of my greatest triumph. If you're not there at six sharp, I'll personally come up and drag you out of bed. Now go."

"All right, Starr, but just one question."

"Yes. Be quick about it."

"Are you *really* going to marry Mrs. Pomeroy?"

"How the hell do *I* know? Don't bother me with trivial details at a time like this. *Em-i-ly!*" he bellowed, and pounded up the stairs.

208

XII

The following week went by so rapidly that every day still seems like the one before or the one after to me. My wife, being more systematic, keeps a sort of diary—not a journal exactly, but a booklet with little things like appointments with the dentist, luncheon engagements, people's birthdays, and anything noteworthy that may have happened jotted down in more or less chronological order. It is to her that I am indebted for even the foggiest recollection of these action-packed days of shooting *Valley of the Vultures*. At least the book helps me to remember where Starr (and I) happened to be and when. And so I shall quote from my wife's day-book and then expand as best I can.

MONDAY. *Hair—10:30. Gr. chiff. dress, P's bl. suit—Tintoria Francesa. Write kids, Mother, M&O.*

Monday dawned clear, fair, and hot, like all the other days in Mexico City. By the time I bolted down some coffee and got out to the patio Starr was pacing up and down dressed in a style reminiscent of the late Cecil Blount De Mille. The only other person who'd managed to arrive that early was Lopez, the cameraman, who had brought with him tons of the most expensive and impressive-looking equipment. Having taken on, once again, the shackles of capitalism, Mr. Lopez wore the neat pin stripes and worsteds, the button-down collars, the sober ties of a young man forging ahead in banking. He trotted a pace or two behind Starr drinking in every one of his millions of words, differing with him from time to time, and occasionally making a suggestion. From the respect and deference paid him by Starr, I figured that he must be an exceptionally accomplished cameraman, and indeed he was. "Now Lopez, my dear, we start shooting here on page seventeen where Doña Ana-Rosa and her husband have just completed building the hacienda. I usually like to start right from the beginning and go through in perfect sequence so as not to break the mood for the actors but . . ."

"But dat's kinda costly. Yeah, I dig."

Indeed, Starr had made more than one film in perfect sequence, doing scene one in a studio in Hollywood, loading all the cast and crew onto a special train to film a second scene that lasted less than a minute on location in Kansas, putting them back on a train for another brief scene in Hollywood, piling them aboard a chartered ship for a quick shot on the Beach at Waikiki, shipping them back to Hollywood, and so on. These pictures rarely took less than a year to film, transportation costs came to more than the payroll, and if the actors could even remember the names of the characters they were playing after being herded through stations and freightyards and hotels and piers and bus terminals, they were a lot smarter than I think they were.

"Now I'll have to ask you to watch out for those telephone wires. Sixteenth century, you know."

"Don't worry about dat, Mr. Starr. I dig."

"Splendid. Anyhow, in this scene Miss James is great with child, and she's praying to . . ."

"Who's great with child?" Lady Joyce and Bunty Maitland-Grim had arrived in the Maitland-Grim Rolls-Royce, bearing a thermos of coffee.

"Monica, my pet. You're fourteen minutes late."

"But about fourteen hours early, knowing the way you work, Leander. Do you want us to change now?"

"If you would, my dear. Just leave that coffee with me. Dennis, do show them into my apartment. That will be the women's dressing room. I've assigned the men to your apartment. St. Regis!"

St. Regis poked his head out of an upper window. He was wearing a kimono with an Elizabethan ruff of Kleenex around the collar. Panchromatic make-up had turned his face, hands, neck, and ears the color of a ripe apricot. "Yes, Mr. Starr, I'm just getting into my make-up."

"Fa God's sakes why," Lopez asked, "ain't he a bird?"

"Please show Lady Joyce and Mrs. Maitland-Grim to my bedroom. Dennis, you'll find their costumes, suitably marked by scene and page number, in my living room. Then you can take the men's things to your place. Now, Lopez, as I was saying . . ."

A dozen or so costumes hung from the huge silver chandelier in Starr's living room. They seemed a bit sleezy to me— felt and flannelette passing for velvet, some of the skirts not even hemmed, and everything hastily basted or pinned together. Interpreting my look correctly, Lady Joyce said, "Don't worry, my dear. This tatty stuff photographs a lot better than the real thing. With the right lighting it will look lovely. That's one thing Leander does know. And at least everything is clean." Bunty giggled. "Oh, Monica, I'm nervous as a witch." "Right up here, your ladyship," St. Regis called.

Then I picked up a great load of capes and doublets and tights and boots and swords—all neatly pressed and labeled —and hung them around our own living room. By the time I got back to the patio, another actor had appeared. He was a middle-aged Mexican who had done so well being sinister in Hollywood South-of-the-Border epics during the thirties that he had returned to Mexico, retired, and now was immensely rich through dabbling in real estate, acting only when he felt like it. He spoke glib, rapid English with all of the actory intonations, but with every statement tinged with the pressures of big business. His speech, off camera, contained almost no punctuation. "Good morning oh yes how do you do I've read some of your books in English of course they lose so much in translation awf'ly glad to meet you at last just tell me where to change and what's to be done about make-up if anything and I'll be right with you I do hope this flick won't take too long three days for me and no more Mr. Starr said you see I'm trying to put together this parcel of land on the Reforma and . . . Oh yes of course I don't want to disturb your wife I know how it is with the ladies must have their beauty sleep the bathroom will do splendidly be with you in a shake thanks ever so."

Out in the patio Starr and Lopez were setting up in the corner where Dr. and Miz Priddy lived. In addition to a saint of some sort set into a niche in the wall, there were some very pretty flowering bushes and interesting dappled shadows cast by a pepper tree. They had been joined by Mr. Guber, natty in a play suit and a straw sombrero with "Souvenir de Mexico" woven into the front of it. "Great day in the morningue," he was saying, "when I left home I never dreamed I'd be makingue a movie with the great Leander Starr. Will this be awright for like a pee-on's costume, Mr. Starr? Gee, will Shirl ever be thrilled if it plays at the Queen Anne in Teaneck."

My wife came hustling out of our apartment, clutching her peignoir to her, to report that there was a naked man in our bathroom.

Lady Joyce and Bunty emerged from Starr's apartment, hair scooped back into great Renaissance buns, skirts held high above the dust, glowing English complexions innocent of make-up or else enhanced so subtly that no traces of cosmetics were evident even in the sunlight. It was the first time I'd ever realized how very pretty Bunty actually was. "Will this do, Leander? I copied the hair from a portrait hanging in Bunty's bar. The period is authentic." Lady Joyce could be very businesslike when back in the traces. "You look ravishing, my dears. Now be still." Bunty stifled a giggle, and then they sat down, after spreading sheets over the chairs to protect their costumes, and studiously reviewed their lines.

"Ever so sorry to give your wife such a start in the biffy couldn't find my jock anywhere do hope she didn't mind all in the business you know." It was the actor who was to play Don Fernando, Doña Ana-Rosa's spouse. He looked very much the grandee, except that he was smoking a cigarette through a Dunhill holder ("have to you know no good lousing up a whole take with these ghastly coughing fits"). Always the actor as well as the realtor, he surveyed himself critically in a long mirror. "Do hope my hair is long enough wigs give me the itch didn't do a thing about make-up but you may want to shade my chops a bit as I'm getting a trifle jowly be fifty-five next month you know now if you've got an extra script I'll give the old lines the once over thanks ever so."

Upon being introduced to his film wife he said, "Good God Monica James I remember you doing a picture with Romney Brent while Lupe Velez and I were slugging it out on the next sound stage poor Lupe how have you been my dear?" The three of them sat happily smoking and gossiping, while Starr fretted and fumed and consulted his watch and cursed González for being late.

At half past seven Catalina Ximinez made a real star's entrance from her own sumptuous quarters. I gasped at the sight of her. She was made up within an inch of her life, wearing false lashes that looked as though a brace of centipedes had dropped dead on her eyelids. Her hair—if it could be called that—was bleached the color of a brass cuspidor and lacquered and tortured into a towering edifice. In spite of the heat, she was swathed in her dirty white-fox coat. "Good God," Don Fernando said, "it can't be old Catalina Ximinez I thought she was dead but it is by God." In Spanish he said, *"Ah, Catalina, querida! Usted es muy, muy,* muy, *hermosa! Bellísima!* What's she got up as haven't seen anything like it since Mae West playing with Cary at Paramount must have been thirty-two thirty-three. *Bella! Bella!"*

Madame X took the Spanish flattery as her due, not understanding the English, smiled vacantly, and then screamed something in the general direction of her bedroom. In a moment Abelardo and one of the many anonymous servants of Casa Ximinez struggled out with a rose-velvet chaise lounge and a Deauville umbrella to shield Our Star from the ravages of the sun. Mamacita, who had somewhere found an old muskrat cape, followed and bounced happily on one of her tubular chromium chairs. "Mai . . . dotter . . . beeg . . . star," she announced, and flashed her toothless gums around the patio.

I said to Starr, "Look at the Ximinez! What are you going to do about that getup?"

"Don't worry," Starr said. "She's supposed to play a slut and a fool, only she doesn't know it. I'll handle her. By the time I finish with her, she may steal the whole picture."

Emily appeared looking angry and sullen, but at least she was there and more or less willing to play the role of Maria. Just what magic words Starr had found to say to her the night before I shall never know. Three or four actors in costumes of the sixteenth, nineteenth, and twentieth centuries drifted out of our apartment and sat, like very well-mannered children, around the tile table playing cards and drinking Pepsi-Cola.

Even with Starr working at breakneck speed, I soon discovered that making movies, like making war, is mostly a question of "hurry up and wait." At the moment we all seemed to be waiting for González, the film, the lights, and the crew. Sometime after nine the old hog waddled in, all smiles and *abrazos. "Buenos días, mi hermano! Buenos días!"*

"Buenas tardes!" Starr snapped. "Just where the hell have you been?"

Through Heff, Gonzáles went into long flowery explanations: he was late because for his dear brother he went through tortures locating the finest film to be procured, the newest lights, the most gifted crew. The lights looked old, weak, and dangerous. As for the crew, they shuffled about as though they'd never worn shoes before, cautiously fingering and examining everything. It seemed to me that they were seeing a film made for the first time in their lives and were quite awed by the experience.

It was Mr. Lopez, however, who gave González his come-uppance. If González hadn't been able to foist off his own cameraman on Starr, I don't think he'd ever counted on Starr's finding one who was so knowledgeable or quite so fluent and profane in the Spanish language. Lopez grabbed the single can of film that González had brought. "Dat slob calls dis crap film? And one lousy can of it? Ten minutes' worth and short ends at that. Dey use better stuff dan dis for blue movies. An' look at dese lights. Where da hell he find 'em? De old Vitagraph studios? An' looka dat lousy commie crew." While González stood there bug-eyed, Lopez fired questions at all of the men González had brought and dis-covered that not one of them had ever worked on a film before, although the chief electrician had repaired appliances in a shop at Coyoacán. Then Lopez turned on González and really let him have it in his native tongue. I don't know what he said, but it must have been good because all of the Spanish-speaking members of the cast burst into loud ap-plause at the end of the diatribe. I gathered that González wasn't any too popular with them either. Heff, looking sick with embarrassment, was sent off in the Mercedes to pick up ten cans of film to the Lopez perfectionistic specifications. González, puffing with rage, retired to sit in the shade.

"Okay, Mr. Starr," Lopez said calmly, "you may as well re-hearse dis scene, den maybe we can get going."

"Very well," Starr said crisply. "Now you all know what the story's about, you've all been introduced, so we'll start out with Doña Ana-Rosa—Miss Monica James, please—Don Fer-nando and the maid Conchita. May I have absolute quiet? Thank you. And I shall also want the vulture. The vulture has not been written into Mr. Dennis' script. He is my own device. Now where the hell is he? St. Regis!"

"I'll be right down, Mr. Starr," he replied from Starr's apartment. And he was!

None of the performers, not even Catalina Ximinez, had

been able to make such an entrance. St. Regis burst forth from Starr's apartment painted like a billboard. His marcelled hair shone like a copper pot. In addition to his peach-blush flesh, he was rouged like a harlot, his lips the color of a pomegranate, his lashes crimped and beaded with mascara, the lids an iridescent blue, deeply lined and extended with black, and his rather pale eyes awash with belladonna, dilating his pupils so that he groped his way blindly in the sunlight. He looked as though he'd learned make-up at the feet of Mae Murray. But what he'd done to his face and head was as nothing compared to the rest of him. His basic costume consisted of shiny black tights and a leotard fitting so snugly that every rib could be counted. But only God and St. Regis knew what he'd padded the front of himself with— the week's laundry perhaps. *"Qué hombre!"* one of the actors shouted and whistled in disbelief.

"Do I look all right, Mr. Starr?" St. Regis asked, lashes fluttering.

"Yes, considering that your face won't show anyhow. But what in the hell have you got stuffed in *there,* a kangaroo?"

St. Regis blushed beneath the layers of panchromatic make-up. "It was jest that my dance belt was so very snug. . . ."

"Well, whatever it is, take it out. This is a movie, not a freak show."

With St. Regis back to normal, so to speak, and his paint job obliterated by the outsized vulture's head, the rehearsals progressed fairly well. The only distractions were Bunty's nervous giggling, Perro's incessant barking, and Loro's voluble impersonations of Madame X collecting the rents. It slayed the actors, and it certainly lowered the status of Catalina Ximinez, Star of the First Magnitude. Bunty was scolded by Starr, and the animals hastily dispatched to the cellar by Abelardo. By the time they had run through the scene two or three more times, Heff had returned with the new film, the camera was loaded, and we were ready to do the first shooting.

By ordering González's bumbling peons off the set, Starr was able to set up the lights himself. After a few questions from Lopez it became evident that the González sound "expert" had been hastily recruited from a record shop on the Insurgentes, so Starr set up the mike boom and took over the console for the magnetic tape. "Very well," he said, shooting a malign glance at González, "I can handle the sound myself. Sorry, ladies and gentlemen, we seem to be a little shorthanded on the first day, but now I think we can start rolling. Hang on for just a moment." With a practiced eye he flew from one performer to the next dabbing powder against reflection, pinning a costume here, arranging a loose strand of hair there. "Oh, I feel such a fool," Bunty said. "You're sure the old double chin isn't too obvious Mr. Starr always be able to shade it in a mo," Don Fernando offered. In addition to the people who were concerned with the picture, quite a lot of others had happened in. Nothing of much moment ever occurs in our *barrio* without word spreading rapidly, and now upwards of a hundred people—tenants, servants, delivery men, neighbors, and passers-by had crowded into the patio. "Heff," Starr said, "please tell them all that they're welcome to watch, but we must have complete silence, and if there is one sound I'll have to clear the set. Ready, everyone?" he asked the cast as he ducked into his headphones.

The scene began as rehearsed. Don Fernando, who was a miracle of periods, commas, semicolons, question marks, and subtle shadings of speech while on camera, led his lovely wife, Doña Ana-Rosa, in. "Do you like it, my dearest?" "Oh, Fernando , it's beautiful." "Oh, Doña Ana-Rosa," Bunty said. "It's not a hacienda, it's a palace! Finer than a castle in Spain." For once she didn't giggle. "And it's really *ours*, Fernando?" "Ours and our sons' and our sons' sons' and our sons' sons' sons' to build a mighty nation—the land of New Spain." "Oh, Fernando!" "Will you come inside, my heart?" "Oh, señora," Bunty trilled, just barely under control, "the beautiful rooms, the kitchens, the nurseries!" "In a moment,

Fernando, but pray leave me here alone for a little." "Is señora unwell?" Bunty said with a good deal of suppressed passion. "The baby?" Starr's face was working hard, registering all the emotions he had drilled into his actors. "Just a moment alone, I beg you. I shan't be long." "Very well, my dear. Come, silliness, and I will show you the finest nursery a son ever had." It was Bunty's cue to giggle, and she did not hold back. She bobbed off camera in paroxysms of girlish squeals. Very effective.

Alone in front of the camera, Lady Joyce treated the lens to the full radiance of her glorious eyes, then she moved to the statue in the niche and fell to her knees. "Oh, blessed Virgin of Guadalupe," she said, in her thrilling, throbbing voice, "grant to me a son worthy of this land. . . ."

"Doctor, you got your school bag? And your bus fare? And your hard-boiled eggs?"

"Yes, Modesta, my dear, *hasta la vista,* as the Spanish say." A door opened right behind the supplicant figure of Lady Joyce, and Dr. and Miz Priddy stepped out. "Well, well, well, what have we here? Home cinematography, I do believe. Well, as the Bard once said, 'All the world's a stage and all . . .' "

Lady Joyce went into gales of laughter, and the whole silent audience broke up. There stood Dr. Priddy in sunglasses and Bermuda shorts, behind him Miz Priddy in a Hoover apron and amber beads.

"Jesus!" Starr bellowed. "You bumbling old nincompoop! Couldn't you stay in there with your big mealy mouths shut for just thirty seconds more?"

"Well, Ah nevah?" Miz Priddy sniffed.

"Do it again, God damn it, do it all over again."

"It's not dat bad, Mr. Starr," Lopez said encouragingly. "We can just cut from when the broad starts her prayers."

"Ah intind to speak to Miz Ximinez about this outrage?" Miz Priddy said self-righteously.

"Oh, go fluff your duff, my dear," Lady Joyce said. "Now shall we start from where I fall on my knees?"

One more time, and the scene was considered complete. Starr, who in the past had thought nothing of doing fifty takes of a scene, was being very conscious of time and money, and the intensity of his feeling seemed to transmit itself to the actors. Even the most insensitive of them caught Starr's feverish desire to work and work hard and fast. Fortunately, most of them had had stage experience that helped enormously. A performer whose work has been limited solely to movies can blow up his lines, belch, give a bad reading, or take a prat fall secure in the knowledge that the scene can be shot again and again and again until he's fired or—if only by the law of averages—one take turns out to be satisfactory. On the living stage, if you come on with your fly open, trip over the doorsill, or forget your big soliloquy, that's it. The first time is the last time. After the surprise entrance of Dr. and Miz Priddy, practically nothing went wrong. The actors were real troupers. Not only did they memorize their lines, not only did they fall in with every nuance of Starr's direction, they even helped to shift furniture around the patio, contrary to all union regulations. It was all a little thrilling, and it made me think of what the pioneering days of motion pictures must have been like, when movies—and even some great ones—were shot in lofts and greenhouses and parks and open fields, before the formalization, standardization, and sterilization brought on by the mammoth studios of Hollywood. Before we broke for lunch three scenes—short ones to be sure—had been completed and were on their way to the lab to be processed.

As I had anticipated, Starr had a little trouble with Emily during the afternoon session. She made a beautiful-looking Maria in her poor but clean rags and tatters, but her performance in each of a dozen rehearsals was wooden, a little like a Bryn Mawr Baby Greek student reading Aristophanes in front of the class. Not that I could blame her; she had never evinced the slightest interest in being an actress, she was still furious at her father, and the presence of Bruce van Damm, all encouraging smiles and devouring glances, naturally made her self-conscious.

"That wasn't quite right, my darling," Starr said patiently. "Perhaps you don't quite realize the enormity of the situation. You're standing here in this shabby patio listening to this damned fool of a woman—begging your pardon, Miss Herrera—" he said to the raw-boned character actress who was playing Emily's aunt.

"Pairfeckly ollraite, Señor Starr," Miss Herrera said generously.

"You know that the crops for the year have amounted to a handful of grain, that the hacienda is mortgaged right up to the roof, that everything is falling apart. And you know that your aunt knows it. But she still lives in the past, trading on a great family name, believing that because the place has prospered for the last nine hundred years it will again. And you are trying to . . ."

"Yes, I understand all that," Emily said coldly. "I'll try again."

Emily and Miss Herrera began once more. Miss H. was a seasoned old warhorse who for the past fifty years had played unsympathetic roles such as the haughty infanta, the strait-laced duenna, the cruel stepmother, with the same tried and true competence. She wasn't brilliant, but you could depend on her. You could depend on Emily, too. As sure as the sky was blue, she was dull, mechanical, and thoroughly bad. Starr was just about to break into the scene when suddenly a great change came over Emily. In the space of less than a second she turned from automaton into spitfire. In a trice her well-bred, nicely modulated voice rose a full octave, and she began to scream at poor old Miss Herrera. "Oh yes, Aunt Mercedes, I know. I know. We are the rightful heirs of the kings of Spain, the rulers of the earth. Well, look at the earth we rule—dust and filth and rubble!" With that, she picked up a handful of dry dirt and flung it in the poor old lady's face, bringing on a terrible wheezing attack. In astonishment I turned to look at Starr, and then I saw the inspiration for Emily's sudden burst of fury. Mrs. Worthington Pomeroy had arrived, had tiptoed up behind Starr, and was now making ringlets of his hair around her pudgy index finger.

"That will do, thank you," Starr said. "We'll try a take now."

"But, Daddy, I really don't . . ."

"Are you ready, Lopez?"

"Sure t'ing, Mr. Starr. Very well. Places please." Starr put on the headphones and adjusted the sound console. "Quiet please. Camera. Action." Miss Herrera began the scene in the same professional way she had always rehearsed it. Emily was sullen and seemed on the verge of tears. It was a rather long scene, and as it progressed I watched Starr with mounting interest. First he reached out for Clarice's all-too-eager hand. He was seated where the gesture couldn't have been lost on his daughter. The pitch of her performance began to rise. Still in his headphones and still twiddling with the dials on the console, he put his free arm around Clarice's thickening waist. The fury mounted still higher, with Miss Herrera, slightly surprised by the turn of events, almost matching Emily for fury. At the climatic moment Starr pulled Clarice, simpering hideously, down onto his knee. Then the dam broke.

". . . dust and filth and rubble," Emily cried. "Well, take your precious earth and live on it if you can. *I* won't!" She swept up a load of dust and gravel and let poor old Miss Herrera have it square in the eye, whereupon the saintly Miss H. screamed *"Madre de Dios!"* and fetched Emily a haymaker that sent her staggering. Then they both burst into tears. It wasn't in the script but it was sensational.

"Cut!" Starr said, unceremoniously dumping Clarice to the ground. "That was superb, my darling, superb! Kiss Daddy."

With a sniff Emily said, "If you don't mind, I'd rather not. I believe that's all you wanted of me—for today?"

"*All* I wanted of you, my precious. It was more than one could reasonably expect from Maggie Leighton. Oh, my beloved . . ."

"Then if I may be excused. I'll be with you in a moment, Bruce," Emily said, and marched prissily to Starr's apartment while Miss Herrera was led off by a couple of volunteers to the Farmacia Corazón de Jesús for first aid.

Sadistic as it may have been, Starr had really dragged a performance out of his daughter. By that time most of the actors were finished for the day and had gone home, leaving our apartment a wasteland of Kleenex, cigarette butts, empty bottles, and forgotten articles of clothing. It was now time for Our Star of Stars, Catalina Ximinez, to do her stuff, and I was curious to see how Svengali was going to handle this particular Trilby. I felt that he had bitten off more than he could chew, but as usual I was wrong. Madame X was, to begin with, unable to read a manuscript in English, and Starr had not bothered to explain the plot or her role to her. Totally indifferent to anything as unessential as a story, la Ximinez simply assumed that she was the star, that she was going to be all sweet and sympathetic and that her acting would range from archly coy to coyly arch with lots of fluttering gestures and saccharine simpers. I knew that her limitations in English were such that most of the dialogue in her scenes would have to be spoken *at* her by better linguists and, accordingly, I had limited her speeches to mostly "yes" and "no" and "oh" and "please" and "thank you" and "good morning" and "'good night." The longest of her speeches, like a telegram, ran to just ten words, and I was prepared to cut that. I also knew that she was to play Doña Isabel, the vain nineteenth-century chatelaine whose stupidity and cupidity had brought about the turning point in the fortunes of the family and the hacienda. What I *didn't* know was how Lucifer himself was going to get a vain, conceited, no-talent

222

cow like Catalina Ximinez, whose only interest in *Valley of the Vultures*—if, indeed, she even recalled the title—was to see herself once again on the screen as a radiant young beauty admired by one and all, to turn in work that wasn't downright ludicrous. But again I hadn't reckoned with the evil genius of Leander Starr.

Having sprawled on the chaise longue like a Matisse odalisque all morning, Madame X had disappeared into her own quarters for lunch and had not reappeared, but I gather that she'd been keeping an eye on things from her bedroom window, because when it was time for her to do her scene, she made yet another grand entrance—this time in costume. Either that bull dike from the Institución de Masaje had beaten tons off her middle or else she'd been laced in to the bursting point. She was dressed in a wasp-waisted gown of the eighteen-eighties—white with red polka dots and faintly flamenco dancer in feeling—with the most prominent bustle ever seen. I wondered whether it was just a monument of wire, horsehair, and crinoline or if her excess poundage had simply been outer-directed. She carried a matching parasol, and to that rather fussy costume, bouncing with ruffles and tucks and pleats as it was, she had added, from her own astonishing wardrobe, a number of fans, stoles, mitts, artificial flowers, pins, clips, necklaces, earrings, bracelets, a towering celluloid Spanish comb, a cotton-lace mantilla, and harlequin sunglasses. "La Ximinez ees raidy," she announced. Mamacita, in transports of joy and also dark glasses with skittish seashell frames, followed, moved her chromium U.S.O. Club chair to the very edge of the set and sat bouncing orgasmically.

I suppressed a gasp. "Good Lord, Starr, who dressed her?"

"Same designer who did the rest of the costumes—not all of it, perhaps."

"Well now, who's going to *un*dress her? She looks like a rummage sale."

"Be patient, dear boy. She may bring more to the character

of Doña Isabel than you ever did. Ah, Catalina, how beautiful!" She removed her dark glasses and batted her Gordian knots of eyelashes. The only thing that Starr was firm about was the removal of the blood-red lacquer that had been applied to her artificial nails. Madame X was not pleased, but after I, Starr, the wardrobe man, her manicurist, and even Mamacita assured her that liquid polish had not been invented in the eighties, she grumpily consented to dunking her talons into acetone, from which they emerged looking cold, gray, and dead.

When Catalina had appeared in her costume plus the plethora of dowdy accessories, I thought the wardrobe man was going to have a fit. When she started reading my lines, I was certain that I was. Starr had selected two extremely strong actors to appear in most of her scenes with her: one was the feckless, decadent husband; the other played the role of the overseer of the hacienda—a good and honest farming man who is driven to rebel against her.

Through Heff, Starr started to explain the action to her. "You, my dear, are a lovely aristocrat, sweet and kind and adored by all. But the overseer is a slothful, lazy, inefficient son of a bitch, shifty and dishonest, and you have lost all patience with . . ."

"Leander," I said, feeling outraged, "that's not at all what I . . ."

"Shut up," he muttered. Miss Ximinez beamed, and flexed whatever facial muscles she had that could still move under the burden of make-up into vacuity, idiocy, and grouch, which I suppose were to signify breeding, sweetness, and impatience. "Now, Heff, please ask Miss Ximinez if she knows her lines."

"Oh, ove coorse. Oll ove dem. 'Yais.' 'No.' 'Darrleeng Don Pedro.' 'Deess monn eess lousy. . . .' "

"Lazy, Catalina. 'This man is lazy.' "

"Ah, ove coorse. 'Deess monn eess lay-zee.' " 'ow we do know he don't steal?' 'Ai om bore now. Most drass for de Heneral's boll.' " She smiled in triumph. Still bouncing in her chair, Mamacita applauded enthusiastically.

The two actors who were to appear with her had been coached separately, so that not too much time was wasted on rehearsal. The scene was to be played directly in front of Madame X's own impressive doorway. The sun had descended, throwing the area into shadow, and Starr had arranged the most flattering lighting possible. If you didn't know who it was, Madame X almost looked good—and not more than thirty-five.

"Very well, Lopez," Starr said. "I hope you've got lots of film. We'll be needing more than one take of this. Now, Heff, Señorita Ximinez is to make a stunning entrance right through the front doors. When you hear Don Pedro say 'Stupid, dirty Indians, who cares if they're hungry,' you give la Ximinez a slight push and she comes on. You'll explain that to her, won't you?"

Heff, who tried to be as pleasant and helpful as his father managed to be repulsive and destructive, nodded and led Our Star into the house.

The scene between the soft Don Pedro and the upstanding man of the soil went as scheduled, the overseer warning of discontent among the field hands, the master being indifferent to the plight of the workers.

"Stupid, dirty Indians," Don Pedro said with a fine lift of the lip, "who cares if they're hungry?"

With a twiching of ruffles and kicking of trains, Madame X hove into sight, paused on the top step a little like Carmen, her parasol open like a windmill behind her head, then she stepped forward, tripped on the hem of her dress, and went down like a sack of meal, cursing and clawing in the gravel.

"Save that footage," Starr said to the cameraman, "we may be able to use it." Then he bounded forward. *"Catalina, querida!* Are you hurt?" I was so undone that I had to go to my apartment and mix a quick drink to pull myself together. By the time I returned, Miss Ximinez, dusted off and freshly powdered, was playing the scene as though she might have been Yvonne Printemps about to burst into song. I mean it was unspeakably bad. When she was finished, Starr embraced her. "Brava! Brava! And now, *querida,* would you do it just once more. The lights weren't quite right. And would you also do it without the artificial eyelashes. They seemed to dim the luminosity of your eyes." Heff translated, and Madame X, always the gracious star, magnanimously consented. In a twinkling Starr had the lights rearranged and this time—even I could see it—Miss Ximinez looked exactly like what she was, a shrill, silly, vain old frump. Following Starr's nervous gestures, Lopez panned the camera in on the action, getting many a grisly close-up. When it was done, Starr kissed her on both cheeks and said she had been magnificent and that would be all for the day. I saw Mamacita's hairy old mouth working, so I saved her the trouble. "I know. Your daughter big star."

With surprising speed the costumes were put away, the lights and Lopez's camera were stowed in the big blue-tiled storeroom that had been the convent kitchen. The last remaining actors, the wardrobe man, and González's Indians said good night and made for home. Starr, Lopez, González, the long-suffering Heff, and I were all who remained. González, looking pained and petulant, waddled over to Starr, his stomach swaying gently from side to side. "Leandro, Ai lak to tok to you."

"I'd like to talk to you, too, Aristido. Will you begin or shall I?"

"Alone."

"There is nothing you have to say that can't be said in front of Mr. Lopez and Mr. Dennis. Without them I don't know where we would have been today."

Heff began to translate, but Lopez took over in a torrent of furious Spanish. His speech lasted for a good fifteen minutes, and I can't believe that he even paused for breath. When he finished, González was too furious to speak.

"What was that all about?" Starr asked, so impressed by Lopez's eloquence that I thought he might even cast him. "Señor Lopez has said to my father . . ." Heff began. Again Lopez interrupted.

"I told dat fat pig where ta get off at. What da hell, he's s'posed ta be producin' dis flick, and he don't do nothin' but sit on his ass. He calls dat a crew? A sound man? A grip? An' I told him that tammara I want same help on the set—real help—or I'll report him ta the unions." More translation and a horrible torrent from González.

"Well," Lopez said, the wind somewhat taken out of his sails, "I guess I ain't hardly in no position ta report nobody, but I'm not crappin' when I tell ya that this Spic is strickly fum herring. Good luck, Mr. Starr. *Hasta mañana.*" He put on his little Madison Avenue snap-brimmed Homburg and strode off, every inch the young Republican.

With Heff looking sick and ashamed, but still serving as interlocutor, Starr and González had it out. Amazingly calm and patient, Starr pointed out that González had been late, had brought only one can of inferior film, completely inexperienced technical help, and had done nothing but sit. In his own behalf, González said that the first day was always the hardest, that there had been a mix-up when it came to ordering the film and the lights, that some agency had double-crossed him when he had hired the crew, that it would never happen again, that they were devoted brothers, and a few opinions of me that seemed to lose a good deal in translation. There was an *abrazo,* effusive kisses on both cheeks, and González & Son were off, promising to be back with the dawn of tomorrow.

Alone with Starr, I said wearily, "Well, it's a good thing you refused to listen to me and you didn't actually sign anything with González."

"Why do you say that, dear boy?"

"Because now you can dump him. Keep Heff, if you like. He's at least useful. But get rid of that old crook before he . . ."

"My dear Patrick, I couldn't."

"Why the hell not? You saw what he was like today. He's forgotten whatever he once may have known about producing a picture. He brought the worst of everything and did nothing except make trouble. Lopez is dead right. He's an old has-been, a phony, and a crook. And for this you're paying him a thousand bucks a day. Give him a hundred and tell him it's . . ."

"But you see, I can't."

"Why not, please?"

"Because González has the money."

"*Money?* He hasn't got a single centavo. You saw that crumbling pleasure dome he lives in. He *literally* hasn't a pot to . . ."

"He has all of *the* money. The *Valley of the Vultures* backing. I gave it to him last week."

"You *what?*"

"I gave it to him. It was the only sensible thing to do. With all the judgments out against me. With Guber breathing down my neck. If I'd banked it, someone would have found out and attached it or . . ."

"You . . . gave . . . one . . . hundred . . . thousand . . . U. . . . S. . . . dollars . . . to . . . that . . . fat . . ."

"It's customary, my dear," Starr said, flushing slightly. "He's the producer. He's supposed to pay the bills. I know nothing of figures. Besides who else . . ."

"You blathering old fool! You could have given that money to St. Regis, to Emily, to my wife and me, to Bunty or Monica—even to Mr. Guber—and it would have been in safer hands than with that . . . Oh, Starr, I give up. I'm finished."

In my dirty clothes I slammed across the patio to our own apartment and ran headlong into the Warburtons, the proper American couple my wife had invited to dinner. They were wearing evening clothes and warm smiles. "Patrick! You look just like a peon. You bohemians! Well, here we are, better late than . . ."

"Nobody home!" I roared, and slammed the door in their faces.

TUESDAY. *Lydia's b'day. Get children's tickets. Write Trust Co. Call good divorce lawyer. Starr's rushes.*

Tuesday, like Monday, involved only the principals working in Casa Ximinez. My wife, who by then had given up speaking to me, went grimly around the apartment tripping over actors in various states of undress, picking up other people's clothes, and thinking they were mine, hanging them up in closets or sending them to be laundered. One particularly ugly mustard-yellow sport jacket was given outright to Guadalupe, and the young actor who owned it had the devil's own time getting it back.

González turned up almost on time, bringing with him a very few extra pieces of electrical equipment, a man who seemed to know at least the rudiments of lighting and, to handle the sound, a sinister fellow who looked as though he'd made his livelihood tapping telephones. They were something of an improvement, but they still didn't know as much about their trades as Starr or Lopez.

Lopez said grimly, "We're gonna see some rushes tonight," and managed to get rid of González for long periods at a time by sending him off to the processing laboratories in his Mercedes every time a can of film was completed. Heff was kept around as interpreter and general handy man. The only actual trouble González caused was when he reached out and pinched Catalina Ximinez and she indignantly broke her parasol over his head. I'd always suspected that that wasn't *really* a bustle.

During the morning we finished up the rest of the patio shots. After lunch we did Doña Ana-Rosa's agonizing labor in

Starr's big carved walnut bed. Actress and director got into rather a heated argument as to just how a woman felt when she was giving birth, and Lady Joyce won it hands down. Mr. Guber suggested that someone say "Tear up some clean linen sheets and get all the boilingue water you can," a cliché I'd only heard about five hundred times in the movies, but with an authentic sixteenth-century tiled kitchen at our disposal, we squandered a few feet of film on it with Bunty, a steaming caldron, Guadalupe, and Mamacita all racing around in a frenzy. Guadalupe was enchanted to earn fifty pesos as an extra, and it proved to be a turning point in Mamacita's life as she soon learned from Heff to say "Ai . . . beeg . . . star."

Maidless, owing to the prior demands of art, my wife got our living room tidied up and then furiously stood by and watched while we used a corner of it to show depraved Don Pedro trying to seduce a simple Indian maiden.

Mr. Guber generously volunteered his own quarters. With the removal of a serape, a plastic guitar, two sombreros, framed photographs of Shirley, the children, and the Tea-neck J.W.V.'s annual post dinner-dance, it did nicely as Don Fernando's estate office, although Mr. Guber was a trifle offended when we refused to use his portable computing machine as one of the sixteenth-century props.

Emily, still angry and silent, had nothing to do that day but traipse moodily out to the dried-up well, crank up an empty water bucket, and then shake her fist tellingly at the flock of vultures wheeling above. Rehearsals and shooting took her all of ten minutes, and then she was off with Bruce.

As on the preceding day, the most time and trouble were squandered on Madame X. She had a number of costume changes—riding habit, ball gown, negligee, two lavish day-time dresses, and a cloak—which kept her out of everyone's way most of the time, and to the designer's fury, Starr allowed her to junk them all up with gewgaws of her own. As before, he did all of her scenes two ways—once with the eyelashes, the subdued lighting, and the camera keeping its distance; and then a second time with her own eyes, the make-up toned down, realistic lighting, and plenty of weird angles and close-ups. I couldn't imagine how *any* of the footage could be used for anything except frightening children, but Starr was lavish in his praises.

By sundown we'd used up all of the film, done all of the scenes Starr and Lopez had planned, and were still an hour ahead of schedule. "We'll see the rushes in my living room tonight at nine o'clock sharp," Starr said. "Don't be late." To Catalina Ximinez he said, "Querida, you come to my place, ten o'clock," and gave her plump arm a squeeze.

There was quite a crowd of interested spectators gathered in Starr's living room to view the rough rushes that night. Lady Joyce and Bunty had been invited, and even Henry Maitland-Grim seemed quite *compos mentis.* Angry as she was, Emily was too curious to stay away, and Bruce was being all smiles and protectiveness next to her on the sofa. Invited or not, González, with Heff as his mentor, sat furious on a straight chair, his thighs and buttocks overhanging the seat by a good foot on each side. Mrs. Pomeroy, as chief backer and director's inspiration, was very much there. Lopez, looking like a vice president of the Chase Manhattan Bank, was fussing around with a projector and the tape machine. The lights went out. A few false starts at co-ordinating the sound with the action, a couple of unprintable words from Mr. Lopez, and we were off.

I don't truly remember now exactly what I had expected— not much, my wife claims. At any rate, I was surprised and most agreeably so. The shabby old patio photographed as though it had been built yesterday, and a coat of Casa oil on the battered Priddy front door made it gleam like freshly polished walnut. Through Bunty's glissando of giggles we watched the scene involving Doña Ana-Rosa, Don Fernando, and Conchita the maid. Lady Joyce looked about twenty the way Starr had lighted her, and Lopez had caught her best angles. The shoddy costumes photographed like something straight from the court of Spain, and even the hoked-up lines I had provided took on a certain importance and dignity under Starr's direction. The unexpected emergence of Dr. and Miz Priddy during Doña Ana-Rosa's fervent prayer, Starr's outburst, and Lady Joyce's complete breaking up provided such enormous comic relief that Lopez had to halt the showing until everybody finished laughing. After that everything was down-to-earth and businesslike. Even though everything was out of sequence, leaping senselessly from the sixteenth century to the eighteen-eighties to the present, even though everything needed cutting and editing, you could still tell that it was a good picture. St. Regis, on the silver screen at *last,* was suitably sinister and even passably balletic in the role of the vulture. He cooed with pleasure from the rear of the room. Emily's scene with poor old Miss Herrera came as one of those thunderbolts of realism that the artier film critics would be talking about for years. Her pains were rewarded by a spattering of applause led by my wife, who, up until now, couldn't have been more anti-*Valley of the Vultures.*

But the greatest scenes of all—and here there had been some quick cutting and splicing—were those involving Catalina Ximinez as the vicious, empty-headed Doña Isabel. Just for one more laugh, we were treated to her initial dive off her own doorstep, which sent everyone—even Emily—into such gales of laughter that Lopez had to run it again. Then we all settled out and watched the Starr version, as against the Ximinez version, of Doña Isabel. She was terrifying. In Starr's harsh lighting, with the ridiculous eyelashes off, the garish make-up toned down to just that point where she looked like a woman of the eighties who had dipped too deep into the rouge pot, I could see immediately that Starr had been right to let her overdress. She looked old and mean and stupid and cruel—but these natural qualities were intensified by the camera, the lighting, and the direction. Her performance was electrifying, the close-ups were especially eerie. Spellbound, we watched the scene with her husband and the overseer, with which she had made her cinematic comeback the day before, as well as three of the scenes she had made earlier in the day. When it was finished, there was a moment of total silence and then a loud round of applause.

"Jeest," Lopez said, "if dat broad don't watch it she'll cop an Oscar."

"Ooooooo," Bunty said with a convulsive little shudder.

"It's unbelievable," Lady Joyce said. "Simply uncanny. She seemed so commonplace, so sort of stupid and bovine. And yet when she's in front of the camera . . ." Even the sullen González sat up and took notice.

"Now remember, everyone," Starr said. "This is not exactly Catalina's conception of the role. She'll be here very shortly, and the rushes that she will see are entirely different from these."

As an encore, Lopez ran off some old film clips that he'd found. One of them depicted a lot of gentry racing through the verdant countryside in Victorias. The actual locale was Sussex or Surry, but it was filmed from such a distance that no one would know the difference. He'd also picked up some old footage of cattle grazing, a Spanish colonial village (Santa Fé, if the truth were known, which it wouldn't be), lush fields of waving grain, and some other odds and ends that would add a great deal of grandeur, scope, and authenticity to the picture without costing anything. Just as we were viewing a lot of aristocrats waltzing beneath a mammoth crystal chandelier—ideal for the General's ball on the eve of the uprising—there came a discreet scratching at Starr's door. "This will be Miss Ximinez," Starr said. "Just don't get your cans of film mixed up, Lopez."

Madame X swept in as though she might have been one of the old Hollwood's several Marquises de la Falaise de Coudray. Under what used to be called a silver-fox "chubby," she wore a yellowing white-satin evening dress of the early

Carole Lombard period. Her gilded hair, finally released from its moorings, was severely parted, exposing the salt and pepper roots, completely covering one eye in the manner of Veronica Lake, and hanging in uneven scallops to her shoulders. Mamacita followed, prouder than Mrs. Temple, Mrs. Coogan, Mrs. Lyon ever could have been of their get. The ladies shed their pelts, acknowledged the enthusiastic applause, and sat down to watch the rushes. In the dim light reflected from the screen I watched Madame X's face—the expression of weary patience, the polite boredom, the slight sneer at Lady Joyce's performance, the screeching laughter at the unscheduled appearance of Dr. and Miz Priddy. They were the same old rushes, all right, until we got to the Ximinez scenes. Then Lopez snapped on the lights, quickly switched film cans, and reloaded the projector. What came on next was too horrendous to be believed. In the hazy, soft-focus light the men looked fragile and effeminate, like Meissen figurines. Owing to something Starr had done with the sound, even their voices had become slurring and syrupy. But the laugh riot of all time was Madame X, photographed always from a distance, and always at whatever angle could be considered her best; she made me think of nothing so much as the late Julian Eltinge playing in *The College Widow* or perhaps St. Regis doing *Charley's Aunt* (one of his great triumphs at Alhambra High). I could barely control myself. Bunty couldn't. She choked into her handkerchief, struggled to her feet, and fled up the stairs, knocking over a drink en route. Even the poised Bruce van Damm had a hard time keeping a straight face. But Señorita Ximinez and Mamacita were in raptures. Madame X leaned forward in ecstasy, enthralled by every flutter of the antennae of her eyelashes, whispering *"Bella! Hermosa! Guapa! Dulce!"* at every fatuous gesture, every toned-down squawk of her cockatoo voice. It seemed incredible that anyone could be quite so self-delusive when the ghastly truth was projected on a screen not ten feet away, but Madame X managed. I had managed to keep a hold on myself fairly well until the last of Doña Isabel's scenes, when she did a trick with the eyelashes over and through the plumes of a dusty feather fan that left me helpless. I joined Bunty upstairs. When we were able to return, Madame X, lanquidly dragging her furs on the floor behind her, was doing her big exit. "Tonk you, Señor Starrr. Ai mus go 'ome an' slip for tomorrow." Mamacita proudly jerked a thumb toward Catalina. "Mai . . . dotter!" The door closed behind them.

"Ecktualleh, I liked her better the second time," Henry Maitland-Grim said.

WEDNESDAY. *Ball scene. Chignon. Children's tourist cards. Eye make-up? Starr—rushes.*

Wednesday marked the last day of shooting at Casa Ximinez, the first day with enough extras to constitute a mob scene, and *my* debut as a movie actor. The problem of extras, which Starr had confidently placed in the pudgy hands of Aristido González, was a very simple one. Only three kinds were needed: happy, well-fed farmhands for the big feast of thanksgiving that Doña Ana-Rosa was graciously throwing at the close of the first episode; starving, rebellious ones to burn down the tottering empire of Doña Isabel; and rich, haughty haciendado types to cavort decadently at the General's ball. I can only believe that González chose them from a local home for the feeble-minded. A more unprepossessing lot I have never seen. Starr fired half of them on first sight; the remaining ones, given to scratching themselves in unmentionable places while supposedly drinking toasts to the mistress of the manor or storming the hacienda or sipping champagne in marble halls, were just as expendable. Lopez really blew up this time and literally chased González out of the patio. I was again amazed at how fast the man could move, for all his excess weight, when he really had to.

"So we waste da whole day callin' up S.T.P.C.?" Lopez asked darkly.

"Certainly not," Starr said furiously. "We've got enough

235

people right here—plus the cretins González brought. Dennis! Guber! take off your clothes!" Within half an hour, he had rounded up enough people within the four walls of Casa Ximinez to make a pretty fair showing. Not only were all of the servants and their children and relatives rounded up, but so were the tenants. Mr. Guber was in seventh heaven. Given an opportunity not only to appear on the screen but to wear some of her more recherché souvenirs, Miz Priddy soon got over her indignation and fell right in with Starr's plans. The Doctor played hookey that day and, scrawny as he was, looked quite convincing under a layer of body paint. A honeymooning couple from Midland, Texas, of whom nothing had been seen or even heard, except for a steady succession of slaps and squeals, postponed whatever it was they were planning for *that* day and entered into the spirit of things with the sort of terrifying enthusiasm that, I suppose, made Texas what it is today. Bunty placed an emergency call to her house, and before long Henry Maitland-Grim came stumping in on his wooden leg, a splendid Savile Row tailcoat over one arm, followed by his household staff. Heff volunteered to serve, but explained that he couldn't see a foot in front of his nose without his spectacles. Starr said that that was perfectly all right and if Heff fell down a lot that would only add to the realism. Miz Priddy whistled up her singing and dancing urchins. Clarice summoned all the servants from Casa Ortiz-Robledo and even consented to *walk* all the way home, put on her major jewels, and appear as a dress extra in the ball scene, although she didn't feel that she'd be right as a peasant. St. Regis was eagerness itself to play *any* role, but Starr firmly clapped the stifling vulture mask over his head and told him that he was too valuable as a bird. By nine o'clock that morning Starr had Emiliano Zapata's guerrilla army on his hands. He jumped up to the top of a table, whistled for silence, and, through Heff, announced that he was very grateful to them all and that the producer, Señor González, would pay every man jack of us fifty pesos for the day's work. Loud cheers. The wardrobe man passed out our prosperous, sixteenth-century clean rags and tatters—just shirts and kerchiefs; trousers didn't matter as most of us had our legs under the thanksgiving table. As a matter of fact, I played the whole harvest-festival scene in bathing trunks, sitting next to Mr. Guber who was still in his pajama bottoms. For authenticity—and a Starr touch that recalled his devil-may-care days of the thirties— Starr sent around to the local grog shop for several gallons of tequila, as well as Coca-Cola for the kids, who philosophically spiked it with the grownups' tequila. It was quite a bacchanal for ten in the morning, but as far as authenticity went, it was the most festive festival ever filmed. Starr urged us to make a lot of noise, as though that were necessary, and spent a lot of time on close-ups of men swigging tequila, people licking their fingers, interesting facial planes, the *vigilante* relieving himself against the jacaranda tree, which, I feel sure, will never bloom again, and of Guadalupe's cousin, the lottery-ticket salesman, passing out into a bowl of beans. Then we were all told to shut up in no uncertain terms while Lady Joyce, looking beatific in the widow's weeds of Doña Ana-Rosa, made her final speech about the glories of the land, and St. Regis, as the vulture, slunk up and symbolically enveloped the whole table.

Starr was besieged with requests for information as to exactly when *Valley of the Vultures* would be playing at the Variedades theater. Tonight? Tomorrow? The day after? What famous stars would be in it? Silvia Suarez? Maricruz Olivier? Francisco Rabal? Cristina Rojas? Manolo Fabregas?

Over the noise of the revelry, the squabbling, the impromptu singings, and the half dozen or so transistor radios, Starr culled out the kids, the ones who were too well fed or too drunk, and explained to the rest of the extras that the time was now only eighty years ago, that they were all poor and starving, that they all hated Catalina Ximinez who was rich and mean—here a great cheer went up—and that they were out to get her and to burn her house down. If he wanted realism he couldn't have chosen his words better. In impoverished, nineteenth-century dirty rags and tatters, which looked exactly like the sixteenth-century ones, the mob played the scene so convincingly that I was almost afraid that Madame X's head would end up on a pike. They stormed her elaborate front doors with such gusto that the hinges gave and the doors fell flat inside the Ximinez hallway, carrying with them a load of two dozen men kicking and thrashing. "Magnificent!" Starr shouted.

I thought that Madame X would feel differently, but I was wrong. After her triumph of the night before, she would have let them sack the whole house. "Don't motter. Very old. Ai get *beeg* place nax year."

True to his word, Heff had fallen down and been slightly trampled. Mr. Guber had suffered a mild black eye, and there were a few minor cuts, abrasions, and contusions to be treated by the Farmacía Corazón de Jesús, which had doubled its volume of business in the last three days.

After lunch we all got into musty old rented costumes that must have been salvaged from a stranded road company of *Dame aux Camellias* during the exact period of Doña Isabel's reign of terror. I looked and felt like a damned fool in a ruffled evening shirt and a moth-eaten old tailcoat that was green with age. My wife did somewhat better in rotting plum silk. Not much could be done with Miz Priddy, but she was passable in black satin with a mantilla—her very own "and authintic?"—covering most of her face. The Doctor drew an evening suit that was big enough for two of him, but sitting down with a lot of pins up the back it didn't matter much. The Texas honeymooners looked handsome, and Henry Maitland-Grim was very splendid in his own duds, once his British decorations had been forcibly removed. Lady Joyce and Bunty were permitted to be in the scene as long as they kept their backs to the camera so as not to be recognized. So was Emily. Bruce, oddly enough, flatly refused to appear, which struck me as strange in such a poised, co-operative young man who was trying to court favor with Starr. The old *vigilante,* Guadalupe's alcoholic son, the lottery-ticket salesman, and a couple of the Maitland-Grim servants were judged sober enough and distinguished-looking enough to appear—well in the background—as frivolous gentry at play. Mr. Guber was not. Clarice shouldn't have been, but as she was wearing half a million dollars' worth of diamonds, one could hardly rule her out. Knowing what Starr had done to Madame X in her scenes, I shuddered to think how Clarice would come out or, for that matter, how *I* would.

All we had to do was stand around Madame X's grand drawing room sipping ginger ale from plastic champagne glasses and looking lofty as all get-out at the General's gala ball, while lovely Catalina Ximinez drifted through, flapping her fan, on the arm of Henry Maitland-Grim who, wooden leg and all, had won the Man of Distinction contest hands down. By this time Madame X was so entranced with her own image that she had taken to "improving" her part no end, and the results were devastating, what with trills and winks and wrinklings of the nose and wrigglings of the shoulders and switchings of the hips. But since we were supposed to be at a party, laughter was permissible, although some say that Bunty went *too* far. Three takes—one in which Our Star tripped over Henry's wooden leg, one done the Ximinez way, and a final one done the Starr way—and we were finished for the day.

"Four o'clock and already done," I said to Starr as I removed the period wig he insisted on my wearing. "Come on to our place and have a drink. You've earned it."

"Thanks, dear boy, but I can't. Heff has to rush these takes off for processing, and then I have to spend the rest of the afternoon doing shots of Catalina."

"What shots? She's done everything she has to except two or three small bits out on location."

"This is just to keep her happy. Nothing we'll use. But as long as she thinks that she's the star of this picture . . ."

"Leander," I said, "did it ever occur to you that what you're doing to poor old Madame X isn't exactly honest?"

"Many times, *carissimo;* I toss and pitch every night. But she is great—when she does it *my* way."

"Starr, when this picture's released, she'll be in a frenzy. She'll kill you. Here she thinks she's the most beautiful thing since Madeleine Carroll and . . ."

"My dear child, you are talking to a man who may not know much but one who knows actresses backward and forward. When this picture is released and she gets someone to read her notices to her—and Lopez is right, she just *might* get an Academy Award as best supporting actress—she won't care if we shot her with x-ray film. By then she'll think the whole thing was her idea."

Madame X appeared in a peach maribou negligee, hair piled high, a box of Ivory Flakes under one arm. "Ai om raddy."

"Ah, yes, *querida. Now* for that exquisite scene in the bubble bath."

From the rushes shown that night—first just for Starr, Emily, my wife and me and, as before, a special late show for Madame X and Mamacita—I realized that my future was not as an actor. Perhaps Bruce had been wise to stay out of the picture. It always embarrasses me to see people I know performing unless they are very, very good. Dr. and Miz Priddy, Mr. Guber, Henry Maitland-Grim, my wife and I were not. Mrs. Pomeroy, as the Marie Antoinette of Guerrero province, came off more like Peggy Hopkins Joyce. Then I realized that that was exactly what Starr had intended—but it hardly seemed the way to begin a marriage made in heaven. Indeed, it struck me as a foolproof way to end an engagement, and maybe that's what he intended, too. But whether I was embarrassed, whether Starr was married or single, engaged or jilted, the rushes were great. Leander had the knack of making you think that you weren't seeing black and white and gray people projected on a screen but that you were really there. Even knowing exactly who and what and how, I found the scenes of the day so thrilling that for a weird moment I almost felt that we were seeing real life.

THURSDAY. *Location. Lunch basket. Gin. Cigarettes. Sun lotion. Take book. Starr—rushes.*

As I said before, the main advantages of using the Carretera del Desierto de los Leones were that it was nearby and encompassed every kind of scenery we would need to portray three centuries of rise, decline, and fall. To get there one bowls out the Insurgentes, past the Estudios San Angel on the Antiguo Camino de Acapulco; there one hits the Carretera, which leads past a variety of countryside—deep ravines and a miserable settlement of squatters who have no water; thus the highway is lined with tin containers, each marked with the name, number, or sign of the owner, waiting to be filled each day by the Departmento Central. If that wasn't grim enough for Starr, I didn't know what would be. The road goes on and gradually passes through fine trees and flossy houses, past the Colegio Militar, and eventually through fine forest to a convent that is erroneously named Desierto de los Leones.

Early in the morning we left Casa Ximinez in a most exotic sort of convoy. González led off in the Mercedes-Benz lolling voluptuously in the back while Heff drove. Starr followed with Mrs. Pomeroy, the omnipresent Mr. Guber, and several bottles of champagne in the lavender Cadillac. Next came Bruce's Continental, Emily in the front, St. Regis in his vulture costume, my wife, and I in the rear. We were followed by the Maitland-Grim Rolls; then Our Star with Mamacita and Guadalupe, doubling as lady's maid, in the Hispano-Suiza; Lopez and the sound man with all of their equipment in a Volkswagen bus; a Fiat truck piled high with stagehands, lights, reflectors, costume trunks, props, and two tents for dressing; a three-wheeled Isetta, containing the wardrobe man and his languid assistant; and finally an old Fifth Avenue double-decker bus, overflowing with extras from Casa Ximinez and, on the upper deck, Miz Priddy and her band of children in gaudy native costume. One almost longed to see a plain old Ford or Chevrolet, and from the array of bottles, hampers, and suntan lotions, the whole procession had more the air of a very eccentric picnic than grim business.

For the location work, Starr had economically decided to start working at the middle of the picture, when the oppressed peonage rises against the indifferent landlords and burns down the hacienda (the actual conflagration to be accomplished by destroying a small cardboard model) and mean Doña Isabel, on her knees in the ashes, swears vengeance. In this way Madame X, the more expensive actors, and most of the extras could be dispensed with first, saving a lot of trouble and money.

In his reconnoitering, Mr. Lopez had found a burnt-out structure of indeterminate original purpose and vintage standing out in the middle of a barren wilderness. A corner of it would do splendidly for Madame X's final spiel and for some starving farmhands to be seen scavenging around. A grimmer site could hardly have existed even in the real Valley of the Vultures.

A few of the principals had arrived before the convoy, and, in the heat of the sun, had already removed as many clothes as the law would allow.

"How do you like it?" I asked Starr.

"My dear boy, if Mexico needed an enema, here is where they'd plug it in. Now, be a pearl and try to get everyone organized."

It was easier said than done. Miz Priddy's urchins had gone suddenly wild, chasing lizards and each other all over the landscape. The women's dressing tent suddenly collapsed, leaving a thrashing, throbbing lump of something under its many folds and some muffled curses in Spanish. It was Catalina Ximinez who emerged disheveled and begrimed and furious. It was also an unexpected stroke of luck; Madame X had originally planned to go through fire, sacking, and looting, and still end up in spotless white. As it turned out, she did the first take *her* way and for the second —or Starr—take, a sudden fitful breeze came up, covering her with more dust and ashes than the city of Pompeii.

We finished at five o'clock, and those extras who had completed their work were clamoring to be paid. By a strange coincidence, Mexico's Number-one Producer, Aristido González, had been called back to town on a mission of the utmost urgency, and all that the extras saw of him was the roll of fat over his collar through the rear window of the Mercedes-Benz as it sped back to Mexico City. Starr assured them all that they would be paid, and, more or less satisfied, everyone called it a day.

FRIDAY. *Location. More suntan lotion. Cucumber sandwiches? Extra Thermos. Rushes.*

A considerably diminished company. Emily was being used, along with Felipe, the young Indian who played her sweetheart. That meant that we would have Bruce's company, as well as Clarice's. Neither of them seemed willing to allow the object of his or her affection out of arm's reach for very long. Lady Joyce and Bunty had short scenes. Catalina Ximinez had been given the day off and had accepted Henry Maitland-Grim's invitation to spend it in and around his swimming pool. The Gonzálezes, father and son, were also on hand. All of us had grown fonder and fonder of Heff as we had become less fond of Aristido. He and Starr were barely speaking. He and I were not. Lopez used him only to scream at and to blame whenever anything went wrong. That day he made the fatal error of pinching Bunty, Emily, and Lady Joyce within the space of five minutes and incurring everybody's fury—even Starr's. It was hot and dusty and we were all in vile moods.

We were down to half a dozen extras, all recruited from

Guadalupe's family of full-time eaters. As the *vigilante* worked all night, he was perfectly content to sleep most of the day on location and collect his fifty pesos. The lottery-ticket salesman, whose cadaverous face had made him invaluable to Starr, was less willing.

"Señor," he said, "ees necessary for Ai to work." (It was the first I had heard of it.) "Three days now Ai do only the *cine* but no sell lottery tickets. Ees not possible do peecture more an' no sell lotería."

"Damn it!" Starr snarled. "Tell him he's making more by being an extra than he ever did selling lottery tickets. Everybody in Mexico who doesn't sell silver jewelry sells lottery tickets."

"Yes, but he hasn't been paid," I said.

"Tell him I like his face, and we'll give him double—a hundred pesos—for one more day's work."

I told him. "He wants the hundred pesos, but he also wants to sell tickets for the Monday lottery. It's for two million pesos."

"Oh, all right. I'll buy a ticket. How much?"

"Ten pesos."

"How much is that?"

"Eighty cents."

"Sold. Now tell him to take off his shoes and look miserable."

"He wants to sell a whole *cachito*."

"What's that, his sister?"

"No. He wants to sell a whole block of tickets—twenty of them. He says if you buy twenty, you can win the whole two million."

"He's nothing but a blackmailer. That's—let me see—fifteen or sixteen American dollars. He's holding us up. If I hadn't started using him in Emily's scene yesterday, I'd kick him out of the whole picture. He's got us over a barrel and he knows it."

"I really don't think he's quite that cagey or quite that

hep when it comes to film making. He just wants to get on with his regular work—as do I."

"Is there *no* gratitude to be found in this benighted land? Very well. Tell him I'll take all twenty. They're probably counterfeit at that."

The lottery-ticket saleman burst into great smiles, exposing the rotting teeth that Starr found so photogenic. "*Gracias, Señor. Doscientos pesos.* You pay now pliz."

"Can't the idiot see that this suit has no pockets?" Starr exploded. True, he was wearing a bikini and a lot of suntan lotion and had become the color of mahogany. "Dennis, be a dear and give him the money. Here, St. Regis, take these useless tickets and *don't* use them to pad your dance belt. Places everyone!"

The day did not go well. A terrible duststorm blew up, which was photographically satisfying to Starr and Lopez but put everyone else into even viler tempers. Old Miss Herrera suffered a touch of the sun and had to be taken home—after her last scene, fortunately—in the air-conditioned Cadillac, moaning deliriously. Clarice was so cloying and so omnipresent that I thought that Starr was going to belt her. And Bruce, in his self-appointed role as peacemaker, got in between Starr and Mrs. Pomeroy with all the charm and tact of a rather dimwitted nursery governess trying to keep peace between two naughty precocious children. So Starr turned on Bruce, and then Emily turned on Starr. Lady Joyce, who had been saintly up to then, sided with Starr, while Bunty took up the cudgels for Bruce. St. Regis got into a fearful quarrel with the wardrobe man's lissome assistant and later suffered a heat stroke in his vulture suit. The *vigilante* and the lottery-ticket salesman took drunk at the luncheon break. Lopez and González got into their most heated quarrel, which was interrupted only by the arrival of two very tough-looking specimens who claimed to represent some sort of Mexican film-making union. The questions they asked embarrassed González no end. Naturally I couldn't follow the conversation, but Lopez could. It ended—or was at least postponed—with González reaching into his pocket and handing each of them a wad of banknotes, which marked the first time I had ever seen him pay out money to anyone. They went away, but not with what you'd call smiles of joy on their faces. Then Lopez blew up. "I knew it! I knew it! Dat fat crook ain't done a t'ing. Not one mudder-lovin' t'ing about unions or nutt'n' else. He ain't fixed nobody, ain't made no arrangements. Dis is a scab show an' yer never gonna get it past da Dirección-General de Cinematografía. T'ousands of dollars an' hours wasted wid dat crook." Then he let fly at González in Spanish and eventually had to be physically restrained by Bruce and me from flying at that fat throat.

Somehow we got through the day. But seeing the rushes in Starr's cool living room that night cheered everyone up. Showers, dinner, and drinks had helped, of course; even so, any fool could see that it was going to be an excellent picture.

SATURDAY. *Location. How long, oh Lord, how long?*

On Saturday the shooting all took place at the edge of a majestic forest filled with shade trees and twittering birds; there were green rolling fields, a babbling brook, and gentle zephyrs. Only our three leading ladies and a dozen actors were needed. There was a holiday air to the whole thing. The only mishap of the morning was when the mike fell from its boom, clunking Catalina Ximinez squarely on the head, but even she claimed to be amused by having been knocked senseless. St. Regis and the costume assistant made up their differences of the day before, and arranged to meet at the Hombre Alegre Bar at ten that evening. Over lunch he confessed that he had perhaps been too influenced by the elegant names of such performers as Carlyle Blackwell, Colin Clive, Clive Brook, Elliott Dexter, and C. Butler Clonebaugh when he had selected his pseudonym. In fact, he confided, he had chosen Alister because it was so close to Albert, and St. Regis because Starr had been staying in the St. Regis Hotel (still unpaid, I feel sure) when he delivered a bouquet of flowers to the first Mrs. Starr and had never quite got around to leaving. "The ee-nitials was the same as Albert Schmackpfeffer, which was convenient for my monnygrams. And there was such an air of ellygunce about that lovely place. But now with all these new stars, Rock Hudson, Rip Torn, Tab Hunter, and now that I'm reely in a picture, maybe I should try something more up-to-date." He went into fits of giggles as names such as Tack Hammer, Shad Roe, and Ruff Trade were volunteered. Catalina Ximinez even offered to give Lady Joyce some of her make-up hints. That's the kind of congenial day it was.

I dozed off under a tree during the afternoon's shooting, as they weren't doing much but taking long shots of people flitting through trees or racing across meadows into each other's arms. At four o'clock I was awakened by Starr's shouting, "That's it. We're all done. Take off your duds and go home, kiddies. I said ten days, and we've made it in *six*, thanks to a troupe of real, old-fashioned pros. There's nothing to do now but some atmosphere shots, which Mr. Lopez and I can do alone. We can't even use our vulture, Rock Bottom, né Albert Schmackpfeffer, for those." St. Regis went off into gales of laughter. "I wish I could give you all a big party—booze and cold cuts and a combo and all the traditional studio fixings. I can't. But I can say . . ."

"Oh, but *I* can give a party, Leander," Clarice cooed. "You and I can give it together. My house, the Casa Ortiz-Robledo tomorrow night—say at ten?" There was general applause.

"Well, ladies and gentlemen, you heard what Mrs. Pomeroy said. Tomorrow night at ten. You'll get your party *and* your salaries. Until then, thank you and God bless you."

"Jeest," Mr. Lopez said with tears in his eyes. "Dat Starr. What a guy. Six mudder-lovin' days an' he's shot the whole picture. What a genius!"

XIII

On the seventh day He rested. I did not. Having been threatened with everything from expulsion from the Authors' League to the Malay boot by my agent if I didn't turn in the cute story about Salli, Mr. Right, and the broccoli, I finished every last adorable word of it and then read it aloud over the telephone to the pitiable woman in New York who types my manuscripts while she took it all down on her machine. "But I've got people coming for dinner," she kept saying. "But I *can't* take it to your agent tomorrow, I promised to . . . 'Gloriosky?' What kind of word is that? I'd have said . . . Sally with an 'i' instead of a 'y'? You're kidding!" The telephone bill will probably come to more than the thousands of dollars that sterling household magazine pays for good clean trash like the saga of Salli, but still it was finished. And so was Starr's movie! My obligations, moral and otherwise, were paid up. I could start the novel I had tentatively promised my publisher for a year hence, I could drive Thos. Cook & Son mad by making and remaking plans for dragging our children through Switzerland in the summer. We could start accepting invitations—and even tender a few ourselves as long as we, and not Guadalupe, did the cooking. But after having appeared in a genuine movie, Guadalupe was too far above cooking even to turn out the usual daily barrels of rice and beans for her family. We could hire a car and take a short jaunt somewhere or we could just sit and loaf. At the moment I was in favor of nothing quite so much as a long nap.

"I'm for the sack," I said to my wife. "How about you?"

"As soon as I finish writing the children to remind them not to bring skates and skis and things like that when they come for Easter. I'd also like to get the grit of Desierto de los Leones out of my scalp. After that I'd be delighted." She turned on the tub at its mightiest trickle and went back to banging the typewriter.

I climbed up to our bedroom and observed the patio in its Sunday quietude. It was all but deserted. Earlier in the day Starr, Lopez, and, of course, Mr. Guber had gone into the hinterlands to get a few of the atmospheric shots Starr was so famous for—wheeling vultures, dozing lizards, scaly plaster walls, interesting clouds, and so on to add to Lopez's hoard of film clips. Dr. and Miz Priddy had driven some miles to attend some banal native jam session. St. Regis and his new friend, the wardrobe assistant, had set off on some sort of sentimental journey. The Texas honeymooners had finally got themselves unpried long enough to motor into town for lunch. Two overworked girls from the Vog Salón de Belleza had come to prepare Our Star *and* Mamacita for the Pomeroy shindig. Bruce's car was parked out in front, glistening in the sunlight, and I supposed that he and Emily, looking like clean-cut American youth, would be off on some athletic mission. Well, let them all do whatever they wanted. I needed a nap.

I took off my clothes, glanced at myself fore, aft, and side-ways in the mirror, and shuddered. Although life with Leander Starr could never ever be described as "soft living," the weeks spent almost exclusively in his society had left their mark—a slight bulge in front, two in back. I picked up a copy of *Look Better, Feel Better* and read the inscription, "This ought to put even *you* back in shape—Stuart." Looking through the sketches of some tragically incomplete men drawing themselves up from knee to groin, navel to neck, coccyx to nape, I thought how nice it would be to look that trim once again, contemplated running through a series of

Mensendieck exercises, then said, "To hell with it," and flopped down on the top of the bed.

I have no idea how long or how deeply I slept, but I dimly remember dreaming of Miz Priddy multiplied by a dozen, all saying, "Isn't it quaint . . . Isn't it sweet . . . Absolutely authentic, my dear . . . Just think, four hundred years old . . . Not just ordinary Catholics but the daughters of the finest . . ." There was a sharp scream. I opened my eyes and saw a gaggle of middle-aged women of the sort once caricatured by the late Helen E. Hokinson standing in the bedroom doorway, staring aghast at my nakedness.

"Well, I never!" one of them, presumably the leader, gasped.

"Well, neither have I," I said. "Just what the hell do you think you're doing in my bedroom?" As my robe was across the room, I felt that the better part of *savoir faire* would be to pull in my stomach and play it straight.

"We are Las Damas de San Angel."

"You're what?"

"Las Damas de San Angel and we *arranged* this house tour with Señorita Ximinez months ago."

"Oh. In that case, don't let me get in your way. But would you mind tossing me that dressing gown? I don't feel that I'm properly dressed for the occasion."

"Come, ladies," the leader sniffed. Flower hats bobbing indignantly, they marched down the stairs in their sensible shoes and stormed out of our apartment, slamming the door so hard that a picture fell off the wall.

In a moment my wife was upstairs, wrapped in a towel, hair hanging in long, wet strands. "What in the name of the Lord was that? They came barging right into the bathroom and I got soap in my eye and . . ."

"Those were Las Damas de San Angel—whatever that may be."

"Oh, yes. They're those frightful old American clubwomen who tour historic houses. Mother corresponds with one."

"Well, I think your mother may well be writing her in care of some historic house of correction if they just pop into people's bedrooms uninvited, unannounced, unwanted."

"Well, Madame X certainly didn't say anything about their coming to *me*. If she had, I'd have tidied up a bit and certainly not have been in . . ." She was interrupted by an ear-splitting scream and a babble of high-pitched American voices. I raced to the window just in time to see a perfect stampede of pastel suits and flower hats pouring out of Starr's apartment. *"Well,"* the leader said, "this is the *last* time we *ever* visit Casa Ximinez! The two of them there blatant as you please. *Come,* ladies!" Twitching with indignation, they stomped out of the patio.

Too undone, as well as too curious, to go back to bed, I stood there watching through the blinds. In a couple of minutes Bruce stamped out of Starr's place looking angry, frustrated, thoroughly shaken, and none too well kempt. He stormed out to his big car, slammed the door shut behind him, and drove off in a cloud of dust, scattering children, dogs, cats, and chickens in his wake.

"What are you looking at?" my wife asked, busily toweling her hair.

"Nothing. Just local color."

Clarice's party for the cast and crew of *Valley of the Vultures* was a full-scale affair. She had democratically desisted from inviting any of the Mexican stagehands or extras—"They'd feel so self-conscious and out of place here, sweetie, that I thought it kinder not to ask them at all"—but had augmented the small array of stars and principals with her own list of flamboyant nobodies. She had now had plenty of time to wreck the elegant Casa Ortiz-Robledo with plenty of highly personalized touches, such as a full-length portrait of herself in brocade and diamonds, lots of photographs of herself in the company of Grade C notables, and a tall stack of enormous morocco-bound scrapbooks containing full coverage of her brilliant social career—her name, underlined in red, listed as having taken tables at charity balls and public banquets, canned press releases announcing that Mrs. Worthington Pomeroy had arrived at dozens of publicity-minded hotels for a short visit, commercial photographs of herself and other overdressed people leering at the camera from night-club tables. The archives of her meteoric rise all formed a fairly depressing picture of just how far one can go on money and money alone.

The garden was a blaze of light and gave the immediate impression that Clarice had read, clipped, and heeded every article ever printed on "Clever Things to Do with Your Terrace." There were fairy lamps strung in the trees, votive lamps surrounding the pool, hurricane lamps on every table, Hanukkah lamps on each step, lily-pad candles floating in the illuminated swimming pool, kerosene torches stabbed into the earth, *luminarias*, a spotlight with changing colors playing on a statue of the Virgin of Guadalupe, and, for good measure, some Japanese lanterns. A mariachi band played incessantly, and there were two bars and the long buffet piled high with food.

Clarice herself outdid all the party decorations in a tight lace sheath designed by someone who truly must have hated her. She was very much Miss Show Biz that night and stunned her chums with lots of inside movie-making terms whether used correctly or not. One could see that it wouldn't be long before Mrs. Goldwyn, Mrs. Warner, and Mrs. Zanuck would be asked—or told—to move over.

Starr arrived with Lopez, looking flushed and triumphant. "Well, dear boy," he said, "we did it. We did it all today. Lopez motored me out to a dried-out lake bottom on the way to Teaco or Texcoco or some such appalling spot, filled with garbage and squatters and vultures—swarms of them. We also got a few feet of a beautiful sandstorm. . . ."

"That sounds terribly pretty," I said. "You didn't, perhaps, shoot a cholera epidemic or a few people dying of bubonic plague?"

"No, but we did get some divine rats. Fastest picture I've ever done. All I have to do now is edit, add some suitable background music, and the whole thing's done. Not a holiday treat for the Radio City Music Hall, perhaps, but a relentlessly depressing little gem that will have the art-house syndicates on their ears. Ah, good evening, Clarice, my dear."

"Yer late," she said. "I thought I told you to . . ."

"My dear girl, I was out with Lopez finishing the picture."

"Then it's *done?*" she asked. I didn't like the look in her eye as she said it. I could almost hear the wheels turning under her platinum-blond gamine wig.

"Uh, well, uh, yes, in a manner of speaking—all except for the final cutting and editing. By the way, has anyone seen Mr. González, our producer?"

No one had. Heff was on hand, and he seemed a trifle vague about the whereabouts of his father. "My father took the motorcar and drove to the laboratories"—he pronounced it la-*bore*-a-trees in his best British fashion—"early this afternoon. He said he might be late for the party but . . ."

"What da hell?" Lopez said. "On a Sunday? The lab ain't open."

"I believe that my father made a special arrangement. I don't know the details. He simply told me to take the omnibus to Mrs. Pomeroy's party and that he would arrive later."

"Beats me," Lopez said.

"He may simply be getting them to speed up the work," Starr said.

"It's done—except what we shot today."

"Well, I'm sure he'll arrive. I do hope so. He's got the checks for the actors."

The Maitland-Grim household swept in looking as though they were about to attend the Queen's birthday gala. Naturally, Clarice lost no time in lionizing them with her pals. "May I present my dear old friends, Lady Joyce and Major and Mrs. Maitland-Grim." Twenty minutes of the most desultory conversation seemed to comprise a lifelong bond as far as Mrs. Pomeroy was concerned. She called Lady Joyce

Lady Monica quite incorrectly, pointed out Henry Maitland-Grim's connections to two or three earldoms and a marquisate, which embarrassed him into complete speechlessness, and spoke of Bunty's mad, mad parties—to none of which she had ever been invited—as though she had personally stamped the invitations and helped to set the table. One could see plainly that Mrs. Pomeroy wasted no time in taking full possession of anything or anyone that caught her fancy.

With Emily she was insufferable and almost the stage mother, referring to her as "my little girl" and "my little deb." Emily was looking fairly grim, and I noticed that Bruce never left her side.

Catalina Ximinez and Mamacita had spared no efforts in preparing for Clarice's party. Lacquered, enameled and corseted, Madame X had crammed herself into a siren's dress of chartreuse that made her rather sallow skin look as though she had been left underwater for several months. Even Mamacita had been treated to a pair of old golden slippers, a jet capelet, and a cluster of artificial corkscrew bangs insecurely pinned to her sparse hair. About the only person who could keep a poker face in their company was Henry Maitland-Grim, but then his many years in some regiment or other had given him better training than most of us had.

Dr. and Miz Priddy arrived, he in a greenish old black-alpaca suit with a tinkling festoon of Phi Beta Kappa keys and other honorary baubles of higher education hanging from his watch chain like shrunken heads. Miz Priddy had fashioned herself a most original evening costume from the spoils of her travels. Reading from north to south, she sported a tortoise-shell comb (Seville), coral earrings (Venice), seed pearls (Yokohama), a yellowing lace blouse (Brussels), a smallish sari (Bombay) worn hooked over her elbows as a stole, some gold filigree bracelets (Istanbul), a length of multicolored brocade (Damascus) wound around her as a skirt, a scarab pin (Cairo) to keep the skirt together, and some Enna Jettick sandals (Chattanooga) dyed almost to match the skirt. She was perfectly willing, whether admired or not, to tell you exactly when, where, and how she had acquired each object. "The Doctor and Ah were in Turkey in 1946? While he had a fellahship at the Amerikin University? Well, Ah wint inta the Bizarre with all those twistin' corridahs and Ah saw this old Moslem womin sellin' filigree?" Dr. Priddy contented himself with quotes from Byron ("On with the dance; let joy be unconfined; No sleep till morn, when Youth and Pleasure meet"), Wordsworth ("Is it a party in a parlour?"), and Ecclesiastes ("A man hath no better thing under the sun, than to eat, and to drink, and to be merry"). To an already leaden party they added precious little leavening.

St. Regis, the hair a tangle of reddened ringlets, the lashes curled until they nearly scraped his brows, the lips just suspiciously pinker, was dancing attendance on the wardrobe assistant, while the latter's employer looked on with ill-concealed dislike.

The actor who had played Don Fernando turned up with a sensational-looking wife many years his junior. A lot of the guests recognized him from old pictures he had made in Hollywood, and, being as celebrity-conscious as their hostess, all wanted to tell him how wonderful he'd been. He was gracious, but when it came to showtalk he would have none of it. Real estate was, apparently, his only love. "Remember this house very well turned it over in forty-two to some German fellow sitting out the war and then again in forty-seven at a mark-up of very nearly a million pesos but of course that was nothing compared to the coup I pulled on the house King Carol took during . . ." Miss Herrera seemed well, managed to stroll at the pool's edge without falling in and to eat and drink without mishap. She did, however, keep her eye on the entrance, and once I heard her ask another of the actors where Aristido González was and when the actors would be paid. Still there was no sign of Gonzáles, and Heff looked unhappier and more put-upon than usual, answering dozens of questions in Spanish and English concerning his father. The actors, I gathered, weren't the only ones waiting to be paid. The sound man, the wardrobe man, the head electrician, and a number of other minor executives—those of a level exalted enough to be numbered among Mrs. Pomeroy's social circle—were all grimly hanging on for the appearance of our producer.

In a bumbling attempt to be cheering, I brought Heff a drink and said, "Cheer up, Heff. I'm sure that your old man has found a beautiful blonde who can't resist him, and he'll be along as soon as he's eased her tensions and fulfilled her insatiable demands."

"Mr. Dennis," Heff said with a look of horror, "my father has been totally impotent for nearly twenty years. I thought surely everyone knew that." Then he walked away.

The party went on for hours, but you could hardly call it gay. Plenty of music and talk and noise and food and drink to be sure, but it lacked cohesion. People drank more deeply than usual and got drunk, but they didn't appear to be having a very good time in the process. The press arrived, summoned by Clarice, and dutifully took pictures of everyone, misspelling names from left to right; the notices of the affair, duly printed a couple of days later, made it sound like a real bash, but I don't think anyone, with the possible exception of Clarice, was having fun. Still, nobody had the sense to call it quits and go home, and those who had been connected with *Valley of the Vultures* were still waiting for Gonzáles and their money.

It was after two o'clock and the party had been dead on its feet for some time. It simply wouldn't lie down. That was when Clarice decided to drop her bombshell. I suspect that she was a little drunk, like most of the guests, and it didn't make her any more attractive. Ordering the mariachi band to play a fanfarade, she climbed gracelessly up on a chair and shouted, *"Quiet* everybody. I have an important announcement to make." There was a lot of murmuring and shushing, and in due course the room was still. "I want everybody here to congratulate Mr. Leander Starr, the famous director, because very soon he's gonna be directing *me*. Yep, we're engaged to be married, and you're the first to know it." Applause and then lots of buzzing, while the females of Clarice's "set" rushed up to rub cheeks with her and caw unfelt effusions. Starr looked stunned, and he was *just* able to accept the congratulations of the merrymakers.

And then Emily tossed a little pineapple of her own. Jumping up on the same chair and in almost the same shrill, vulgar style of Clarice, she said, "And everybody can congratulate Bruce and me, because I'm going to become Mrs. Bruce van Damm of Fairfield County and Gracie Square." Starr looked positively ashen, and I must say that for a girl who was supposed to be madly in love and just freshly engaged, Emily didn't seem much better. There was lots of applause and whooping and screaming, and Clarice ordered champagne all around.

"Let's go," my wife said after a couple of dispirited toasts had been drunk, "my feet are killing me."

"All right, and don't take forever thanking our hostess."

"Don't worry."

We fought our way through the crowds and out into the hallway. In a little reception room I could hear Starr talking to Emily.

"Yes, darling child, he seems a very nice young man, but couldn't you have talked it over with me first?"

"We were never alone or you were never home," Emily said defiantly. "Besides, why should I? Did you ask *my* permission to marry Mrs. Pomeroy?"

"That's entirely different. I'm a great deal older."

"And so is Mrs. Pomeroy."

"Even if you don't consider me," Starr said, "you might at least think of your mother—*and* Mr. Strawbridge. Mind you, my dear, I'm not saying that I disapprove, but . . ."

"I telephoned Mummy this afternoon. Don't worry. I reversed the charges. She and Bunny are flying down tomorrow."

We were just about to go when Bruce arrived, all dark eyes and white smiles. "Going so soon, Pat?" Having resented being called "sir" by Bruce when first we met, I now resented his calling me by my first name. Simply impossible, my wife calls me.

"Yes," I said. "It's late."

"I do hope you'll both be at my party tomorrow night?"

"Oh?"

"Yes, Emily's mother is coming down, and I want to give a big party to celebrate our engagement. I do hope you'll come."

"Well, we'd . . ."

"I'm going to rent all of El Paseo. That's sort of a special spot for us. We first fell in love there while Willy was playing *our* song."

"Who's Willy?" I asked.

"Why, the owner. I thought you knew him well."

"Oh, you mean Mr. Shelburne."

"Yes, I thought I'd go in and have a talk with him tomorrow morning and then drive out to the airport to meet Emily's mother and stepfather. Shall we say nineish?"

"Let's say nine."

"Good night."

"Good night."

XIV

My wife and I had foolishly expected that things would get back to normal at last, without taking into consideration the obvious fact that when Leander Starr is in the vicinity things are *never* normal.

Dressed in my most casual, I was having a second cup of coffee in the patio and considering inviting myself for a dip in the Maitland-Grims's pool when Starr appeared in one of his dandiest London-dandy outfits—gray worsted, bishop's cuffs, hacking pleats, double-breasted waistcoat and all.

"The bridegroom cometh," I said.

Starr looked a little startled, but he said, without too much conviction, "Clarice has many sterling qualities."

"Sterling and gold and diamonds and oil and . . ."

"Shut up and give me a cup of coffee. Emily has convinced me that it would be the part of wisdom to go out to the airport with her and Bruce to meet Caroline and that man they insist upon calling Bunny. I don't mind telling you that I'd far rather be at the lab cutting my film. Howsomever . . ." His conversation trailed off, but I was beginning to get the picture. Now that he was back on his feet again, had made a picture, had every expectation of getting out of debt and into the chips, wild horses wouldn't have prevented him from turning up at the airport just to show Caroline that he was still a man of parts.

I yelled for Guadalupe to bring out an extra cup, and she shuffled onto the scene with her usual gloom. But when she saw Starr she brightened. "Ah, Señor Starr, *buenos días!* We make peecture—me, mai dotter, mai sohn, mai oncle, mai cozeen. You pay now. All come to . . ."

"Ah, yes, yes. But I'm not the one to pay you. Señor Aristido González is the producer. He has the money and, of course, he will be around this morning to pay the extras —as well as everyone else."

I said, "He even owes me a day's pay as an extra—fifty pesos. My wife, too."

"Sixty, dear boy. Dress extras are paid more. For *ton,* you know."

"Well, I plan to collect every centavo of it—even if we give it to the Red Cross. Anything is better than letting that hog get his fat hands on it."

"Ah, poor dear Dennis. Thank God I haven't your small, narrow, suspicious mind. We did a superb picture together, did we not?"

"You did. Lopez did. The actors did. But I don't know what González did except make trouble and one thousand U.S. dollars a day."

"You simply do not understand Aristido."

"I'm afraid I do and what I also understand is . . ."

Emily came out looking as though she were about to meet weekend guests at the Paoli station. "Good morning, Mr. Dennis," she said. She seemed rather nervous—and who could blame her, what with a meeting between her father and Caroline in the immediate future. "I wish Bruce would get here. Their plane is due at . . ."

"Don't worry, my dear. We've plenty of time. Remember, they have to go through the *aduana* and all that business about tourist cards and health certificates. We have hours."

"I still don't like to keep Mummy waiting." I didn't blame her.

The conversation dwindled to spiritless questions and answers about more coffee, where I thought Caroline and Bunny would like to have lunch, whether the Bamer was a suitable hotel for the Strawbridges or whether the Maria Cristina would have been more their speed.

Eventually Bruce arrived, all slicked up for meeting still more future in-laws. He greeted Emily with a kiss that made me think more of mouth-to-mouth resuscitation than betrothal. I had to look away, and I noticed that even Starr, as the proud father of the bride, seemed uneasy.

"Well," Bruce said, coming up for air. "I've arranged everything with Willy."

"Willy?" I asked again, knowing perfectly well what he was talking about.

"Shelburne. I've taken all of El Paseo for tonight. Now I'll have to round up some guests. Just a sort of spur-of-the-moment party. You're coming, of course?"

"Oh, of course. I wouldn't miss it for anything."

"I shall have to leave on the early side," Starr said. "I actually shouldn't be wasting the whole day when there's my film to cut. But anything for you, my dear," he said, patting Emily's hand.

"Daddy, Bruce, I think we really ought to be going. Mummy hates to be kept waiting."

"Don't I know," Starr said, wearily rising to his feet. "Well, dear boy, until tonight." They all piled into Bruce's glorious car, and then they were off.

I busied myself doing such important things as reading the Mexico City *News* and the morning mail. My wife breezed past, dressed for town, and departed in a taxicab with the information that she was going to patronize such fine old Mexican establishments as Richard Hudnut and I. Miller in preparation for Bruce's party. I was in the midst of an elderly issue of *The New Yorker* when I noticed a respectful delegation of some twenty-odd people standing around me. They were Guadalupe's many relatives, servants from the other apartments in Casa Ximinez, and various people from the *barrio*. All of them had been extras in *Valley of the Vultures*. Abelardo, who knew the most English and who was the most politically advanced, served as spokesman.

"Señor Dennis, sir, please, sir."

"Yes, Abelardo?"

"Señor Dennis, sir, all of us have served as *supernumerarios* in Señor Starr's film, as have you yourself, along with Señora Dennis."

"That's right," I said to him as though he weren't quite all there.

"Señor González, the impresario, has promised us all that we would be paid our fifty pesos for each day of working on the film. I realize that it does not seem very much money to a wealthy Americano such as yourself, sir, but to all of these people in the *barrio* fifty pesos is a large sum, and some of them have worked for two days, even three days."

"Mm-hmmm." I wondered just what he was trying to get at.

"But as of yet Señor González has not paid any of us."

"I know where he lives," I said, hoping that they might just string the old crook up. "It's out in the Pedregal."

"Ah, yes, Señor Dennis. We know also. A very grand establishment. We have tried very many times to reach him on the telephone. Impossible."

"Yes?" I said almost eagerly. "I believe that he said his telephone was broken."

"No, sir, I am sorry, sir, but the telephone of Señor González is not in a state of disrepair. It has been unconnected for many, many months by the company. My cousin Rosario works for the company—a junior executive, sir—and I have it on his own vow that Señor González has not paid. It is for that reason that the telephone in his fine house is no longer functioning."

Guadalupe sputtered something in Spanish.

"Also, sir, Guadalupe says that a cousin of hers was employed for many years by Señor González and was dismissed without the salary of her ten terminal weeks. He has not a good reputation, and all of these people worry because he say that he pay and yet he don't pay. We know that you are his friend. . . ."

"His *friend*? I hardly know the man, and what I do know I don't like."

This was translated, and there was a feverish jabbering. "In that situation, then señor, the *supernumerarios* of the film have elected you as *delegado*—delegate for negotiations —to see Señor González. You are to be head of the Men's Committee while Guadalupe will be leader of the Women's Committee."

"What are you talking about?"

"We have chosen you, señor, to visit the home of Señor González to collect the money that has been promised to us. Here is the list of names and amounts."

"But I . . ."

"Were you not also in the picture, señor?"

"Well, yes, but . . ."

"Have you been paid, señor?"

"Well, no, but it's only . . ."

"Then we have correctly done you the honor to elect you as the most diplomatic of us to represent the *barrio* in its disputation with Señor . . ."

"*Diplomatic?* I can't speak Spanish worth a damn, and González can't . . ."

"I will accompany you as interpreter, señor."

"And then his place in Pedregal is a long way from here. I don't even know exactly where . . ."

"I will act as guide and chauffeur with Señorita Ximinez's automobile. Señorita is occupied with my cousins from the Vog Salón de Belleza. She will not need the Hispano-Suiza —or know that our delegation is employing it."

I didn't want to get mixed up in this thing, which seemed strictly a localized fracas, but looking at the eager faces of the rest of Starr's extras, I knew that I'd hate myself forever if I said no. "All right," I said. "When?"

"As soon as señor changes his clothing?"

"Change my . . . What's the matter with what I've got on now?"

"Oh, no, señor, this must be a formal delegation. You have perhaps an evening suit?"

"No, I *don't!* Not down here. Would black tie do?" In the

end we settled for an earnest navy blue with hat and tie to match. Guadalupe was dressed in her best black silk and some elaborate earrings. A white carnation was hastily tucked into my buttonhole, and we were ceremoniously helped into the back of Madame X's Hispano-Suiza. A meticulous list of the names of the extras—including Dr. and Miz Priddy, Major Maitland-Grim, Mrs. Worthington Pomeroy, Mr. Guber, the Texas honeymooners, and us—was placed in my hands. It contained names, addresses, and number of days worked. The total was a bit over five thousand pesos—not quite four hundred dollars—but I knew how much it meant to the people in the *barrio*. There was a resounding cheer as we set off.

The only time I had ever visited the González place before, it was locked up tighter than Paradise. This time the gates were wide open, and Abelardo drove right up to the front door, which was also standing agape. Guadalupe and I politely rang the bell. No sound could be heard. Then I pounded at the open door. Still no reply. I walked into the house. All of the old Riveras and other pictures were gone. The living room still had its furniture, its stumps of candles. The fireplace was overflowing with papers. It reminded me of the last time I had visited Starr's grand offices above Fifth Avenue. I had a sinking feeling that all of this had happened before and that our producer had flown the coop, but with the eager, trusting faces of Guadalupe and Abelardo gazing hopefully into mine, I had to make some pretense of putting up a search. I lifted the telephone receiver and jiggled the cradle. It was still dead. There were still no lights. On the terrace down below, the swimming pool had been drained and nothing but a couple of puddles of stagnant water and some nasty sort of submarine growth remained.

"We try upstairs?" Abelardo said. "Sleeping quarters?"

There were only two rooms above. A very small one, obviously belonging to Heff as it contained books and magazines in English. A hopeful sign was that the drawers contained a few—not many but a few—things like shirts and socks and underwear. The other room was enormous. It held a vast canopied bed with a nest of stinking, tumbled sheets that couldn't have been washed less than a year ago. There was some ponderous baronial-looking furniture and a tremendous oil painting of a fat nude of the sort that used to hang over bars in the gay nineties. But everything that was portable had gone. Dresser drawers gaped emptily. The wardrobe had been stripped of everything except an old, sprung, elastic garter. By now it was obvious to Abelardo and Guadalupe —González had simply decamped, taking with him whatever was portable, including, I knew, the money Starr had given him to pay for all of the expenses connected with the picture.

"It looks," I said inanely, "as though no one is at home."

"I understand, señor," Abelardo said. "We thank you very much all the same. You would like to drive back now to Casa Ximinez?"

"First, let's go to the police," I said.

"Señor Dennis, that would be an impossibility."

"Why? The man's a thief. He's promised you money for work you did, and now he's gone. You know he's gone, don't you Abelardo—not a shirt, a suit, a tie left. The house wide open. The pictures missing. No sign of his car . . ."

"Yes, señor, I understand well. But I also know, señor, that no person in the *barrio* is a member of the union of cinematic performers. If we were to go to the police, they would only laugh at us and then be angry because we had appeared in Señor Starr's picture. It is hopeless, señor. Please to get in. I will drive you back to Casa Ximinez. And thank you again, Señor Dennis. It is a very handsome suit."

"Tonk you, señor," Guadalupe said, looking at me with welling eyes. "You vairy good."

Back home I shut myself into our apartment and tried to think—and also tried not to think—about Starr. It was one thing for thirty people in the *barrio* to be out a few pesos each, but if González had actually done what he so obviously had done, poor old Starr would be out every penny he had been able to raise toward producing his film. Nor had anyone involved with the picture a leg to stand on. Like the extras, everyone had gone into it without the comforting advantages of contracts or union protection. González had arranged it that way, and now there was no one to turn to. I placed a number of expensive and fruitless long-distance calls to New York. My agent was sympathetic but not very helpful. Yes, John Steinbeck and Bertita Harding had both had unsavory things to say about González, but unless contracts were available for examination . . . Using a lot of words I didn't understand, my lawyer said things about extortion being proved, peculation, and absconding with funds. He also mentioned examining the contracts—if any—and suggested calling in the police and a Mexican-American law firm of his recommendation. A friend in the film business said that it was all a crying shame and that Starr was—or at least had been—a great director, but anyone who was fool enough to get involved with a thief like González deserved anything that happened. A harsh judgment, perhaps, but one that coincided exactly with my own. More discouraged than ever, I rapped on Starr's door. No one was there but St. Regis, who was setting a bowl of caviar into ice and squeezing little rosettes and curlicues of some repulsive goo onto rounds of melba toast.

"Heavins, Mr. Dennis, just the very one I wantid to see."

"I'd like to see Mr. Starr too. It's very important."

"And Mr. Starr would like to see you. He tellyphoned this very minit and says that you and Mrs. Dennis *must* come for cocktails. He says it's urjint."

"Well, tell him that what I have to say to him is urgent too."

I went home and systematically telephoned all of the Lopezes in the Mexico City telephone directory. None of them was the correct Lopez. There being nothing else to do until I could see Starr alone, I did nothing.

How urgently Starr needed the backing of his friends was immediately evident at his cocktail gathering held in honor, more or less, of his third wife, Caroline Drexel Morris Starr Strawbridge, and her second husband. The guest list was small and strangely selective. The second Mrs. Starr, now Lady Joyce, was present along with her hosts Bunty and Henry Maitland-Grim. The prospective fifth Mrs. Starr, now Mrs. Worthington Pomeroy, had not been invited. Emily Starr, the only spawn of four marriages and now the future Mrs. van Damm, was on hand, of course, with her fiancé. My wife and I had been rung in, and that seemed to close Starr's book of "respectable people."

Caroline had aged gracefully, as the saying goes. She looked like an idealized advertisement for Bradford Bachrach Photographer of Women or one of the many Mrs. Exeters who model dresses for those no longer young in the pages of *Vogue*. Her hair had gone gray early, and she had wisely made the most of it. Her figure was still good, and she had what is known in the trade as a "beautiful carriage." To look at her summoned up all the visual clichés of snob advertising. You could almost see her pouring tea from a seven-piece International Sterling silver set while discreetly and expensively clad in a dress from Rosette Pennington, the skirt lifted just high enough to reveal McCallum stockings and long, narrow pumps from Frank Brothers. She would be saying to a man along the lines of Baron Wrangel or Commander Whitehead that she never worried about money because the Guaranty Trust did all that for her. She would be surrounded by Williamsburg reproductions from Kittinger. In the background one would surely see a stock maid hefting a pile of Wamsutta sheets and a lovable old retainer bearing a tray filled with Calvert, Justerini & Brooks, Black and White, and House of Lords whiskies. Through a window draped in

Scalamandre silks, a terrace furnished in Woodward wrought iron would be visible; beyond that a Rolls-Royce, a Lincoln Continental, and a Chrysler Imperial in the driveway; and beyond *that* the Davey tree-surgery-ed verdure of the stately estate hastily mocked up by the studio assistants. Seeing Caroline toying with a canapé and a Martini, the discreet glitter of diamonds from Caldwell, the sober elegance of her Nan Duskin dress gave me a twinge of nostalgia for the old Wonderlax "class" ads. I almost wished that the future Mrs. Starr could be there to take a few lessons from her predecessors.

To see Caroline was one thing. To hear her, however, was quite another. Her voice and diction, never attractive to begin with, had developed into a perpetual whine. No sentence was ever quite begun or quite finished. One simply listened for an occasional noun or verb from someplace in the middle of what Caroline was saying and tried to deduce her meaning. ". . . class of people . . . Assembly . . . hardly ever go now . . ." ". . . Jews . . . Bala Cynwyd . . . Main Line ruined . . ." ". . . Nat Burt . . . perfect traitor . . . wife went to Miss Hewitt's . . ." ". . . Liv Biddle . . . couldn't read it . . ." (The literary references, if indeed that is what they were, were delivered for my benefit, for Caroline was scrupulously polite, and thoughtfully included everyone in her sparkling conversation.) Her mind had also developed, if that is the word I want, into a very efficient filing system. Names, addresses, genealogies, social connections, schools, and scandals that had occurred within the past three decades were tidily tucked away in a series of pigeonholes behind her alabaster brow, waiting to be plucked out at a moment's notice. Caroline remembered me. She was one of those women who never forget a name or a face, a time or a place. By some electronic miracle she was able to press the Dennis button and have at her fingertips a mysteriously perforated and slotted card that contained all pertinent information about me. "Yes . . . American Field Service . . . Chicago . . . school with your sister . . ."

Caroline had also worked up an efficient classification system whereby, without even appearing to interrogate, she could ask fewer than half a dozen questions and immediately place anyone in his proper social niche—assuming, of course, that the answers were true and delivered in correct English and a good accent without any hemming or hawing. Neatness counted and, as always, acquaintanceship with any Morris connection earned extra points. My wife passed with flying colors. ("Vassar . . . know Liz Wadsworth . . . Connie Irwin . . . maiden name . . . cousin of mine . . .") I was *so* proud of her! It was easy to visualize Caroline presiding at a dinner party, tenderly stroking a Philadelphia Chippendale highboy, or heading the Ways and Means Committee of some socially impeccable Worthy Cause, but to imagine her going to the bathroom or having a baby or performing any truly basic function was almost impossible. And the picture of her flopping passionately into Starr's bed—even all those years ago—still refused to come into focus.

Nor could I imagine many steamy moments with Mr. Strawbridge. He had several first names, but Bunny—a most ill-fitting apellation—was all he was ever called. He was about forty-five but looked much older. He had gone to chunkiness rather than to fat. He had also gone to Episcopal High, Lawrenceville, and Princeton. He was in banking, I think, and had also served some very minor function as some sort of sub-under-assistant secretary in the Eisenhower cabinet. Mr. Strawbridge—I *can't* call him Bunny—was perfectly willing to talk in short, telegraphic sentences punctuated by reticent chuckles, but Caroline was not anxious to hear him say much of anything and terminated his every statement, no matter how brief or vital, by whining, "Oh shut up, Bunny." I can't say that I got to know him very well.

Caroline had processed Lady Joyce and found her passing. One could almost hear the mechanism of her classification system clicking away: English, one point in favor; title, one point in favor; widow, one point in favor; married to Starr, one point against; divorced from Starr, one point in favor;

actress, one point against; attended Roedean, one point in favor; flat in Belgravia, one point in favor; acquainted with Caroline's friend Lady Dullard, one point in favor; and so on. Henry Maitland-Grim was *summa cum laude* with Caroline. Bunty had obviously been found wanting but was to be tolerated because of peerage associates and marriage to Henry.

Bruce was getting the fish eye from his prospective mother-in-law, although he seemed to be filling in all the blanks on Caroline's simplified short-form questionnaire perfectly. But if Caroline was of two minds about her daughter's choice of mates, Bruce had nothing but adoration for both the Strawbridges. Filial love all but oozed from every pore. "Of course, we want to get married as soon as possible, Mrs. Strawbridge. Down here would be nice, but if you prefer . . ."

". . . Philadelphia . . . reception at home . . . much more suitable . . ."

"Mummy, I don't *want* a big wedding."

". . . your grandmother's veil . . . the bishop . . . lovely lawn going to waste . . ."

"After all, heheh, Caroline," Mr. Strawbridge offered, "it *is* Emily's wedding, heheheh."

"Oh, shut up, Bunny . . . some sort of trousseau . . . announcements engraved . . . believe you said Yale, Bruce . . ."

It was not the time or the place to tell Starr that Aristido González was nowhere to be found.

Starr was very much onstage. He was looking brown, lean, and distinguished. Caroline betrayed more than a flicker of interest every time he spoke—and that was often. He bubbled over with talk of his new film, how sensational it was going to be, how good Emily had been in it, on and on and on. I hadn't the heart to tell him the news. Nor was I able to get him alone once that night. My wife and I were spirited to El Paseo with the Maitland-Grims, while Starr was transported by Bruce. At the party there was no hope of speaking to him at all.

Bruce had certainly done things with a high hand. He had taken over the whole restaurant and even hired a small band to play when Mr. Shelburne was not presiding at the piano. The buffet put to shame even the cornucopias laid out at Casa Ortiz-Robledo, and champagne flowed in rivers. Bruce was winningly modest about it and kept saying, "It's just a little impromptu sort of thing with a few people I called at the last moment." It was those last-moment people, I think, who rather detracted from the air of well-to-do refinement.

Clarice Pomeroy and Catalina Ximinez were invited—they more or less *had* to be—but they did very little to the tone of the evening. In fact, when Caroline first laid eyes on Clarice, her firm jaw literally dropped all the way to her sternum. "You say you are *marrying* Leander . . . amazing . . . very interesting . . ."

One would have expected a woman as possessive as Clarice to be a bit annoyed with two former Mrs. Leander Starrs in the same room, but she seemed to welcome both Lady Joyce and Caroline Strawbridge with open arms—perhaps because of the social aura surrounding each of them. "After all, sweetie, there's no reason we can't be civul-ized about it."

The other people at the party left really a lot to be desired, and I could sense that Caroline's automatic grading system was working overtime adding up negative points. I had never before met any of Bruce's Mexico City chums, in fact, I didn't even know he had any. He had—a couple hundred of them, and all the very sort of people he had disapproved of so when I first met him at Bunty's luncheon party. The Van Damm visiting list seemed to comprise every phony in the Federal District. They were not as blatantly vulgar as the people who came to Clarice's parties, and yet they were more so, for they all had pretensions to intellect or breeding instead of just good, dirty money. It was the kind of gang that turns up at art openings. There was an almost tangible trampishness about the women and a sort of epicene quality to the men. They were youngish—about Bruce's age I guessed

—and very pose-y in a gauche way I can't quite describe. The air was thick with the names they dropped. Fashionable people, places, shops, addresses, and vices made up almost all of their conversation: "Bergdorf . . . Alfa-Romeo . . . Portofino . . . Elsa . . . no, darling, Cap Ferrat . . . Mainbocher . . . the Winston Guests . . . Onasis . . . Hobe Sound . . . but of course he's gay . . ." They were the kind of people who talk the way the people in "People Are Talking About" are supposed to talk, and it sounded every bit as genuine and original. However, they were all deeply impressed by Starr, by Mr. and Mrs. Strawbridge, by Lady Joyce, by the Maitland-Grims, and even by Emily. Emily didn't seem to have met any of them before, and she looked rather uncomfortable when it came to making conversation with them. It struck me quite suddenly that Bruce was either very naïve or not nearly as discriminating as he had always appeared to be. I felt that he had made a tactical error in laying on so large a party composed of such a motley bunch. The part of wisdom, I thought, would have been a little black-tie dinner in the private dining room, far more geared to the Caroline Drexel Morris Starr Strawbridge ethos than this crush of the half-world. However, that was Bruce's problem. Oblivious of Caroline's disapproval, he was in his element, presenting Starr and the Strawbridges as though he had invented them. It was an easy party to leave.

"Starr," I said, as my wife and I pushed our way past him on the way to the door, "I've got to talk to you."

"Yes, dear boy, in the morning. So you see, my dear," he said to the ghostly-looking young brunette who was hanging on his every word, "there we were doing this picture about pearl divers when this monsoon blew up and . . ."

"Starr . . ."

"Run along, dear boy. We'll talk in the morning before I go off to cut the picture. Good night, *mes chers*. Well, as I was saying, this monsoon blew up . . ."

It was hopeless.

While we were waiting for the doorman to find a cab, Bill Shelburne appeared with a suitcase. "Skipping town?" I asked.

"Just going up to New York for a couple of days. Business. Maybe catch a couple of plays. If I did a party like this every night, I could afford to stay there for a year. As it is, I'll be back on the weekend."

"Just who were all those people?" I asked.

"Aren't they friends of yours?"

"Friends of *mine?* I never saw any of them before and hope I never do again."

"That's funny. The Van Damm boy said . . . Oh-oh! Mind if I take the first cab? The plane leaves at . . ."

"Be my guest," I said, opening the taxi door for him. "Have a good trip."

When we got home, Lopez was stamping up and down the patio, a trail of cigarette butts behind him.

"Lopez," I shouted, "where . . ."

"Where da hell have alla yez been at? Jesus, I been waitin' here since . . ."

"I've been trying to get you on the telephone all day. González . . ."

"González has run off wit da whole God-damn picture."

"He's what?"

"Dat's why I been tryin' ta find Starr, fa Crissakes. I went ta da lab late dis aftanoon wit' da stuff we shot yesterday. Da whole picture's gone. Dat big slob went around dere on a Sunday, gottum ta open up da place, paid for da lab work, loaded all da cans of film inta his car, an' disappeared. He's gone an' so's da whole God-damn movie."

"And so's the money," I said dismally.

"Poor Starr. I tole him . . ."

"Poor, *poor* Starr."

XV

"Go directly to bed. Do not pass Go. Do not collect two hundred dollars" was the message I got from the brief and unhappy interview with Lopez. I did so.

"But what's the matter?" my wife kept asking.

"Don't ask me, please. It's so terrible I don't even want to talk about it. In the morning, yes, but not just now."

Lopez apparently kept his impatient vigil in the patio and I know that he found Starr. Flushed as the great director must have been from his triumph at Bruce's party, he was not beyond grasping the terrible facts of life that Lopez had to offer. Sleeping as soundly as we both do, at something past four in the morning we heard the air split with an animal cry that sounded eerily like a mother who has just learned that her newborn child has been fed to werewolves. For all of the human and animal noises emanating from Casa Ximinez during the hours of darkness, Starr's wail of anguish had a wild, unearthly quality that turned my blood to ice water.

"What was that?" my wife said, sitting upright.

"Starr, I'm afraid."

"But what *is* all this?"

"Don't ask me now. I'll tell you in the morning." Then I turned over and fell into a tortured slumber filled with nightmares of González in the role of a great athlete racing across a map of the world with a bag of gold under one arm and a very old fat woman who looked like Clarice Pomeroy under the other.

Dawn dawned. With the best intentions in history I told my wife a carefully bowdlerized version of what had happened. But instead of being the Good Little Woman who is also a Pillar of Strength, she burst into tears and dashed up the stairs sobbing something about poor Starr. I tried to tell myself that Leander was as crooked as a dog's hind leg and deserving of no sympathy—after all, look at what he had done to me—and that the González flit by moonlight, or sunlight or whenever he had chosen to abscond, was purely poetic justice. Somehow, I couldn't make it hold water. Starr, for all of his vagaries, had intelligence, taste, charm, and—don't ask me why—even a certain sweetness. There should have been a comedic value in his finally having been bilked after gypping so many others. Somehow, there was not.

With great bravery I decided to leap out of bed and knock at his door to be of *some* usefulness, even if it only amounted to holding the crying towel and, from time to time, wringing it out. With even greater cowardice, I did not. Instead, I wrote long letters to each of our children, wrote to my parents, my mother-in-law, my sister, my niece, my business manager, my agent, my old friend Ned in Atlanta, Georgia —to more people than I had written during the past year. It was after eleven when all of the senseless letters were finished. Then I realized that Starr would *have* to be visited.

I rustled, rather than knocked, at his door. St. Regis answered. His eyes were red from weeping, traces of brown mascara and blue liner made a curious gallstone smudge from cheekbones to eye sockets. "I'm ever so sorry, Mr. Dennis, but my imployer is out." Then he broke down entirely. Emily came to the door. "I suppose you know," she said, gazing frigidly upon me, as though I had introduced the iniquitous González into the family. "I suppose you know that Mr. González has disappeared with all of Daddy's money *and* the movie."

"Yes. I'm afraid I do know."

"Well, don't be too upset," she said. "And please don't

worry. *I'll* see that Mummy and Bunny are kept busy all day. D-daddy hasn't e-e-even gone to b-bed. He really is o-out." Then Emily fell sobbing upon St. Regis' neck. Leaving that touching scene, I quietly closed the door and tiptoed away.

The telephone was ringing when I got back to our own place.

"*Quién habla?*" I said, being accustomed to wrong numbers.

"Patsy? It's Bruce." We had now, apparently, progressed from Sir to Pat to Patsy. I wondered when he was going to start calling me Pretty Lamb, as my maternal grandmother did up until the day I had my curls clipped.

"Hello, I was just about to call and thank you for a lovely evening," I lied.

"Good thing you didn't, Patsy. My phone's out of order. I'm calling from a booth in Sanborn's. I wondered if you could have lunch with me."

"That's very nice of you, but as a matter of fact, I . . ."

"It's terribly important. I need your advice."

"Well, I'm rather busy, but . . ." Bruce had used the magic words. Who is ever too busy to give advice? Like him or not —and I mostly didn't, albeit without reason—my curiosity had been piqued, and there is nothing so devastating to indifference, dislike, or even loathing as a good nudge in the mind-somebody-else's-business zone.

"Oh, I know you are, chum"—really, *chum,* we certainly were on cozy terms—"but this is terribly important. It's a question of taste."

That was the real hooker. If superior knowledge can't pull a sucker in, superior taste can. "Well," I paused, feeling my hair and beard, "I *should* pay a call on the barber, but . . ."

"Where do you usually go?" Bruce said, a trifle like the mother of a very plain subdebutante asking the mother of six eligible sons about summer resorts.

"Corner of the Reforma and Calle Napoles," I said almost coyly.

"Then shall we meet at Focolare? One o'clock, say?"
"Focolare. One."

Focolare is my least-favorite restaurant in all of Mexico. At almost all times there are plashing fountains the very sound of which make me feel that I ought to go to the bathroom, whether I need to or not. When the waterworks are shut off, a whole band of musicians comes trooping down a great staircase like show girls in some old Ziegfeld *Follies* to fill the air with every corny Latin-American melody ever composed on Seventh Avenue. Visiting school teachers adore it. During lunch it is filled with up-and-coming young Mexican businessmen who order Scotch because it is expensive and therefore chic, and then douse it with ginger ale, Seven-Up, or Coca-Cola to make it more palatable to them. I arrived a bit early, but Bruce was waiting for me at the bar among the young businessmen, nervously breaking up Fritos and fried-shrimp chips.

"It's noisy here in the bar," he said before I could even sit down. "Shall we get a table?" I needn't have answered. In the very perfunctory Spanish that all Americans who live in Mexico eventually learn to speak, Bruce asked to have the bar chit put onto the luncheon check and guided me, glided me, to a table directly in the spray of a fountain.

Bruce was rather too grand over the menu, trying to force upon me, as a first course, bits of fish and flesh that I didn't want, a well-manicured hand gesturing airily. To show my own pretty fangs I ordered eggs and bacon, when I would far rather have had something like Tournedos Rossini—talk about cutting off one's own nose. In the end it proved the better part of wisdom.

Having been summoned to deliver advice, I waited more or less patiently for The Question. It was not immediately forthcoming. Bruce had a bottomless fund of social chitchat, and he dipped from it frequently. He discussed his party of the evening before, referring to assorted guests as Jaime and Dolly and Pietro and Jenny and Sonny (or Sunny) and

Chip and Bobo—the gender of people named Bobo has always eluded me. I was rather at a loss to follow very closely, and itching with curiosity to find out just why he was taking me to lunch. It probably reveals a nasty segment of my own character, but I am not ashamed to admit that when some-body I don't know well offers to pay for an expensive luncheon, he is after something more than the pleasure of my palate, and whenever he says that it is "important," he means that it is important to him and not to me. Never having been exactly *pro* Van Damm, I found myself becoming a little more anti-V.D. (in the Van Damm sense of the term) with every social nicety. He was *so* nice! Bruce had the kind of manners that made me conscious of my own many failings, yet I still felt wary. But for one rare time I was correct. He suddenly turned off the charm like the fountains in the restaurant and with the too-brief preamble of "Well, Patsy, I've taken up too much of your valuable time. . . ." got right down to the subject—but not quite directly.

"Do you like this star sapphire?" Bruce asked, showing me a stone set in a big, thick, man's gypsy hoop, which was suddenly produced from his jacket pocket. Hating all male jewelry as I do, I couldn't comment frankly. Still, the sapphire was exquisite, set in a circle of what looked to be magnificent small diamonds.

"It's sensational," I said truthfully. "The most beautiful star I've ever seen."

"I plan to get it reset for Emily. It's an heirloom stone. What jeweler do you suggest?"

"My God, how would *I* know? Every other shop in Mexico City is a jewelry store. Fifty of the best of them must be within a stone's throw of this restaurant."

"Yes, but you see I don't want just *anything* for Emily. Her family is ve-ry wealthy. Am I wrong?"

Suddenly it occurred to me that Bruce *was* wrong. Wrong, wrong, *wrong!* This was simply one of my many hunches. They are usually wrong, wrong, *wrong,* too, but I always

278

feel that they are right and, in my case, feeling is even worse than *knowing*.

"I think that Caroline and"—I took a deep breath—"Caroline and *Bunny* know where the next meal is coming from. But remember, Philadelphia money, like Boston money, doesn't show the way that New York money and Chicago money shows. It stays in the bank."

"Uh, you've done quite well at writing, haven't you, uh, Patsy?"

"Fair to middling," I said, feeling my spine stiffen. "Why?"

With a lovely display of eyes and teeth, Bruce began getting down to cases. "Well, uh, Patsy, I've been living pretty high on the hog lately and, uh, now that I'm getting married, uh, you see, uh, the stock market is, uh, acting rather strangely and, uh, my trustees, uh, advise, uh . . ." He gave it up and reached for his drink. The glass was gone. Why is it that people who want to get something out of you always wait until the table is cleared before getting down to cases?

Bruce was in a state of confusion, offering brandy and stingers to me, ordering a stiff Scotch and soda for himself. I was in no confusion at all. I suddenly realized that here was someone I had never very much liked and now I found myself detesting him. But what fascinated me was the bumbling, boyish, almost gauche way this patently charming, suave young man was trying to put the bite on me. I waited.

"Well, Patsy, the point is that I find myself rather short on funds, and I wondered if you could let me have a couple of thousand until Emily and I are married."

"A couple of thousand what?"

"Why, dollars."

"That's a very easy question to answer. No."

He looked almost wounded, like some child who has entered the circle of grownups, sung his song, recited his poem, performed his Chopin étude, bowed to all the ladies, shaken hands with all the men, and still not been allowed to stay up past his bedtime. All his social accomplishments lavished on me for the past weeks had gone to waste. There was no tip, no piece of cake, no champagne glass filled with ginger ale forthcoming as his just reward. He began to turn a trifle nasty—not really, because utter lovability had become such a habit with him, but I could sense that our honeymoon was over. "I believe," he said without much conviction, "that your wife has private . . ."

My wife is the softest touch in the world. I took care of this little matter for her. "In trust, Bruce. My wife and I also have two children to educate, two taxes to pay, two establishments to run. . . ." I stopped. What I really meant was that I didn't like him, didn't trust him, wouldn't give him a dollar if I had money to burn.

"Of course, Leander must have a good deal tucked away. But I don't think I ought to . . ."

"Right, Bruce. You certainly oughtn't. And I wouldn't suggest asking Caroline or even Emily." The boy was a total jerk. "What about your own family?"

"Well, there's hardly anyone left. My brother David is in automotive engineering, but he has children to support. My sister spends almost everything keeping up her estate—we've always lived in Fairfield County—her gardens . . . her conservatory. . . . Well, I don't want to trouble them. I suppose I could always sell my car. It cost ten thousand, and down here it would bring . . ."

"It would bring one of the stiffest jail sentences you ever heard of. It's absolutely against the law to drive a car into Mexico and not to take it back out. The only crime a tourist can commit that's worse is to pass a bad check." I don't know what made me settle on that particular felony, but if I'd squirted Bruce full in the face with the soda siphon he couldn't have reacted more violently.

"What do you mean?"

"Just that. To pass a bad check in Mexico—even a check

drawn on insufficient funds—carries a prison sentence. No diplomatic immunity, no . . ."

"About how long does it take a New York check to clear?" He gripped his glass so hard that his knuckles were white.

"Three weeks—four maybe."

He relaxed again. Once more I was allowed to bask in his warm smile, his sincere gaze. "Laws are funny, aren't they?"

"Uproarious," I said.

"Well, perhaps you could give me a word of advice about this." From an attaché case of black alligator he produced a small unframed painting. "It's a Pavel Tchelitchew. I'm a little tired of it, and I might just unload it on the right collector down here. Tchelitchew is still fashionable, I suppose." How very Bruce that statement was. This well-bred imbecile didn't care if a picture was good or important or even pretty as long as it was fashionable. Oddly enough, this particular painting wasn't even that. In terms of pure vogue, it was decidedly *un*fashionable. It was a gouache painted in the last faint rays of the setting surrealist sun sometime during the late thirties. It depicted a not-very-attractive man, naked but for a long red cape studded with real paillettes. All the tired tricks of the window-trimming trade were in it —the exaggerated false perspective, the ghostly light, floorboards running into infinity, a tattered banner in the best Eugene Berman tradition, a couple of red carnations scattered on the ground. It was all beautifully conceived and painted, obviously the work of a master draftsman, but so slick and chichi and dead that it was almost comical. The only thing that surprised me was that a boy as young and as stupid as Bruce would even have heard of so special an artist or would have owned a painting of such a dubious period, which must have coincided roughly with the date of Bruce's birth. Bruce was the sort of square young man who would know the obvious painters—Picasso, Matisse, even Dali—but not the Tchelitchews, the Carringtons, the Bermans, and Ernsts. It was like trying to sell a zoot suit.

"It's a Tchelitchew all right," I said. "Done about thirty-six or seven."

"And very valuable." It was a question rather than a statement.

"I shouldn't think so. It's a little old-hat—or at least it is just now."

"But do you think some art gallery . . ."

"You could try. The Calle Niza is full of them. This whole section is." The time had come to break away. "Well, I'm sorry I haven't been more helpful, but thanks for lunch. . . ."

"Oh, yes. *Mozo! La cuenta por favor!*" As the check arrived, Bruce excused himself. I waited. I waited five minutes, ten minutes, fifteen minutes. The restaurant was empty but for me. Our table, however, was not. The Tchelitchew painting, the sapphire ring, Bruce's gold cigarette case and lighter smartly stamped B van D were there. So was the alligator attaché case. I couldn't help noticing that it had a red-morocco lining and that it was stamped L B B and not B van D. Waiters hovered. After half an hour I called the captain. "Will you please look in the men's room and see if Mr. van Damm is ill?" I asked.

"But he is not here, sir. Two men came in and he went away with them."

There was nothing for me to do but pay the check, pack up Bruce's artifacts, and go home.

It doesn't take long for news—good or bad—to travel around our *barrio,* and needless to say the Americans residing at Casa Ximinez had become about as popular with the natives as a general tax levy, simply as a result of Starr's film. I was prepared to run the gamut of sullen faces in the neighborhood, but I didn't expect the full-scale mob scene that eddied and flowed through the patio for the rest of the day and night. The first person I saw was Bill Shelburne waiting in our living room.

"What are you doing here? I thought you were in New York."

"I was. I'm back."

"Talk about a quick trip, did . . ."

"Listen, this friend of yours—this Bruce van Damm who got engaged to Leander Starr's daughter . . ."

"Friend of *mine*? Bill, I *know* him but . . ."

"When he came charging into my restaurant yesterday taking over the place as though he were Bonnie Prince Charlie, he gave you as a reference."

"*Me?*"

"Yes, you. He also gave me a check for three thousand bucks that isn't worth . . ."

"Bill. What are you talking about?"

"This." He flourished a check drawn on a fine old New York bank. "This happens to be my bank. Your Bruce van Damm gave me this . . . this lovely piece of baby-blue paper last night just before I flew up north. So long as I had to go to the bank anyhow, I thought I'd just deposit it."

"And he can't cover it?"

"*Cover* it? He doesn't even have an account there. They never heard of him. So here I am stuck for tons of food, gallons of booze, a staff of thirty-three, a band. . . . He even gave me a *tip*—a check for one hundred dollars for singing my own songs in my own place, and it's every bit as worthless. You certainly run with a fast set."

"But he's not a friend of mine. I've only known him for a couple of weeks. I don't even know where he lives."

"I do. Or at least where he *lived*—a very posh flat on the Hamburgo. I've just been there and had a little talk with his landlord who's stuck with the same blue paper as I am—but not for so much. His just came back from the bank. And in addition to this three-thousand-dollar item, Mr. van Damm has also signed a couple of dozen tabs in the restaurant that are . . ."

"How *dare* you speak to my daughter that way, sir!" From

the patio issued the frappé voice of Caroline Drexel Morris Starr Strawbridge in one of its rare moments of passion.

"Now see here, uh, whoever you are . . ." Mr. Strawbridge offered.

"Oh, shut up, Bunny! I don't know who you think you are, but . . ."

"Private detective, name's Fairfax, lady. Here's the credentials. It seems that your daughter's gentleman friend, a certain Bruce van Damm, took some things that dint exactly belong to him from our client, uh, Lucien Brooke Barney of New York—a Lincoln Continental car, some pictures, a star-sapphire ring, watches, cuff links, cloze, and some other stuff amounting to quite a load."

I went to the window. Emily was in tears. Caroline was busy being the outraged mother eagle, and Bunny was just Bunny. They were being confronted by a small, wiry, little rat terrier of a man in a too-sharp gray drip-dry suit and a ditto straw telescope hat dyed gray to match. "It might also interest you folks to know that Mr. Barney has been keeping your, uh, fiancé, for the past two years. But no sooner do he and his ole lady go off on a li'l trip than the cute boy skips. Sorry to spoil the wedding plans, but I think the ceremony may be delayed ten to twenty years."

"Wh-where is Bruce now?" Emily asked.

"Where d'ya suppose, sweetie? In the cooler."

"And just why do you come here to tell me all this?"

"I'm here for what *you* can tell *me*. There's this sapphire ring, some pitcher by this painter"—he consulted a list—"Cello-chew, a few other things we're tryin' ta trace. *Chairshay la fam,* like they say. And so if you'd just hand over these few items, you'd be saving your, uh, boyfriend, yourself, and I quite a bit of unpleasantness. Let's have 'em, baby."

"Don't you touch my child!"

"Now, see here, sir. Our lawyers back in . . ."

"Shut up, Bunny. . . ."

I picked up the attaché case, the picture, and the ring and stepped out to the patio. "Are these what you're after?"

"Who are you?"

"That doesn't matter. Is this the stuff you're looking for?"

He consulted a list again—a fairly comprehensive one. "Well, yeah, but . . ."

"Then take this foul junk, *and* your foul mouth *and* your foul mind and go."

"Hey, now, listen."

"Out," I said. *"Now."*

"Is . . . is this true?" Emily asked.

"I'm afraid it is, Emily."

". . . *knew* it . . . moment I saw him . . . related to Mrs. Chauncey van Damm . . . dead for years . . . didn't even know it . . . ghastly party . . ."

"Mummy, please . . ."

"Yes, uh, Caroline, poor Emily . . ."

"Oh, shut up, Bunny. Minute you came down here to that worthless father . . ."

"Now what?" Starr came into the patio. He was still wearing the suit he'd had on the night before, and he looked drained. All he needed now was this.

"Daddy!" Emily cried. Once again the whole story came out while Bill Shelburne and I stood pointlessly around wishing we were somewhere else.

"There, there, baby," Starr said. "Mexico is full of con men, and you and I are con-man-prone. It's a family trait."

"But, Daddy, I thought he loved me and . . . and all he . . . he wanted was . . ."

"Don't cry about it, darling. Lots of people do terrible things for money."

"I hold *you* responsible for this, Leander Starr," Caroline shouted. ". . . perfectly nice boy of her own class back home simply dying to marry her . . . minute she comes anywhere near you . . ."

"Caroline," Starr said, "have you forgotten that moonlit

night in the heart of the pygmy country when I broke my whangee stick over your rather spare backside?"

"Forget? How could I forget? . . . bear the marks . . . this day . . ."

"That was but a love tap as compared with what I will do to you now if you don't close your big, loud mouth."

"Now, see here, Starr . . ."

"Oh, shut up, Bunny! Well, I've had enough of this foolishness, Emily . . . coming back to Philadelphia and marry Dick just as you'd planned to . . . telephoned him from the hotel this morning . . . be down on the first plane he can . . ."

"Howdy neighbors! Anythingue unusual goingue on?" It was Mr. Guber, a perfect sight in his crumpled seersucker.

"Yes, Mr. Guber," Starr said. "A good deal. My daughter Emily has just been bilked by a fortune hunter, and Mr. González has skipped off with every penny of the money I raised to film *Valley of the Vultures* and also with the film itself. Otherwise it's been a quiet day."

"That's appallingue!"

"Appalling is right. So you might just as well bring out the handcuffs, the leg irons, the bloodhounds—all the rest of it. I'm a broken, defeated old fraud and I'll go peacefully."

"Señor Starr! Señor Starr!" In a moment the patio overflowed with all the extras from the picture. Guadalupe's relative the lottery ticket-salesman was at the head of the phalanx brandishing a newspaper.

"Señor Starr," he shouted. "Now you pay us. For me two days at fifty pesos, one day at one hundred pesos. For Guadalupe . . ."

"I'm sorry," Starr said. "I can't pay you. I'm a ruined, bankrupt old pauper—a phony and a fraud. I don't have a hundred centavos."

"But you rich man, Señor Starr. Now you pay."

"Would that I could but I can't. I'm flat, stony broke."

"No, Señor Starr. You rich man. See," he shouted, unfurling the newspaper. "You look. Here you name. You win the big lottery!"

XVI

Two million pesos is a pretty piece of change in any land and any language. Even after the Mexican government bit into the big prize for its fifteen per cent income tax, Starr was left with one hundred and thirty-six thousand United States dollars.

"Starr," I said, "it's a miracle! Do you know what this means? You can get in the clear with the government. Guber will settle. They'll strike a compromise just to get your name off their books. No more flitting around from country to country. You can go back to Hollywood and be a big man again."

"I'm a big man *now*, dear boy. At least big enough to pay the people who've given their time and money to *Valley of the Vultures*."

Mysteriously meticulous and businesslike, Starr called a meeting of all his creditors—Madame X, Lady Joyce, Bunty, and Mrs. Pomeroy, the big backers; the actors; the extras; the technical help. He explained what had happened, apologized, and paid them off to the penny. He even paid Dr. and Miz Priddy and my wife and me for our work. Mr. Guber also received his four dollars for appearing as an extra, but that's all he got. I've never seen so much money go so fast.

Lopez, at last a thousand dollars richer, turned up the next day with Heff by the collar. "Here's da kid, Starr," he said. "Now maybe we can find out where dat slob went wit' da movie."

"Please," Heff said. He seemed dazed and not quite in this world.

"I found 'im in the Zócolo beggin' handouts. Now, yuh gonna tell us where yer dad is?"

"I don't know," Heff said. Lopez fetched him a blow that sent him halfway across the patio where he fell in a heap. For a small man he packed quite a punch.

"I don't know, I tell you. I haven't seen him since last Sunday. I haven't eaten since then. They've taken the house. I've been sleeping in the park. I . . . ."

"Still stickin' to dat old script, eh? Okay, let's try again." Lopez swept him up off the ground and slapped him across the face.

"Please don't. I tell you I . . ." Then he fainted.

"Stop it, Lopez," Starr said. "The boy's telling the truth. He's been left in the lurch by his father the same as we have." Almost tenderly, he revived Heff and told St. Regis to give him a meal and put him to bed. "I also owe the boy a good deal of money."

"Owe *him* money? After what his ole man done you kin say . . ."

"Once and for all, Lopez, he cannot be blamed for his father's shortcomings any more than my poor Emily can be blamed for mine. I employed him. He did his work well. I shall now pay him, and I don't wish to hear any more about it."

Starr also covered Bruce's bad check to El Paseo. "But I can't take this, Mr. Starr," Bill Shelburne said. *"You* don't owe this debt."

"Yes, Mr. Shelburne, in a way I do. If I'd been a better father to my child—paid some attention to her, been with her, shown her the ins and outs of life as it is lived other than on the Main Line—there wouldn't have been a Bruce van Damm. She would have seen through him immediately, not that I did myself. I was too busy thinking of Leander Starr and not busy enough thinking of Emily."

As for Emily, other than a perfectly understandable humiliation, she got over Bruce in short order. Caroline's candidate, Dick, arrived with a pretty, square-cut diamond ring as well as a *receipt* for it, and even I must admit that he wasn't bad. He may have lacked the dark good looks, the boyish charm of Emily's most recent attachment, but everything about him was genuine.

Starr gave a party in honor of the young couple and even had El Paseo do the catering. "I've done so well out of all of Emily Starr's engagements," Mr. Shelburne said, "that I really ought to propose to her myself."

"Happy?" I asked Emily while Clarice was jockeying Caroline for a few good Philadelphia introductions and Lady Joyce for some good London names.

"Yes. Really I am, Mr. Dennis. I feel like an awful fool, of course."

"Not nearly as foolish as you would if you'd really married Bruce."

"No, not nearly. I'm used to Dick. I've known him forever. He's comfortable. Not exciting, but comfortable."

"When you've been married as long as I have, you'll find that comfort beats excitement six ways from Sunday."

"And I hate to admit it, but all along Mother knew best."

"Your mother, if you'll forgive my saying so, is a consummate ass."

"Perfectly true. But still she was right. Right about what was best for me."

"Well, she had a fairly eventful first marriage herself. Talk about excitement."

"But she didn't learn anything from Daddy. I did."

"Such as?"

"Such as I'm not going back to Philadelphia and have Mummy's big wedding with the bishop and the marquee on the lawn and settle down in Wayne. Life à la Daddy is too rich for my Morris blood, but life à la Mummy is too poor for my Starr blood. Dick and I are going to be married simply and quietly. Then we're going to take a year off—maybe two

—and bum our way around the world seeing things and people we've never seen before, learning things. . . ."

"That's nice if you can do it. Lovely. But isn't it going to be rather expensive?"

"That's all taken care of. Daddy did it."

"Daddy did what?"

"This." She opened her purse and proudly displayed a certified check for twenty-five thousand dollars. Attached to it was a note in Starr's wild scrawl. "Blessed child—I've never given you anything. Now I give you this. Take it and live a little. Daddy."

My knees literally gave way. On Tuesday Starr had received a hundred and thirty-six thousand dollars. On Wednesday he had paid out a hundred thousand of it to the people connected with his abortive film. And now this. Just what he was planning to give Mr. Guber was an interesting question.

"I . . . I hope you'll be very happy," I said.

"I know I will. And now good-by. Back to Philadelphia on the midnight plane," she kissed me, "but not for long." And then she was gone.

The next day we were sitting in the patio casually plotting how Starr might make the best use of his remaining money when the strangest of the many strange visitors of Casa Ximinez arrived. She was a woman who looked to be somewhere in her fifties, but it would be hard to tell. Although she was meticulously neat and clean, the mark of poverty was upon her. It is a look that anyone with a modicum of observative power can spot on the street, in buses and subways, in parks and cafeterias, and it becomes more pronounced with time. It is a colorless look. The clothes, even if brand new, are no-color clothes—rusty blacks, tobacco browns, muddy grays—that become more and more poverty-stricken with wear. With time the colorlessness spreads to the wearers themselves, to their skins and their hair, to the way they stand, sit, and walk. There is a diffidence and a resignation to them. This woman was a textbook case. She advanced slowly, ploddingly, toward us. "Excuse me," she said, "but I'm looking for a certain Mr. Starr—Leen-der Starr."

"I am Le-an-der Starr," the old maniac said grandly.

"I'm Mrs. van Damm. Mrs. Rose van Damm."

Even Starr was nonplussed. Finally he was able to say, and rather foolishly, "I—I see."

"I'd like to have a word with you," she said. Then she cast a questioning look at my wife and me.

"I think, Mrs. van Damm, that there is very little we will have to say to one another, and certainly nothing that you cannot say before my dear old friends Mr. and Mrs. Dennis."

Taking this as more or less—mostly less—of an introduction, I shuffled to my feet and gave an embarrassed little bob of my head. My wife, from her chair, nodded and murmured nothing too. Then she said, "Won't you sit down, Mrs. van Damm?" She did, heavily and hopelessly.

"The—the reason I come to you, Mr. Starr, is I think you're the one can tell me the most about Brucie. I don't understand all of it, but I figured you'd know something."

For once Starr didn't ham it up with a gala performance of outraged dignity. Instead he said, and rather quietly for Starr, "Well, madam, I am sorry to tell you that your son is in con-sid-er-able trouble. With a restaurant, with his landlord, with my daughter, with the Mexican Government, *and with me.*"

She took that in slowly, absorbed it, nodded, and said, "Go on, please."

"He has lied and cheated and passed bad checks. He has apparently stolen a valuable automobile in the States and— even worse—he has attempted to sell it down here. If you want to know where he is at the moment . . ."

"I know. I just been to see Brucie."

"Well then," Starr said, but not unkindly, "there is little more I can tell you, except that it looks bad. Very bad. There is always the American Embassy. . . ."

"I been there too. I wasn't able to get very far with the—uh—party I talked to. I just wanted to come here and apologize, like, for Brucie. He's not really a bad boy, Mr. Starr."

The classic phrase. What poor, mystified, bedraggled mother of what thug, mobster, thief, mugger, extortionist, or murderer doesn't invariably say, "He was always a good boy."

"But Brucie was always odd, like. Quiet, like, and inside of himself. Even when he was a little boy in Bridgeport, he never played with the other neighborhood kids. Instead, he was always trying to be something better than he was. It's prob'ly my fault. If his dad hadn't of died maybe I could of stayed home and looked after him a little more. But I don't know. His brother Davie made out okay. Married, owns his own home and his own service station. My girl, Rosalie, she settled down with a nice nursery-farm boy. . . ."

I could hear Bruce van Damm all over again: ". . . always lived in Fairfield County . . . my brother David is in automotive engineering . . . my sister's gardens . . . her conservatory . . ." Nothing had *quite* been a lie.

"Brucie was always a nice-lookin' boy, clean-cut. People liked him. He didn't have no trouble getting good jobs. Office jobs, I mean. Not like the rest of us. But then he never seemed satisfied. Spent all of his money on fancy clothes, a tux, even. 'Where can you wear 'em?' I'd ask him. And he was always sending off for books. Not stories, like. Nothing anybody would wanta read. There was one that cost a terrible lot, and it was nothing but a list of high-society people in New York. I can't recall the name."

"The Social Register?" my wife suggested unhappily.

"Yes, ma'm. That's the one. And then there was even this big English book he found secondhand, all about lords and ladies. And fancy catalogues. And then there was this old book about the van Damm family, and Brucie was always trying to see if we was relatives. He even found out that we were, but like I told him, it's a big old Dutch family. Then he moved to New York and got mixed up with a whole lot of rich loafers didn't hafta work or do much of anything but go around to a lot of fancy clubs and like that. . . ."

Again I could hear the debonair Mr. van Damm discoursing on that eccentric relation of Tuxedo Park and electric-car notoriety, on how he had discovered one of my novels in the Knickerbocker Club library. Everything he had said about himself had been technically true. He had simply known when and where to stop.

". . . next thing I know he's moved into a place with this fancy New York society fellah. Barney somebody . . ." This, I gathered, would have been the elegant and orchidaceous Lucien Brooke Barney and the "funny little hole in the wall in Gracie Square." Mrs. van Damm plodded onward with the sordid story that was so obvious to everyone but her. "Brucie stopped comin' home—not even for Chrissmuss—and began running around with a bad crowd. . . ." Many people, less down-to-earth, better acquainted with the gossip-column elite, and more easily impressed than Mrs. van Damm, would have considered it a very *good* crowd—the best. I sided with *her;* my wife and I had met Lucien Brooke Barney & Co. ". . . . then this Barney fellah all of a sudden turns against Brucie for no reason . . ." Well, to be eminently fair, it seemed to me that a ten-thousand-dollar automobile, some valuable pictures, and a lot of clothes and jewelry did constitute a pretty good reason to be annoyed. And hell does have a fury greater than a *woman* scorned. It was all so clear—that gold cigarette case, the standard equivalent of a wedding ring in Mr. Barney's circle; the big star-sapphire hoop scheduled to be reset for Emily's finger; the sick, slick, Pavel Tchelitchew painting that Bruce "might just unload to the right collector down here." My heart went out to this pathetic mother bravely, blindly trying to blame herself or life or society or bad companions or *anything* for the mess her son had become.

"So I come here from the . . . from the jail, Mr. Starr, to

ask you not to be mad with Brucie. He just couldn't help himself."

Starr cleared his throat. "I'm not angry, Mrs. van Damm. I'm sorry. Sorry for you. Even sorry for the boy. But now I'd like to ask you just what you intend to do about getting your son *out* of all this."

"I already had a letter from this Barney fellah's lawyer." She took a carefully folded sheet of paper from her shabby plastic handbag and showed it around almost proudly as though it might have been a royal grant. "He says that if Brucie sends back the auto and . . . and some of Mr. Barney's other things, that'll be okay. Mr. Barney don't wanta make Brucie any trouble." I glanced at the letter written on the one hundred per cent rag paper of an ancient New York law firm whose founders could never have dreamed that any client of theirs—and surely not a *Barney*—would ever be involved in anything quite so messy. Through the chilly legalese it was easy to read that while Lucien Brooke Barney would have loved nothing more than lots of trouble for Bruce, the law firm was just as anxious to avoid that sort of trouble's attendant publicity for Mr. Barney. "He was meaning to return them right after he got . . ." Even Mrs. van Damm couldn't bring herself to finish the sentence. She colored and choked and worried at her purse with her plain, square working woman's hands.

"What about the . . . uh . . . what about the other . . . uh . . . problems, Mrs. van Damm? The debts, the bad checks? Passing a bad check is a prison offense in Mexico."

"That's just it, Mr. Starr. It's a lot of money—a whole lot. More'n five thousand dollars in debts, and then there's the fines and paying the lawyer. It'll come closer to ten and . . . and . . ." Her big brown eyes—the same fine eyes she had handed down to Bruce, if nothing else fine—filled with tears. Her face began to crumple. "Mr. Starr, we're poor people. I work in a cafeteria. I got nothing put by. I had to borrow the money from my younger son to come down here. They'll send

B-Brucie to prison—to a dirty Mexican prison—and I . . . I can't do nothing about it." She buried her face in her hands and sobbed hopelessly. My wife and I sat paralyzed with pity and embarrassment, not even daring to look at one another.

Starr got wearily to his feet. "Don't cry, Mrs. van Damm. Please. I'll be back in a moment." Except for Mrs. van Damm's sharp, dry sobs, there was silence. Starr returned almost immediately, a package in his hand. "Here, Mrs. van Damm," he said, placing it on her lap. "Take this please."

She looked up with streaming eyes. "Wh-what is it?"

"It's a hundred thousand pesos—about eight thousand dollars. Use it to get your boy out of here."

"*Starr!*" I cried. "Are you . . ."

"Shut up!"

"M-Mr. Starr," the woman said, "I can't."

"Yes you can. You must. There's nothing very much else *for* you to do, is there?"

"Mr. Starr, you don't know what this means to me."

"And you don't know what it means to me. St. Regis!"

"Yes, Mr. Starr," St. Regis said, bobbing into sight at the doorway.

"Will you please be good enough to put my guest into a taxicab? Come Mrs. van Damm."

"Mr. Starr, I'll pay you back. I swear I will."

"Of course, of course."

"If I have to work all the rest of my life."

"Of course you will. And now good-by and good luck."

"Mr. Starr, you've saved my boy. I can't just leave like this without . . ."

"Oh yes you can. I despise prolonged leave-takings."

"But Mr. Starr . . ."

"To the taxi, please, St. Regis. Good day." A moment later and we were alone.

"Starr," I gasped, "you are out of your mind?"

"Probably."

"But this was your nut, your nest egg, your eating money until you got started again and that woman . . ."

"That woman, my dear Dennis, could very easily have been *my* mother."

There really wasn't anything to say, but I said it anyhow. "Starr, will you please tell me just what you're planning to do now. You began with a hundred and thirty-odd thousand free and clear. A hundred went to pay off on a movie you don't even own—don't know where it is . . ."

"An honest debt. Would you want me to stick a lot of poor Mexicans for their time and trouble *and* money?"

"Another twenty-five thousand went to dower Emily who needs it about as much as . . ."

"Who told you that?"

"She did."

"After all, dear boy, she's my only child. I've never done anything for her—never even seen her. It seemed the very least I could do—a gesture, really."

"Some gesture! And then this last final gesture—eight thousand bucks to spring a little he-whore like Bruce van Damm, plus another three to cover his bad check to El Paseo. That leaves you . . ."

"I've always envied your head for figures, dear Patrick. That leaves me flat. Well, I've always said that having a lot in your pockets ruins the hang of a suit."

"But Starr, what about your future? What about settling with the government so you can go back to making movies in the States?"

"Oh, don't bore me with all that just now, dear boy. At the moment I have such a pleasant sense of well-being that . . ."

"Well-beingue?" Mr. Guber had stolen across the patio. "And you certainly should have. I've just been talkingue to the department over longue distance—amazinguely good reception. And a very good reception, too, Mr. Starr, when it came to presentingue your particular problem."

"Which particular problem is that, Irving?"

"Why, your back taxes. What else? I couldn't quite get them to settle for ten cents on the dollar, which was my original intention, but they did strike a compromise that you should find very attractive after I explained how you'd taken so much of your lottery winningues to pay the poor slavingue people in *Valley of the Vultures* and all. But my chief gave me full authority to settle your whole indebtedness, six per cent interest and all, for a flat . . ."

"They're not going to settle for one red cent, Irving. The money's all gone. I'm as poor today as when I came into the world."

"Home for the holidays. Shirl and the . . . *What?*"

"You heard me, Irving. It's gone, gone, gone. Every last centavo. And you know what, Irving? I don't really give much of a damn."

"Are you crazy or somethingue? One hundred and thirty-six thousand *ferblundgit* dollars you had, and now it's . . ."

"Gone, gone, gone, I repeat."

"Starr, you *derschlugeneh meschugeneh!* Practically I'm knockingue myself out for you to get a decent settlement, and now you go and tell me . . . I ought to get extradition papers and haul you back to . . ."

"Go right ahead. But let's travel first-class and you *will* make arrangements for the luggage and my body servant?"

"Starr, you've gone off your head. I all but kill myself gettingue you the most favorable settlement so you can go back and start in again at the top. For a paltry little sum of . . ."

"Of how much?" I turned and saw that Mrs. Worthington Pomeroy had been standing in the patio unnoticed, an almost incredible fact as she was wearing low-slung slacks and a very brief top with a large expanse of abdomen, diaphragm, and navel exposed in between. "Leander, sweetie, poor little Clarice has been sitting all alone in that great big lonely house and not even so much as a ting-a-ling on the telephone.

297

You've been neglecting me, sweetie. What seems to be the trouble, Mr. Guber?"

"Trouble? Here I go and work the biggest deal in the history of the Department of Internal Revenue—a discount like that on *my* taxes I should get—so Mr. Starr can pay up and go back to the States a decent, law-abidingue citizen, and what does he do but go out and blow the whole bank roll. It's disgustingue!"

"Oh come now, Mr. Guber," Clarice said with a sharklike smile. "I'd be only too happy to pay up Mr. Starr's little bill with you folks—sort of a wedding present. Shall we say tomorrow afternoon—*right after the ceremony?*"

"Clarice, my dear. So soon? The papers . . . licenses and all that . . ."

"My Mr. Overton has fixed all of that. He'll take care of you, Mr. Guber, as soon as we're married. We'll be filing our taxes jointly after that."

"Clarice . . ."

"It'll be just a simple wedding in the garden. Of course all of you will come?"

"We have to meet our children at the plane at three . . ." my wife said.

"Bring them, too. I love children. Heavens, look at the time! I gotta rush. So many things to do. People to call. Flowers to order. You just come along with me, Mr. Guber, and I'll attend to everything. *Husta man-yana!*"

XVII

The airport at Mexico City is always a busy place, but on the last Friday before Holy Week it's a madhouse with practically everyone in the district trying to leave it for vacation. The mariachi band was out playing for all it was worth, the peafowl were strutting their stuff, luggage was being lost, children strayed from their families, taxis rammed into one another, people were cursing and screaming and weeping—a real holiday spirit in the air.

My wife and I got there good and early to learn that our children would be arriving good and late—two hours late. "Oh, dear," my wife said, "that means we'll miss Starr's wedding."

"Good. Somehow I don't think I could stand there and see Clarice slip the noose around the old bandit's neck."

"How did he seem this morning?"

"Surprisingly calm and self-contained. St. Regis was much more nervous. They were packing."

"All set for the big move into Casa Ortiz-Robledo, poor saintly man."

"Well, I suggest that we wend our way up to el bar and do our waiting there, unless you want to be trampled to death by all the holiday makers."

"I'm with you," she said.

The bar was a little oasis of peace and quiet—no one except the waiters and us. We got a table near the window, ordered drinks, and settled down for the long wait.

"I thought I'd hire a car, and we could take the children

to see Chapultepec Castle and possibly the floating gardens at Xochimilco and then . . ."

"Jesus!" a voice boomed out.

I looked across the room to the entrance and saw two Episcopal clergymen—one flat on the floor. The younger was dressed in black clericals and a large panama hat with the brim turned down all the way round. "Oh, sir, have you hurt yourself, uh, father?"

"Help me up, brother, and be quick about it." Once back on his feet the senior reverend was the picture of a Dickensian English country vicar—gaiters, shovel hat, and the thickest pair of spectacles I have ever seen. "Just get me to the bar, sister."

"Yes, father."

The vicar groped his way blindly to the bar, knocked over two stools, took the Lord's name in vain, and then squared things by adding "Amen."

"What'll it be, mother?"

"A daiquiri, please, father."

"Ah, my good man, a daiquiri for my curate and a big planter's punch for me."

"Si, padre."

"Happy carefree Latin children, sister. Even though they embrace a faith different from ours, I feel certain that Hhhhhe has a special place for them in Hhhhis capacious heart."

"Yes, father."

"Now you've got the tickets—Mexicancan or whatever it is, brother?"

"Yes, father. Nonstop to Montreal."

"One of the Seven Cities of Sin, isn't it, mother?"

"I've always had a lovely time there, father."

"Ah, yes, that dear little vine-covered church—St. Leukemia of the Mounties. And a jolly rectory as well."

"Excuse me," I said to my wife. I sidled up to the bar and stood beside them.

"And you left all of our excess luggage with Father Dennis?"

"Yes, father."

Their drinks were set down on the bar before them. "Peace on you, brother," the vicar said, hefting his glass.

"Peace on both of you—you big clowns," I said.

They wheeled around, and when they saw me I thought they were both going to faint.

"Starr, what in the name of God are you doing here in that getup?"

"Please, dear boy. Not so loud. We're traveling incognito."

"You couldn't be more conspicuous if you were wearing neon lights. Where did you get those goldfish-bowl glasses and that dominie's drag?"

"A farewell gift from St. Regis' friend, the wardrobe assistant."

"Farewell? Is Clarice hauling you off on some long honeymoon trip and why in clericals?"

"I don't know quite what Mrs. Pomeroy's plans are. My own call for flying direct from Mexico City to Canada without once touching on my native soil. I feel like Philip Nolan."

"But what about the wedding?"

"*Malheureusement*, dear boy, I shan't be able to attend it."

"You look as though you were officiating at it. But Clarice?"

"Cad though I feel, Clarice and Mr. Guber will be left waiting at the altar while I am winging my way to Canada—a fugitive from justice perhaps, but a free soul. Oh, I took the liberty of storing a few odds and ends in your apartment. Nothing much—six trunks, my golf clubs, photographs, a few old costumes, and theatrical mementos. When I settle in Canada I'll let you know where to send them."

"But you're just flying off like this when . . ."

"Yes, dear boy. I owe Clarice nothing. Every cent of her investment has been paid back. My money is hers, but Leander Starr is mine."

"Not so loud, father," St. Regis said.

"Oh, shut up, sister."

"All passengers departing on Mexicanadian Flight 113 non-stop jet to Montreal will please embark through gate three," the public-address system squawked. For good measure it repeated the message in Spanish. *"Todos los pasajeros . . ."*

"That's our flight. We're off, dear boy. Thanks ever so for all you've done and do write and tell me how the wedding went." He bussed me resoundingly on both cheeks and blew a kiss to my wife. "Come, brother," he said to St. Regis.

"Yes, father." With that they were gone.

"Ole! Padre! La cuenta!" the bartender shouted.

"Never mind," I said. "This round is on me."

"Now what?" my wife asked when I got back to our table.

"We're not the only ones who are missing Starr's wedding. He is too. The old escape artist is at it again."

"Good!" my wife said.

"Bunty, darling, you've got to get control of yourself. Your face is a perfect river of mascara."

"Oh dear, and they swore this stuff was waterproof. Well, I don't care. I shall turn old and ugly and haggard and never so much as *look* at another man. Oh, Monica, the humiliation."

"A drink is what you need, Bunty. And so do I."

Lady Joyce entered the bar, all but supporting Bunty Maitland-Grim. Bunty, dressed in the blackest of black, carried a number of fur coats. She was weeping a fountain of tears.

"May I?" I said, unloading the furs.

"Oh, thank heaven, there's at least *one* man who has some consideration for me." Then Bunty caught a glimpse of my wife and, with a thunder of bracelets, collapsed into her arms.

"Thank heaven is right," Lady Joyce said, sinking onto a chair and ordering two double whiskies.

"What's the matter with Bunty?"

"It's Henry."

"Is he dead?"

"Oh, no. Bunty could bear that. Far worse. He's run off. Run away with none other than Catalina Ximinez!"

"No!"

"Yes."

"It's all my f-fault," Bunty sobbed. "I should have locked his leg up at night. If he'd run off with the cook I could understand it, but that broad-bottomed Mexican c-caricature. O-o-o-o-oh." She was off again.

"I'm sure it won't last," I said.

"The sacrifices I've m-made for Henry. G-gave up a career as a Bluebell Girl with a heavenly tour of the C-continent and now I'm cast aside like an old . . ." She couldn't finish.

"Poor darling. I'm taking her home with me for a little rest until Henry comes to his senses. I hate to miss poor Leander's wedding, but with Bunty in this state . . ."

"You're not the only one who's missing it," I said. "Look."

A great silver jet was poised directly beneath us waiting to receive its few passengers. Two servants of the Lord were at the very head of the first-class queue.

"Mexicanadian? Isn't that that strange airline that's owned outright by some odd American woman who . . . Oh, do look. Really, that dear little C. of E. vicar. He looks like my father."

"Look a little more closely," I said.

At the mouth of the plane Starr turned, removed his shovel hat, and bowed deeply in the general direction of the bar.

"Leander!" Lady Joyce said. "So he's standing her up. Bully for Starr!"

"Just like a man!" Bunty sobbed. "Brutes, all of them. Darling, do get me another whiskey. I'm that shattered."

"He's made it," I said. "Safe from Clarice Pomeroy at last."

"And that little tax man?"

"From him too—for the time being."

"Poor Clarice," Bunty sniffled. "We're just toys to the whole pack of you."

"Mexicanadian isn't wasting much time on the ground," my wife observed. Already the motors were beginning to turn over, the doors closed, and the stairway was being removed.

"Heavens, do look!" Lady Joyce said.

I turned. There was a lot of confusion on the field, and I saw a man and a woman racing hell-bent for leather out toward Starr's plane.

"Why, there she is now," Bunty said. "*There's* Clarice Pomeroy."

"*And* Mr. Guber," my wife added.

Together they flew up the stairway, the door opened, and they got into the plane. Then it began rolling across the field.

XVIII

Things just aren't the same at Casa Ximinez. Our children are here and that's nice, but there's very little in the way of local color to show them. Starr is gone, and so are Emily and St. Regis. Lady Joyce and Bunty are back in England. Henry Maitland-Grim and Madame X have departed for points unknown. Mamacita has learned to say "Mai . . . dotter . . . Inglis . . . laddy," but she doesn't do it with the same old spirit. Mr. Guber and Mrs. Pomeroy have not been heard from. Even Dr. and Miz Priddy have gone off to some quaint spot for Holy Week. Perro has given up barking almost entirely and, with no dog barking or rent collecting to set him off, Loro roosts silently in the patio.

Nor is our apartment the same. What with six of his trunks and a few tons of other memorabilia cluttering up the place, it is not easy to forget Starr. In addition to his silver-framed photographs of late notables, we are also about to come into *Valley of the Vultures*. The film and González have been found in a miserable little town down on the Guatemala border—González dead of a knife wound, the picture very much alive. Lopez and Heff have gone down to give the old crook a burial—at a public crossroads with a mahogany stake through his heart would be my suggestion—and to see how much of Starr's stolen money can be found among the dead man's effects. If any, I hope they give a liberal reward to the one who stabbed him.

Guadalupe has just slapped the morning's mail down on

my desk. In addition to the usual bills and ads there is a very proper card from Philadelphia saying that Mr. and Mrs. Llewellyn Cadwalader Strawbridge announce the marriage of her daughter Emily, etc. There is a letter from that virtuous women's magazine, which I quote in part:

"*All* of us here in the fiction department *flipped* over your story about Salli, Mr. Right, and the broccoli. Simply *adorable*. We loved it so that at today's ed meeting we decided to inaugurate a whole new series called *The Right Set*. It is to concern Salli and Mr. Right in their years as young marrieds. We *definitely* want *six* a year for *three* years with an option for *three* more years. No author since Ethel M. Dell has ever been so honored. Congratulations!"

A letter from Boar Hall announced that Henry Maitland-Grim had "come to his senses at last" and was seeking a reconciliation with Bunty, but that he was being held prisoner in Yucatán—without his leg—and that Bunty was in Paris having her face peeled.

Finally there was a letter from a YMCA in Los Angeles, the I's in Patrick and Dennis dotted with voluptuous O's. I quote it in its entirety:

Dear Mr. Dennis,

I am writing to you because you have always been such a good freind to my imployer Mr. Starr and I.

The trip to Canada was not a success. Through the use of my Mexican freind's clever disguises Mr. Starr and I was able to get onto the Montreal airplain but could not take off before we were discovered by Mr. Guber and that awfull Mrs. Pomeroy.

As Mrs. Pomeroy owns the whole Mexicanadian Airline she ordered the pilot to land in Los Angeles—not even caring that we had all bought tickets non-stop to Montreal ! ! !

She was so mean that she even had the radio operater send ahead for "G. Men" to be at the airport waiting for poor Mr. Starr. (If any man made it so obvious that he did not care for *me* I would be too *proud* to demein myself so!)

But it was dark and raining when we got to Los Angeles ("sunny California" ha-ha!) Mr. Starr was the first one out of the plain and when we got to the imigration desk he was nowheres to be seen. He just vanished into the thin air!

But that is not all. In all the exitement he seems to of picked up Mrs. Pomeroy's jewel case instead of his own hand luggage so that mean lady is now charging him with the theft of more than a million dollars worth of her ugly diamonds. Some people just are not well bred ! ! !

Noone has seen hide or hair of Mr. Starr since then. I am ever so worried! But with Mrs. Pomeroy's jewel case at least I know that he is not in want.

But in the mean while I am in a very unpleasant situation as Mr. Starr has all of my money. I would not presume upon your freindship if I was not going to be locked out of my room at the end of the week. If you could loan me $100 I will pay it back as soon as I find work. I spend my days making the rounds of the studios (there is very little casting) and the nights waiting for my imployer to contact me. Where ever he is, I know he will return.

Thank you for any help you can give me. My best wishes to you and Mrs. Dennis for a very happy Easter.

Your freind,

Alistair St. Regis

I have just wired a hundred dollars to St. Regis, and now I'm waiting in the silent, lonely patio for my wife and children to come home for lunch. A voice just called out, "Dennis, dear boy!" I leaped from my chair with shock, but it was only Loro, the parrot. He has, at last, learned something new.

I look up at the windows of his apartment and expect that he will suddenly appear, imperious, ridiculous, and demanding. Yet he is not there. A family from Cleveland have leased the place as of Monday. Starr has, as usual, disappeared into thin air.

And yet I know that he has not. Somewhere, somehow, he is hard at work—ordering people about, complaining about the accommodations, the service, the cleaning, the pressing, the credit. And someday, at some inconvenient time, he will return to our lives like—*can* I say it?—like a bad penny, getting me out of bed, out of the tub, out of the middle of the golden-wedding anniversary of Salli and Mr. Right (and the broccoli) , ready to charm me and con me, beleaguer me and bully me, take my money and the shirt off my back (while criticizing its cloth and cut). Starr is gone, but never for long. He will be back and be back fighting—saint and sinner, innocent and ingrate, benefactor and blackguard, charmer and charlatan, sage and scoundrel, gallant and grifter, wit and wastrel, sophisticate and simpleton, rebel and rake, dreamer and dope, but always unabashedly and unaffectedly a genius.

Casa Ximinez
Mexico City
Good Friday, 1962